THE BREAK IN

THE BREAK IN

KATHERINE FAULKNER

RAVEN BOOKS
LONDON · OXFORD · NEW YORK · NEW DELHI · SYDNEY

RAVEN BOOKS
Bloomsbury Publishing Plc
50 Bedford Square, London, WC1B 3DP, UK
Bloomsbury Publishing Ireland Limited,
29 Earlsfort Terrace, Dublin 2, D02 AY28, Ireland

BLOOMSBURY, RAVEN BOOKS and the Raven Books logo are trademarks of
Bloomsbury Publishing Plc

First published in Great Britain 2025

Copyright © Katherine Faulkner, 2025

Katherine Faulkner has asserted her right under the Copyright,
Designs and Patents Act, 1988, to be identified as Author of this work

This is a work of fiction. Names and characters are the product
of the author's imagination and any resemblance to actual persons,
living or dead, is entirely coincidental

All rights reserved. No part of this publication may be: i) reproduced or
transmitted in any form, electronic or mechanical, including photocopying,
recording or by means of any information storage or retrieval system without prior
permission in writing from the publishers; or ii) used or reproduced in any way for
the training, development or operation of artificial intelligence (AI) technologies,
including generative AI technologies. The rights holders expressly reserve this
publication from the text and data mining exception as per Article 4(3) of the
Digital Single Market Directive (EU) 2019/790

Bloomsbury Publishing Plc does not have any control over, or responsibility for,
any third-party websites referred to in this book. All internet addresses given in this
book were correct at the time of going to press. The author and publisher regret any
inconvenience caused if addresses have changed or sites have ceased to exist, but can
accept no responsibility for any such changes

A catalogue record for this book is available from the British Library

ISBN: HB: 978-1-5266-7543-9; TPB: 978-1-5266-7544-6;
eBook: 978-1-5266-7542-2; ePDF: 978-1-5266-7539-2

2 4 6 8 10 9 7 5 3 1

Typeset by Integra Software Services Pvt. Ltd.
Printed and bound in Great Britain by CPI Group (UK) Ltd, Croydon CR0 4YY

To find out more about our authors and books visit www.bloomsbury.com
and sign up for our newsletters
For product-safety-related questions contact productsafety@bloomsbury.com

For Arthur

Part One

Afterwards

Later, Alice's memories of it are like broken pieces, with edges that don't match up. A door handle juddering up and down like a malfunctioning lever. Stella's pale face. A chair clattering to the ground, followed by the champagne bottle and flutes. A floor that glittered dangerously with broken glass.

Her husband, Jamie, tries to convince Alice that the details aren't important.

'People like him have such chaotic lives,' he tells her sadly.

Jamie understands this, because of his job. His charity tries to straighten the chaos out for people, calm the storms that engulf their lives. Alice has always been protected from these storms. Until now.

The police ask Alice what she and her friends – Yas and Stella – were talking about, just before they saw his face at the window. Alice tells the detectives she can't remember.

She only realises later that the detectives don't actually care what the three of them were talking about. They are just checking their stories, seeing if the details match up. Looking for signs that one, or all, of them are lying. And Alice has failed their first test.

Alice can remember the details, if she really has to. It's just that whenever she thinks back to that day, the same nightmare showreel starts in her brain, like those picture montages that start up unbidden on your phone. A gunshot smash of glass, a silver flash of knife. A silent leak of crimson on her kitchen tiles.

Evening Standard
17 July 2023

A mother arrested for fatally wounding a teenage intruder is waiting to hear whether she will face a murder charge, the Met has said.

Ezra Jones, 18, died after his botched raid of the East London property of Jamie and Alice Rathbone on 14 July.

Alice Rathbone, 42, was holding a 'play date' at her £1.2 million house in Hackney with friends when the intruder broke in through their basement door.

Unemployed Jones, also from Hackney, was repeatedly asked to leave but it is claimed he seized a kitchen knife, before attempting to enter an adjoining room where the couple's nanny, Becca Cox, was supervising the children.

Mrs Rathbone admitted hitting Jones on the back of his head with a metal stool. Jones was rushed to hospital but later died as a result of the injury.

Mrs Rathbone was initially arrested on suspicion of murder and released on bail. A file has now been passed to the Crown Prosecution Service which will consider 'what, if any, further action will be taken', the Metropolitan Police said.

Scotland Yard said in a statement that it had informed Jones's family and is keeping them abreast of developments.

A representative for Mrs Rathbone, an art restoration expert, has previously said she had been 'terrified' during the incident and had simply done 'what any mother would have done', after fearing the children were in danger from Jones, who had been 'brandishing a knife and making threats'.

Her husband, Jamie Rathbone, a senior executive at the troubled families charity Handhold, was not at the property at the time of the incident. A spokesman for Handhold said neither 'Ezra Jones, nor any member of his household' had ever been in contact with the charity.

Detective Chief Inspector Luke Barnes said: 'This is a tragic case for all of those involved.

'As expected with any incident where someone has lost their life, my officers carried out a thorough investigation into the circumstances of the death.

'A file has now been passed to the CPS as required under the guidance and they will consider what, if any, further action should be taken in this case.'

A source added that all possible charges were being considered, 'up to and including murder'.

Inspector Barnes continued: 'There will also be an inquest in due course, which will provide a chance to further review the circumstances of Mr Jones's death.'

ENDS

COMMENTS (79)

@east17er
All fun and games living in a £1m house in an 'edgy' area until you get robbed isnt it

@mamapukka
I heard they was all drinking champagne and left there kids in the other room watching TV with a nanny, couldn't even be bothered to make sure the house was secure when they had young kids there, disgraceful

@chardonnay008
Classic snobby-arsed middle-class mother, this area is full of them now, used to be a nice working class area now no one can afford because these types drive up the prices

@alyssa_writes
I think she was justified if he had a knife and her kid was there??
@jonesyboy
How did he even get in, didn't they even have the brains to lock there doors
@kittyheels
Why does she look so miserable in every photo get some botox love
> **@pink_lemonade**
> Botox? She looks well young for 42!
>> **@jonesyboy**
>> Only because she looks like a teenaged boy. Can't be doing with little skinny women like that

@redwall4
Posh woman in '£1.2m house' how much you wanna bet she gets off scot free?!
@oldlabour444
How is that house worth £1.2m, that area down by the canal is so dodgy? Ppl are insane
@SarfLondon
She looks like a stuck up b*%tch and her kitchen is so try hard get some taste
@nasturtiums77
Why was that poor child stuck in another room with the nanny while she drank champagne? Honestly, I don't know why some people have children if they don't want to spend time with them
> **@KarenClarke2**
> I thought the same thing, pretty clear this so-called 'restorations expert' has prioritised her career and that fancy house over her child

@Lulabella
Sad that he died but she did what any parent would of
@shaggy5
Gentrification is mental, How is this a £1.2m house, London is insane
@roman_road
She shud go to jail, ridiculous

@mrsosman
He was only a kid, obviously had problems but deserving of sympathy not a violent death, thats whats wrong with this country there is nothing for these kids at all

[CLICK FOR MORE COMMENTS – PAGE 1, 2, 3....... 124, 125]

ALICE

When the officers finally let her go home, Alice does not get dressed for three days.

She staggers around different parts of her house, her hair in the same wilting ponytail from the day before, or the day before that. She clutches her phone, sometimes plugging it in to charge and crouching there, by the plug and the wire, so she can keep holding on to it. She checks news sites obsessively for stories about the break-in. When she can find nothing new, she just sits, staring out of the top window at the toy shapes of boats on Regent's Canal, the snaking railway tracks that sound every few minutes, day and night, with the low clatter of overground trains.

Sometimes Alice looks down at her hands, thinks about what they have done.

Jamie does the school runs, the cooking of pasta, the polite fielding of calls and messages from concerned friends and colleagues, the job of reassuring Alice's Aunt Sarah – who is all that remains of Alice's biological family but who they find difficult company at the best of times – that no, she really needn't leave her health food shop in the hands of someone else and come and stay, that they had things in hand. Jamie organises for the basement door to be replaced, then drives to the DIY shop and purchases extra locks for the new door, a ring doorbell, a set of bars for the basement window, and wordlessly sets about installing them himself.

Alice listens to the sound of him sawing and hammering, but cannot bring herself to join him downstairs. She loads up more news clips about the break-in on her phone and watches them over and over. The coverage becomes disorientating. In it, Ezra is no longer a snarling burglar, it seems, but a baby-faced boy, a teenager. New pictures – supplied, she assumes, by the family – show him with football medals, in school uniform, in a colourful T-shirt on holiday, one arm slung around his mother. One picture shows Ezra with his father – who died, the reports say, when he was a young teen. A bereaved little boy. And Alice killed him.

There is one clip Alice is unable to stop watching. A brief interview by the ITV local news with a woman stood on the threshold of her council flat, gripping the doorway for support.

He was going through a lot. He didn't deserve this, is all the woman manages to croak. Then she waves the cameras away, eyes moistening behind her glasses. She pulls the door closed, and the clip cuts out.

The caption beneath her reads:
Linda Jones, Mother of Ezra Jones.
Alice is haunted by *Linda Jones, Mother of Ezra Jones*. She must have watched this clip a hundred times or more. At night, unable to sleep, she replays it on her phone between checking for any new stories about the break-in. She combs the articles for anything that could suggest why it happened. Why Ezra had come to her house in the first place. What had been behind it all. But she finds nothing. And then, even though she knows she shouldn't, she scrolls down, to read the comments people have written underneath the articles. There are so many now.

Her lawyer, Jessica, tells Alice to ignore what people are writing, what they are saying online. 'It's all nonsense. None of it makes any difference to the facts. Your home and family were under attack. The case that this was self-defence is abundantly clear.' She tells Alice not to speak to the journalists. 'Just keep your head down,' she'd said. 'It'll all be over soon.'

And so, Alice waits for it to be over. She nods but makes no comment to the reporters and photographers that buzz around her doorstep for a week or so, before moving on. For the first few days, she had smiled at the cameras. But then one paper called her 'the smiling killer'. After that, she had stopped smiling, but that seemed to annoy people even more. Readers commented on how miserable she looked, how she could do with getting Botox.

In the beginning when the details were scant – a 'burglar' who had died after being attacked by a 'homeowner' – people had been ready to defend her. But as more details about Alice leaked into the coverage – her age, the fact she had a nanny, the champagne detail (where on earth had they got that?), her so-called 'high flying career in the art world', the current market value of her London house – the readers commenting below the line had started to turn on her.

Jamie and Jessica are right. It is a form of self-harm, reading the comments. Alice knows that. But she cannot seem to stop. It is shameful, probably, how much she cares about them. The unfiltered, anonymous opinions of people she has never met. Most of whom seem to have made their minds up that Alice is a bad person, a bad parent (an 'older mother', one had called her). Lots of them think Alice is a murderer. And that if she gets away with this, it will only be because she is rich, or at least middle class.

She can see that Jamie is disappointed to find his wife is the sort of person who cares about all this stuff. Who lacks the courage to just let the anonymous Internet people hate her. He doesn't understand why she can't just click the browser window closed, and return herself to him and Martha, to the life they shared before.

Finding her squatting on the floor again one night, stabbing at her phone screen, Jamie snaps.

'Enough,' he tells her. 'The charges are going to be dropped any day. We have to try to move on from all this.'

He takes her phone gently, like a crisis negotiator. Presses the button on the side so that the screen goes black.

'What is done is done, Alice,' he adds softly. 'We can't change it. It is just something we have to live with.'

Just something we have to live with, Alice thinks bitterly. Easy for Jamie to say.

Jamie didn't smash someone's skull in.

UNKNOWN
19 July 2023
4.12 a.m.
City Road Basin, Regent's Canal, North London

She rides harder, until she reaches a part of the canal that she doesn't know so well. Here, the banks yawn wider, and this is what she wants.

She'd considered the stretch near Baring Street, close to Alice and Jamie's house. But the water there is shallow; in the daylight, you see everything under the surface. The gaping mouth of a Tesco carrier bag, a bicycle handlebar. Once, even a child's Buzz Lightyear, his wing cracked like that was why he crashed.

At least if she'd dumped it there, though, it would be done. She wants the solid weight of it gone from the pocket of her jogging bottoms. The ancient battery still hot from being left on, like something radioactive.

But she knows she needs to get further away. So, she has taken a bike – cheap, with a flimsy lock – from the rails near the canal. She'll dump it later, in the water, somewhere deep enough. Once she has got rid of the phone.

She'd bought the black jogging bottoms and jumper from a charity shop. She'd paid cash. No balaclava – perhaps that would have been over the top, anyway. She'd found the black face mask scrunched in a coat pocket, left over from Covid times.

She'd hoped the canal would be quiet this early. But even at this hour, the city is awake: cars, night buses, Ubers. There is always the chance of a drunken reveller, a homeless person dozing under a bridge. She has seen city workers running on the towpath before dawn, heading south for the bleak glitter of Canary Wharf in their Lycra and AirPods.

What would these people do, though, if they saw a cyclist, masked and hooded, speeding along a quiet stretch of canal path at 4 a.m., then flinging a phone into the water? Something to do with drugs, they'd think to themselves, privately. Gangs, or county lines, or all of the above. Most, she thinks, would obey the urban instinct to avert one's eyes, to not get involved.

Rain starts to fall, the surface of the water dancing with the drops. She makes herself focus, picks up speed as the canal broadens out, bends a little towards the west. She races past a queue of squat narrow boats, carries on along the bend, until she can't see anyone around. There are no bridges here; the walls between the canal towpath and the pavements above are built high. As she passes under the shadow of a ragged silver birch tree, she takes the phone from her pocket and tosses it, spinning, into the middle of the canal, where it sinks without a trace.

She turns and pedals back the way she came, until she is forced to stop, her heart beating too fast in her chest. She brakes under the bridge.

There is no one here, she reassures herself. No one can know you were here. Her real phone is still switched on and plugged in beside her bed, setting off – she has been assured – the telltale pings that will later indicate she was there, asleep, this whole time.

Only now does she pull the hot mask down from her face and breathe. There is a predictable stench of piss, the foaming mass of sticks and litter at the edges of the black water. She waits for her pulse to fall, looks out at the starless sky. She wonders what will happen now. Whether this will be the end of it all. Or just the beginning.

ALICE

They've agreed that they will get back to normal this week, that Jamie will go back to the office. But now the time has come, Jamie is hovering by the door, turning his keys over and over in his hands.

They've had the door repainted, but the colour isn't right, Alice realises. It stands around Jamie offensively, framing him. Is it just because the paint is new? Or had she misremembered the colour? She'd been sure it was called setting plaster, but it had come out a fake, sugary pink, not the warm, womb-like hue she remembered. The stools are new, too. They don't match. Her kitchen looks unfamiliar and wrong.

And then there is that space, between the island and the stairs, where he fell. Nothing marks it; the blood was wiped clear, or it must have been, at some point, between the day it happened and Alice coming home. Had it been easy, she wonders, to wipe it clean? Or had someone had to get on their knees, and scrub the traces of him away? Alice does not know, and has never found a way to ask.

'Mummy, you forgot the blueberries.'

Martha is looking up at Alice from her bowl of porridge.

'Sorry, love.' Alice shakes the thoughts from her mind, finds the punnet at the back of the fridge, tips the remaining berries carelessly into Martha's bowl. Martha looks down at them and pouts, her lip starting to wobble.

'You normally cut them, Mummy. And this one is yucky, look.' She holds up a berry. It is, indeed, rancid, a band of white fur around its middle, its watery blueish insides leaking onto Martha's fingers like a fish eye.

Becca, their nanny, sweeps the bowl and the mouldy blueberry away and hands Martha a wipe for her purple-stained hand. 'Here,' she says. 'Let me.'

'I'll get going then,' Jamie says uncertainly, fiddling with the clip on his bike helmet. 'Shall I?'

Jamie hasn't exactly said he really needs to get back into the office this week, but Alice suspects that is what he is thinking. It is what she would be thinking. Alice has always hated taking time off work. Objectively her job is not important, not like Jamie's. But it is important to Alice. If she stays away too long from her paints, her easel, her coffee cup, her chair by the window, she finds it exerts a sort of umbilical pull on her. She starts to long to be in the studio, with the paintings, with her earplugs in, enjoying the quiet company of her own mind.

The last time they spoke to Jessica, the lawyer, she'd said they should both get back to work as soon as possible.

'It looks good,' she'd said. 'Shows the police your employers have no concerns, reminds them you're two professional people, getting on with your lives. Just keep your heads down, stick to your bail conditions and everything should be fine. I'd expect to see the charges dropped any day now.'

'Of course,' Alice tells Jamie, with a smile. 'You should get going.' But when their eyes meet, Alice can tell he is still not sure. Maybe because last night, he found her again, at two in the morning. Curled up in a ball in the blue light of the loft, and watching the clip of Linda, the mother, again, the clip Alice had promised to stop viewing. Her cheeks had been wet with sobbing.

'You said you'd stop doing this.' Jamie had sounded exhausted. Had her crying woken him up? Or had he been reaching for her in the night, hoping she would be there to return his touch? Hoping they could start to piece that part of their former life back together, too.

Before Alice could reply, the tinny speakers of her phone had sounded. Linda on its small screen, holding a hand up in front of her face like a stop sign, eyes moistening.

He was going through a lot. He didn't deserve this.

'I'm sorry,' Alice had sniffed, muting the phone. 'I'll switch it off. I will try to stop.'

But Alice still cannot seem to stop.

Becca replaces the bowl in front of Martha, blueberries refreshed.

'Mummy,' Martha says, 'where is the key ring I made you?'

Martha is staring at the hooks by the door, where Alice keeps her set of keys.

'What, darling?'

'The star-shaped one,' Martha prompts. 'With rainbow colours. I made it for you in art club.'

'I still have it, darling. I love it,' Alice says, although she can't now remember the last time she saw the key ring which Martha had excitedly presented to her on Mother's Day, wrapped in pink tissue.

'It's not on your keys, though. Look.'

Alice looks up at her keys. Martha is right. The key ring is gone.

'Oh,' she says. 'I'm sorry. Maybe it fell off. I'll find it, sweetheart.'

Martha's small face is clouding, eyebrows knitting into a shelf of worry over her eyes.

'I'll find it,' Alice says again.

'But what if you *can't*?'

Alice is pained by how little her reassurance seems to wash.

'We'll find it, Squidge,' Jamie says. 'Don't worry.'

Martha returns to her breakfast. Alice watches her daughter, the impossible sweetness of her pale face, her small nose, her messy hair, tucked behind the pink seashell of her ear. It is pointless for Jamie to tell Martha not to worry, when it is in Martha's essential nature to worry about everything. Monsters. Thunderstorms. The pigeon they once saw outside the National Gallery, limping on a single ulcerated leg.

'Mummy says we can go to the open-air pool today.' Martha tilts her chin towards Jamie for confirmation. Has her daughter decided, like her husband, that Mummy can no longer be trusted?

'Are you sure about that, Alice?' Jamie looks at Alice in that different way he looks at her sometimes now, as if he is talking to someone on a bridge, poised to jump at any moment.

'Yes. Of course. Martha wants to go. I'll be fine. And Becca can help.'

Becca is standing near the fridge now, wiping crumbs from the sideboard into a cupped hand.

'No,' Martha blurts, suddenly tearful. 'I want just Mummy to take me.'

'Martha!' This is unlike her, Alice thinks. She adores Becca.

'That's OK,' Becca smiles. She turns to Martha. 'Hey, you. How about I stay here and finish tidying up?' Becca tips the crumbs into the bin. 'You go to the pool with your mum. And then I'll meet you there a bit later, maybe?'

Martha nods, and Alice tells herself that today, she will be better. A proper parent – present, resilient, practical. More like Jamie. More like Becca.

Jamie is still lingering by the door. Alice would rather he just leave now.

'Honestly, Jamie. We are fine. Have a good day. See you later.'

'OK.' Jamie pauses. 'You will make sure you lock up properly, won't you? Both of you?'

'Of course,' Becca agrees.

Jamie finally leaves with a nod at Becca, a dry kiss brushed onto Alice's cheek, another on Martha's head. He holds out his hand so that the door will close softly behind him – Alice cannot manage sudden noises now – and flicks her a final glance before he leaves.

Once Jamie is gone, Alice stands, straightens her spine. She takes out bread and a knife. Becca clears her throat.

'Alice?' Becca asks. 'Can I speak to you about something, please?'

Alice looks up at the clock on the wall.

'Can it wait, until a bit later? I want to get Martha to the pool before it's hot.'

'Oh,' Becca says. 'Yes. Sure.'

Becca leaves the room and Alice starts cutting sandwiches, rolling beach towels, finding hats. She makes sure she packs the sunblock. She can already feel that it is the sort of day on which a child is likely to burn.

ALICE

Martha tosses her scooter against the railings, works the clasp on her helmet with her small fingers. Alice gently covers her hand and releases it for her. Then she pulls the dress over Martha's head, so that she is just in her swimming costume and sandals.

Martha's costume came from a children's boutique on the edge of Victoria Park. It is a Danish brand, a pale blue printed with lemons, two frilled straps criss-crossing sweetly at her back. Alice still allows herself to buy these things occasionally – souvenirs of a version of motherhood she knows to be a lie, a carefully curated Instagram fantasy, but the aesthetic of which she still finds seductive.

Alice badly wants to give Martha the summer she'd had in her mind when she bought this swimsuit. She wants her daughter to have a childhood so happy she has no idea how happy she is. She is determined Martha will know nothing of the darkness that now lurks in Alice's mind.

Martha points across the pool.

'Mummy, that's Frankie!'

Alice stiffens. Frankie. That means Stella is here, too. Alice hasn't seen Stella since the day of the break-in, or exchanged any messages with her. Technically, she is not allowed to speak to her, or Yas, until the threat of charges is officially dropped. Luckily, Becca was exempted from this, Jessica having made the argument that Becca needed to communicate with Alice in order to work, and was not a key witness, having been in another room when it happened.

'Let me just put a little more of this cream on your face, Martha.'

Martha hops from one foot to the other, twisting away, craning to see what Frankie is doing. There is something heartbreaking about the skittish way Martha interacts with other children. It's as if she is always frightened they will run off and talk to someone better.

'They are having a water fight!'

'Wait...' But Martha is gone, running towards the golden arcs of water.

Alice surveys the scene for a free sliver of grass between the prams and picnic blankets. She had imagined that they would be arriving before the crowds, but even though it's barely ten, the scorched lawn around the pool is packed. There is no space to lay towels in the shade of the chestnut trees, as Alice had planned. She sets them out on the only remaining scrap of space.

Alice has been dreading coming here, in truth. But Martha loves it, and it is very hot, and Alice can't keep her locked up at home all summer.

The sun climbs in the sky, white and menacing. The park's concrete paddling pool is slippery and perilous – the mums all joke about what a death trap it is. There has been talk of the council shutting it down. Alice needs to watch her daughter closely. She can feel sweat gathering between her shoulder blades, can feel the heat on the rise of her cheeks. She presses her sunglasses firmly onto her face.

'Excuse me? Alice?'

A bearded man, tall, a bike helmet cupped in one hand, has walked over, is standing over her, casting her in shadow. He looks vaguely familiar – is he a school dad? Or does she know him from Martha's nursery days? It's hard to keep track of all the parents on the class WhatsApp group, which children they match up to.

'I just want to say, Alice – we're all thinking of you.'

Alice feels a prickle all over her body. She braces herself, but it's no good.

'I really hope the police see sense in the end. You did absolutely the right thing. Anyone would have done what you did.'

Alice knows she is expected to be polite, even thankful, for this sort of interaction. But she does not feel thankful, nor does she feel like being polite. Who even are you? she feels like asking him. Who was waiting for your verdict?

Before she can say anything, though, the dad is clapping a hand to her shoulder, locking eyes and looking at her gloopily.

'Anyway, I just wanted to say that. And just so you know, no one around here thinks any different. No one thinks for a second you're some sort of... *murderer.*'

Alice glances over at Martha who, luckily, is playing with Frankie on the other side of the pool, too far away to overhear.

'Right, OK,' she manages. 'Well, thanks.'

The man stares, one hand cupped over his eyes. It's clear he was expecting something more, that she has disappointed him by not appearing more gratified. She watches a flicker of irritation cross his face before he replaces it with a smile, raises a palm goodbye and walks away. Alice's hands tremble a little as she smooths her skirt, pushes her sunglasses back up her nose.

Murderer, murderer. The word whispers at the edges of her consciousness all the time now. Alice keeps telling herself – keeps being told by others – that she will soon be free to get on with her life just as before. But Alice is slowly realising things will never be quite as they were before, even if the charges are dropped. Chance remarks of strangers, the brightness of the sun, the tinny noise of Martha's iPad games in the back of the car, are all now capable of igniting something in Alice's nervous system, quick as a struck match.

Her phone vibrates. Alice gropes for it at the bottom of the bag, under the towels. The screen reads 'Unknown number'.

'Hello?'

It is the same as that call she had before. A fizzing sound, but no voice on the line. The first time, she'd waited for the telltale clicking, the voice asking about PPI or an accident. But there had been none.

She moves her thumb to hang up. But then something different happens this time. There is a voice.

'Alice.'

'Hello? Who is this?'

There is no answer. Just a sort of sizzle, like fat spitting on a stove.

'Who is this?'

The fizzing sound again, louder now.

'Hello?'

Still nothing. Alice is irritated. 'I'm hanging up.'

Now the voice returns.

'You should know. There was a reason he was there that day.'

Alice's whole body reacts, adrenaline flooding her system. *He.* This is about the break-in. It must be. But who is it? Not the mother she saw on TV, surely. The voice sounds different, younger. Who, then?

'Is this – is this about Ezra?'

More static, a crackle so loud Alice moves the phone from her ear.

'He isn't who you think he is.'

'Ezra?' Alice is desperate now. 'Who is this? The line's really bad. Who am I speaking to?'

'You don't need to know who I am. You just need to know.'

'Know what?'

'That you need to be very careful.'

Alice stands up. Her stomach contracts. The threat is unmistakable. There is also something wrong with the voice now, or the line. It sounds odd, distorted. One moment it sounds female, then suddenly electronic, and deeper.

'What? What do you—?'

Three beeps. The call has gone dead. Alice holds the phone in front of her face, stares at the screen.

'Mummy!'

Martha is racing back, her voice breathless. 'Mummy, did you bring a water pistol for me?'

Alice stares at her daughter. 'What? No.'

'But Frankie and the others are having a water fight! I told you! I need a water pistol!'

Alice feels suddenly outside of herself. She wants to shed all this. The day at the pool. The sandwiches. The towels. Martha.

She cannot do it. She needs to be somewhere else. Somewhere she can think about what has just happened. What she just heard.

'I think we should head back.' Alice is speaking to herself, as much as her daughter. Her breathing suddenly feels heavy, effortful. 'It's – it's too hot.'

'But, Mummy, you said…'

'Look,' she snaps. 'I can't do this today. I'm sorry, Martha. I thought I could, but I can't.'

Martha's whole face drops. 'But we've only been here for, like, a minute!' Martha has tears in her eyes. 'Please, Mummy.'

'Alice! Is that you?'

Alice turns around to see Stella walking over with Frankie. Stella is smiling, pushing her sunglasses into her hair. Her pale linen dress shows off her toned, slender, lightly tanned arms. Newly painted toenails glint from her box-fresh sandals. Alice feels exhausted just looking at her.

'How are you, Alice?'

Stella's voice is kind but neutral.

'I've been thinking about you all the time since…' Stella frowns. 'I wanted to call, but, you know.'

Alice nods, still unable to speak.

'Hey – are you OK? You look…'

'Mummy! Mummy!' Martha is tugging at Alice's top. 'Can we have ice cream?'

Alice recovers a little. She looks at Martha. 'What? No.'

'But Frankie is having one!'

'I said no,' Alice snaps. She feels things souring, the day having already run off course. 'You don't need an ice cream. We just had breakfast. And anyway we're going home.'

'But why does Frankie get to stay and have an ice cream?'

Alice glances at Stella, who makes an apologetic cringe face, mouths 'sorry'.

'Oh, no, it's fine.' Alice waves her apology away. 'Martha, just because Frankie is having one, doesn't mean I'm going to buy one.'

'But that's not fair if Frankie is getting…'

'Just stop, Martha!' Alice shouts suddenly. 'Stop whining, all the bloody time! You sound like a spoilt brat!'

Alice registers the hush that has fallen around them. She looks down to see her daughter's lip starting to wobble, her face starting to pinken and crease into crying. So that's it. The nice trip to the pool is ruined. And for what? What a pointless complaint to make, anyway – if her daughter is spoilt, then whose fault is that? Alice might as well shout out, 'I'm a bad mother, as well as a murderer.'

Murderer, murderer.

Alice thinks about Linda Jones, hiding her face behind her hand, closing the front door.

He was going through a lot. He didn't deserve this.

About the voice on the phone.

He wasn't who you thought he was.

About Ezra, about what he said, how he seemed to be looking for someone, and how that had played on her mind, even though the police said they couldn't find any evidence that he was anything other than confused.

'Alice?'

She feels someone's touch on her arms, and flinches automatically. She looks down and realises that Stella has reached out to her.

'I was just wondering,' Stella says softly. 'Do you want me to take the girls for a bit?'

Alice swallows, shifts her gaze from Martha's sobbing face to Stella. She tries her best to focus.

'What?'

'It's no problem. It'll make my life easier if Frankie's got someone to entertain her.' Stella grins at Martha. 'We'll have fun, right, Martha?'

Martha looks as surprised as Alice, but she has stopped crying, and is not obviously horrified by the idea.

'But what about…' Alice makes a face. Is this against the rules? Stick to your bail conditions, the lawyer had said. Alice should not have any contact with Stella or Yas until the charges are dropped. Or Ezra's family. Or any of his associates. Whatever that means.

Stella shrugs. 'I'm sure it's fine,' she says quietly. 'You didn't contact me, did you? We are just here in the same place, our kids happened to get talking.' She shakes her head, as if to reassure herself. 'And we've made our statements. The charges are being dropped any day, right? That's what I heard.'

Alice is relieved Stella has heard this too.

'Still... I can't ask you to do that.' Alice likes Stella, but she wonders whether their friendship – formed this year at the school gates – is robust enough to withstand all this – this favour, everything else that has happened. She still can't quite believe what happened, on a play date in her kitchen, a terrible thing, a trauma that Alice feels responsible for exposing Stella and her daughter, Frankie, to.

On the other hand, Alice feels desperate.

'Honestly, it's not a problem,' Stella says again. 'Take your time.'

'OK.' Alice nods, then looks at Martha. 'OK. Thank you, Stella. Thank you.'

Alice mumbles some logistics, promises to message Stella Becca's details.

'Becca can pick you up, Martha, OK?' Alice pulls a confused Martha in for a quick, awkward hug. As she walks away from the pool, she realises guiltily that she is almost giddy with relief. And, before she has made a conscious decision to do it, she starts walking east, in the direction of the canal. Towards the home of the man she killed.

ALICE

The estate can't be more than a mile from where she lives, but it is as unknown to Alice as a foreign country. It borders a dead stretch of the Regent's Canal she has only ever walked straight through, on her way to Broadway Market or London Fields. She has never given this estate, or the people who live in it, much of a thought.

A map at the entrance has all the buildings laid out and labelled, like beige puzzle pieces. It is not the worst sort of estate, but not the best either. Weeds sprout from the cracks in the hot paving stones. Four huge wheelie bins stand grimly by the staircase. A sign reads: No Ball Games. A boy and a girl play in the small, tired playground, taking turns to push the bars of a squeaking roundabout. Alice smiles as she passes, but they don't look up.

Alice takes out the crumpled piece of paper where she wrote down the last-known address that was read out in court. As she gets closer to the right flat number, she recognises details from the clip she has watched so many times: the small front garden with its clothes dryer and folding chairs, the NO JUNK MAIL sticker on the glass, the sad line-up of potted plants, living ones jostling with dead.

Alice is not going to knock on the door of Linda's flat. Obviously. She is not stupid. That would be a clear breach of her bail conditions; the sort of thing which could result in her being put back in custody.

So why is she here? She wants to see where Ezra lived, before he died. *There was a reason he was there that day*, the person on the phone had said. Alice wants to know what it was.

Maybe there will be some clue here, something that will help her understand.

Alice's phone vibrates in her pocket. She picks it out. Two missed calls from Jamie, one unread message. Has he found out that she has left Martha with Stella and gone AWOL? She decides to ignore him, puts the phone back. Jamie would be horrified if he knew she was here, of course. But Alice is tired of inaction.

The clothes dryer creaks as she squeezes past it, careful not to upset the pots. She glances into the window. Beyond the net curtains, Alice can see that a light is on. Something, or someone, moving inside.

Alice panics and turns on her heel. In doing so, she knocks over a pot. It smashes, breaking neatly into halves, like an Easter egg. Alice gasps.

What can she do? She can't knock to apologise. She has no choice but to leave.

She walks quickly, almost breaking into a run, struggling to shake the feeling that she has been seen, that someone is watching her making a hasty retreat. The heat is intense. As she leaves the estate she sees a small parade of shops on the main road, a coffee shop among them. She decides to duck inside there, to catch her breath and gather her thoughts.

Alice orders an iced coffee and sits in the window, clinking the ice cubes together as she stirs the straw, feeling her pulse return to normal. Through the glass, she watches a little gathering of babies and toddlers under the shade of some trees on a green space opposite. An NCT group, she guesses. The toddlers waddle around with snacks in their hands, older children climb the low branches of the trees. On the railings, laminated signs flap in the breeze, advertising the sorts of music groups and stay-and-plays Alice used to take Martha to.

Alice is staring at the mothers on the grass, which is weird of her. It is making her strangely sad, this reminder of how her life was, when Martha was a little baby. It's silly to feel this way. Alice had hated many things about the baby stage: the relentlessness, the exhaustion, the loss of herself. She'd spent much of her maternity leave – when she and Yas were off work with Martha and Iris – as a tearful, soggy mess, convinced she was doing everything wrong, guilty that she longed so hard for Martha to nap longer, to be old enough to watch TV, just so she could have a break. But now, watching this cast of younger mothers doing all the same things she and Martha used to do, Alice feels a sense of loss. Like when you go back to your university town and a new cast of young people are there, living a life you thought had belonged only to you.

Alice had been relieved to return to work after maternity leave. Back in the studio, Martha happy at home with Becca, she'd felt like she could breathe again. But now that Martha is a child, a full-fledged person, Alice sometimes finds herself grieving the baby version of her. She sometimes wishes she could start again at the beginning, do a better job. But of course, nobody gets a second chance with their children.

The coffee shop is quiet, and Alice's nursing a single iced coffee over nearly an entire hour goes unremarked upon. Her phone vibrates again, and then falls silent. Alice wonders if the battery has died. She had seen it was low – she forgot to charge it last night. But anyway, she had sent Stella Becca's number – Stella will call Becca, won't she, if there's any problem?

Alice opens her wallet, stares at the picture she keeps inside it, of herself, Jamie and Martha, outside the ice-cream place in Rye. It was their first ever holiday as a family of three. They'd rented a glass-fronted house right on Camber Sands, called Gull Cry. They'd been back several times since.

Alice stares at Martha's chubby cheeks, Jamie's tanned, handsome smile, and then, finally, her own face. She'd been obsessed with how much weight she'd gained, embarrassed to take her dress off on the beach. But now all she sees is how smooth and line-free her face was, how her hair was still dark and thick and yet to feature the rogue greys she now regularly has to pluck out.

Alice suspects she should probably have had some sort of therapy after Martha was born, like the doctor had suggested, and as Jamie had constantly badgered her to. Would that have helped? Maybe if she had, they'd have had another baby when Jamie had still wanted to. Alice had never wanted Martha to be an only child, but when Jamie had wanted to try again – around the time of this holiday, she guesses – the thought of being pregnant again so soon had felt horrifying to Alice. Her reaction had been so emphatic that they'd barely spoken about it again. Until a few weeks ago. Just before the break-in. And apparently, Jamie had changed his mind about wanting another baby. So that was that.

Maybe if she'd had therapy, he'd feel differently. Maybe she'd be different and better. Happier, more balanced. Less likely to do what she did, even. As usual, Alice finds herself raking over the break-in in her mind, looking for some wobbly pencil line of logic from one thing to another. She wonders why she can't accept that, as Jamie says, such a line might not exist.

'We're closing early today, everyone.' A girl with a bored voice comes out from behind the counter. She starts collecting coffee cups and napkins. Alice replaces the photo in her wallet, stands up to return home, via the canal. But as she crosses back through the estate, she finds herself slowing her pace outside Linda's front door.

Alice pauses, just for a moment. Could she knock? Own up about the pot, and offer to replace it? That wouldn't be so bad, would it? She could take a tiny glimpse inside, that way. To the place where Ezra had lived.

Even in her own mind, it sounds ridiculous. It is ridiculous. *You need to leave this place*, she tells herself. *You need to leave now*. And she is about to – she will tell herself later that she was absolutely intending to do just that – when the door opens.

Blood rushes to Alice's head. She stares down at her hands, as if she might have knocked without even realising she had done so. But she hadn't. She hadn't done anything. It is as if she caused the door to open, just by being near it.

Linda steps out, holding an empty milk bottle. She places it on her step, bending at the knees, not the waist, ladylike. She doesn't seem to have noticed Alice, or the broken pot, at first. Then she suddenly looks up, locks eyes with her through a pair of frameless glasses.

'Can I help you?'

Linda does not look like the haunted woman who Alice saw on TV. There is powder blush on her cheeks, gaudy earrings bobbing at the edges of her face. Her nails are painted the same sugary pink as her lips.

'Oh.' Alice's mouth feels dry, her lips clumsy. 'No, I'm fine, thanks.'

'I thought I saw you here, just before.' Linda's accent is pure East London, her tone polite and curious, rather than hostile. Even so, Alice is flooded with adrenaline. She is not ready for this: actual contact, a confrontation. She braces for Linda to recognise her, from the news reports. But Linda seems to have no idea who she is.

'Is everything all right, love?' Linda prompts again.

Walk away, immediately, she hears Jessica's sharp voice saying. *We'll say you were on your way somewhere, that this was just an unhappy chance meeting. We can rescue this. But you need to leave now.*

Alice has a sudden awareness that she has only one chance at this, at doing the correct thing. But while she does not want to lie, nor can she tell the truth. She cannot speak. She simply cannot. When she opens her mouth, it feels emptied out of moisture. Talking feels impossible.

'If you don't mind me saying, love, you don't look too well.' Linda is looking at her kindly. 'It's been awfully hot today. Would you perhaps like to come in, for a glass of water?'

She smiles sweetly, a neat line of small teeth.

ALICE

Alice sits on the edge of a brown sofa and takes the glass of water Linda has handed to her.

'This is very kind of you,' Alice manages.

'Not at all.' Linda flaps her hand. 'It's nice to have company. Feels very quiet in here sometimes.'

Alice lifts the glass to her face. Linda smiles encouragingly.

'Drink that, lovey. You'll feel better.'

She takes a gulp.

'How do you feel now?'

That sweet line of teeth again, neat as piano keys.

'Fine, thank you so much.' Alice sets the glass down.

'They did say today and tomorrow would be the hottest days,' Linda continues. 'And then – rainstorms again! If you can believe it.'

'Oh, really?' Alice mumbles.

'I never know how much to believe, though, do you?'

'Hmm?'

'People say one thing. Often it turns out to be another.'

Alice looks up at this, alarmed. But the artless smile remains on Linda's face.

'That's why I never look at the news,' she carries on. 'I don't trust none of it. The nonsense people my age put up on Facebook – well, you wouldn't believe.' She gives a rueful smile. 'I'm Linda, by the way.'

It hadn't even occurred to Alice to ask Linda's name, because, of course, she already knew it. Has not asking made Alice look suspicious? She feels hot. What is she doing here? Why did she come in?

She needs to make an excuse, and leave. She can't stay longer, not without telling Linda who she is.

'What's your name, dear?'

Alice swallows. This is it. She has to tell Linda who she is. She has to.

'I'm Alice,' she murmurs.

She watches for the recognition to dawn on Linda's face, for her polite expression to contort into horror. But nothing happens. Linda continues to smile sweetly.

'Do you live around here, Alice?'

'Um – not far.'

'Just passing, then, were you?'

'I... I...'

Alice can almost feel the moment slipping past her. Her mouth feels so dry she cannot seem to form words, her tongue fused to the roof of her mouth. Linda says nothing. Just watches her, expectantly.

'I was... I was visiting a friend, nearby.'

The words just seem to fall out. And then suddenly, it is done. She has told a lie. Alice half expects to hear the scream of sirens outside, a knock on the door, the shadow of officers outside Linda's net curtains. But of course, nothing happens. Nothing at all.

Linda goes on looking at her for a second. Then, her smile falters and her face twists a little, like an electrical malfunction. She stands abruptly.

'Shall we have a proper drink?'

Alice is unsure what to say. Linda is suddenly brisk, turning to the kitchen, not looking at Alice for an answer.

'I don't normally start so early,' she calls behind her. 'Only Jesus God, it's so hot!'

While Linda is in the other room, Alice takes in the details of the flat. It smells musty, like the windows need opening, but it is clean and neat – at least, everywhere but the dining table, which is covered in papers, piles and piles of them, everywhere, flopping off the edges, spilling onto the rug underneath. It's as if Linda was in the middle of a huge sort-out and has given up.

When Linda reappears she is carrying a melamine tray with two cut-glass tumblers, fizzing with ice and lemon. As she sets it down, she winces a little, as if her back is bothering her. Alice wonders how old Linda is. Early sixties, she guesses. On the older side for the mother of a teenager.

Alice takes the glass from the tray and tips it towards Linda.

'Cheers,' she says quietly.

This is surreal, Alice thinks. But the prospect of a stiff drink is not unappealing, now she is holding the cool glass in her hand. The gin hits her in the back of the throat, strong and unexpectedly satisfying. Alice goes back for another sip, then stops with the glass mid-air as her eye alights on a framed photograph behind Linda.

An ordinary family snap, a teenage boy, his arm around his mum. He has, Alice realises, the same upturned smile, the same small, neat teeth as his mother. Linda looks younger, and tanned – perhaps they are on holiday. The picture is cropped close, and it's hard to tell. There is a third person, too, in the photo. A skinny girl, with the same eyes as Ezra.

'Ah. That's my two,' Linda says, seeing her looking, reaching behind her and picking the photo up in her hands. 'My son, his name was Ezra. He died, very recently. A sudden thing.'

Alice fixes her gaze on the ground, unable to look at Linda. What a terrible mistake she has made, by coming here. She hears Linda give a deep sigh.

'He lived here still, with me. He was my boy.' Linda's voice sounds laboured, sort of wet. 'So I'm on my own now. It's quiet without him. Can't seem to get used to it.'

With an effort, Alice forces herself to look Linda in the eye, to say the words she has wanted to say ever since the day it happened.

'I'm so sorry, Linda.'

As soon as she says it, Alice is choked with emotion. Even though she knows that she is cheating, that she doesn't deserve to feel better, she does.

'Thank you, love.' Linda looks down at the picture, crooks a finger to rub at a mark on the frame.

'He'd got himself into something,' she says, still rubbing with her finger, her voice loosened a little. 'Something he had no business being part of. It wasn't his fault, really. It all just got out of hand.'

Alice stares at Linda, suddenly alert. Her heart is thumping in her chest. So there *was* something – something that led Ezra to Alice's door. Alice is desperate to ask for more information, but of course, doing so directly is impossible, so she lets Linda keep talking.

'He was a bit of a handful, Ezra.' Linda is sighing now, rubbing one eye. 'Had a lot of problems. Couldn't get on with school. Couldn't settle to things. He was getting to be like his father.'

Linda sets the photo down in her lap then picks up the glass again. Alice watches her glug until the liquid is gone. What problems is she talking about? Alcohol? Drugs? Something else?

Linda stands up, replaces the framed photo, then retrieves the gin bottle from the kitchen, before returning and topping her own glass up another inch. Alice watches her pour, the slight tremor of her hand. She thinks about Ezra's slurred speech, his confusion. The tremble of his hand on the knife. They say alcoholism runs in families, don't they?

'Are you all right, dear?'

Alice hadn't realised she had closed her eyes. She snaps them open.

'Don't tell me,' Linda says gently. 'You've lost someone too? Is that it?'

Alice stares at the orange swirls in the carpet.

'It's a bit complicated.'

'I see.' Linda bows her head, signalling a respectful retreat from the topic. Alice steals another glance at the picture, at the girl with the same pale eyes as Ezra.

'Is that your daughter?'

'Yes,' Linda's tone hardens a little, 'that's Jade.'

'Ezra's sister,' Alice prompts.

'His twin.'

Alice swallows. Ezra was a twin. Why had none of the endless news stories mentioned the sister?

'I expect they... were close?'

'Oh, yes.' Linda looks away. 'Always close. Too close.'

There is a sharpness in Linda's tone. She takes another sip from her glass, which must be basically neat gin now. Her eyes are unfocused for a moment as she tips it back.

Alice wonders what she means, what this Jade is like. She wracks her brains for what else she can legitimately ask.

'Has Jade been supporting you? Since it happened?'

Linda's face clouds a little.

'Jade does her own thing,' she answers eventually. 'Always has. She's been coming and going. When it suits her.'

Alice tries to piece together the dynamics of this family. An adored but troubled son. A difficult daughter. The father dead.

'Ezra loved Jade.' Linda is looking away into the middle distance now, almost as if she has forgotten Alice is there. 'He was protective of her – not that she needed protecting. She can look after herself, that one.' Linda gives her head a little shake. 'I think he looked up to her, in a funny way, even though they were the same age. Jade was always a bit more switched on, you see. Whereas Ezra was... easily led. Which is probably why he ended up—'

Linda jerks her head at Alice, seeming to suddenly remember the stranger sitting with her.

'Oh, never mind, love. Doesn't matter now.'

Alice sips her drink, her mind racing. Linda was about to say something then. About Ezra. About whatever it was that led him to her. For the first time since it happened, it feels like the fog is lifting a little, that she is nearing an answer. But she needs to tread carefully.

There could be more clues, Alice thinks suddenly. Here. In his flat. Maybe among his things.

Alice glances down Linda's hallway. She sees a double bed with a pink bedspread in the room at the end. There are two other doors. A bathroom, she supposes, then another bedroom.

He lived here still, with me.

'Linda, would you mind if I used your bathroom?'
Linda looks at her strangely, for a beat. Then her face clears.
'Of course, love. Just on the left.'

Alice treads softly down the orange carpet, pressing her palms to the walls.

Alice decides she has to look. She might never get this chance again. If Linda asks, she can say she got the wrong room.

Alice pushes the door of Ezra's bedroom and presses the switch. The central light flickers on, a bright white bulb in a blue shade that makes a faint fizzing sound.

Ezra's bed is unmade, the sheets creased, a sports holdall shoved half-under the bed. There are energy drink cans on his desk, a laptop, a coil of wires, thick as a rat's nest, underneath. A Nintendo switch. Two pairs of trainers, one pair neatly stacked, the other kicked off, with laces trailing, as if he just stepped out of them, and vanished.

Then Alice sees something else. Lying on the floor, between the wires and the trainers.

Alice stares at it, then has to close her eyes and look again. Because it cannot be here. It is in the wrong place.

A home-made star-shaped key ring with rainbow stripes. The key ring her daughter made for her at her after-school art club.

It is here, on the floor of Ezra's bedroom.

LINDA

I knew who she was, of course I did.

Saw her mooning about outside, peeping through my curtains, knocking over that old plant and I thought: I knew you'd come.

I couldn't see her well, through the nets, but I'd have known that guilty face anywhere. I'd kept all the papers. There was a picture of her online, too, on her work website, where she did her job fixing paintings and whatnot. A black and white portrait of her, her hair falling about all soft and messy in that way posh women wear it. In the news articles they'd said she was forty-two, but in the portrait she'd looked younger – one of those childish faces. A shirt with a strange old-fashioned collar, trendy probably, something a slim girl like her can wear.

She didn't look nice like that today, though. She looked a right mess. Hair all lank like she'd not showered in days, purple half-moons under her eyes. Looked like she'd aged ten years. *Well*, I thought. *Good*.

I wasn't ready for her, the first time, so I was relieved when she lost her nerve and ran off. But I guessed that she would come back, try again. Interesting that she came, knowing how much trouble I could get her in, with the coppers, for coming. I reckon she had to have really wanted to come, to take that sort of risk.

I wondered why.

I sat a little while, had a drink, let myself settle. I found my picture of Ezra, the one I keep by my bed, and I moved it right behind the sofa. I wanted to see her face, when she saw his. The face of the person she killed.

When she came back, I waited for her to knock, but I soon saw I'd have to take matters into my own hands. So I took a deep breath and opened the door. I wasn't going to make it easy, though. Better to pretend not to know who she was, wait for her to own up to what she'd done.

But then she sat on my sofa, and didn't say anything. I kept waiting for her to come out with it, but she didn't.

When I realised she wasn't going to come clean after all, that she wasn't going to admit who she was, what she'd done – well. I felt myself getting a little bit cross. What had she come for, then? To gawp at me?

I needed to get away from her for a bit. A drink seemed like a good idea. I found my hands were shaking as I mixed the gin and tonic. I couldn't cut the lemons properly, and the slices came out all wrong, all thick at one end, translucent the other. Things like that get to me, asymmetry, unevenness. I had to throw them in the bin, start again.

When I put the gin bottle back, it occurred to me that all of John's old medicines were still there in the cupboard, from before he died. Sleeping tablets, muscle relaxants. All sorts. It would be so easy, I thought. She was skinnier than I'd imagined, not much bigger than Jade really. It wouldn't have taken much.

But no, I thought. I wanted to have an eye on her. I needed to see for myself whether she cared enough, felt guilty enough, about killing my son.

The funny thing was, as it went on, I found myself feeling a bit sorry for her, with her lank hair and twitchy fingers. She was cut up about it, I could see that well enough. And of course, I know what it is to have done a terrible thing. To have sinned in the eyes of God.

I tried to work out how much she knew, about what had come before. As far as I could tell, she was in the dark about it all. Which is no bad thing.

I think that's why she came, though. She can feel there's more to it, that the truth is hovering somewhere out of her reach. I know she pretended to need the loo, and had a poke around in his bedroom. I've a feeling she even took something of his, though I'm not sure what.

When she'd gone, I poured myself another drink – well, can you blame me? Jade would, she says I've got a *dependency problem*, that I *use alcohol as a crutch*. By the time it got dark, the bottle was gone. Perhaps she's got a point.

I popped it in the recycling, started again on my piles of papers. I need to get everything sorted out – I haven't much time. But somehow, I keep losing track, having to start again at the beginning.

I put the latest letters from the doctors on top of the throwaway pile. I don't know why they keep on at me about these appointments – aren't the NHS supposed to be on their last legs? Well, they can keep their drugs, their scans, their radiation, thank you very much. I know I don't have long, and that's fine by me. None of it matters any more. I'll leave it in the hands of the Lord.

I have my regrets, of course I do. I think everyone does. I'll never forgive myself for the things I've done. For all the secrets, all the lies.

That's why I've decided to write it all down, just like this. Ezra doesn't need his laptop any more. It's just been sitting there since the police finished with it. I haven't known what to do with his things. It feels sort of nice to switch it on, have it warm and buzzing on my lap, with all his silly stickers on it. A little piece of him.

I'm not the fastest at writing it all out. My fingers aren't what they used to be, thanks to arthritis. It's one thing after another at my age, was like that even before I got sick. But anyway. Not much longer. I can feel that somehow.

I don't know who I'm writing this for exactly. I don't even know if I'll be able to finish it in time. But at least then I've told the truth, in some sort of way. And maybe it'll be like the Bible says. The truth will set me free.

ALICE

Alice is in the hallway, her empty coffee mug in her hand. She can hear the creak of Jamie's office chair as she passes his study at the back of the ground floor. Jamie has a load more parcels piled up in the hallway, from 'securitysolutions.com'. Alice sighs. She suspects it's just a displacement activity, his new obsession with security. He wants to feel he is doing something. Even if there is nothing to be done.

She considers going into the study, to collect his espresso cup and ask if he wants anything, then hears he is on a work call. He has a specific voice for these calls – energetic, relentlessly upbeat. The voice of the Jamie she was first drawn to, the Jamie everyone is drawn to, the parent whose energy her daughter so obviously prefers.

Alice is used to people looking over her head for Jamie at parties, breaking into delighted smiles when they see that he is there. To waiting, coat on her arm, while he finishes his chat with the bartender or the taxi driver or whoever he has struck up a connection with. He is just so good at other people, at listening.

It was the same when they met. He turned up the dimmer switch on her life. She'd told herself there were advantages to not having a partner, or any sign of one, in the latter half of her thirties. She had, albeit through unhappy circumstances, her own house, her dream kitchen, decorated the way she liked, with colour and pattern choices that Aunt Sarah had made faces about at first, before later admitting it 'had turned out rather nicely, in the end'. She had her dream job, working with some of the most extraordinary paintings in the world. She had the freedom to go to an art gallery, a spin class, take the Eurostar to Paris whenever she liked. (She hadn't done that for years, but she theoretically could.) She had built a life she loved, was the point. And she was fine. It was only when she met Jamie that she had thought how dull, how colourless that life had been, in comparison to a life with him in it, a life in which she and Jamie could go to Paris together.

She listens to Jamie on his call for a while. She can only hear his voice, not anyone else's. He must have his headphones on. He is talking about the charity's brand vision for the next five years, what their strategy should be, the possible impact of a change of government.

This sounds like an important meeting, and listening to it gives Alice an uneasy feeling. Jamie had said his work would be quiet in August, that he didn't have any meetings he couldn't do on Zoom. She wonders now if the real reason he is still at home is because he is genuinely anxious about their security. Or worse, because he still thinks Alice, who doesn't start at her new job until next month and is at home until then, is going slightly mad. Either way, him being around today is annoying. It means she'll have to make up some lie about where she is going.

Alice shoves her hand into the pocket of the oversized cardigan she wears around the house, and closes her fingers around the key ring she found at Ezra's. She finds herself doing this several times a day, feeling each point of its star between her fingers in turn, checking it really exists.

She still hasn't said anything to Jamie yet, about visiting Linda, and finding the key ring in Ezra's room. She wants to get it straight in her mind, first, how such a thing could have happened. What the various explanations are. And what each one might mean.

She had considered the possibility that she herself had the key ring in her bag all along, and had somehow dropped it that day as she crept into Ezra's bedroom. But after careful thought, she had discounted this. Before they'd left for the pool, Alice had searched her rucksack from top to bottom for the key ring, just as she had Martha's school bag, and all the other tote bags hanging on hooks by the door. And she was consciously being quiet when she went into Ezra's room – she'd have noticed if she'd dropped something.

Her key ring must have got there some other way. Except, she'd never been to that flat before. And it couldn't have been that Ezra took it during the burglary at Alice's home – because he'd never made it back. Thanks to her.

Had Ezra stolen it at an earlier date? Along with her keys, perhaps as part of a plan to burgle her? Perhaps he'd removed the key ring, fearing it was too distinctive, and retained only the house keys, and that's how it had ended up on his floor.

But this made even less sense. Alice hasn't lost any house keys, just the key ring. And if Ezra had been smart enough to steal Alice's keys to burgle her house, why on earth would he have shown up when Alice was at home, and broken the basement door down instead of using his key?

Alice had been left with only one other, uncomfortable thought. Had Ezra taken other things? Had he been stalking them? Watching them – or watching her? And if so, why? Why them? What had Alice been to him?

Alice has decided there is only one way to find out. She needs to go back and see Linda, apologise for not being honest the first time, and just tell her the truth about who she is. How she came because she is haunted by what she has done and cannot move past it. And she will also tell Linda about the key ring, and ask her what she thinks it could mean, what the connection could have been between Ezra and her.

Of course, she knows she is taking a huge risk, and that there's a possibility Linda could tell the police. But Alice has convinced herself the chances of Linda reporting her are low, that she is both kind and old-school enough to instinctively dislike the prospect of grassing someone up to the cops.

She is also sure that Linda knows something, about whatever it was that Ezra was involved in before the break-in. *He'd got himself into something, something he had no business being part of* – that was what she'd said. Alice has thought about those words, over and over, wondering what they meant.

Alice ducks her head into the living room, where Martha is watching cartoons.

'You need to leave for tennis camp in five minutes,' she calls. 'Becca's going to walk you.'

'But none of my friends go to tennis camp,' Martha objects.

'Yes, they do. Frankie does. You are still friends with Frankie, aren't you? You had a nice time with her at the pool?'

Martha pouts. 'She's OK. But she always copies me.'

'That's not very kind, Martha,' Alice's admonishment is half-hearted. She is impatient to get on with her day. 'I'm sure you'll have other friends there too. Can you get your shoes on, please?'

Martha doesn't even look at her, her face television-dulled.

Alice rubs one of the points of the star, the glitter scratching softly against the pad of her thumb. She feels guilty about having so easily abandoned her fantasy of spending the summer holidays just hanging out with her daughter, before she starts her new job in September. But she just can't stop thinking about Linda and Ezra, and the anonymous call, and the key ring. She has decided at the last minute to sign Martha up to a tennis camp Stella had mentioned, that Frankie is going to. Only for a few days. A week at most. Alice just needs a little bit of time to herself. To work out what she is going to do.

Alice carries her mug down to the kitchen, where Becca is standing by the sink. Becca is working a tea towel in her hands.

'Hey, Becca.' Something about the way she is standing makes Alice pause. 'Are you OK?'

'Me? Fine.' But Becca looks grey, drained of colour. 'I just wondered, though, if you might have time for that chat this morning?'

Alice had forgotten that there was something Becca had wanted to talk about. She doesn't want to do this now. Having made the decision to go back to Ezra's home, she is anxious to leave, flooded with the adrenaline of it. But Becca looks like she might combust if Alice puts her off again.

'Sure,' she says breezily. 'Of course. What's up?'

Becca is still holding the tea towel, folding it and refolding it in her hands. She clears her throat.

'Can we – shall we sit down?'

Becca sits down and Alice takes a seat opposite, on one of the new stools that she doesn't like. Becca is wearing wide linen culottes which cling to her hips, a cropped sleeveless shirt which shows her blotchy upper arms. Alice always used to think that Becca just had an eccentric dress sense, but she has recently realised all the younger people in East London dress like this now, in these weird, unflattering high-waisted trousers, big trainers, cycling shorts. She'd been shocked to realise this had happened to her – that people had started looking young, wearing clothes she didn't understand.

Becca, though, never looks quite right in her generation's fashionable clothes. There is something unfinished about Becca, an unsteadiness, like a child in adults' things.

Becca puts the tea towel to one side, then pushes a strand of her long hair behind her ear, her eyes darting from the windows to the table to the floor. She looks like she is about to cry.

'Is everything OK, Becca?'

As soon as Alice asks the question, Becca's eyes moisten.

'Oh, Becs. I'm sorry. What is it?'

Alice tries to work out what she has missed. She tries to think when she and Becca last had a proper chat. They used to. Becca was very private – she has never spoken to Alice about dates or boyfriends or anything like that – but she had told Alice a bit about her family, in Devon. Alice had got the impression her upbringing, as the adored only child of conservative Christian parents, had been somewhat oppressive.

Alice had even wondered, sometimes, if she and Jamie felt almost like a surrogate London family for Becca, a family who had chosen her and who she could be herself with. Alice had liked the idea of being that for Becca. Alice had been lost at Becca's age, too. She'd had no parents or siblings, no real family at all, apart from Aunt Sarah, who – although Alice knew she'd done her best – always felt like she was in Alice's life more through obligation than anything else. From what Becca said about her own parents, there were parallels.

And Alice loves having Becca around. She has always felt more like a friend than an employee. She is so conscientious that Alice has never really had to keep track of her expenses, or her holiday days – she has never really asked for much, and if she has ever wanted time off, Alice has never wanted to deny her it.

A few months ago, Becca had seemed happy. She'd been talking about buying a flat, had said her parents were going to help her with a deposit. Alice had got the impression there was a partner of some kind on the scene, too. But more recently – in the weeks before the break-in – Becca has seemed different. Withdrawn, monosyllabic, even a bit moody. She has gained weight, too, and seems to have stopped paying so much attention to her appearance. She has been coming in with lank hair, lumpy leggings, stopped bothering with make-up. When had all that started? Was it a break-up? Or something else?

'I've been trying to find the right time,' Becca murmurs eventually. 'And it never seems to be... I know it's a terrible time for you both, and I feel so awful, doing this now.'

It takes a minute for Alice to understand, for the panic to rise in her chest.

'Oh,' Alice says. 'Oh, no.'

Becca talks falteringly, seemingly close to tears but with a dogged determination to get the words out that is almost painful for Alice to watch. She talks about how much she has loved seeing Martha grow up, but how her return to school in September 'just feels like a natural time' for Becca to 'move on'.

So this is what it's all been leading up to, Alice thinks. All the days she has been calling in sick, all the weird moods she's been in when she is here.

But you *can't* quit, Alice thinks. We talked about this just a few weeks ago. I told you about the new job I'm starting in September – the long hours. I won't be able to manage without you. But of course, all that is about Alice, what *she* needs.

'I thought you were happy to stay another year,' she says gently. 'Did – something change?'

Becca looks away, and Alice feels awful.

'Sorry. Perhaps that's a silly question. The burglary must have been horrible for you, Becca.'

Clearly, she and Jamie haven't thought properly about how the break-in has affected their employee, which is remiss of them, especially as they've ensured Martha, who barely even remembers it, has full access to an expensive therapist (apparently her main comment was 'I was just watching *Encanto*'). Becca is so young. They have a duty of care to her. Should they have given her time off? Arranged counselling or something? At least offered?

'It's not just that,' Becca mumbles.

Alice can't ask more questions now, because Becca is wobbling, crumbling into a soggy mess. Has something else been going on with her, something Alice hasn't seen, through the fog that has enveloped her own life?

She knows it is selfish, but this is going to be so bloody stressful, replacing Becca before her new job starts. Also, she hates the idea of their undersized family unit shrinking further. She realises with sudden clarity that Becca is probably the closest thing Martha will ever have to an aunt, or sister. But maybe Alice was wrong to think she could somehow purchase such a thing for Martha.

Alice reaches out for the younger woman's hand and squeezes it. Becca is upset – her own disappointment will have to wait. She takes a breath, gropes in her mind for the right thing to say, the right advice.

'Becs, we will be very sad to lose you, but you must do what's right for you. You must always do that. When will you leave?'

Becca exhales noisily, then looks away abruptly, brushing at a tear forming on her bottom eyelash.

Alice feels furious with herself for not knowing what it says in Becca's contract – the document that keeps their very lives going. Surely it should be three months? She has a horrible feeling this is not the case, though. Is it two months? Surely it can't be just one?

'Will you… still come to Rye with us at the end of the summer holidays?' Alice ventures. 'Martha is so looking forward to it.'

Taking Becca on a free holiday each year has always felt like a price well worth paying for her willingness to help in the day and in the evenings. Alice knows how hopeless this makes her, but for her and Jamie, the holiday will feel a lot less like a holiday without Becca there. Is this normal, Alice wonders? How reliant she feels on Becca to prop up her own hit-and-miss parenting, how panicky she feels at the thought of not having her around?

'Um, oh. OK,' Becca nods, sniffing. 'Sure.'

'Oh, good. Please don't be upset. We'll work this all out.'

Alice hopes she is saying the right things, supportive things. Becca sniffs wetly, holding the tea towel up to her face.

'I knew you'd be like this, Alice,' she mutters. 'So kind about it. It makes it even harder…'

Becca collapses into sobs. *For goodness' sake*, Alice thinks. *Stay here, if it's so hard, don't leave us. We can work this out, whatever 'this' is.*

'Becca,' she says, reaching for another squeeze of her hand. 'Is there… is there really nothing I can say to change your mind?'

But this time Becca pulls her hand away abruptly from Alice. A blotchiness rises to her eyes and cheeks, a tremor in her fingers as she pushes a piece of hair behind her ear, once, then again, as if it won't stay put.

'I just need to leave here, OK? I need to leave.'

Alice is silenced. Becca's tone is final, like a slammed door. And Alice is sure she can feel it now, the shadow of something else, something bigger, moving under the surface of the conversation.

ALICE

She presses Linda's doorbell gently, practising the words she had prepared for when Linda comes to the door. She has a box of the sensational coconut macaroons from the Violet bakery packed carefully in a tote bag on her shoulder. She grips the strap of the bag, trying to quiet the voices in her head telling her she should not be back here, taking this stupid risk. That Jessica would kill her, not to mention Jamie.

Just wondered how you were. Wondered if you fancied a cup of tea.

Linda, I need to tell you something. I need to tell you the truth.

Alice waits a while. She can't tell if the shuffling sound she can hear is coming from inside the flat. The broken pot has been left on its side, and the plants on Linda's patio look in worse shape now, after two more weeks of summer heat, their straggly tendrils colourless and crisped. Linda's windowsills are newly grubby, her formerly clean windows fogged by a layer of dust.

The person who eventually answers the door is not Linda, but a much younger woman.

The girl is small and slight, not much taller than Linda, her slim figure drowned in a T-shirt and baggy tracksuit bottoms. Thick, tinted eyebrows and curves of synthetic eyelash sit uneasily on a childish face. Alice recognises her from the picture. It is Jade.

'Oh right. It's you,' Jade says, staring up at Alice.

Alice is thrown, the words she had prepared evaporating. Surely Linda hasn't told Jade about their encounter? Jade must think Alice is someone else. But who? Does she recognise her from the newspapers? But if she does, why isn't she angry?

'Well, are you coming in, then?'

'Oh,' Alice mumbles. 'Yes, please. Thank you.'

Jade stands to one side to let Alice pass. Before she knows what she is doing, Alice is past her, inside the flat.

'I'll show you through here, shall I?' Jade turns around. 'It's funny, you sound different than you did on the phone.'

Alice blinks. The phone? For a single mad moment, Alice wonders if Jade could be talking about the calls from an unknown number, if she is confessing to being the one who called her at the pool.

The flat is messier than when she was here last. There are clothes and shoes everywhere, used cereal bowls and coffee mugs strewn over the orange-swirl carpet. Jade picks a path through to the cramped hallway. They are heading to Ezra's bedroom, Alice realises. Before she has had time to process what is happening, Jade opens the door.

The room looks entirely different. All Ezra's things are gone, packed away. It has been stripped of furniture, and piled with boxes. There is a battered buggy in one corner, a few shopping bags.

'The cot will need to fit there.' Jade gestures to a corner of the room where the carpet is worn almost completely away. 'Do you do car seats, as well? On the phone you said it depends what you've got in. I need everything, basically. I don't even know what I need! Someone gave me a pram, but I dunno, the wheel sticks a bit. It's like a wonky trolley.'

For the first time, Alice notices the curve under Jade's baggy tracksuit top. A neat sphere, as if Jade has a football stashed under there. She is, Alice would guess, five months pregnant. Maybe more.

Jade picks at her eye with a single finger, making a visible effort not to dislodge her eyelashes. She extracts a small blob of black goop, holds it in front of her face to examine it.

'You worked there long?'

'Sorry?'

'At the baby bank.'

Alice finally understands what is happening. Jade thinks Alice is here from a baby bank. Alice has heard of baby banks, she knows what they are – like food banks, but for baby stuff. Jamie has mentioned them to her. His charity sometimes referred expectant mothers to them.

That's why she is being so calm. She thinks Alice is a charity worker. She has no idea that Alice is the person who killed her twin brother. Alice clamps her jaw shut in a bid to control the rising nausea.

'So?' Jade says. 'What do you think, about the pram?'

Alice forces herself to concentrate on what Jade is asking her. She follows her gaze to an old buggy covered in scuffs and stickers, the material blotchy with stains.

'There's only a chair thing, you know?' Jade puts her hands on her hips, stares at the buggy. 'I dunno whether you can even, um... put a baby in that.'

'You would need a bassinet,' Alice hears herself saying. 'For a newborn. They – they need to lie flat.'

'Oh, yeah, I thought that, too,' Jade replies quickly, with a bravado that is slightly heartbreaking.

'You might be able to find a bassinet that fits that pram, though,' Alice says, trying to be helpful. 'A second-hand one, online maybe.' Alice is aware she is still talking. Why is she still talking?

'OK,' Jade nods. 'I just don't have that much cash, is all.' She glances to one side. 'You reckon there might be one at the baby bank?'

Alice's cheeks are burning. She needs to own up, tell Jade she's nothing to do with any baby bank. But then she thinks about what Linda said about Jade and Ezra. That they were 'close', even 'too close', whatever that meant. How would Jade react, at being told the truth?

'I... I don't know,' she stammers.

'Right.' Jade nods. 'Well, how should we do it for the other stuff? Do I make a list, or what? Fuck it, I need a cuppa. Want one?'

Alice sits in the living room and listens to the sound of Jade in the kitchen next door, opening a fridge, clinking mugs together. The sofa cushions sag under her thighs. She shifts forward, trying not to sink.

The presence of Jade, rather than Linda, has thrown her. Alice looks at the mess Jade has made of Linda's neat flat, since she was last here. She wonders where Linda has gone, and what Jade has done with Ezra's things, where she might have stored them away. There is no sign of his laptop, or any of Ezra's other things, anywhere. Just the same piles of papers all over the table.

She stands up carefully, and edges towards the dining table. The first stack contains a leaflet from Co-op Funeralcare, a letter from an undertaker. Another from the office of the coroner, stating that Ezra's inquest is due to take place in the spring, giving a list of possible witnesses. Alice is startled to see her own name, right there, on the letter.

She looks away, scans the tops of the other piles, tries to get a sense of what is inside without picking anything up. The next stack looks like bills, missed payment letters. There are multiple letters from the NHS, too, all addressed to Linda. She seems to have a habit of ignoring correspondence. There is talk of missed appointments, blood tests, screenings. What she is being screened for is not clear to Alice; it seems a lot for a sprightly woman in her sixties. Is Linda ill? Or maybe they are routine things, but in her grief, Linda has lost track.

One leaflet is crumpled, as if it's been discarded, then pressed flat again. *Genetic counselling – what you need to know.* Alice has never heard of genetic counselling. Maybe this is linked to whatever is wrong with Linda. Or maybe it's Jade's? Some new thing they do now for pregnant women?

She thinks about taking the leaflet and stuffing it in her pocket, but then she hears Jade's footsteps coming, and is forced to step away.

Jade walks in holding two mugs, a folded piece of lined notepad paper pinched between the knuckles of her right hand.

'I did a list,' she says hopefully. 'Just in case.'

She hands it over to Alice, and Alice stares at it.

Cot, car seat, snowsuit. Babygros for a girl, Age 0–3 months or newborn ones. Jade's handwriting is rounded and childish, the 'i's dotted with bubbly little circles.

A while back, Jamie had suggested they donate some of Martha's old things to the baby bank his charity worked with. Alice knew, from him, how much need there was in their borough, away from their little pocket of gentrification. How families were struggling to afford heating, milk and nappies, let alone cots, mattresses, warm clothes. But somehow, she'd never quite found it within herself to hand Martha's baby things over, and Jamie had never pushed it. Perhaps he'd guessed at how she was feeling.

'I don't like to be asking for stuff.' Jade brushes some imaginary fluff from the sofa next to her. Up close, her Bambi eyelashes are less convincing, and Alice spots a dimpled ridge of acne hiding under the foundation on her jawline.

'My ex, Ryan, he was gonna get everything,' Jade says. She looks briefly sad, before hardening her expression. 'But we're not really together anymore, so.' She sniffs. 'He's decided he's not that keen. About the whole baby thing.'

'I see. I'm sorry.'

'He's a fucking waste of space,' Jade says, with a sudden flash of aggression. Alice startles a little. Then Jade shrugs. 'It is what it is.'

Alice scans the list Jade has handed her, wondering how the morning could possibly have taken this turn. While she might not have actually lied to Jade, it feels very much like the moment when she could have told the truth has already passed. And while telling Linda the truth had felt possible to Alice, Jade is a different creature. She seems edgy, sort of volatile. If Alice tells Jade the truth, she will also have to admit that she was here before, and lied to Jade's mother about who she was. What if Jade reacts angrily, calls the police on her? No – the risk is too great. Alice is in too deep now. She can see no option but to keep lying.

'We'll be all right on our own, me and her,' Jade is saying now.

Alice wonders if she is trying to convince herself.

'You're having a girl, then?' Alice asks, hesitantly.

'Yeah. That's what they told me.' She smiles at Alice, as if it has given her pleasure, to share this news with someone, even a stranger. Alice senses Jade isn't overwhelmed with people to share this news with. Who are happy for her.

'That's great. Congratulations.' Alice pauses. 'If Ryan's not, um... is someone else supporting you, Jade? Your mum, maybe?'

Alice is curious about where Linda is. Is Linda happy about Jade moving in like this, clearing out her beloved dead son's room? Alice wonders.

'Mum's not here any more.' Jade shrugs. 'She had an accident, broke a few ribs and her hip.'

'That's awful. I'm sorry.' Alice is genuinely alarmed. Poor Linda. 'How did it happen?'

Jade looks oddly blank. 'I didn't see.'

'Right.' Alice asks another way, 'Was it – at home?'

Jade gives her a suspicious look. 'Just out there,' she says. 'On the steps outside.' Jade looks away. 'She drinks a bit, my mum.'

'Oh.' Alice thinks of the melamine tray of daytime gin and tonics. 'I'm sorry.'

'Yeah.' Jade's voice is flat. 'She's been up and down. My brother died, not long ago. She's taken it hard.' Jade's words thump between them like heavy things.

'That's – that's so sad,' Alice stammers. 'That you lost your brother – I'm so sorry, Jade. Was it – was it very recent?'

Jade looks at Alice, and for a single airless moment, Alice thinks that Jade is about to tell Alice that she knows exactly who she is, and just how sorry she must be. But then her face abruptly changes, like everything is suddenly wiped clear.

'So,' Jade says. 'What do you reckon?'

'About...'

'The clothes for the baby and that. Can you come back, bring me some bits?'

Alice, stalling for time, lifts up the mug of tea and takes a small sip. It is scalding hot. *Get a grip*, she tells herself. *You are here from the baby bank. You are here to supply clothes.*

She looks at Jade. A mum who is unable to help her, a boyfriend who is not interested, a brother who is dead. And then she thinks about the baby stuff stored under the eaves in their loft. Bags and bags of neatly folded baby girl's clothes, blankets and toys, packed away in big checked laundry bags. An expensive cot, too, that they shipped in from Denmark.

And she also thinks about how much more she wants to know, that Jade might be able to tell her. About Ezra, what was happening in his life, before he died.

'I think we can... find most of it for you.'

It is a good thing to do, isn't it? To donate Martha's baby stuff, like Jamie had wanted to. Helping this young pregnant girl. Helping her baby.

And if she comes back here, and is kind to Jade, then maybe Jade will open up. Tell her things, about Ezra. Maybe then it will start to make sense – why he had the keyring Martha made. Why he came to her house.

Deep down, Alice knows what she really wants to hear from Jade, and Linda. She wants to hear that Ezra was bad. Violent, dangerous, a force beyond anyone's control. Because then it will all feel less, the burden of it. It will feel like something that was out of her hands, that was not her fault. And Alice can finally start to forgive herself, for killing him.

ALICE

Alice tells Jamie she will be spending the morning in the loft, sorting out things to give to a baby bank, like he suggested.

'Oh, great.' He gives Alice a meaningful smile, a little squeeze as he passes her in the kitchen. It makes her feel irritated, like she is being congratulated for having come to her senses on the issue.

Her irritation makes her feel less guilty about lying to him. Well, not lying exactly. It's not *unlike* giving Martha's things to a baby bank. Alice is just cutting out the middleman.

In the loft, Alice pulls the storage bags towards her and starts to locate the things she'd had in mind for Jade: the baby blanket with pompoms in pastel colours, the white quilted snowsuit lined with fleece. These are nice things, expensive things, from brands stocked by the boutiques in Broadway Market and Victoria Park. She remembers bringing them home, wrapped in tissue paper, cardboard labels tied on with ribbon. She'd probably get good money if she sold them on the parent groups, or Vinted. But giving them to Jade will feel better.

Alice rummages through the bags, but can't find any of the really tiny, newborn-sized things. She crawls deeper into the storage space, where the ceiling slopes right down and the dust is mouse-thick on the surface of the exposed joists. Shoved right at the back, she sees one final checked bag – that must be it. As she pulls it out, a black bin bag falls from behind, where it has been shoved. Alice hasn't been up here for ages, but she feels sure she didn't store any of the baby things in one of those.

She reaches for the bin bag, pulls it out with one hand, then opens it up. It contains an unfamiliar black hoody, dark jogging bottoms, a T-shirt. The clothes smell damp and sweaty, like gym gear that Jamie's forgotten to put through the wash. Alice cannot fathom how they have ended up here, in the loft, behind the baby clothes.

Alice takes the bin bag out to put in the laundry, making up her mind to ask Jamie about it later. She pulls the final checked bag out, into the light, and starts selecting the newborn clothes. Another smaller snowsuit, some tiny sets of velour trousers with feet, which she remembers being useful at the beginning. It feels so far away, now, the time when Alice had a baby small enough to place inside this pillowy pink suit and push in the pram through Stonebridge Gardens, her little eyes all wide with the sight of the tree branches in the wind. Alice still remembers the sensation of lifting baby Martha from this padded suit after a nap, her body warm and sleepy, her legs all scrunched up to her tummy, little boxer's fists raised above her head.

Alice shoves the snowsuit determinedly to one side, and the memory with it. She should have done this ages ago. It is ridiculous to have been storing these things pointlessly, when they'd decided there would be no more babies. Or, Jamie had decided. Which amounted, of course, to the same thing.

A few months ago, she told Jamie she thought she was finally ready. That they should go for it. Alice knew plenty of women still having babies well into their forties. It would be different, this time. Everyone said they were more relaxed the second time around. Martha was big enough to help out. It would be easier. It would be fine.

Jamie had burst out laughing.

'Oh, hang on,' he'd said, seeing her face. 'You're not – I thought you were joking.'

Alice tried to smile.

'Is it that ridiculous?'

'Um – I mean, in my head, yes.' He searched her face, bemused. 'I thought we made the call on this, years ago. I thought we decided it wasn't for us. I thought you decided you couldn't do it.'

That was when Martha was still a baby, though, Alice thought. It was different then. *I was drowning.*

'And, honestly?' Jamie scratched his head. 'The more time has gone on, the more I'm relieved we didn't. I think two would be really stressful for us, with our jobs. I thought you thought that too.'

Alice had felt ridiculous then, for having had absolutely no idea that her husband considered the question of another baby closed for ever. The thought made her feel suddenly adrift.

'I did think that,' Alice said flatly. 'But I... I feel differently now. I think maybe I just needed a gap.'

Jamie had sat down beside her, taken her hand. 'You don't think you're just forgetting how hard it was? Don't you feel we're just a bit... a bit too old for all that again?'

The truth was that this was the first time Alice had ever really considered whether she might be too old for anything. Until this conversation, she had taken for granted the constant presence of multiple possibilities about how her life might turn out. She'd assumed all sorts of possibilities were still stretched out wide, like tree branches, ripe for the taking. She'd assumed there was still enough time to flex and change. That the finished picture of her life was ahead of her, not behind.

But looking at Jamie's face, Alice realised the painful truth that at forty-two, her life was no longer a tree with branches spread wide but a static thing, a closed thing, a single path. At some point, without noticing, she had stepped through a series of doors, and others had closed quietly, behind her.

'Don't you remember,' he went on, 'what it was like? Having a newborn? How hard you... How hard it was for you?'

In truth, Alice's memories are a bit indistinct. She'd read some-where that this was the lack of sleep – it prevented you storing the memories of your newborn properly, made them feel blurry, unfocused, when you tried to recall them. Of course, she remembers that it was hard. The relentless, refluxy crying; horrible slick, yellow nappies. The tears when Jamie went back to work. The day she'd thrown her breast pump against a wall in fury. Later, the endless wiping-down of the food-splattered high chair. The winter that a snotty Martha got illness after illness and Alice barely slept for months on end, and she'd actually waited at the front door for Jamie to return from work, holding Martha out in her arms, and shouted at him for getting home even a minute later than he'd said.

But then Martha had got older, and the fog of all that had lifted, and a little girl emerged from it, a girl she now couldn't imagine a world without. She thought of Martha's first wobbly steps here in the kitchen, of her drawings that covered the walls, of Jamie so proud of her when she swam her first splashy ten metres, when she rode her bike across Stonebridge Gardens without stabilisers. And Jamie had turned out to be such a perfect, patient father – so even-tempered, so ready to engage in the Lego and Play-Doh and endless imaginative play that Alice, if she was honest, found crushingly dull. As things had got easier, she'd become convinced they could handle another baby after all – and not just that, that it would be worth it. Just like Martha had been worth every difficult moment. 'But I don't want Martha to be alone,' Alice blurted, in a sudden panic. 'I don't want her to be alone like I was, when you and I die.'

Alice realised that she had recently developed an overwhelming fear of this scenario – that Martha could be orphaned, like she had been at thirteen, left completely alone in the world. Sitting on her garden swing with grown-ups who were not her mum and dad suddenly in their house, coming and going without warning, talking to her in a way that made her feel they weren't talking to her at all but to someone else, their voices overloud and syrupy-sweet. All the real conversations about her happening in whispers downstairs, when she was meant to be in bed. Listening on the stairs in her nightie, her bare feet getting cold.

Jamie pulled Alice into a hug.

'Hey,' he said. 'We're not going to die. Nothing like that is going to happen to you and me.'

'How do you know?' Alice pulled away. 'You can't know that. We're not young.'

Jamie nodded slowly.

'Well, that's partly why I don't love the idea of a baby! You're nearly forty-three. I'm ancient...'

'Hardly! You're forty-eight!'

'All right, but honestly – most people our age are calling it quits.'

Alice felt the sick feeling of having missed something – an expensive flight, a crucial train – the unique powerless sorrow of knowing you should have done things differently, but that it is too late, and the chance has gone.

'I don't know if I agree with you, anyway,' Jamie added thoughtfully. 'That it would be the best thing for Martha. I always feel we don't have enough time for her as it is.'

He means I don't, Alice had thought. *He means I don't have enough time for her.*

'Don't you like our life as it is now?'

Alice had looked up, shocked by the question. 'What? Of course I do, but…'

Jamie sighed. 'We already have so much. Our perfect daughter, our marriage, our home.'

And of course, there was a guilty part of Alice that believed this, too. That she should just be grateful. For owning a house in London, when so many couldn't dream of doing so. For having a child, when so many couples were unable. She'd so often failed to be thankful for these things, instead complaining that the house was too narrow, that it had too many stairs, that the garden was too small. Or that her daughter wouldn't sleep, or eat, or play independently enough; or that the cost of childcare meant they couldn't have the sort of holidays and restaurant meals they had once taken for granted.

'None of our friends are even considering this, Alice,' Jamie went on. 'Look at Yas and Arlo. He's had the snip ages ago.'

'But they have two kids!'

'Yeah, but having Archie was hard on their relationship. You know it was.'

'That's because he was a difficult baby, and…'

'We could easily have a difficult baby.' Jamie looked away. 'You worry about us dying, but I think it's more likely we'd end up divorcing.'

Alice had been as shocked, then, as if he had issued a physical blow. They had never said the word 'divorce' before.

'What are you talking about? Why would we get divorced?'

'Because another baby would put too much pressure on our marriage, Alice. We don't have enough time for each other as it is, or enough spare money.'

'But if I get this new job...'

'Would you feel you could take the job if we were trying for another baby?'

Alice was silent. She had, deep down, wondered about this. The truth was, the new role, as head of restorations at the Cunliffe Institute, was a bigger job than she'd ever dreamed of landing. She was already worried about how much time away from Martha it would mean, let alone if she had another baby.

'Alice,' Jamie says. 'Do you remember my colleague Isobel? You met her at the Handhold anniversary drinks.'

Alice swallows. She remembers Isobel. Isobel was nice.

'Well, she is the same age as you, and she has been trying for a baby for a couple of years now, but she's had three or maybe four miscarriages. It's been devastating for her. It's destroyed her mental health, and her marriage, by the sounds of it.'

Jamie had taken her hands.

'I don't want that for us. I love our little family,' he'd said. 'I love it being just the three of us. We don't need anyone else.'

Alice saw then that for Jamie, the matter was closed. Jamie – typically – saw the positive side of their family's small size. He had come from the worst sort of big family – a disinterested, workaholic father and cold, emotionally negligent mother who'd shipped both him and his three bullying older brothers off to boarding school as soon as they turned eight. In Jamie's mind, a small family was perfect.

'Martha can be enough for us,' he said quietly. 'Can't she?'

Alice felt a lump in her throat. Martha would have to be enough. There was no compromise to be had, not on this. If Jamie didn't want another baby, there would be no other baby.

Alice realises that she is crying, now, which is stupid, and a waste of time. She pushes the tears crossly from her face, wipes her fingers on her jeans. Honestly – why had she kept these things, taking up all this space? Why had she kept Becca on, when they could barely afford it, even when it became obvious there would be no more babies? Of course Becca is leaving. Nannies are for little children, and Alice does not have one of those, not any more.

From far downstairs, Alice hears Jamie's new doorbell ring. The unfamiliar sound is jarring.

Alice hears Jamie stepping out of the study, opening the door. She waits for the telltale beep of a parcel delivery. Instead she hears him talking to someone, then walking back up the stairs.

'Alice,' he shouts. 'Can you come down?'

Alice picks up the bin bag and starts to collect the other things. But then Jamie calls up again, his voice urgent.

'Alice? Can you come now, please?'

'OK, coming.'

Alice leaves the things on the floor and hauls herself downstairs. Halfway down, she meets Jamie, coming up to get her, his face flushed and sweaty.

'Alice,' he says breathlessly. 'They're back.'

'Who?'

'The police.' He turns back around, and heads down to the hallway.

Alice grips the banister. She feels sick. They have found out that she went to Linda's house. Linda and Jade have worked it out, reported her. Automatic recall to prison, that's what they'd said. For any breach of her bail conditions. Alice feels like she might faint, her breath catching in her chest. How could she have been so stupid?

But then she sees Jamie, standing in the hallway now, is smiling, that he is shaking the officer's hand.

'Alice,' he croaks, looking up at her. His face is washed with relief. 'It's over.'

Evening Standard
10 August 2023

A mother arrested for fatally wounding a teenage intruder will not face criminal charges in relation to his death, police have confirmed today.

Ezra Jones, 18, died after his botched raid of the East London property of Jamie and Alice Rathbone on 14 July.

Alice Rathbone, 42, was holding a 'play date' at her £1.2 million house with friends when the intruder broke in through their basement door.

Mrs Rathbone admitted hitting Jones at the back of his head with a metal stool. Jones was rushed to hospital, but died as a result of the head injury.

Scotland Yard said in a statement that it had informed Jones's family of the decision to drop charges against Mrs Rathbone.

A representative for Mrs Rathbone, an art restoration expert, said she was 'relieved' and would not be making any further comment, other than to request 'that her family's privacy be respected'.

She had previously said that she had been 'terrified' during the incident and had simply done 'what any mother would have done', after fearing the children were in danger from Jones, who had been 'brandishing a knife and making threats'.

ENDS

COMMENTS (1,459)

@redwall4
OMG I said all along she'd get off... literally one rule for the rich
@laidback
Seriously will she ever brush her hair
@northlondongirl
Sensible decision from the police, I hope this family get some privacy now and this poor woman can get on with her life
@roman_road
Bro didn't even have a knife on him She said he picked up her knife off the side?! Thats her story but he never came at her house with a knife I don't buy it
@mamaowl
I know he shouldnt have broken in but it seems mad she killed him and there are zero consequences
@southoftheriver
I swear there is more to this, I get such a dodgy vibe from her

[CLICK FOR MORE]

ALICE

Jamie is bouncing in his shoes, unable to control his relief. 'Thank you both, so much,' he keeps gushing to the detectives. 'You've been so great, so professional. We're so grateful, aren't we, Alice?'

Alice, though, feels numb. This is, of course, the news she wanted, and has been hoping for. Jessica called her this morning, she sees now – she hadn't looked at her phone.

She should be happy. She should be grateful the police are on her side, and especially that they never found out about her visiting Linda, or Jade. She should be relieved she's not in any more trouble. She has got away with killing someone. And with breaching her bail conditions. Still, her stomach lurches as she thinks about the things people are going to write, on the Internet.

DCI Barnes is snapping his notebook shut, pulling on his jacket. Jamie is telling Barnes about all the extra security he's been installing, and Barnes mumbles his approval, to Jamie's obvious satisfaction. Is that it? Alice feels like saying. Really?

'Can I just ask...' Alice hears herself saying.

Barnes pauses, Jamie too.

'Of course we're very relieved the charges have been dropped, but – it's still really hard to come to terms with the break-in.'

Barnes looks uncomfortable. Her feelings are beyond his remit, after all. But she cannot help persisting.

'I just... can you not tell me anything more? Anything about Ezra, about what might have led up to this? About why he ended up coming to our home?'

Barnes and his sidekick, Jordan, glance at each other.

'Ezra Jones was a young man with a lot of personal issues.' He looks at Jamie, then back at Alice. 'We're satisfied there was no more to it than that.' It is not the first time Barnes has delivered this line in response to awkward questions from Alice. He is clearly sticking to it.

Jamie smiles at the detectives in an apologetic way. Irritation flares in Alice's chest. Jamie is always so bloody deferential to the police.

'OK,' she says. 'But – there's one other thing. All these messages, online. About me.'

Alice feels herself blushing. Jamie is looking at her again.

'I know people are entitled to their... views, on me, and on what happened,' she continues haltingly. 'But some of these messages feel like threats. A number are very personal. And specific.'

'Alice, we've talked about this,' Jamie says, taking her hand. 'You should just ignore what people...'

'I can't ignore them, Jamie,' she snaps. She pulls her hand away, turns to Barnes. 'There's more all the time. It's – it's horrible. Can't you – can't you stop it, somehow?'

She opens her laptop, which is on the coffee table, and finds the news article where the comments first appeared. Already, she sees, there is a new piece, about the charges being dropped – as usual, the papers seem to have found out before she did. She scrolls to the bottom. 'See? There's more already.'

She watches the detectives read the comments. Comments about her hair, her clothes, her figure, her age. Speculation about her marriage, her sex life. How terrible a mother she may, or may not, be.

'I can appreciate all this isn't easy,' DCI Barnes says gently, pushing the laptop back to her. 'But you're right in what you said first time, Alice. The law would hold that people are entitled to express their views on a matter of public interest. Freedom of speech and all that.' DCI Barnes and Jordan are already heading for the door, and Alice can tell the conversation is over.

When Alice closes the door behind the detectives, she looks at Jamie, and collapses into sobs. Jamie wraps his arms around her.

'Hey, hey, it's all right,' he murmurs into her hair. 'This is a good day. It's over.'

Soon after the police detectives have gone, Becca arrives home with Martha from the park. Jamie relays the news and Becca hugs Alice, thrilled and tearful. Jamie beams at them both, then heads back to his office. Alice puts a movie on for Martha, then goes to have a long soak in the bath to try and relax, but even as she dries her hair, her nerves are still jangling.

Alice finishes packing up baby things for Jade into one of the big checked laundry bags, then carries the bag downstairs to leave in the hallway. When she finally looks in on Martha, she finds she has fallen asleep on the sofa. Alice picks her up, her body limp and heavy. It's nearly seven, Alice realises – time for Becca to leave. She is nowhere to be seen – perhaps she went home already. Alice decides to skip Martha's bath, put her straight to bed.

As Alice slots her arms and legs into pyjamas, Martha wakes a little, and sleepily asks if she can have warm milk in her sippy cup – a babyish habit that Alice has made no real effort to break.

'Of course you can, sweetheart.' Alice picks up last night's empty sippy cup from her bedside table and nuzzles Martha's neck, inhaling the sweet, warm cotton smell of her daughter.

Halfway down the steps to the kitchen, Alice pauses. Becca is in the kitchen. It sounds like she is on the phone.

'Look,' she hears Becca saying. 'I want you to stop calling.'

Alice stops. She doesn't want to invade Becca's privacy. But on the other hand, Martha wants her cup filling up with milk, and anyway, shouldn't Becca have gone home by now?

'It's a no,' Becca is saying. 'I'm not doing it again. I don't know how many times I can say no.'

Alice tiptoes to the bottom step, from where she can see Becca, who is standing at the front of the basement kitchen, by the window facing the street, with her back to Alice. She is winding a strand of her long hair around her index finger, split ends that could do with a chop. Who could she be speaking to? Some horrible boyfriend Alice doesn't know about, trying to pressure her into something?

'No. I said no.'

She sounds really upset. Should Alice say something? Alice sees Becca as something between a little sister and a teenaged daughter – but she has no actual experience of either relationship in reality. She is never quite sure where to draw the line.

'Look, I can't even – I cannot talk now.' Becca drops the strand of hair that was coiled around her finger, and starts worrying at a snagged cuticle instead.

'Because I'm there now! I'm supposed to be working!'

Alice hears something indistinguishable on the end of the line.

'Yes,' Becca answers, lowering her voice a little. 'Of course she's here. She's in the house right now. She's upstairs.'

Alice feels herself gripping harder on the sippy cup.

'I've got to go. This is over, do you understand? Don't call me again.'

Alice watches Becca hang up, stabbing at her phone screen with her thumb, then take a deep breath, her shoulders heaving up and down. She puts her phone in her pocket, then wipes her palms on her strange linen culottes, leaving a smudge of sweat on the legs.

Alice clears her throat.

'Hey, Becs. Everything OK?'

Becca spins around. Her expression is exactly like Martha's when she's been caught climbing up to the kitchen cupboard for sweets.

'Fine. Sorry. I was just looking for my charger.'

Alice is unsure what to say to this obvious lie. Becca's charger is in the hallway. She always charges her phone there, or in the USB attached to the computer in Jamie's study.

'OK,' she says gently. 'You're off for a few days now, aren't you? Seeing your parents?'

'Yeah, that's right.' Becca is looking anywhere but at Alice.

'Great. Well. Have a nice time.'

Becca says nothing.

'Night then.'

'Night.'

Becca's mouth twists, and she dashes upstairs, as if she can't wait to get away.

ALICE

She spoons the pasta into two bowls for her and Jamie and carries them into the front room. Jamie is on his hands and knees, tidying toys.

'Thanks,' Jamie says. 'Martha down already?'

'Yep. She fell asleep on the sofa.' By the time Alice had got back to Martha's bedroom with the milk, after that weirdness with Becca, Martha was already snoring, splayed across her mermaid-printed bed linen. Alice had pulled the duvet over her, headed back down to the kitchen and poured the milk away down the sink.

Alice sits on the sofa, her bowl of pasta on her lap. As she lifts her fork, her phone vibrates loudly in her pocket. She looks at it automatically, then startles. There is a WhatsApp from a number which is not saved in her phone.

Thanks again for sorting the stuff for me. CU tmro. What time? Jade x

Alice had forgotten she gave Jade her number. Was that a stupid thing to do? Can the police monitor her phone? Alice takes her phone out again, deletes Jade's message, then stuffs her phone into the cardigan pocket containing the key ring so forcefully that the rainbow ring nearly falls out, the pasta bowl wobbling in her lap.

'Who was that?' Jamie asks.

'Oh... Just Yas. She got the call from her lawyer about the charges being dropped. Says we should have dinner at theirs, to celebrate.' Yas had sent a message like this earlier, so this isn't really a lie. Stella had messaged too, accompanied by a string of celebratory emojis.

'That sounds good.' Jamie hauls himself up, comes to sit next to her. Alice looks at the pasta, but finds she doesn't want it.

'You OK?' Jamie asks. 'I thought you'd be thrilled about the charges.'

'I am. It's great news. I'm just tired.'

Jamie seems to accept this. He spears a tube of pasta onto his fork and puts it in his mouth.

'We should celebrate, though, like Yas says. Go out for dinner or something. While we still have Becca.'

'Uh-huh.'

'You don't sound very keen.'

Alice wishes she felt relieved and happy, like Jamie wants. But part of her is irritated. How can he be so bouncy?

'I just still feel like we don't have any answers,' Alice blurts, even though she knows it will put Jamie in a bad mood. She watches as his face falls.

'There are no more answers to be had, Alice. We just need to be a lot more careful with our security, that's all.'

Alice says nothing. She knows now that Jamie is wrong about there being no answers. There's too much now that doesn't add up. She also doesn't particularly share his enthusiasm for increased security. But there seems little point in getting into it all again.

'What were you chatting to Becca about?' Jamie asks.

Good question, Alice thinks. She is sure Becca meant her when she said, 'She's upstairs.' Who would Becca have been talking to about Alice?

'Nothing,' Alice says. 'I just told her to have a nice time at her parents'. She's going for a long weekend.' Alice frowns. 'I overheard her having some weird call on the phone just now.'

'Oh, yeah?'

'Yeah. She said something about not wanting to do something, and told the person to stop calling, and then she said: "I'm there now... She's in the house." It was like she was talking about me.'

Jamie frowns. 'She probably just meant she couldn't talk, because her employer was there, no?'

'I suppose.' It had felt stranger than that, though, to Alice.

Jamie takes another spoonful. 'Has she said any more about her plans?'

'No.'

'Nothing at all, about why she's leaving?'

'Not really.'

Jamie rolls his eyes. 'Great. So are we looking for a new nanny? You're starting your new job soon.'

'I know,' Alice sighs. 'She said she'll work two months' notice. We might be able to push it to three. After that... I guess maybe we could just get an after-school nanny?'

Plenty of other working parents at Martha's school have these – local students mostly, with a few hours on their hands. But Alice doesn't want some random student taking care of Martha. She wants lovely, responsible Becca.

'Why do you think she's leaving?' Alice asks Jamie.

'No idea.' Jamie is jiggling his knee. He seems distracted.

'Do you think it's because of the break-in?'

'I don't know, love. You're the one who had the conversation with her. Didn't you ask her?'

'Of course. But she wouldn't say. I thought it seemed like there was something that had upset her, but she couldn't say what.'

Jamie sighs. 'It's a shame,' he says. 'But I guess she had to leave sometime. Is she still coming to Rye?'

'She said she would.'

'Shall I book up some restaurants for us, on the nights when she's babysitting?'

'I guess.'

Alice hasn't really thought about the fact they're going on holiday next week. Jamie seems so cheery about it.

'What?'

Alice makes a face. 'It's just – don't you think it feels faintly absurd to be going on holiday, Jamie? My head is still so wrecked. I don't know.'

'Well, I think it's exactly what we need,' Jamie says, an edge of frustration in his voice. 'Something to look forward to. A break from it all.'

'I guess.' Alice picks up her bowl and takes a mouthful, as an act of will, then puts it down again. Something is bothering her. It takes her a second, then she remembers.

'Jamie – I found a bin bag with some old clothes in the attic. A big black hoody, and some jogging bottoms?'

Jamie's fork pauses in mid-air over his pasta bowl. 'Oh, yeah?'

Alice waits for him to say something more, but he puts his fork down, picks up the remote control and starts scrolling through Netflix.

'Did you mean to throw them out or something?'

'Throw what out, sorry?'

'A bin bag of random old… are you listening to me?'

Jamie turns away from the TV, to face Alice. 'Did I mean to throw out some old clothes? I don't think so. Could they be Becca's?'

Alice considers this. 'I don't know. They looked like men's clothes to me. All black things.'

'OK. Well, possibly.'

'I put them in the wash.'

'OK. I'll have a look.' He makes a face at her, somewhere between worried and amused. 'Is everything OK?'

'Yes, sorry. Fine.' Alice produces a smile, which seems to mollify him.

'It's been a day,' he says, squeezing her knee.

'Yeah.'

'We should get an early night.'

'Uh-huh.'

Alice tries to watch the TV, but can't seem to focus. As the programme finishes, Alice glances over at Jamie. He is still holding the remote. He seems to be gripping it, hard in fact. His wrists are tense, his knuckles white. And even though he is looking in the direction of the screen, she gets the distinct impression he hasn't really been watching the TV, either.

BECCA

Becca watches her mother in the kitchen, the yellowish morning light on her back as she fills the teapot. Becca is sitting at the same oak table where she used to finger-paint as a toddler, eat her toast before school, spread out her GCSE revision guides.

Everything here is always the same. The orangey wood of the kitchen cupboards, the green chequerboard of tiles around the Aga, the trinket dishes on the windowsill. The crucifix on the wall. Baxter, the cocker spaniel, asleep in a sunlit square on the kitchen floor, his speckled tummy in the air, paws twitching.

'How are you and Dad?' Becca asks.

'Fine, love,' her mum smiles. 'I want to hear how it's going in London! Have you had much luck, with the flat hunting?'

Becca keeps telling herself she is going to tell her mum the truth, that she is just waiting for the right time. But when is that? When Mum has filled the kettle, and the milk jug? When she has made the tea, and placed down the pot, and sat down next to Becca, smoothing her skirt behind her? As usual, all that happens, and Becca is still staring at the knots in the oak table, and saying nothing.

'You know, I was thinking,' her mum says. 'I could come and visit you! We could look at flats together! Don't you think that would be fun?'

Becca's head snaps up.

'I... I haven't had much time for flat hunting,' she mumbles.

'Well, you don't want to leave it too long, love,' her mum frowns. 'You'll be priced out. I thought you wanted to find something this year?'

Becca says nothing.

'I'd like to see where you are now,' she goes on. 'I'd like to be able to imagine you. You could take me to your church. And I'd very much like to meet your flatmate, Caz.' Becca's mum pronounces the name carefully, like something she has practised.

Becca's mouth feels thick with the things she can't tell her the truth about. About why she won't be able to buy any flat, not now, maybe not ever. About Caz. About everything that's been happening, all the trouble she has got herself into. Not to mention the fact that she hasn't set foot in a church since the day she booked her train to London, pulled her suitcase, bump, bump, bump down these stairs and left this place and its suffocating sameness to make her own life.

Becca wishes she was more like Caz. Caz would just say, *Look, Mum, I don't go to church any more because I don't believe in it. Sorry if that disappoints you but that's just the way it is. Tough tits.*

But Becca cannot even share this small truth about herself, cannot bear to see the face of her mother – who gave up her whole life for Becca – contort, like a wounded animal. Her mother who always put her pyjamas on the radiator to warm while she was having a bath and cut her sandwiches into triangles. Who for ten years drove her two towns away every Thursday night and sat outside with a lukewarm cup of tea from a vending machine so Becca could go to her hockey practice, and who got into debt paying for Becca to have ballet and piano lessons, only for Becca to give up ballet and piano and hockey and everything else she ever tried and leave school without grades good enough for university or a single idea about what she should do with her life instead.

She is sure her mother is already disappointed in her – she is disappointed in herself. But her mother can't know the truth, the real truth, about what her daughter has become. The church thing would be bad enough. The rest of it would probably kill her.

'Can we take Baxter for a walk?'

They walk around the village. Becca hardly has to talk because every hundred yards, they bump into someone her mum knows, from church, or from her volunteer job in the local town, where she sorts clothes out in the back of the Red Cross shop. Mostly, her mum says, it's clothes from people who have died. It's mainly old people around here. Their children return from London when they die, to empty the houses and put them up for sale. They pile the clothes in supermarket carrier bags and drop them off at the shop. Sometimes they don't even wait for the shop to open, just leave the bags outside, so that they get wet in the rain.

'That's so selfish,' Becca said. Mum just shrugged.

'Grief is a hard thing,' she says. 'When your Granny died, sorting through her things was the worst part. Those awful orthopaedic shoes she had to wear. The bits and bobs of cheap necklaces she'd treated herself to. Her clip-on earrings. The little polyester scarves she'd pretend were real silk, do you remember?'

'I remember.' There is a smile in her voice. Baxter is running up the lane, and Becca can tell he has smelt a rabbit hole. There are puddles in the road, but the sun is shining, the air cool and sweet, the hedgerows giving off the scent of home.

Later, Becca lies in her childhood bedroom, her whole body tingling with energy. She hadn't liked doing it at first, taking the pictures. She'd felt pushed into it, awkward. But tonight she feels bold, reckless. Taking the pictures feels like a relief, a release of the buzzing that has built up inside of her in the choking silence of her parents' house.

She sends one, and the reply pings through on her phone, and she smiles in the darkness at the sugar-rush of danger, the thrill of transgression.

LINDA

All this writing, it turns out, isn't the easiest on your back. There's no desk any more, not since Jade cleared out Ezra's room – without even asking me! – to put her baby things in. She's in the flat all the time now; Ryan too, puffing away on his bloody vape. The pair of them driving me mad.

'What do you mean, you're writing?' Jade asked me the other day, finding me on the sofa with the laptop again. She's always been a slight little thing, so it's thrown me a bit, seeing her thickening out, arms folded over her bump.

'You never write anything.'

'I'm writing you out of my will,' I retorted.

'Oh, boohoo,' she said. 'I'll miss that tenner.' Her eyes narrowed. 'Seriously. What are you bloody writing? Is it one of your boomer Facebook posts? It'd better not be about me.'

'Oh, Jade. Buzz off, can't you?'

Then, I had the idea that maybe I could take the laptop out, to a cafe. For a change. Just to get me out of the flat. I see loads of people doing this now, in the fancy places that've opened up round here since Hackney turned all posh. Sitting with a coffee, tapping away. So maybe I could do that too. Find somewhere quiet, where I could get my thoughts in order. It was hard in the flat, with Jade always hovering about.

Anyway, I never got that far, in the end. One minute, I was leaving the house with my phone and the laptop under my arm. Next I knew, I was opening my eyes in the back of an ambulance.

They kept asking how, exactly, it happened. I told them I just fell – I didn't want the bother.

'Your daughter did mention you'd been struggling with your drinking,' one of the nurses said when she was changing my bandages.

'Oh, did she, now.' Typical. She couldn't just leave it alone.

'For lots of people, an accident like this is a wake-up call,' the nurse said, giving me a look. I said nothing. Later that day, she brought some leaflets, put them by my bed next to a jug of water and a plastic cup like you give to toddlers. I felt like telling her to shove her leaflets up her bottom, but my ribs were too painful.

Now my blood tests have come back, and they've clocked all the other things, the stuff I hadn't told them about. So even though I'm sitting up and all that, perfectly fine, in my view, to go home, they won't let me. They say I need a blood transfusion. And they want me to talk to this consultant and that consultant, something about a treatment plan. More tests, more nonsense.

So there you go. I'm stuck here, bored out of my mind, on a ward with a load of old people who've fallen over, for goodness' sake. And then I remembered about the laptop, still in my handbag, next to my hospital bed.

I'll admit I've been getting a few funny glances, sitting up in the middle of the ward, tapping away. But that nurse has left me alone, mostly. I suppose she's relieved it keeps me occupied, and not causing trouble, like the really old people in here. Edna, in the cubicle next door, who presses the buzzer every time she wants a sip of bloody water, and Bill, in the bed opposite, forever whining on about his dead wife.

My husband, John, he hated hospitals. He hated anyone fussing over him. That's what made it worse, really, when it all happened.

He was a good man, John. Very intelligent, he was, not that he'd ever had much of an education. He was quiet, thoughtful. He loved *The Times* crossword, finished it every day. He liked to read. He was interested in the world, optimistic about it. Even though it wasn't kind to him.

We'd tried for such a long time for a family. We couldn't believe it when it finally happened. A lot of people don't like the idea of twins, but we thought we'd won the lottery. A boy and a girl all in one go, just perfect, he always said.

Ezra and Jade were both good kids at primary school. Ezra didn't get on with the academic side – sport was more his thing – but Jade was very smart. Not just school smart – she was what my mother would call *tricky*. Knew how to get what she wanted from people. Oh, she could be sweetness and light when she got what she wanted. She had another side to her, though, when she didn't.

She was also the image of my sister, Kathleen, by which I mean, pretty. The same long hair, delicate face. Once, when we were shopping up the West End, she got model-scouted. I told them no, thank you very much. I wanted her to use her brains, to know there was more to life than looks. She was furious at me for it. She locked herself in her room and cried. Looking back, maybe I should've let her have a crack. She kept the person's business card for a long time after, stuck on the cork board in her bedroom. Oh, she knew how to hold a grudge, that girl.

Wonder where she got that from, John always laughed, when I said that.

He had a point. I've never been the best at letting things go. But Jade – oh, she's worse than me. She is the master.

ALICE

Alice sits awkwardly on the scuffed armchair in Linda's flat – which now feels like it has become Jade's flat. Ryan, Jade's boyfriend, or ex-boyfriend – it is hard to tell, is taking up most of the sofa, his oversized, trainer-clad feet planted wide apart on Linda's orange swirly carpet.

Ryan is the sort of boy that teenaged girls might find attractive – he has a boyband prettiness, albeit accompanied by a small spray of acne on his neck – and the smirk on his face suggests he is well aware of the fact. As he sits, Ryan holds his phone in one large hand and a vape in the other, emitting little puffs of white smoke that smells like blueberry and tobacco. Tinny blasts of pop and canned laughter escape from the phone as he scrolls with a single thumb.

Jade emerges from the kitchen with a small mug of tea for Alice and an oversized Sports Direct mug for Ryan. Ryan takes his mug without looking up from the screen. Jade flicks a glance at Alice, embarrassed by his lack of manners.

'Thank you, Jade,' Alice says as she takes her tea, trying not to sound too pointed.

Ryan looks up for the first time, regards Alice. 'Who did you say you are again?' He screws his face up a little. 'Social worker, is it?'

Alice fakes a laugh. 'Oh. Ha, ha. No. I'm from the baby bank.'

He stares at her blankly.

'I've brought some things for Jade. For the baby.'

'Oh, right.' At the mention of the word baby, Ryan is instantly uninterested. His gaze slides back down to his phone.

'I thought you were going to college today,' Jade mutters to him.

'Don't start.' Ryan doesn't look up. He takes another puff on his vape.

'I'm busy, Ryan,' Jade tuts, then looks at Alice. 'Come on,' she says. 'We can go in the baby's room.'

Alice sits down on a hard dining chair that has been placed in the corner of the nursery, formerly Ezra's room. She can still hear Ryan's phone from the other side of the stud wall. Him being here is unhelpful. Alice wants to probe Jade a bit about Ezra. Maybe Ryan won't stay long.

Jade has taken Martha's baby things out of the checked laundry bag Alice brought them round in. Her hands slow on the soft, waffle-knit blanket with the pompoms, the label in the back of the padded sleepsuit. A smile flickers at the edge of her mouth. 'This stuff is nice.'

'I'm glad you like them.' Alice remembers the day she bought that sleepsuit for her yet unnamed baby. The expensive blanket was a gift from Yas and Arlo. It feels good to give Jade these beautiful things.

Alice has managed to convince herself that it isn't so terrible to come here, now the charges have been dropped. The police won't be bothered, now the case is over. The thought of that weird phone call and the key ring is eating away at her. She needs answers. And that's more important to her than what Barnes thinks, if he even does find out. If she's not breaking the law by being here, then what is he realistically going to do?

Jade is wearing a bit less make-up today, and looks prettier for it. She holds up the little velour trousers Alice picked out. 'This is a posh brand,' she says. 'Must've been some yummy mummy who donated it.' Jade gives Alice a look she can't fathom. Alice flushes hot, clears her throat to change the subject.

'How are you doing after everything, Jade?'

Alice is relieved to hear the words come out in the exact tone she has rehearsed in her head. Concerned, but casual.

'I'm all right,' Jade says shortly.

'It must have been such a shock. Losing your brother.'

Jade gives a little shrug. 'I don't want to talk about it,' she says, her voice sharper than Alice has heard before.

'Of course. I'm sorry.'

'Jade?' Ryan's voice from the next room, a toddler whine.

Jade stands up heavily. 'I'd better go and see what he wants.' She walks out of the room, one hand on the small of her back.

Alice realises she has been holding her breath. She needs to tread more carefully. There is something different about Jade today. She seems on edge, with Ryan here.

From the next room, she hears a hissed conversation, Ryan's voice rising in irritation, but as much as she strains, she can't hear what has been said. Their voices are lowered. Are they talking about her?

Then footsteps, the front door opening and closing. Ryan's gone.

Alice wonders how long she can afford to stay here, with Jade. Becca is still away, so Alice needs to pick Martha up from tennis camp and pay the woman who runs it. She feels in her pocket for her phone to check the time, but it is not there. She must have left it in her jacket, which is hanging by the door.

Alice walks into the hallway. Jade is standing there, with her hand inside Alice's coat.

Jade pulls her hand out quickly, and looks Alice square in the face, as if challenging her.

Alice blinks. Did she really see that – Jade's hand in her jacket pocket? Alice's wallet is in there with the wad of banknotes for the tennis camp woman – £200 in total. She withdrew the money on the way here, from the cashpoint opposite the estate.

'All right?' Jade looks at her, chin jutting defiantly.

'Yep, fine,' Alice mumbles, as if she is the one caught doing something wrong. 'I was just after my phone.'

Alice glances down at Jade's hand. She doesn't seem to have any money in it, but her cuff has been pulled down, covering all but the tips of her fingers.

'I saw your jacket had fallen,' Jade says airily. 'I was just hanging it up. You want it back?'

'No, I'll just grab the phone from the pocket. Thanks.'

Jade stands and watches Alice reach into the pockets, her heart racing. She finds the phone, and the wallet is in there still too, although Alice can hardly take it out and see if the cash is still there – not while Jade is standing right next to her.

She takes her phone and checks the time.

'Do you need to go?' Jade asks, still watching her.

'I've got some time. I can help you with the other bits.'

'OK,' Jade says.

Alice returns to the room with the cot, trying to shake off the jangly feeling of their encounter in the hallway. She starts sorting out the pieces she carried in with the help of the taxi driver, putting the frame together, pressing in the slats that sit under the mattress. Jade comes in, bringing a fresh mug of tea.

'Thought you might want another,' she mutters. It feels like a peace offering.

'Oh, thank you.'

Jade sinks down onto the hard chair in the corner. The atmosphere lifts a little.

'You must have a kid then,' Jade says. 'Seeing as you know your way around all this stuff.' She gestures at the half-assembled cot, the baby bouncer Alice has set up in the corner. Her voice has returned to a more normal timbre, with Ryan gone.

'Just one,' Alice says carefully.

'Did it hurt?'

Alice puts down her screwdriver.

'Sorry?'

'I said, did it hurt? When you had her?'

Alice pauses. Had Jade said 'her'? Had she told Jade her child was a girl? She supposes she must have done, but she doesn't remember it.

'It does hurt, yes.'

Alice sees a flicker of vulnerability cross Jade's face.

'But you have lots of options for pain relief. You'll know all about that from your antenatal classes, I guess?'

Jade makes a face. 'The hospital offered them, but nah. I hate all that, sitting in a circle. Load of strangers knowing my business. And Ryan would never have come.'

Jade scratches at an imaginary imperfection on one of her fingernails, affecting casualness. Alice wonders how to get back onto more neutral footing.

'Where are you having her?'

'UCLH.'

Alice smiles. 'I gave birth there. It's a great hospital.' She hesitates. 'Is someone... is Ryan, or your mum, going to be able to be around for the birth?'

Jade gives a quick shake of the head. 'Ryan isn't good with blood,' she says. 'And Mum's still in hospital.'

'Oh, no.'

'She's pissed me off, anyway,' Jade mutters. 'She thinks I should of got rid of the baby. She said it again the other day.'

Alice thinks privately that she would probably feel the same as Linda, if Martha got pregnant at Jade's age.

'Not your mum, then,' Alice says carefully. 'How about... a friend, perhaps?'

Jade makes a face. 'I'll just do it on my own.'

Alice stares at her.

'Jade, you can't give birth on your own.'

'Why not?'

'You'll need to have someone with you.'

Jade blinks. 'Is that the rule?'

'I don't think it's a rule, but... Jade, you might need support.'

'Nah.' Jade scrunches her face up, and looks away again. 'I'll be fine.'

Alice half-laughs.

'What?'

'Sorry, nothing.' Alice shakes her head. 'I admire your courage, Jade, honestly. That's all.'

Alice picks the screwdriver up, turns back to finish the cot. She doesn't want to press the point.

'It's not that big a deal,' Jade says. 'Loads of people raise a kid on their own. My mum's been on her own with me and my brother since we were fourteen.'

Of course, the dad who died, Alice thinks, remembering the photo of him and Ezra together. That's not quite the same, she thinks, but she stays silent.

'Do you think you might make it up with your mum?'

Jade shrugs. 'Dunno,' she says. 'I think she blames me, for what happened to my brother.' She looks up at Alice. 'The way she goes on, you'd think *I* was the one that killed him.'

Alice feels a jolt of panic. She cannot meet Jade's eye.

'I'm sure your mother doesn't think that, Jade,' Alice mumbles, her voice thick with guilt.

She senses immediately that she has got it wrong. Jade stiffens. 'What do you know about it?'

'Nothing. I'm sorry.' Alice holds up her palms in a gesture of retreat. 'I am sorry. It's a terrible time for you both, that's all. You must both miss him very…'

'Why do you keep wanting to talk about him, hey?' Jade snaps. 'About Ezra?'

Alice feels jittery, thrown off-balance by this rapid weather-change in Jade's mood, her pout suddenly fierce, like she wants a fight.

'I don't… I wasn't…' Alice stammers. 'I'm sorry, Jade.'

'I just don't want to talk about him the whole time. All right? I've got enough going on.' She gestures at her belly, like it should be obvious.

'Of course,' Alice nods. 'Like I said, I'm sorry.'

Jade starts folding and unfolding the clothes.

'What about your husband?' Jade asks abruptly.

'My husband?'

Alice hasn't mentioned that she is married, has she? But then she realises – her rings. Of course. It's obvious. She is being paranoid.

'Your husband,' Jade repeats her words, as if trying them on for size. 'What's he like? Good husband, is he?'

There is a challenge in her words, somehow.

'He's a good man,' Alice says. 'A great dad.'

'Was he with you? When you gave birth?'

Alice thinks about Jamie's strong hands, clamped around hers through the contractions, his low voice telling her that he was in awe of her strength, that he loved her so much. He'd told the midwife and the anaesthetist to back off when she couldn't talk because the pain was too strong. After, when she and the baby had slept, he'd gone out and returned with the coconut macaroons she loved, all the way from her favourite bakery. He'd been walking around London for hours, he said, to find somewhere that stocked them.

'He was, yeah. He was a big help.'

Jade makes some sort of snorting noise, which Alice does not know how to interpret.

Alice puts down the screwdriver carefully. There is nothing else for her to do. The clothes are folded neatly on the chest of drawers. The cot is made up, a pile of spare blankets and sleeping bags in the drawer underneath. It all looks lovely, but the air in the room has soured somehow. Alice needs to leave.

'You should be all set,' Alice coughs awkwardly. 'But just let me know, if you need anything else. I'll be away next week, but…'

'Oh, sure. Do I just call the main number for the baby bank, if I need you?'

Alice is sure Jade's eyes have narrowed a little. It is almost as if she is trying to catch Alice out. Alice feels suddenly desperate to be out of the flat.

'Yes,' Alice says, with another cough. 'The main number is fine, or you can just text me, like you did before.' How easily these lies come, now. How smoothly they fall off her tongue. 'Like I said, I'm away next week, but someone else will help you, I'm sure.'

'Going abroad, or staying here?'

Alice blinks. 'Pardon?'

'Your holiday. Just wondered where you were off to.'

Alice pauses. 'More of a staycation,' she says slowly. For reasons she cannot entirely explain, she does not want to tell Jade exactly where she is going.

Jade keeps her eyes fixed on Alice. 'Right,' she says. 'OK.'

Jade stands up, presses her hands into the small of her back. She is looking much bigger now, her bump so round on her slight hips, like a bubble ready to detach.

'How long have you got to go now, Jade?'

'Four weeks.'

'Wow.'

Alice stands up, heads to where her jacket is hanging up. Jade stands by the door.

'Thanks,' she says gruffly. 'For bringing the things.'

It seems to cost Jade something, to say thank you.

'You're welcome, Jade,' Alice says, as she pulls her jacket on. 'Good luck.'

Only when Alice is back on the canal path, and well out of sight, does she takes the wallet from her jacket pocket and check it. She is relieved to see the notes are all still there. She counts once, then again, then feels a stab of guilt. She must have been mistaken about Jade's hand being in her pocket. How awful, how ugly of her, to think that Jade would steal her money.

She turns the wallet over, looks at it for a moment before she realises. Something *is* missing. The photo of her, Jamie and Martha holding ice creams by the kiosk in Rye, when Martha was a baby. That photo was here, in the cellophane flap. She's had it in there for years.

She looks inside the card compartments, the zip bit, inside her jacket pocket. But it's not there. The photo has vanished.

ALICE

Yas and Arlo's kitchen extension looks like something out of a design magazine, but it never feels quite warm enough to Alice in the evenings. Probably because of all the glass. There is one big sliding window at the back, and a large skylight positioned over the dining table. Even though it's technically still summer, Alice is chilly in here. She wishes she'd brought a cardigan.

Yas has lit candles in the centre of the dining table. They smell of something botanical, like a forest. Jamie seems relaxed, chatting to Arlo, leaning over to stab an olive with a tiny stick he has picked up from the charcuterie board Yas has set out.

'You OK?' he mouths at Alice, seeing her looking.

In truth, Alice is not, but she is not sure that she can say so, not any more. She increasingly gets the sense that Jamie considers there to be a statute of limitations on the feelings Alice still has about the burglary – one which is fast running out. Jamie's determination to get past it is entirely in character for him. It is not that he is insensitive. He is just not one to hold on to things.

Alice also senses the impatience of others now, too. Everyone else seems to be over it. Stella seemed fine at the swimming pool. And here is Yas, now, setting the dining table with harissa chicken and potatoes and yoghurt, and salad scattered with nuts and avocado and pomegranate seeds, like she always does when they eat here – just as if everything is normal. But Alice does not feel normal at all. She still feels, in these situations, almost as if she is floating some way off from the others, just offstage from the action, looking in. That she lacks their solidity.

'Right! Arlo, get Alice a drink.' Yas sits down at the table, next to Jamie. Arlo passes Alice a glass of champagne, and she notices for the first time that she is the only one without one. Alice takes the glass flute and stares into the bubbles.

'I did ask Stella to come,' Yas says, glancing at Alice. 'But she couldn't make it.'

Alice nods, wondering if this is true. She gets the sense that Yas doesn't actually like Stella that much.

'I just wanted to say, I'm so happy it's all over for us all, and especially for you, Alice,' Yas says. She tilts her glass up and towards Alice. 'Here's to a new chapter.'

The others raise glasses, give their assent, and then sip the champagne. Alice startles. It is the same one that Yas brought over on the night of the break-in.

Does Yas not see this connection? Does it not bother her, the way it does Alice? She tries to copy the others, but the taste of the champagne is unpleasant in her mouth. She finds herself struggling to swallow.

Jamie and Alice first met in this very kitchen. Six years ago, or was it seven? It feels like a lifetime now. Her phone still contains a few pictures from that time, taken at the parties they used to have – usually here, because Yas and Arlo were the only ones rich and adult enough to have bought a big house. Nowadays, those photos look like scenes from someone else's life.

Arlo had invited Jamie. 'He's an old mate from uni,' he'd explained, when Alice had asked – in a tone she hoped sounded casual – about the mysterious male who was joining them. Alice, despite having split with her long-term on-off boyfriend, Tag, a while before, had insisted she wasn't interested in being set up. But in truth Alice didn't love being single as much as she had been claiming, and though she had known, deep down, that it wasn't working with Tag, it had still hurt to see him move on so quickly. His new girlfriend seemed from her social media to basically be a younger, prettier and more successful version of Alice.

'Jamie's a good lad,' Arlo had continued. 'I bumped into him in town the other day. I knew he'd gone to Africa, but I thought he'd just been travelling, bumming around. But he claims he's been working – drilling water wells or some other worthy thing. He said he had a bit of a bad time towards the end, got fed up of the charity or something, so he's quit, come to look for – what do you call them – Third Sector roles, here in London. He was asking after Yas, said he'd lost touch with the uni lot, so I said he should come along tonight.' He had nodded at Alice. 'He's just your type, actually, Alice. You'll like him.'

Alice had rolled her eyes, tried to pretend the idea of this Jamie person was of no interest. In fact, Alice secretly wished that her friends, like Yas and Arlo, would do things like this more. Alice never met unmarried men through her work, and she couldn't bear dating apps – the messages left unread, the awkward dates where you're left dying to go home after fifteen minutes but know you have to stay at least an hour. On one recent date, a guy who had seemed completely normal online had refused to drink the tap water 'because of the fluoride' and asked her whether she thought 9/11 was a hoax.

Obviously, she thought to herself, this will come to nothing, too. But all the same, she'd felt a jolt of something like adrenaline when she saw Jamie at the doorway, just the edge of him, and heard the muffled sound of his laughing as he greeted Arlo, the sound of Arlo slapping him on the back, joking: 'Mate, I told you to have a shave before you came over. You look like you've been living in the bush!'

Alice had immediately retreated into the downstairs loo to apply additional lipstick, cursing her decision not to bother washing her hair. She'd emerged, and wandered into the kitchen, trying to affect an air of casualness. Arlo had raised his eyebrows at her.

'Ah, here she is. Jamie, this is Alice.'

And there he had been, and when he'd met her eye and turned the beam of his smile on her, Alice had thought, *Oh, shit.*

By the end of the night, Jamie was talking only to her. He and Alice had moved their chairs around, so they could talk just the two of them. Alice had seen Yas smiling and saying something into Arlo's ear while looking over at them, and she had pretended not to notice. But she could feel, already, that it was all going to be over now: the scrolling of cringeworthy profiles on her phone, weekday evenings in the gym pretending she had something to do, fixing the U-bend in her kitchen on her own, the soul-destroying Saturday-night dates, the listless, empty Sunday mornings.

By Arlo's next birthday dinner, she and Jamie had been a couple of weeks off from their wedding, and she'd been trying to avoid people guessing she was pregnant.

'Right,' Yas says brightly. 'Food.'

She starts to serve, and Alice tries to concentrate. She doesn't feel at all hungry.

'When are you two off to Rye?' Arlo asks Jamie.

'Next week.'

'You going back to that place Alice always talks about? What was it called? Seagull something?'

'Gull Cry,' Alice sighs. 'No. I wish.'

They'd wanted to rent Gull Cry again this summer. In Alice's mind, it was the perfect holiday home: vaulted ceilings, exposed stone and log burners, double-height windows facing directly out to sea, a terrace that led straight onto the dunes. But this year, when she'd contacted the owners, they'd said the house had been flooded, and would be closed for the rest of the year for renovation.

Alice thinks again about the photograph of the three of them there together in Rye. Of how she'd found Jade's hand in her jacket pocket. Jade must have taken the photograph – she must have done. But why? She feels the coil of worry in the pit of her stomach again, the thought of eating Yas's dinner suddenly unappealing.

'Imagine living in Rye,' Yas says distractedly. 'I'd love to see the sea every day.'

Arlo shakes his head. 'You'd be bored.' He looks back at Alice and Jamie. 'I can't *imagine* wanting to live anywhere but London. Can you?'

'I dunno,' Jamie says. 'Maybe.'

Alice looks up. Jamie's never mentioned wanting to leave London before. Maybe he just isn't really listening to Arlo.

'Bit of a commute from Rye, though, I suppose,' Jamie adds, to mollify Arlo.

'Well, quite. How is work these days, J?'

'Good, thanks, mate.'

'Did you change jobs?'

Alice looks at Arlo, then at Jamie. Jamie is frowning, looking bemused.

'What, me? No. Same old.' Jamie starts slicing his chicken. 'Why do you ask?'

'Sorry, obviously crossed wires,' Arlo shrugs. 'I got chatting to someone who worked at your charity the other day, at a drinks thing, that's all. Can't remember her name now. I asked about you, and she seemed to think you didn't work there any more. She must've got it wrong.'

'No worries,' Jamie says affably, setting his knife and fork down. 'I've just been taking a bit of time at home, that's all. What with everything.' He gives Alice's leg a squeeze under the table.

'Of course,' Arlo nods. 'Understandable.'

'I should probably get into the office more, though, if people think I've left,' he adds, looking at Alice, with an attempt at a laugh.

Alice returns Jamie's smile, but she feels uneasy. It can't be a good thing, if Jamie's taken so much time off that people are starting to think he's left the charity altogether. She needs to pull herself together.

Once they've eaten, Jamie and Arlo stay in the kitchen to wash-up. Yas suggests that she and Alice sit in the lounge. Alice settles into Yas's pillowy sofa, her eye taking in the reassuring familiarity of the objects in the room: the photo from Yas's wedding; another of their children, Iris and Archie, on Arlo's family's sailing boat; the Matisse print over the marble fireplace; the thick, tufted Moroccan rug where she and Yas used to lay Martha and Iris down as babies.

'You doing OK, Alice?' Yas asks.

'I'm all right,' she says.

'It must be a relief, knowing it's all over, no?'

Alice glances in the direction of the kitchen, then lowers her voice. 'To tell you the truth, it doesn't feel like that. Not to me.'

Yas frowns. 'What do you mean?'

'I can't seem to move past it,' Alice says, her voice catching a little. 'I think Jamie wishes I would.'

'Have you spoken to anyone? Like a counsellor?'

'It's not that.' Alice is frustrated, trying not to cry. 'I'm not... traumatised. It's more...'

She trails off. Yas waits.

'I'm just not convinced it's what the police were saying,' Alice murmurs. 'Like... a random burglary.'

'Sorry, Alice. You've lost me.'

Alice lowers her voice further. 'I think the boy, Ezra – I think he targeted us, that he was looking for us specifically. And there must have been a reason. I don't know what. But – well, no one agrees with me, and the police don't want to know, so...' She trails off, with a little shrug. 'I know Jamie just wants to forget it. But I'm finding it hard.'

Yas hesitates. The sides of her mouth twitch a little, as if she is struggling to find the right facial expression.

'To be honest, Allie, I think Jamie's probably right, isn't he?'

Her voice is gentle, but Alice can't help feeling the stab of disappointment. Even Yas doesn't believe her.

'I mean, what you're doing, it's a normal impulse – to find a reason, or someone to blame,' Yas goes on kindly. 'It's somehow harder to accept that these things are...' She searches for the words, but lands on a shrug. 'Basically, random bad luck.'

Alice feels a lump rising to her throat. She had wanted so badly for Yas to listen. She'd been ready to confide in her about the anonymous phone call, her visits to Linda and Jade. About how she'd found her key ring in Linda's flat. And now, the missing photograph of the three of them at Gull Cry, that she was sure Jade had taken from her jacket pocket.

But now, she looks at her friend, and realises it would be pointless. Yas's mind is made up. Just like Jamie's, and Arlo's, and the police's, and everyone else. They have moved on. And left Alice behind. She is totally alone.

'Alice? What is it?' Yas looks concerned. 'Is there something else?'

Alice opens her mouth, but then Jamie and Arlo are coming back into the room, and the moment has passed.

'No,' she mutters. 'It's nothing.'

They return home before eleven, not wanting to keep Becca up too late.

'You were quiet tonight,' Jamie says, as he pushes the key in the door.

'Sorry.'

Jamie closes the door behind them, softly.

'I don't know,' Alice says irritably. 'The whole evening was a bit weird. A champagne toast to me getting away with murder? Didn't you think?'

Jamie sighs. 'I think Yas was just trying to be nice. She is hoping you can lay it to rest, you know? That we just drop it. Move on with our lives.'

Alice says nothing. But she is not done with it. Not even close. And if Yas isn't the person she can confide in, and who can help her find out what really happened, she needs to find someone else. Someone who will listen.

ALICE

'So,' Stella says, dipping a herbal teabag on its string in and out of her cup. 'You want me to do some digging.'

They are sitting at Ladybird, her favourite of the cafes by the canal. The towpath is overgrown, huge beanstalks of buddleia arching over the path, tangling with cyclists. The water of the canal is still and bottle green. On its surface, a pale-green confetti of algae swirls, its patterns like a fine lace. In the light, you can see right through to the bottom, where the beer cans glint like a treasure hoard.

Alice often comes to Ladybird. She likes its wobbly tables, its muted colours, its peaceful vegan scruffiness. Jamie loves the coffee here, and their pancakes are Martha's favourite. Alice finds it fascinating to watch people on the towpath. Runners in full Lycra and Fitbits, earbuds in. Cyclists on trendy fixie bikes. East London parents with their toddlers in tie-dye Crocs and linen dungarees, looking for ducks. On the way here, she'd nearly been knocked into the water by a cyclist blasting reggae from speakers attached to the bike frame. Once, walking with Yas when the girls were babies, they'd seen a heron diving for fish. They had turned the buggies around so Iris and Martha could watch it spread its pale wings and lift up over the water.

'I'm curious,' Stella says, when the waitress delivering Alice's coffee has retreated back inside. 'How come you don't buy what the police have said? I mean, the detective told me that Ezra Jones was just – you know. "Troubled".' Stella had raised her hands, making quote marks in the air with her polished fingernails.

'They said that to me too.' Alice makes a face. 'Well, for one thing, why was he shouting: "Is he here?" They still have no idea what he meant by that. Who he was looking for.'

'Was it "he"?' Stella frowns. 'I thought it was "she". "Is she here."'

Alice tries to remember. 'I guess he was slurring – it was hard to tell.'

'Yeah.' Stella pauses. 'The slurring is what made me think he was, you know, drunk, or high, or just confused?'

'I admit it did seem that way,' Alice sighs. 'But, it's just…'

'What?'

Alice wonders if it is really such a good idea to tell Stella what she has been doing, and thinking. But the truth is Alice feels desperate now, and feels she has no one else that she can tell. Yas thinks Alice should forget it and move on, and none of her other friends feel close enough for this scale of confession – especially since Alice has noticed other mum friends from Martha's school pulling away from her lately, as if they want to put distance between themselves and what she did. Martha doesn't seem to get invited to many play dates and parties any more – is this Alice's imagination? Her old boss, Stanley, hasn't spoken to her much either since she left her job at his studio, where she'd been for years. Her ex-colleagues haven't been in touch over the summer, which Alice has found a little hurtful. Which only really leaves Aunt Sarah – who wouldn't understand – and Jamie. Who, Alice knows, would go completely mad if he knew she'd been to see Ezra's family.

So, Alice is left with Stella. And Stella is a journalist. Maybe she can find things out that Alice can't.

'Stella,' Alice lowers her voice, 'if I tell you something, do you swear to keep it to yourself? I need to tell someone. I feel like I'm going mad.'

Stella blinks, and Alice cringes, worried that she has scared her off already.

'Of course. I promise.' Stella tears the croissant, the soft, buttery flesh parting between her fingers.

So Alice takes a breath, and then, she tells her everything. The weird phone call she got that day at the pool. About going to Ezra's home. How she'd ended up meeting Linda, and then Jade. The key ring. The photograph. Once she starts, she finds she cannot stop. She has badly needed to have someone to unburden herself to.

'OK,' Stella says, puffing out her cheeks. 'Wow.'

'I know it sounds insane,' Alice sighs. 'You probably think I'm insane. Everyone else does.'

'No, no,' Stella says. 'It's just – well, it's a lot. And it's all incredibly strange. What did the police say about the phone call? Can they trace it?'

Alice flicks her eyes down at the table. Stella raises her eyebrows.

'Ah,' she says. 'You haven't told them. About any of this.'

Stella's voice is devoid of judgement. Alice bites her lip.

'Jamie either? Or Yas?'

Alice shakes her head. Stella just nods.

'I see.'

They sit in silence for a moment. Stella looks deep in thought.

'Look,' Stella says slowly. 'I guess I could make some enquiries at work, if you think that would help.'

Alice looks up. 'Really?'

'Into Ezra, I mean,' Stella clarifies. 'Who he was, what his deal might have been; see if I can find any clues that might help explain all this. I mean, I'm curious about it too. Especially now.'

Alice shifts in her chair. 'What will you do exactly?'

Stella shrugs. 'Just the usual journalist stuff. Electoral records, financial records. Any sign of him popping up in relation to other crimes. Anything that might suggest a connection, a reason he was there. That he might have targeted you. Of course, there might not be one. But – if it would put your mind at rest a bit, then – maybe it's a worthwhile exercise?'

Alice looks across the water, then down at her untouched coffee. She thinks about the nights she has spent, lying awake at 3 a.m., anxiety still roiling in her stomach, pictures of what happened replaying in her mind. The horrible online comments. The nagging sense of dread that has stayed, even now the charges have been dropped. The way her house feels unfamiliar and unwelcome, the disconnection she feels, from her husband, from Martha, from everything.

'Yes,' she nods. 'Yes, please, Stella.'

COMMENTS (5 NEW)

@mamaowl
I know he shouldnt have broken in but it seems mad she killed him and there are zero consequences
@southoftheriver
I swear there is more to this, I get such a dodgy vibe from her
@hatchetjob
The Rathbones are scum
@hatchetjob
Alice Rathbone is a murdering whore
@hatchetjob
I'll never forget what you did
@hatchetjob
Don't worry, you'll get what is coming to you
@hatchetjob
I know where you live, bitch

ALICE

'Is this our holiday house, Mummy?'

Martha is staring into the bay window of the holiday cottage, which is splattered with seagull shit: thick, white diagonal flecks across the glass like white paint.

'Yes, it is,' Alice says brightly. 'Let's have a look, shall we?' Alice jams the stiff key in the lock, lets them both in.

Alice walks around the downstairs, silently trying to work out how she has been tricked. How the owners managed to crop the photos, so that you couldn't tell the cottage was so poky inside, and so overlooked, so squashed up on top of all the other houses on this side of Rye.

'We'll have a nice time, I promise,' Alice says firmly. 'And we're so close to the beach. You'll love it when we get there.'

'What beach?' Martha looks out of the kitchen window, which directly faces a long queue of bins.

Becca swoops in through the open door, setting down two suitcases and taking Martha's hand. 'Let's go up and find your bedroom, shall we?' She grins. 'I want top bunk.'

'No, me!' Martha giggles and races after her.

Martha is thrilled with the bunk beds, so Alice is able to contain her own disappointment about the dated tiles and ancient shower curtain in the bathroom, the underwhelming views from the windows. She thinks of the perfect azure rectangle of swimming pool that Yas posted on Instagram this morning from their Greek island villa.

'What? This is fine.' Jamie gives Alice's shoulders a squeeze. 'Martha loves it. It's great being in town. We're right by the best ice-cream shop.'

Alice tries to smile, but it isn't just the house. She is struggling to get into the summer holiday spirit. There have been more comments about the break-in online. Different, this time. There is one particular commenter who has started turning up on all the articles about Alice anywhere on the Internet. At first the comments were just nasty. But recently they've spilled over into things that sound to Alice like threats. Implying they know things about her, and her family.

Alice wants to ask the detectives again about the comments, but Jamie thinks she should just ignore them. Alice is in awe of Jamie's ability to just ignore things if he thinks they might make him unhappy.

Alice pulls away from Jamie, and he sighs.

'Please don't be gloomy,' Jamie murmurs, glancing up the stairs towards where Becca and Martha are. 'Martha will have a lovely time. Most kids in London would give their left arm for a holiday like this, you know, Alice.'

Alice hates it when he brings his work into things like this, guilt-trips her with tales of deprivation.

'I'm sorry. I promise I will cheer up.' But she folds her arms rather than reaching out for him. She can feel herself closing off from her husband, the growing list of things that she is not telling him about starting to harden between them.

Once they are unpacked, Jamie says they should walk down to the harbour and get fish and chips on the front. But the walk is longer than Alice remembered, and when they finally get there, they realise there is no vegetarian option for Becca. She says she doesn't mind, that she will just have chips. As soon as the food is handed to them, the gulls cock gimlet eyes at them and start dive-bombing. They hurry a terrified Martha home.

'Never mind. We can reheat the chips in the oven,' Jamie says, trying to keep things cheerful.

As they walk back up the cobbled hill to the cottage, it starts to rain. They pass the ice-cream place with their heads down; even Martha doesn't suggest they stop. Alice glances up as they pass the place where the photograph was taken, the one that she used to keep in her wallet. It makes her feel a bit shivery.

Alice is almost sure that Jade took the photograph. But why would she do that? Is it because Jade hasn't bought her story about the baby bank, and is trying to work out who Alice really is?

Or maybe she already knows. Maybe that's why these messages have started. Maybe they are coming from her. Alice has another disturbing thought. Could Jade have used the photograph to work out where Alice would be going on holiday? She tries to remember how much of the background was visible in the image. Was the name of the ice-cream place visible? Would Jade have been able to work out that the picture was taken in Rye, and put two and two together?

Alice dismisses the thought. She is being ridiculous. Nonetheless, even having these thoughts is surely a sign she should end this now. She needs to stay away from Jade, and Linda. Forget they were ever in touch.

Except, if Jade has worked out who Alice is, then maybe things have gone too far already. Maybe Alice is no longer in control of what is going to happen next.

STELLA

Stella paces along the floor of her newspaper office, holding her little cardboard tray of two hot drinks, looking into the glass meeting rooms.

As usual, most have been taken. In one, the news editor is dispensing a bollocking to two terrified reporters. Stella winces for them, hurries on. In the next, her own boss, Annie, is on the phone, swathed in her usual statement jewellery and colourful silks. She gives Stella a little finger wave, and Stella smiles awkwardly. She'd hoped to avoid Annie today. The chances of her meeting her deadline on this week's mag piece are slim to none. Stella has been otherwise occupied.

Finally, she finds who she is looking for: Oscar, from the investigations team. He is sitting with Emily, Stella's favourite of the in-house lawyers – a woman not much older than Stella, also a single mum. Emily looks tired, her face grim. Her messy bun has a pencil stuck in it, and beneath her shift dress she is still wearing the trainers she walks to work in. Stella gives Oscar a wave. Oscar rolls his eyes, makes an imaginary gun with his fingers and holds it against his head, then breaks into a smile. Then he holds up his fingers to indicate he will be two minutes.

Stella waits awkwardly until Emily stands up and collects her stack of files from the table. Stella holds the door open for her.

'Thanks, Stella,' Emily says, shuffling past her with the files. A worried look comes over her face. 'Were you looking for me?'

'Not this week, you'll be pleased to hear.'

Emily is visibly relieved. 'Thank God.' She shifts the files in her arms, tries to blow a strand of hair out of her face. 'Sorry, I didn't mean that. It's just – dealing with Oscar alone is a full-time job.'

'I heard that,' Oscar calls from inside, where he is slouched in his chair, a pen in his mouth.

'You were meant to.' Emily fixes her gaze on Stella. 'I felt sure you were going to say you had something big for me, Stella. I've seen you in the office late every day this week.'

'Better than being in the flat on my own,' Stella says, with a sad smile. 'Hugo's got Frankie this week. He's taken her to Tuscany with his new girlfriend.'

Without Frankie, Stella's life feels small and quiet.

'That's rough,' Emily says, grimacing with what Stella knows to be real understanding. She tilts her head to one side.

'Look, Stella – this piece you're working on. If it's the same thing as before – we really do need people to go on the record. If the victim's not cooperating...'

'I know,' Stella says, forcing a smile. 'Don't worry. I'm working on it.'

'OK. Good.' Emily turns back to Oscar. 'And Oscar? Let me know when you've put the calls in, all right? Much will depend on the right of replies. I don't want to see it on the list until we've been through them.'

'Got it.'

Oscar grins in a way that he presumably hopes Emily will find charming. She rolls her eyes, then reaches out, gives Stella's arm a squeeze.

'See you, Stella. Let's grab a coffee sometime.' Stella nods. She needs to keep Emily and the other lawyers onside, if she's ever going to pull this off.

'Definitely,' she replies.

Stella edges into the room and places the coffee in front of Oscar.

'What's that?'

'A bribe.'

Oscar laughs. 'Don't let the lawyers hear you say that word. I'm already in Emily's bad books.'

'You're always in her bad books.'

'Only because she's so bloody risk averse. All our lawyers are these days.'

'Tell me about it.'

Stella takes the chair that Emily has vacated. As she does, Oscar smoothly collects the papers they'd been discussing into a neat stack and turns them face down, placing his closed notebook on top. Despite coming off like a lazy public schoolboy, Oscar is a consummate professional. Even though he and Stella are friends, he is always scrupulous about keeping details of his investigations and sources confidential.

When they were trainees together, Stella had got more scoops than Oscar. It was her everyone talked of as the rising star. But then she'd got pregnant, and taken a year's maternity, and had had to ask for flexible working, for Frankie, and, well, her career had stalled, if she is honest. Now Oscar is a paid-up member of the media elite, the sort of journalist who exposes corruption, and wins awards. And Stella – for all her Instagram following (mainly PRs) and offers of freebies (mainly sponge bags and eye masks) – is stuck on the other side of the office, between Fashion and Travel, in what Oscar's obnoxious reporter mates call 'the shallow end'.

'So what am I on the hook for if I drink this?' Oscar doesn't wait for her to answer before he takes another sip.

'It's the same thing as before. I need your help.'

Oscar swallows, makes a face. 'Oh,' he says. '*That* thing.'

'Yeah, that thing.'

Oscar gets up, closes the door behind Stella, then sits back down again.

'I can't do what you asked,' he says.

'Why not?'

'Because, Stella. I'm not even convinced it's *legal*.'

Stella tilts her head to one side.

'You've done it before, Oscar. I know you have.'

Oscar makes a face again. 'Only under legal advice. Having established the public interest with the Editor. You know what the lawyers are like.' He gestures vaguely in the direction that Emily went.

'There is a public interest here,' Stella insists. 'I told you what this guy did.'

Oscar sighs. 'I know,' he says. 'And I'm sorry about what happened to your friend. But it's not clear-cut. I only have your word for half of it...'

'I'm not lying,' Stella says petulantly.

'It's irrelevant whether I believe you or not,' he replies, evenly. 'I can't *prove* it.'

Stella doesn't need Oscar to mansplain journalism to her, but she supposes she was asking for it.

'And even if we did... go down that road,' Oscar continues. 'Covert recording. You know it wouldn't wash without legal sign-off. Which we'd never get. Not in this sort of case.'

Stella sighs. 'So what now?'

'It's like Emily says,' he shrugs. 'You need to get the girl on the record.'

'I have tried. She won't do it. At the moment.'

He and Stella look at each other.

'This isn't just about me,' Stella says. 'It's a massive story if we crack it.'

'I don't doubt that. But we need proof, and we can't get it without people on the inside. You know we can't.'

Stella stands up. 'OK,' she says. 'I'll get someone.'

Oscar raises his eyebrows.

'I will,' she snaps. 'I'm not letting this go, Oscar.'

Oscar laughs. 'I got that.'

Stella snatches up her coffee cup and steps outside, resisting the temptation to slam the door. She jams open the next meeting room, where a group of graduate trainees are hunched over their MacBooks.

'Sorry, guys,' she lies. 'This room is booked.'

They look up, like frightened rabbits. She can tell immediately that they haven't booked it, and they won't put up much of a fight.

'Oh. Sorry. Sorry.'

Stella holds the door open for them as they file out, head bowed, headphones and empty coffee cups between their fingers.

Stella closes it behind them, exhales and positions herself facing the glass, so that she can see anyone who might approach the meeting room, and so that the screen of her laptop is not visible to anyone outside.

While her laptop ticks into life, she tries to think.

Then she loads up her browser and, not for the first time, types the name CLARA LAYWARD into the search bar.

ALICE

They trudge down to the beach at Camber Sands, the poles of the UV tent they have dragged from the cottage digging into Alice's back through her canvas bag. She is relieved when they finally settle on a spot on the soft white sand of the bay. The sun is high in the sky, and as Alice watches Martha runs into the surf, Becca following behind with her hat. Two seagulls soar overhead, their shadows chasing each other across the white sand-dunes like black snakes. She wonders aloud whether they need more shade for Martha to play in.

'I'll go and get one of those big umbrellas,' Jamie offers.

Alice sits down on her towel and watches him walk to the shop. After a while, she starts to relax. She reclines on her elbows, enjoying the healing tingle of sunlight on her skin. Jamie returns with the umbrella under one arm, sets it up, then takes a cold Diet Coke from the cooler and hands it out to Alice.

'Heaven,' she says, taking it. 'Thanks.'

Alice cracks the ring pull, takes a sip, then closes her eyes briefly. Breathes in the familiar summer smell of salt, the call of seabirds.

'Coming here always makes me wonder why I live in a big city,' Jamie says, sitting down next to her on the towel.

'I know what you mean,' Alice says idly, closing her eyes again. 'But imagine how depressing it would be in the winter.'

'Do you think?'

'Definitely.'

'That's interesting. I was wondering whether you'd find it sort of healing, maybe. Moving away to somewhere like this. After everything that's happened.'

Alice opens her eyes, cups her hand over them to look at him properly. 'What do you mean?'

'I just know how hard you've been finding things lately,' he says. 'Coming here – it got me wondering whether a move might help you on? A fresh start, in a place where you're not reminded of it all the time.' He sighs. 'I just want you to be happy, love. If that means moving – then I'd be all for considering it.'

Alice sits up now, turns away from the sun, to get a better look at her husband, as if scanning his face will give her a clue as to what is going on here. She remembers his comment at Yas and Arlo's. She'd forgotten about it until now.

'I don't want to move,' Alice says flatly. 'And certainly not out of London. I love London. Martha's happy at her school. I've just got this great new job…'

Jamie makes a face.

'What?'

Jamie rubs his chin. 'I just think maybe you shouldn't dismiss the idea out of hand. It might be good for Martha, too. Our garden is so tiny. Look how she loves all this open space.'

He gestures to Martha, who is crouched at a castle she has dug in the sand, the sun on her back, chatting happily to Becca, who is gamely kneeling with her on the sand, digging a moat for her.

'Imagine growing up somewhere like this. She could play on the beach every day. We could even get that dog she keeps asking about.'

Alice blinks in disbelief. 'You don't want a dog.'

'I want whatever is best for Martha,' Jamie sighs. 'I don't care about being in London. Martha just needs a mother who is happy and healthy and present. I want that for her, and you. I want you both happy. And safe.'

'I am present, Jamie! We are safe!' But Alice's voice is high and reedy, and she is losing her conviction because the pictures are coming again: the juddering door handle, the broken glass, blood on their lovely tiles.

'We love our house,' Alice croaks weakly.

'Well, it's your house, really,' Jamie says.

'It's our house,' she corrects him, feeling hurt. 'And I love where we live. That hasn't changed.'

'But things have changed. *You* have changed.' He runs a hand through his hair. 'Can we just be honest for a second? You're not coping, Alice.'

Alice opens her mouth to protest, then closes it again.

'And I really get the sense it's not helping you,' Jamie says more gently. 'Living in the house where it happened, having the memory of it there in front of your eyes, all the time.'

'It's not that, Jamie,' Alice insists. 'It's not being in the house that's stopping me from "moving on".' Alice does the quote marks in the air, rolls her eyes, even though she can hear how petulant, how defensive she sounds.

'So what is it?'

Alice folds her arms.

'What?'

She sighs. 'There is no point talking about it, because you won't even consider the other possibilities.'

'What other possibilities?'

'I still don't think we know the truth, about what happened. I don't think it was just some random attack. I think there was something the police missed.'

Jamie rolls his eyes. 'Not this again.'

Alice hesitates. If it helps convince him that she's not going mad, then maybe it's worth it.

'Don't go nuts, all right, Jamie? I should have told you this earlier – I was trying to work it all out first.'

'Work what out?'

Alice hesitates. 'On the morning of the break-in, I got this anonymous call…'

'What? Why didn't you tell me?'

'Well, because at the time I thought it was probably nothing, you know? Some cold caller asking about PPI or car accidents, or whatever. Except the call was silent. Just a sound like someone was breathing on the other end.'

'OK, but…'

'Listen, OK? I thought it was nothing – and with the break-in, I forgot all about it – but then the day you went back to work – while I was at the pool with Martha – I got another call. I am sure it was the same person. It was the same weird fizzing noise. And this time there was a voice, except the sound was all distorted. They said that I should be careful. That there was a reason Ezra had been at our house that day…'

Jamie's eyes are wide. 'Hang on,' he says, holding a hand up. 'They actually said Ezra?'

'Well, no, they just said "he" – but it was obvious they meant him. And they said "he" wasn't who I thought he was. And then they hung up.'

Jamie is shaking his head in disbelief. 'And you didn't tell me this?'

Alice is silent.

'Alice… the police need to know about this! Why on earth didn't you tell them, when they came back?'

Alice looks down. 'Because they were coming to tell us the charges were being dropped – I suppose I didn't want them raking it all up again. I wanted… I wanted to work it out myself.'

'Yourself?! By doing what?'

Alice bites her lip. If it's not a secret, then maybe it will stop eating at her. Maybe it will feel smaller, less of a big deal. And she will feel better if she tells him. She and Jamie have never had secrets.

'I went to Ezra's flat.'

'You did *what*?'

Martha looks up from the sandcastle she has started to build. Thankfully, Becca is out of earshot, having been sent to sea by Martha to fill up a bucket with water for the moat.

'What the hell, Alice?'

The people next to them on the beach exchange a look. Jamie ignores them, his eyes fixed on Alice.

'I wasn't going to knock,' Alice mumbles. 'I just wanted to see her, Linda, the mum. I… I don't know what I was doing. I thought maybe it was her that had called me. Or that I might be able to find some... some clue, or something, by going there. About who Ezra was, why he broke into our house.'

Jamie drops his head into his hands.

'I cannot believe what I'm hearing, Alice. How could you have been so stupid? Is that even legal? Didn't the police say we couldn't go near his family?'

She says nothing.

'You didn't speak to her, did you? The mother?'

Alice says nothing. He looks at her.

'Oh no. Oh, God...'

'I wasn't planning to...'

'Oh my God, Alice. I cannot believe you would be so fucking stupid! I can't believe she didn't report you. I can't believe she would even let you in!'

'She didn't know who I was,' Alice says quietly.

Jamie's face contorts. 'What?'

'She just thought I was lost, and needed a glass of water.'

Jamie's eyes widen, his Adam's apple bobbing in horror.

'Please tell me,' he growls, 'that you told her the truth?'

Alice looks away. 'I was going to. But... they both just assumed I was someone else and then I just... found I couldn't say it.'

'For God's sake!' Jamie hesitates. 'Wait – "they"? I thought you said it was just the mum?'

'It was. The first time.'

'The first...'

'The first time I went it was just Linda, the Mum.' *You might as well tell it all*, Alice thinks. *Jamie will be angry, but then he will calm down, and he will know what to do. He always does.*

'The second time, Ezra's sister was there. Her name's Jade. They were twins.'

Jamie's face has shed its colour. He is looking at her as if she is completely insane.

'But listen, Jamie,' Alice says. 'When I was there, the first time. I found my key ring. The one Martha made for me. It was *in their flat*. In Ezra's old room.'

'Key ring?'

'Yes! My key ring, from my keys, that went missing. I found it in Ezra's bedroom. Don't you think that is bizarre? That it must mean something?'

'Maybe you just dropped it in there while you were... doing whatever you were bloody doing in his bedroom? Which was what, by the way?'

'No.' Alice shakes her head. 'I'm sure it wasn't that. And, Jamie, that's not the only thing. Linda said that, before he died, Ezra had got involved with something he shouldn't have...'

'I bet he had,' Jamie hisses. 'And I'm pretty sure I know what it was. A bottle of vodka and a side of narcotics.'

'And then,' Alice continues, ignoring him, 'the next time I went to see Jade, a picture went missing from my wallet. A photograph of the three of us. I think Jade took it...'

At this, Jamie explodes. 'Why the hell did you go back to see Jade? Why? When?'

'I... She's pregnant. I just... I just took her some baby clothes.'

Jamie's face is pale. 'Oh my God,' he mutters. 'Enough – *Enough!* Jesus, Alice.'

Jamie stands up. Alice has never seen her husband so furious.

'This stops *now*,' he hisses. 'Do you understand? You need to stay away from them.'

Alice blinks. She knew he would be cross, but she is floored by the ferocity of his tone. He has never spoken to her like that before. He is actually sweating.

'I know,' Alice says. 'But, Jamie, I...'

'No buts, Alice! What if...' He lowers his voice. 'What if the police found out you breached your bail conditions?'

'Jamie, you aren't hearing me,' Alice pleads. 'You keep telling me to move on. But I can't. Not until I know what happened, what made him choose our house. He had my key ring! That means he was following me, or he'd been to our house, or something, before all this. It wasn't random, like the police said. There was a reason. There must have been.'

'We know the reason, Alice,' Jamie snaps. 'We live in a nice house in a dangerous area of a big city. Anyone after a few quid would have a reason to break into our house. OK?'

Jamie takes a beer from the cooler. He pops it open with an aggression Alice rarely sees. His hands are shaking.

'You know,' he says. 'Yas thinks the same as me. She thinks you're driving yourself crazy. Obsessing about what happened, about the news coverage, about what people think, about all the idiotic shit that idiots have written online about you. She thinks you need to stop it, move on. We all do.'

Alice stares at him. Yas is her best friend. When has Jamie been speaking to Yas about Alice behind her back?

Becca is here now, with the bucket, saying something about a pink plastic spade of Martha's, that they had yesterday but now can't find. Alice doesn't want Becca to overhear their argument.

'Let's talk about this later,' she mutters to Jamie, as the sun slides behind a cloud.

Once Martha is in bed that night, Becca says she is going to head out for something to eat.

'Is there anything you need from the shops?' Becca is already pulling on her denim jacket, reaching for the door handle. Alice suspects she has picked up on the continuing tension between her and Jamie, and is dying to escape. Alice sighs. She had hoped that this week in Rye might provide a chance to find out a bit more about what's been bothering Becca. Maybe even what that weird phone call she overheard was all about. But Alice has been preoccupied.

'Of course,' Alice says. 'Sorry, Becca. We will get some nice veggie food in for the four of us tomorrow night, won't we, Jamie?'

Jamie, who is flicking through his phone on the sofa, barely looks up.

'It's OK,' Becca says kindly. 'You two should go out for a meal or something. Spend some time together.'

Alice feels the colour rising to her cheeks. Jamie still doesn't even look up from his phone as Becca closes the door behind her.

Alice walks around the back of the sofa where Jamie is sitting. He is looking at houses on Rightmove on his phone. She looks over his shoulder as he flicks through a picture gallery for a timber-framed house with a garage to one side. There is a big shiny kitchen Alice would never choose, a white leather three-piece suite set around a ludicrously large TV, bifold doors out to a lawn striped with two shades of green.

'Where's that?'

'Wadhurst,' Jamie mutters, without looking up.

It's obvious from his tone that he is still annoyed with her.

'Where's that?'

He glances up. 'Edge of Kent,' he says more gently. 'Near Tunbridge Wells. There's fast trains into London. And it's only forty-five minutes from here. We could come to the beach whenever we liked.'

Alice reaches for the wine in the fridge and pours herself a large glass, the pleasing glug, glug of it making her feel slightly calmer.

'I'm just looking at what's out there,' Jamie says defensively.

'Uh-huh. You want a drink?

'It was named the best place to live by the *Sunday Times*,' Jamie says, ignoring her question.

'Oh, well then, it *must* be the answer to our problems.'

Alice immediately regrets the sarcasm, which is not her style, but she can feel her hackles rising. Jamie turns to face her.

'You won't even speak about it?'

'I don't know what you want me to say!' Alice throws her hands up in the air helplessly. 'You sprung this idea on me three hours ago. You've never even mentioned moving out of London. Now suddenly you're Aunt Sarah, trying to move us out to the suburbs, to save our child from the horrors of urban life!'

'Well, maybe Aunt Sarah has a point. Maybe there is a reason families move out of London.'

'Yeah, usually because they can't afford a house like the one we are lucky enough to live in! Or because they need more space. Which we don't, since we're not having any more children.'

Alice tries to stop this last part sounding bitter.

'They move because it's safer, and you know it. All the people we know live in a dreamworld about London. They think if they live in big Victorian houses, it'll never touch them. The drugs, the crime, the violence, all the darkness of it. But I see it, Alice. I see how close it gets to us. To Martha.'

Alice has never heard Jamie talk like this before. She is really unsettled now by the change in Jamie, cannot fathom his sudden obsession with a house move he has never, during their whole marriage, expressed any interest in.

'You never worried about any of this before the break-in,' she points out. 'We love where we live. We *love* London. I love the parks, the canal, the market. So do you. And yeah, OK, it's rough around the edges, but we don't care about that – we used to laugh at people who couldn't see past those things.'

Jamie's face is unreadable.

'And you more than anyone,' Alice goes on. 'Jamie, you've always been so...' Alice searches for the right words. 'So sympathetic to people with... difficult lives. You understand it! You help them!'

'No, I don't.' Jamie makes a dismissive gesture with his hand, like swatting a fly. 'It's all rubbish. I see that now, since it happened. It's all nonsense. The charity is a waste of space, Alice. The caseload is beyond help. I'm not bothered whether I stay in that job or not. I think a fresh start would be great, actually.'

Alice is shocked into silence. Jamie has never spoken like this before about his work.

'This isn't about all that, though,' he says, dismissing the job that keeps their family afloat with a flap of the hand in a way that Alice finds slightly alarming. 'I don't care about it any more. This is about you. We need to move on. Do you honestly think you can, while we're in that house?'

Alice sits down carefully next to him, cradling her wine.

'It is making you unwell, Alice, living in the house where it happened. I see it on your face, when we're in the kitchen. I *see* it.'

Alice hangs her head. She didn't think he'd noticed her thing about the kitchen. They never spoke about it. About the space where it happened. But Alice always avoids it, if she can. She hates standing there. Stepping over those tiles. It feels like walking on his grave.

'I hear what you're saying,' Alice says, recovering her composure. 'But you know what that house means to me. I can't imagine moving.' Alice turns to look at him. 'I always thought we were happy there.'

Her voice is shaking, a tuning-fork tremor of emotion. But Jamie only shrugs, as if he has no idea.

'I'm just asking that you look at the alternatives,' he says. 'Some of these homes – the size of them does make you think. Check out this one. It's bigger than Arlo's house!'

Alice frowns at this. 'Who cares if it's bigger than Arlo's house?'

'I'm just saying, it's huge.' Jamie changes tack. 'You could have one of the bedrooms for a study. And it's got a nice village primary, grammars nearby. And a deli and a pub. It looks like there's a bookshop, too, and an independent art gallery.'

The mention of the study – something she's always loved the idea of – and the gallery is for her benefit, she knows.

'Let's have a look, then,' she says, softening a little.

'OK,' he says. 'Hang on. Look at this one – this one is more you.'

He hands his phone over and she flicks through the pictures. The house is nicer than the last one. The kitchen has an Aga, a double-aspect master bedroom, a garden with mature trees and rose bushes. The asking price is less than what they'd get for their current place.

'I'll have a look at some later,' she concedes.

Alice hands back his phone, and takes her glass of wine to the sofa opposite Jamie. She looks around the room, noticing again how gloomy and tired it is, how scratched the paint on the walls is. She imagines she is in Gull Cry instead, next to the log burner, looking out to sea from the double-height windows. Or sitting on the balcony at night, like she did that first summer, with baby Martha falling asleep in her arms, warm and limp. The soft music of ice cubes clinking together in her glass of rosé, the call of seabirds.

The sagging sofa is comfortable, the sound of the rain outside soothing. Alice closes her eyes, rests her head against a sofa cushion.

She is woken by a slamming noise.

Alice jumps, wine spilling from her glass. It is dark outside. The rain is falling heavily now. Alice feels disorientated. In her dream, she'd been at Gull Cry – or she had at first, but then it had changed to a new house, one not familiar to Alice, with a shiny white kitchen, and Jamie sitting at a blood-red stool at the island, smiling.

Now she sees she is in neither of those places, but here, in the cramped holiday cottage in Rye, and it is dark, and late. Had she fallen asleep?

'What was that?'

She looks for Jamie. He is no longer on the sofa opposite her. After a few seconds, she hears the back door close, and Jamie crossing the kitchen and coming back into the lounge.

'What was that noise?' Alice asks him.

Jamie shrugs. 'No idea. I was just taking stuff to the bin out the back.'

'It sounded like someone was slamming against the front door, Jamie.' Alice knows how this sounds, but she cannot help a rising note of panic creeping into her tone. 'It really freaked me out.'

'OK, relax,' he sighs. 'I'll check.'

Jamie opens the door, pauses, then shuts it again. He walks back into the lounge, then through to the kitchen. Alice can hear him rummaging around in the cupboards.

'What? What is it?'

'Nothing. I'll sort it out.'

'Sort what out?'

Jamie emerges from the kitchen with a dustpan and brush in his hands.

'It was just a gull.'

'What?'

'That slam must have been it flying into the door window.'

'You mean it's dead?'

'It looks it. It doesn't look very nice. I'll clear it up before Becca gets back.'

Becca is still out? Alice pats around for her phone to see the time, but can't find it. How long had she nodded off?

'It's OK, Alice. Just perhaps not a very nice sight for a vegetarian.'

Jamie is trying to make light of it, but Alice feels anything but. Jamie is being shifty, doesn't want Alice to look for herself.

'I want to see.'

Jamie makes a face, but doesn't stop her as she marches to the front door and opens it.

The bird is obviously dead. At first, Alice thinks it is missing its head – all she can see is its two skeletal wings, spread wide, like a broken angel. But then she sees that the bloodied head is lolling behind one wing, a sticky mass of blood and cartilage where the two were once joined.

'Would it – would it look like that if it had just flown into the door?'

'I'm not an expert on dead gulls.'

But Jamie looks unsettled, and Alice is pretty sure that even he would admit that a gull does not end up like this on a doorstep at random. Any more than a man ends up at an address at random and breaks a door down, or their daughter's hand-made key ring ends up inside a flat where Alice has never set foot in her life.

Part Two

The Day Of

ALICE
7.26 a.m.

Alice is standing at the worktop, slicing blueberries for Martha's porridge while it hums brightly in the microwave.

Her phone vibrates. Alice's first thought is that it must be Becca. She is usually here by now, and Martha needs to get dressed soon. She is still in her pyjamas, sat on a stool at the island drawing, a rainbow of her pen lids scattered over the terrazzo floor.

Alice glances at the screen. The call isn't Becca, but an unknown number.

'Hello?'

Nothing. No sound on the line, just a sort of fizzing.

'Hello? Becca, is that you?'

The fizzing gets louder. Is it a mechanical noise, Alice wonders? Or is it the sound of breathing?

'Who is this, please?'

Her tone is different now, and Martha looks up, surprised to hear the sharpness in her mother's voice.

More breathing. Alice feels unsettled, the hairs on her arms lifting from her skin. Then she hears a click, and the call is gone.

'Who was that, Mummy?'

Alice forces a smile to her face, ruffles Martha's fringe.

'Not sure,' she says brightly. 'Probably a wrong number.'

The microwave dings. Alice presses the door open. She takes Martha's bowl of porridge, slices some blueberries over the top and drizzles it with honey so the surface glistens with gold.

'Can I have more blueberries?' Martha asks with a grin, as she sets the bowl down.

Alice pushes a lock of Martha's fringe from her eyes. 'You'll turn into a blueberry if you eat many more.' But she takes the punnet back out of the fridge and starts to wash and slice, discarding the rancid ones in the food waste.

'Eat up, quick, OK? We need to get dressed.'

A message pings through on her phone. Alice flicks the screen open. It is Becca this time. She reads it and sighs.

'What's wrong, Mummy?'

'Oh, nothing. Becca says she can't come today because she is a bit poorly, that's all.'

Alice thinks through the hours of her day, the various things she needs to do. She can hear Jamie in the shower. He won't be able to help.

Becca used to be so reliable. Who gets sick this much in summer? Maybe Alice needs to have a chat with her. Alice has never needed to have that sort of chat with Becca before. She hates the idea of it.

'Does that mean you're going to pick me up from school?' Martha asks.

'Me or Daddy.' *Almost certainly me*, Alice thinks.

'Can I still go to the playground? Becca promised we could.'

Alice sighs. 'Sure, love.'

'Yay. Shall I make a picture for Becca?'

The look on Martha's face punctures Alice's bad mood. Drawing pictures is her daughter's love language. Cats and dogs and horse after horse, just like Alice remembers producing as a child. *To Daddee, love Martha. To Becca, love Martha.* A line of upright kisses along the bottom edge, like plus signs. *Another masterpiece by Martha plus plus plus*, Jamie always says, as he pins them to the noticeboard.

As Alice tips in the extra blueberries, a memory comes to her, of being made to clear her pictures from the kitchen table ahead of silent breakfasts with her aunt, the relative who had been landed with Alice after her parents' death. Alice wasn't allowed to get her drawing things out at the breakfast table at Aunt Sarah's, and there was never honey or jam, or even much conversation. Only cork place mats, clear Tupperwares of Alpen and shredded wheat, the watery skimmed milk Aunt Sarah thought would keep her slim, and silence.

'I'm sure Becca would love a picture,' Alice tells Martha, cupping her soft face with one hand. She adjusts the bowl and the pot of pens, so her daughter can draw as she eats.

Alice should probably call Aunt Sarah more often, should probably arrange to visit her this summer. After all, she is on her own. But she is so awkward on the phone, and Alice finds the conversations painful, so instead she sends Martha's drawings to her through the post, pretending Martha drew them for her. Alice usually receives a polite text a few days later thanking her, and asking how they all are. The exchanges rarely gather momentum, and usually peter out after two or three messages.

Aunt Sarah continues to find Alice, and her life choices, unfathomable. She has never warmed to Jamie – although, as Alice has always reassured him, she hasn't warmed to anyone else either, to Alice's knowledge. She also doesn't approve of where they live, thinks they should be saving to 'move out' somewhere with a 'proper' garden for Martha – by which she means a semi in a nice, safe suburb like hers. When she visits them – very occasionally – Jamie and Alice have to struggle to keep straight faces as they watch her glance at the graffiti, the council estates, the drunks asleep in Stonebridge Gardens. She has no concept of how lucky Alice is that her inheritance stretched to a small, terraced three-bedroom Victorian house, bought in 2009, before gentrification, and right when the market had dipped.

The house was worth much more now – if Alice had waited even three years, she'd probably have struggled to afford one like it. But Alice barely thinks about this, because she cannot imagine selling the house. She loves everything about it. She has painted the bedrooms in all her favourite colours – stormy indigo, mustard yellow and plaster pink – and covered them with prints and paintings, mostly from art school friends. There are several art works on long-term loan from Stanley, who has exquisite taste and far more art than he can fit on the papered walls of his Chelsea bachelor pad. The furnishing has taken her years of scouring flea markets and eBay, the little shops in Camden passage.

Alice hears the soft footsteps of her husband entering the kitchen. She watches him give Martha a kiss, then lean to kiss her mouth.

'Morning, wife.'

Jamie smells soapy from the shower. He starts making their espressos, being careful and precise with the machine, getting them just right. Behind him, the morning light is starting to slant into their little garden, with its terracotta pots and tangled climbers, framed by the glass sliding doors Alice has never once regretted the expense of installing.

Alice sits down opposite her daughter.

'Becca has called in sick,' she tells Jamie. He looks up from the machine.

'Again?'

'I know.'

Jamie rolls his eyes. 'What's up with her?'

'I'm not sure,' Alice says. 'She says she's ill, but she's not herself lately, is she?'

'No.'

'I wondered whether it was boyfriend trouble, or something,' Alice muses. 'Not that she ever tells me anything about her love life.'

Jamie makes a face. 'I really can't do pick-up, today,' he says. 'I've got so much on.'

'OK.' Alice expected this. 'Can you do the drop-off, though?'

Jamie can't usually do the school run, and nor can Alice, which is part of the reason they've kept Becca on, even though it feels increasingly extravagant to have a nanny for a single school-age child.

'OK,' he sighs. 'Sure.' He hands Alice her coffee, then gives her a squeeze from behind.

'Thanks,' Alice says, squeezing him back. 'It's just, you know, I was thinking I should probably tell Stanley today. About the new job.'

Jamie detaches from her. 'You're definitely going for it, then?'

Alice looks up at him, surprised.

'I honestly don't know why I wouldn't. We've been through all this, I...'

'OK, OK, I know.' Jamie holds his palms up. 'You should do whatever you want to do.'

Alice's gaze catches on his collar. She doesn't recognise it. Jamie rarely buys new clothes.

'New shirt?'

'Oh. Yeah. I got some new work things. My shirts were feeling a bit snug.' Jamie attempts a laugh, but Alice can see he is a bit embarrassed, tugging at the fabric. 'I think I'm getting a dad-bod,' he sighs.

'You are not,' Alice protests. Jamie is a bit fleshier than he used to be now that she looks at him, but it doesn't bother her.

'Maybe I'll get back into cycling to work, now it's warmer.'

Alice stands up and wraps her arms around his waist. 'I'd rather you alive with a dad-bod than crushed by a lorry.'

'What, Mummy?' Martha looks up in alarm.

'Mummy was just joking, Squidge.'

A couple of months ago, Jamie had come home looking like he'd been beaten up. He'd had a collision at Old Street roundabout with an Uber being driven too fast. He had black eyes and was covered in scratches, and his bike and the laptop he'd had in his bag were all smashed. Since then, she'd been anxious about him cycling. And despite having replaced his old bike, she'd noticed he'd been using it less, leaving it idle in the storage shed he'd lovingly built at the front of the house. She has felt a mixture of relief and guilt about this. Jamie loves cycling, and she suspects he has only stopped because of her.

Jamie walks up behind his daughter. 'How's my blueberry monster? Didn't you leave any for me?'

'No!'

Jamie nuzzles Martha from behind, tucking his fingers into her armpits until she tenses and giggles.

'It's sweet how you still slice the blueberries,' Jamie laughs, turning back to Alice. 'You do realise she is five years old and the proud owner of these twenty perfect teeth?' Jamie tips Martha's head back to look at her teeth and pretends to count them. She giggles.

'I know,' Alice smiles at them both. 'Just habit.'

'Right,' Jamie says. 'Guitar lessons today, Marth? I'll grab your bits.' Jamie leans to give Alice another kiss. 'Go on, you get going. I've got this.'

Alice accepts the kiss without moving. 'You don't think I'm doing the right thing.'

It's not a question.

He shrugs. 'We'll make it work.' Alice says nothing, but Jamie's continued uncertainty about the new job has dulled it for her. The thought of the conversation she needs to have with Stanley lies uneasily in her stomach, like sour milk.

She picks up her bag, blows Martha a kiss. As she grabs her phone to leave, she wonders briefly again about the phone call, the fizzing sound. Whether there had been a person on the other end of the line, or not.

6.11 p.m.

The downpour has come on suddenly, in a crescendo of white noise. The rush of it at the windows stops their conversation.

'Blimey.' Yas heads to the sliding doors out to the back garden to have a closer look. Alice can make out the two ridges of Yas's shoulders under her cream jumper as she stares out at the rain. Beyond her, the doors are a wobbling cinema screen of grey. A low roll of thunder sounds; a downpipe gurgles. Later, the grass of Alice's small, square lawn will be washed a verdant green, the heads of the roses heavy with the weight of water.

'I knew I should have had my bloody gutters swept,' Yas sighs.

Alice had been about to run the bath, start warning Martha it was time for bed. She had been planning to say it loud enough to signal to Yas and to Stella that it is time for them to take their children home. But it would be rude, to send them out in this rain.

Alice thinks about Jamie, who will be on his way home from work. Her husband rarely thinks to take a rain jacket, or an umbrella. He is the sort of person who always thinks the sun is going to shine. He will be soaked when he arrives, she thinks. Any minute now.

'You two should stay,' she says to Yas and Stella, only because she feels she should. 'The kids can watch until the end of the film.'

At least it doesn't matter, Alice thinks, if Martha goes to bed a bit late. It is Friday, after all, and nearly the school holidays. The teacher has probably given up ages ago.

Yas glances at Stella, then back at Alice.

'If we're staying, shall we all have some of this?' Yas stands, heads to the fridge and pulls out a bottle of champagne. Alice looks up at her, surprised.

'Did you sneak that into my fridge?'

'Of course I did!' Yas grins and waggles the bottle, holding it by the neck. 'It's for you, silly! Happy new job.'

Alice laughs. 'You didn't need to do that, Yas,' she protests, even though she knows it's pointless. Yas is already popping the bottle, finding Alice's glasses. Yas loves champagne, and is a firm believer in celebrations. She takes them seriously, and is practised at the art of them. It is one of the things Alice likes most about her.

Yas takes out Alice's fancy coupe glasses. 'One for you, Stella?'

Alice holds her breath, hoping that Stella will respond with enthusiasm to the idea. This will make Yas more likely to warm to her. As much as Yas ever warms to new people. While Yas and Alice have been friends since university, Alice has only known Stella since their daughters started at the school at the beginning of the academic year, and she is not sure how well Yas knows her, if at all.

Stella hesitates, shifting in her chair. She glances at the expensive-looking label on the bottle. 'Oh. No, thanks. I'm fine.'

'Have one!' Alice smiles at her in a way she hopes is encouraging. Maybe Stella feels awkward about accepting champagne from Yas, who she has only just met. *Don't worry*, Alice wants to tell her. *Yas can afford to share.* Yas and Arlo live in a listed house twice the size of Alice's. Yas has a French-door fridge, a live-in nanny-housekeeper, a personal trainer, a successful career, a happy marriage, one child of each gender and an incredibly chic capsule wardrobe – everything you are supposed to have at forty-two. In fact, Yas had most of that stuff before she was out of her twenties.

'Oh, all right, then. Thank you.'

Yas fills the glasses nearly to the brim. Alice selects one and holds it up to be clinked by each of the other two in turn.

'Cheers.'

Alice takes only a tiny sip. She doesn't like champagne all that much – it tends to give her a headache. Is it strange that she has never felt she can admit this to Yas, even though they have been friends for well over a decade? Alice has been unable to shake the suspicion that Yas would view it as a sort of personal flaw.

'This is lovely,' Stella says.

'Isn't it?' Yas agrees.

'So come on, Alice,' Yas says. 'I want to hear all about the new job. What is the actual title?'

Alice clears her throat. 'Head of Restoration,' she says. 'At the Cunliffe Institute.'

'Incredible,' Yas beams. 'Do you know it, Stella?'

'Of course,' Stella smiles. 'I love it there.' She makes a self-deprecating face. 'I mean, I don't know much about art. But I like the cafe!' They all laugh.

'When do you start?' Yas asks, turning back to Alice.

'Not sure yet,' Alice says. 'I only just handed in my notice today.'

'Oh. How was that?'

'Awkward.' Alice has spent the afternoon trying not to think about Stanley's disappointed-dad expression, the way the corners of his mouth twitched down as he mumbled his polite congratulations.

'I'm hoping to take a few weeks off. The Cunliffe have agreed to delay my start date until September.'

This had been Jamie's idea, so that Alice could spend time with Martha over the summer holidays. She had worried it was asking too much of the Institute, delaying by so many weeks. But Jamie was right – the new job would mean longer hours, at least at first. She'd feel less guilty about it if she'd at least taken some time out to be with Martha over the summer.

'It sounds so prestigious, Alice,' Yas says. 'You must be thrilled. Did they headhunt you?'

'Sort of.'

Alice allows herself a little frisson of pride at how she was hunted down so fiercely for the role – by the Cunliffe Institute, of all places. She usually dismisses talk of her career – Jamie, after all, is the one who does the really important work, work that helps people, that makes the world better. But the truth is Alice loves her job, and knows she is good at it. Stanley always says she has a 'rare eye' for what a painting needs, a natural instinct for finding solutions. When to be bold, and when to be gentle. And the truth is that because Stanley has always given her the flexibility she needs with Martha, she has ended up staying at his small restorations firm in Mayfair much longer than she really should have done. She should have been pushing for a more prestigious role like this years ago.

Even with a boss as understanding as Stanley, Alice has found primary school hours hard to manage. After a week of picking Martha up looking tearful and alone in the playground, Alice had quickly realised the school's wraparound care wasn't going to work. They'd decided the best thing was just to keep Becca on, at huge expense, for another year so Martha could be collected every day at 3.15 by someone she knew. It was only just financially manageable, but Alice told herself it wouldn't be for ever.

Now, Alice thanks God they have kept Becca on. The new role will mean even longer hours, and the whole thing is only going to work because they have her.

'You feeling all right about the new job, Allie?' Yas cocks her head. 'You just seem to make this weird face whenever I mention it.'

It is typical of Yas to see through Alice's cheery front and place a slim finger on the exact spot where she is most tender. Alice is excited, but also nervous about the change – not helped by her latest phone conversation with Aunt Sarah, who had sniffed that it sounded like 'an awfully big job for the mother of a young child'. And as much as she loves Becca, and knows she is privileged to have her, Alice already feels guilty that Becca often has to relay key information about Martha's new life at school – which day is PE day, which reading level she is on.

However, she doesn't want to admit all this agonising to Yas. She wants to be more like Yas is about her banking career: ambitious, unapologetic.

'Of course, I'm thrilled.' Alice sets the champagne down on the table. 'Why wouldn't I be? It was difficult telling Stanley, that's all. I've been there a long time.'

A clattering sound of crockery causes the three of them to pause and look up. Becca is in the kitchen and has started unloading the dishwasher.

'Sorry, guys,' Becca says softly.

'Don't be sorry,' Yas calls. 'Do you want a glass of champagne, Bec?'

'Oh, no. Thanks, Yas.'

Having called in sick this morning, Becca had messaged at pick-up time to say she was feeling a bit better, and would come and help with dinner. It had struck Alice as a bit of pointless martyrdom – something Becca was prone to – but by that time Alice had agreed to host two children, so she decided to accept the extra help.

Becca does look a bit tired and unwell. She is wearing fluffy house slippers, leggings and a shapeless cardigan. She sets things on the sideboard in piles: a neat rainbow stack of IKEA children's bowls, parts of a blender, a kitchen knife.

'Oh, Becca, I meant to introduce you properly – this is Stella,' Alice says. 'Stella's daughter Frankie is friends with Martha.'

'Oh,' Becca says vaguely. 'OK. Hi.'

'Hi, Becca,' Stella smiles warmly. 'We met the other day in the playground, I think?'

'Oh. Yeah. OK.'

Becca's seems distracted, trying to push the dishwasher closed. She struggles, has to go back for a second attempt. Then she pauses, as if to steady herself on the worktop. Are her hands shaking a little? Alice wonders. And do her eyes look pink around the lids?

Becca pads off to the TV room where the children are watching their film. As she pulls the door to, she meets Alice's eye again, just for a moment, and Alice tries to reset her stare into something friendlier as the door closes between them.

6.31 p.m.

The champagne glasses are empty now, warm and fingerprinted. Alice's basement kitchen seems darker. The rain intensifies, as if the sound has been turned up.

'So, what's everyone doing over the summer?' Alice asks, over the rain.

'We're off to Kefalonia again,' Yas says. As Yas outlines her holiday plans, Alice notices Stella's expression tighten. She keeps changing the way she is holding her champagne glass, as if she is worried she is going to do it wrong.

Alice worries Stella is finding Yas intimidating. She hadn't intended to have them over at the same time. It was just that she'd offered to collect Iris for Yas as a favour, and then when they'd bumped into Stella and Frankie at the playground on the way home, Iris and Martha had begged for Frankie to be allowed to come for tea too. Which meant Stella had joined them. And then Yas had come to pick Iris up, and then the rain had started. So now, here they all are.

Alice glances at her phone. There is no word from Jamie. She is feeling tired now – the champagne hasn't helped. She would like to get Martha to bed to allow enough time for her to soak in the bath. She wonders how she can bring things to a close with Yas and Stella. Can she send them out in this rain?

She decides to pretend Jamie is nearly home, to signal to them both that it is time to go.

She picks up her phone with more emphasis this time.

'Oh, that's Jamie.' She flicks her thumb, pretending to read a message. 'He'll be home in a couple of minutes.'

'Anyone want another glass?' Yas asks, ignoring her.

'I'm all right,' Alice mutters.

'I'll get the bottle.' Stella jumps up and yanks the fridge door open, the light inside bathing her face in a watery spotlight as she closes her hand around the neck. For a moment, Alice thinks Stella looks troubled, as if she is searching for something else, but can't find it.

And then a noise outside causes them all to startle, and look up.

6.37 p.m.

When Alice realises that the sound is Jamie's feet on the basement steps, her relief is instant. He appears at the doorway, and she feels an unusually powerful surge of affection at the sight of him, his hair wet, his blue shirt darkened by the rain, clinging to his shoulders.

'Enjoying the summer everyone?'

Jamie grins at the women, but his joviality doesn't really land for some reason. Stella is just staring at him. Jamie closes the door behind him, dulling the sound of the rain, marches on the spot to dry his feet on the mat, then takes his trainers off.

'You poor bastard,' Yas mutters, a hand clapped over her mouth. 'Look at your trousers!'

Jamie sighs theatrically.

'Glass of fizz?' Yas asks him.

'Oh, nice. Yes, please. What are we celebrating?'

'Your wife's professional brilliance.'

'Ah. Of course.'

Jamie throws a smile at Alice, and she feels better as their eyes connect. Yas and Stella will go home, and she and Jamie will have dinner, and everything will soon be calm and cosy and normal.

Yas pours Jamie a glass of champagne and he takes it, then raises it slightly in Stella's direction.

'Hi,' he says brightly. 'I'm Jamie.'

Alice had forgotten that Stella and Jamie have never met.

'Sorry, Jamie, this is Stella. Stella, Jamie.'

Stella smiles back limply. 'Hi.'

Yas reaches over to pour the last few dregs of champagne into Alice's glass.

'You must be so proud of Alice,' she says to Jamie.

'Of course I am.' Jamie gives Alice's shoulder a squeeze from behind. 'What have you done with the kids?'

'They're watching *Encanto*.'

'Ah.' Jamie pulls open the door, sticks his head in, calls hello to his daughter. The women overhear a vague whining that he is blocking the TV, the sound of Jamie remonstrating with Martha. Alice notices Stella watching Jamie's back as he talks to his daughter.

Jamie closes the door, rolls his eyes.

'What shall we do about dinner?' he asks Alice. 'I'm starving. Shall we get a takeaway?'

'Sure.' The champagne has mentally eased Alice into relaxation mode, and she doesn't feel like cooking.

'Great.' Jamie pulls the fridge door open. 'Ah. We've got no milk, though, for Martha's bedtime. Shall I go and grab some?'

Alice will remember this moment later, the sudden, irrationally strong sense she has that she does not want Jamie to go anywhere. That she wants his continued presence here in the kitchen, which signals, she hopes, that now is the end of the play date, the beginning of their normal Friday night.

Stella stands up suddenly, clutches her leather jacket from the back of her chair. 'I can go for you, if you like?'

Alice looks at her.

'To the shop. For milk.' She is pulling the jacket on, as if she is in a hurry to go. 'I really don't mind. I think I was the one who used the last of it, for my coffee earlier.'

Alice blinks. Yas is raising her eyebrows.

'Nah, don't be silly,' Jamie says with a smile, nodding at Stella's champagne glass. 'Finish your drink. I'm soaked already. I'll only be two mins.'

Jamie leans down and gives Alice a wet kiss on the cheek. Stella sits down, slowly, in her chair.

The door slams shut behind Jamie. The thunder comes again, a low growl, and Alice finds she is counting in her head, waiting for the flash.

6.41 p.m.

'I'll just check Martha isn't freaking out about the thunder.'

Alice says this more because she feels like standing up than for any other reason. She turns towards the room where Becca and the children are. But then Yas speaks.

'What— what the fuck?'

Her voice changes the atmosphere. Alice turns around to look at Yas and finds that she is pale, looking out of the window at the front.

Alice follows her gaze.

The man – she will remember later that she definitely thought man, not boy – is at the front window of her basement kitchen. A black hood over his head, his eyes in shadow, but the bottom of his face visible. An open, panting mouth with small, yellowish teeth. The man is standing right up against the glass.

Alice screams and drops her champagne flute. And then, as if he is not a person, but an animal of some kind, the man – or boy – hurls himself against Alice's basement door.

6.42 p.m.

The slam of his body against the door is like a starting gun. Yas gulps, Stella claps her hands to her mouth. They both look at Alice. But Alice does not have an answer.

'What is he...'

Another slam, louder this time, like an explosion. And now the door is open, hanging off one hinge, as if its neck is broken.

With a sort of stumble, he is inside, the hooded man – his body, the heat of it, is there, inside her kitchen. Alice can smell him, and the smell of the rain, which washes in now, from where the door was, just a second ago.

'Where issshe?'

The man looks young, but there is something greyish and unwell about his skin, his teeth. Stella looks again at Alice.

'Where the fuck isshe? Isshe here?' A slur in his voice. He is drunk, then, and confused. Maybe not even dangerous. But Alice thinks this, rather than feels it. What she feels, on a cellular level, is the opposite. Her throat is dry. Her blood pulses hotly with adrenaline.

'Why don't we just calm down,' Alice tries.

'Don't talk to me, you fuckinbitch!'

He grabs at something on the sideboard, sending IKEA children's crockery in pastel shades clattering to the floor. When he turns around, he is holding the kitchen knife Becca left on the side. There is dirt under his fingernails. His knuckles flash pink and white as his grip tightens on the handle of the knife.

'Put that down!'

Alice hears her own voice, its schoolteacher tone unfamiliar to her. Her fury has made her different than she thought she would be, in a moment like this.

'Shut the fuck up!' He kicks a stool, one of the tall metal stools from Alice's island, and it comes flying at her. She throws her hands up to defend herself, twists away, and the next thing she knows there is more glass on the floor.

Alice slowly bends to pick up the stool. She does this without taking her eyes off the man. Her jaw is locked. She feels more angry than scared. This is *my* kitchen, she wants to say. You get the *fuck* out of *my* kitchen. She thinks of Martha, and her gaze flicks towards the door to the room where Becca and the children are.

A mistake.

The man catches her looking. He spins towards the door.

'Isshe innere?'

'No one is in there.' But Alice's voice could hardly sound less convincing.

He glares at her, his pale face turning red with fury. 'You're lying,' he pants. 'You're a *liar!*'

He turns around, and starts towards the door to the TV room where the children are. The atmosphere changes. Stella and Yas both move forward, Yas gasping as she steps on a piece of glass.

Alice's thoughts speed up. How long has Jamie been away? Four minutes, maybe five? He will be back any second now, she tells herself. Any second. Could Jamie take this man, this intruder? Will his male body somehow know what to do, in a way that Alice's does not? Jamie is strong, and averagely fit, but he is in his forties now, hardly some sort of SAS hero. And this man is holding a *knife*.

The man twists at the door handle. Alice hears Stella scream.

'Not there!' Stella cries. 'Get away from there!'

'I need to talk to that fucking *cunt*,' the man snarls.

Alice feels her hands stiffen on the stool. This man is not in his right mind. He has a knife, and he is heading for the room where the children are. Jamie, hero or no hero, is not here. There is no time.

Alice is behind him before she even knows that she has moved. Close enough to feel the heat, the sweat under his black clothes, to hear the soft, wet pant of his breath. And her hands are hardening around the legs of the metal stool. Holding it, up, up, until it is aloft, over her head.

The man senses her there, starts to turn around.

'You wait, you fuckinbitch. Wait till you hear, when you hear what...'

But already, a surge of something, something like a jolt of adrenaline, or electricity, or instinct of some other primal kind, is coursing through Alice, and she is bringing the stool crashing down.

She will remember later the clap of the metal as it cracks his skull, the way it splits open, like an egg. And then the way he lies there, the stool on top of him, a crimson pool spreading out around him like paint.

Yas stands still for a second, as if frozen to the spot, then shakily pulls her phone out.

'I'll call an ambulance,' she mutters. She glances uncertainly down at the blood, blooming like an ink blot.

Stella sinks to her knees beside the man, one hand pressing against the wound on his head, the other searching the rest of his body. She is muttering something about pressure, airways, secondary wounds. But Alice cannot make sense of anything.

There is silence then, except for Yas on the phone, and the dull sound of the rain. And then another sound. A soft moaning noise, that Alice only belatedly realises is coming from her.

Part Three

Autumn

ALICE

Martha's school rucksack looks so big on her, its thick straps sliding off her narrow shoulders. Alice replaces them, tucks a lock of Martha's nearly grown-out fringe behind her ear. Her skin is still a little pink from the short blast of sun that arrived in Rye for the last days of their holiday.

'Are you all set, love?'

Martha doesn't reply. She looks nervous.

'Look at my big girl,' Jamie grins. 'How did she get so grown up?'

Alice doesn't respond. He looks at her in that way he does sometimes now, like she is a puzzle he no longer has all the pieces for.

'What?' he asks, with a note of impatience. 'You look worried about something.'

'I'm just... not looking forward to seeing all the other mums, you know?'

'Oh, that. Just ignore them.' Jamie zips his bag up sharply. Alice suppresses a flash of exasperation. That's Jamie's answer to everything these days. Ignore it. Ignore the other mothers. Ignore the weird anonymous calls, the online threats, the rotting bird that was dumped on the doorstep of their holiday rental. The obvious signs that something is very wrong.

'Have you got a lot on today?' Alice asks Jamie pointedly. He is pulling a tie into a Windsor knot. There is a small red flick of a shaving cut just under his chin. Ties don't usually get much of an outing from Jamie's wardrobe, and she can't remember the last time she saw him wearing a suit like this.

Jamie looks up. 'What? Just meetings. Usual stuff.' Jamie crouches down next to Martha, his trouser legs riding up to reveal the pattern of his socks. His shoes are polished to a mirror shine. 'What about you?'

'Not much,' Alice says vaguely. She hasn't told Jamie that she plans to meet up with Stella later, to find out what Stella has found out about Ezra. It doesn't seem worth another argument.

Jamie isn't listening to her reply in any case. He is rummaging in his bag for something for Martha.

'Ah, here it is,' he grins. 'For your first day back.' He pulls a wrapped present out of his backpack and hands it to her. Martha, who lost the first of her teeth on the way back from Rye, bursts into a gappy smile.

She rips the paper open, then holds the present up to Alice. 'Unicorns! Mummy, Daddy got me a unicorn water bottle!'

'Wow. Well done, Daddy.' Alice had completely forgotten that Martha's water bottle was lost, that she'd promised her a new one.

Alice goes to fill it up. Over the sound of the water, she hears Jamie telling Martha she is his best girl, that he is so proud of her. She screws the lid on tight, her hands feeling clumsy. The water bottle doesn't seem very good quality. She wonders what happened to the old one. She has lost her sunglasses, too. She could have used them to hide behind, when she sees the other mothers.

Alice searches, but cannot find either item on her cluttered surfaces, or in the messy sideboard drawers. Disorder has crept into her previously ordered home these past few weeks, things pushed away haphazardly in cupboards or down the back of sideboards. This past week, she keeps noticing more things that have gone missing. Her favourite gold earrings of her mother's, which she was sure were in a little bowl by the front door. The camisole she likes to sleep in when it's hot. A notebook where, since Martha was tiny, she writes down all the funny things that her daughter says or does.

Alice is gutted about the notebook – it was something she'd wanted to keep adding to as Martha grew, that she wanted to pass on to her. But the earrings bother Alice the most. Alice wonders whether maybe Becca borrowed them and lost them – although it would be unlike her not to ask first, or to at least own up, and offer to replace them. But the earrings were from the 1920s, given to her mother by her father for her wedding day, and like her mother they are not, she thinks with sadness, easily replaceable.

'Jamie, do you know where my sunglasses are? I'm sure they were here on the side.'

'What? No, sorry.' Jamie is bouncing from one work shoe to another, tying his laces, like he suddenly has an excess of energy.

'You know, I was just thinking about this move stuff,' Jamie calls over to Alice. 'Shall we put the house on the market, just to see?'

Alice blinks. 'What?'

'Just as an experiment. To test the market. See how much we'd get for it. I was talking to Barney about the best way of doing it.'

'You spoke to Barney?'

Barney is Alice's financial adviser, the person who was entrusted with looking after her interests after her parents died. She wasn't aware that Jamie ever spoke to Barney. Certainly not without talking to Alice first.

'Yeah,' Jamie says. 'He was saying that if we sold, we could put the money in the bank, then rent somewhere for a bit while we work out which area we want to buy in.'

Alice buries her head in her hands. Just the idea of 'renting for a while', the casualness with which he says it, sets her nerves on edge.

'Jamie, I cannot have this conversation now,' she says. 'It's Martha's first day back – can we just focus on that for now?'

Jamie raises his palms in retreat. 'All right, all right, I'm sorry,' he soothes. 'We can talk about it later.'

You're bloody right we will, Alice thinks furiously. But she smiles, for Martha's benefit, untucks the collar of her checked school dress from inside the neck of her jumper.

'Are we moving house, Mummy?' Martha's voice is quiet, and worried.

'No, darling. We're not.'

Alice avoids looking at Jamie. Martha seems somewhat reassured, but glances at her father with a flicker of suspicion. When Alice hands Martha the water bottle, she grips it tightly, hugging it to her chest with both hands.

ALICE

After the morning she has had, dropping a reluctant Martha off at school, Alice has been looking forward to seeing Stella for a coffee, and hearing what she has found so far. While Stella is in the bathroom, Alice can't resist having a flick through the papers she has left in a pile on Alice's kitchen table. The papers are still warm from the printer in Jamie's study. Stella said she didn't have one in her flat. 'It's a bit small for things like that,' she had said, and Alice had noticed her glance enviously at the high ceilings of Alice's hallway.

Alice skims through the documents one by one. At first they look exciting – birth and marriage certificates, electoral records, newspaper cuttings. Alice tries to take in the names, dates, places. But she knows a lot of these things already. She rummages further, impatient for something new.

When she hears Stella returning to the kitchen, Alice places the papers back where they were on the table and masks her disappointment with a brisk smile.

'Coffee?'

'Oh, sure,' Stella says. 'Lovely.'

Alice stands up and starts the espresso machine, fumbling over the capsules.

'Your house is gorgeous,' Stella says. 'I love how bold you've been with all the colour.'

'Thank you,' Alice smiles.

'Have you lived here long?'

'I bought this place in my twenties. My parents died,' Alice adds, by way of explanation.

'I'm sorry,' Stella nods simply. 'You made a great choice. I'm so glad we moved here. I love being by the canal.'

'Where were you living before?'

'Leyton?' Stella says it like a question, and Alice has to admit she isn't exactly sure where that is, other than some way east. 'It was OK. Much nicer round here. The flat's smaller, but I love being on the water. Frankie saw a heron from her bedroom window the other day.' Stella smiles at the memory, then gives herself a little shake. 'Sorry, you want to see what I've got. Let me show you.'

Stella starts spinning the papers around with her fingers and pushing them towards Alice. Alice sets the coffees down, and looks politely at what she has found, as if it's the first time she has done so.

'This is Ezra's birth certificate – they're publicly available, you just have to pay a tenner or something,' Stella says, pointing. 'See – from 2005. It names his mother as Linda Mary Jones, née O'Brian, and father as a John Ezra Jones. They had their children quite late in life – she was forty-two.'

Alice blinks. Stella – who Alice knows recently celebrated her thirtieth birthday, so is more than a decade younger – takes a beat to register Alice's unease.

'Sorry,' she mumbles. 'I know that's – I didn't mean that forty-two was late in life per se, just that...'

'It's fine,' Alice says, forcing a laugh. She blinks away her sadness at the memory of Jamie's words, when they'd talked about another baby. *Most people our age are calling it quits.*

'I wonder if she struggled to have children, maybe?' Stella says more carefully. 'She and John had been married two decades, look. They married in 1985. And look, here's the birth cert for Jade Marie Jones – same birth date, in 2005. She and Ezra were twins. Did you know that?'

'Oh. Twins.' Alice is not sure why she is feigning surprise. She knows all this. None of this is helpful.

Stella looks a little deflated.

'Also,' she says, 'it looks like Ezra's father died in his fifties. Ezra and his sister Jade would have been about fourteen. That's young to lose your dad, isn't it? It must have had an impact on him. On both of them.'

Alice doesn't see much point in mentioning she already knew this, too. Then she remembers something Linda said about Ezra. *He was getting to be like his father.*

Alice sees that there is another certificate in Stella's pile. *Death Certificate. John Jones.*

'Did you find out what the dad died of?' Alice asks, reaching for the death certificate. Before she can take it, though, Stella grabs most of the papers and scoops them up into a pile, stuffs them in her bag.

'Heart attack,' she says briskly. 'Cardiac disease, I think it says on there, which is the same thing. He died at the flat. He and Linda have lived there since the eighties. Look, here's the electoral roll entries. No Ezra and Jade on it – under sixteens don't show up, and even after that it's only if you're registered to vote which it looks like they never have.'

Stella shows Alice the electoral roll copies, and a few other things, but most are familiar to her. Cuttings she has already seen online. A picture of Ezra, as part of a group in the local paper, when he was in primary school. He'd won some sort of local football trophy. He is grinning at the camera, a gap-toothed seven-year-old. Alice has to fight the urge to look away.

'So... nothing else?' Alice asks. 'Nothing that links him to me or Jamie?'

'Not that I've found. Sorry.' Stella pauses. 'But maybe that's... reassuring?'

Alice hesitates.

'Did you look at the sister, Jade, much?'

'Not really. Why?'

'No reason,' Alice says weakly. 'I just keep thinking about the photograph Jade took from me. It's got me thinking. What if the key ring was nothing to do with Ezra? What if *Jade* took my key ring? And made the phone call, and posted all these horrible messages online?'

'I see,' Stella says, though she doesn't look as if she does.

'I guess I was just wondering,' Alice says, clearing her throat, trying to sound less worried than she really is, 'if there's any evidence that Jade could be a bit – you know. Unpredictable.'

For a moment, Alice wonders whether she should mention the other things that have gone missing from her home. Or the dead gull. She is starting to believe it is at least possible that Jade has been stalking her, breaking into her house, even that she followed them all the way to Rye and placed a dead bird outside their holiday home. But she can't seem to find words in her head that don't make her sound like some kind of paranoid lunatic.

Stella hesitates, but then makes a note. 'OK. Focus on Jade. Got it. I'll have another look.'

'Thank you.' Alice pauses, while Stella writes down something Alice can't read.

'Is – is there any way of finding out if someone has a criminal record, Stella?'

'Not usually,' Stella says, looking up. 'Why? Are you thinking of Ezra?'

Alice makes a face. 'I was actually wondering more about Jade.'

Alice wants to know everything possible about Jade. She wants to know who she is dealing with, exactly how dangerous a person Jade might be if – as Alice suspects – she has worked out who Alice really is. That she is the person who killed her brother.

'I do have a police contact,' Stella says slowly. 'I don't know if he'll help me. It's trickier these days, with the cops. It might be asking a lot.'

'Sure.' Alice nods.

'But I will try him,' she says. 'And I'll try some other things, too. And I will let you know if I find anything else.'

'Thanks.'

Stella sits back in her chair, stretches her arms above her head. 'Thanks for the coffee,' she says. 'You're not working today?'

'No, I'm not starting my new job until later this week. I wanted to be around for Martha's first day back.'

'How was she at drop-off?'

'I think she was OK,' Alice grimaces. In truth, she barely remembers how Martha was. She'd been too focused on the other mothers, on who was looking at her.

Everyone is on your side, Yas had texted her that morning. But Alice saw the curious glances, the reappraising looks, from mums she used to chat to. She doesn't even blame them. Who could resist stealing a glance at the woman who'd been in the news during the summer holidays for killing a burglar with a metal stool? Wondering if, faced with the same *extremis*, they themselves would be capable of doing what she did, of killing someone. She knows this because she herself would have the same questions. She would look at someone differently after that, too.

The truth is, she looks at *herself* differently. She can't reconcile her image of herself with the fact of what she has done. She doubts it will ever settle, this cognitive dissonance which makes her own life feel unreal to her now, as if she is inhabiting the life, the body, of another person. Which has made her feel apart from her own life, her friends, her daughter, even her husband. Which makes her turn away from him at night when he tries to draw her close.

'I find it hard to tell how Frankie is finding school,' Stella volunteers, dragging Alice back to the present. 'She gets so quiet.'

'Oh, Martha does the same,' Alice agrees. 'I'm so glad she's found a friend in Frankie.'

'Me too,' Stella says. 'They're so similar. I think Frankie really loves that art club they go to together. She's always so happy when I pick her up afterwards.'

'Does she?' Alice feels a twist of Mum-guilt. 'Our nanny, Becca, usually does that pick-up.'

'Oh, yes, Becca. She seems great.'

'She is. She's leaving us, sadly, at the end of September.'

Stella looks sympathetic, but not surprised. Alice wonders whether she could have known this information already. Did Becca ever chat to Stella, perhaps, at art club pick-up? Alice supposes there is no reason why she wouldn't. Except Alice is sure Becca had given her the impression she didn't really know who Stella was.

'I don't really know why she's leaving.' Alice glances at Stella again.

'Getting the right childcare is so hard.'

'It is.' Alice briefly wonders whether Stella is deliberately side-stepping her attempt to gather information. Then she realises that Stella is probably talking about how hard it is being a single parent, and mentally admonishes herself for being so self-centred.

'How do you manage it with Frankie?'

'Oh, I mostly work from home, so I just try to muddle through as best I can,' Stella smiles. 'It was easy when she was at nursery. The school hours are hard. I would love a Becca.'

Alice smiles, says nothing. She knows she and Jamie are so privileged to be able to afford a nanny, especially one as wonderful as Becca.

'Then again,' Stella says, 'I don't know how Frankie would react to another person looking after her – she's so used to it just being the two of us.' Stella makes a face. 'Must be because she's my only one. Poor kid gets all my neuroses projected onto her.'

'I'm sure I do the same.' Alice pauses. 'Do you ever worry about Frankie being an only child?'

Alice regrets the question as soon as she has voiced it.

'Sorry, Stella – that's such a personal question. Ignore me.'

'No, I don't mind.' Stella is smiling again. 'You mean, do I worry about her being lonely, that sort of thing? Yeah, I do sometimes.' She pauses. 'Do you?'

'A bit,' Alice admits. 'I would like – would have liked – another, to be honest. For Martha, mostly. I didn't love being an only child. Jamie doesn't agree, though. He had a difficult family life, couldn't stand his brothers, doesn't really speak to any of his family now. I think he'd have loved to be an only child.' Alice forces a laugh she doesn't feel.

'Really?' Stella frowns. 'I can't imagine that. My little sister and I were thick as thieves when we were kids – we had our own secret language, whole imaginative worlds, that belonged only to us. We were best, best friends.'

'That sounds nice.'

'It was.' Stella is staring down at the knots in Alice's mangowood table, her fingers pulling at a gold hoop earring that seems to be bothering her.

'Well, you have plenty of time,' Alice says cautiously. 'You're so young.'

Stella laughs. 'I don't know. I mean obviously we've split up, her dad and I, so sibling opportunities are limited.' She gives a rueful smile. 'I probably worry more about that, to be honest – whether I've, you know, damaged her forever by making her a child from a broken home, by not giving her a "proper family".' Stella makes the quote marks in the air with her fingers, flashes a pained smile that doesn't reach her eyes.

'I'm sure you haven't,' Alice says. 'And I'm sure you had good reasons.'

'Oh, I definitely did. My ex was *extremely* unfaithful.' Stella says it like a punchline, holding her coffee cup in front of her smile.

'I'm sorry.'

Alice has thought before that there is a fragility about Stella, behind her curated outfits, her cheerful earthiness. Alice has often got the sense she exists under the weight of something. Well, this must be it. Alice cannot even imagine how difficult it must be. To find the partner you share a child with has been unfaithful, and you must somehow find the strength to leave, and parent alone. Especially as, from what Alice can make out, Stella's job – as a features writer on a national newspaper – is one of those creative-industry jobs that sounds prestigious but doesn't actually pay very much for the work it demands. Alice wonders, not for the first time, whether Stella's flat on the canal is owned or rented. How much support she gets from Frankie's father.

'It must have been hard, splitting up, when you have a baby.'

Stella looks thoughtful, rather than guarded.

'The actual splitting up was not as scary as you imagine,' she says, after a pause. 'Expensive, but a relief, really. The stressful part was all the stuff that came before it.' She looks down to her fingernails. 'I had this perfect baby daughter, and I just wanted us to be perfect too, but I just kept getting this horrible feeling. And if I ever asked him outright, he'd say it was my hormones, or whatever. We'd have a perfect weekend, the three of us. And then I'd find a receipt, or a weird message would pop up on his phone. I'd catch him lying about little things. Pointless things. It took me a while to realise. If they lie about small things, it means there are bigger things, too.'

It is a familiar story, and yet beyond Alice's experience. Alice has never had time for the sorts of men that Stella is describing. Her on-off ex-boyfriend, Tag, who she dated for most of her twenties, was a bit hopeless, but never unfaithful. And Jamie has always been so straightforward about wanting marriage, family, monogamy. He always is so sad to hear of any couple splitting up. Alice has always found it quite touching.

'I'm glad you had the guts to leave,' Alice tells Stella. 'Many women wouldn't.'

'I'd never have stayed with him, once I knew,' she says. 'Not even for another sibling.' Stella pulls herself up, paints on a bright smile. 'But I can't regret my marriage, because it gave me Frankie. And our surname, which despite the associations, I love and will never surrender.'

'What's your surname?'

'Glass.'

'Stella Glass,' Alice laughs. 'It is a great name.'

'Isn't it?' Stella chuckles. 'Like a spy.' She raises one eyebrow, then laughs. 'But yes. It is a shame, for Frankie. That she's missed out on a brother or sister, and that I chose such a hopeless twat to be her dad. Co-parenting with Hugo is a nightmare. He lets her down, all the time.'

Alice can hear a lump in Stella's throat, her voice going a little jagged.

'She'll sit at the window,' she goes on. 'With her rucksack all packed. And Hugo just won't come. Or other times, he will act like the perfect father, and spoil her with stuff I can't afford, just to spite me. Last Christmas, he knew I had saved up to surprise her with tickets to *Frozen* the musical – so he just took her one day, on a whim, a couple of weeks before Christmas. Front row seats. Just to spoil it.'

Alice stares at her, aghast.

'Another time, he told her I was mean for not letting her have sweets – that when she was with Daddy, she could have ice cream for lunch and dinner. He took her to the parlour at Fortnum and Mason, and let her eat as much as she wanted. She was sick all night when she got back home.'

'Oh, Stella, I'm sorry,' Alice says, shaking her head.

'I know it sounds awful,' Stella sighs. 'But I sometimes think Frankie would be better off if her dad was dead.'

Alice looks up, wondering if she misheard. But Stella is smiling, talking in the same tone she just used to talk about her daughter's art club and *Frozen* tickets.

'I just think it would be so much better for us all,' she shrugs. 'If Hugo was dead, I could tell Frankie a lovely fairy tale about how wonderful he was, how much he'd loved her. This way, he gets to break her heart again, and again, and again. And there is nothing I can do to protect her from him, or from the message he is giving her: that she is not really worthy of love. Because the law says that access to her is his right.'

Stella is standing up now, plucking up the coffee cups for the dishwasher, as if what she has just said is no big deal. And yet there is something about the coolness of Stella's hatred that makes Alice's hair stand up on end.

'Some men are just toxic, Alice.' Stella tips the mugs upside down, slots them neatly onto the dishwasher shelf and presses the door closed. 'And the world would be a far better place for our daughters, if they did not exist.'

Evening Standard
10 September 2023

An inquest into the death of a teenager who was killed after he broke into a £1.2m home in East London will take place in the spring, a coroner has said.

Ezra Jones, 18, died after his botched raid of the East London property of Jamie and Alice Rathbone on 14 July.

Alice Rathbone, 42, who had been holding a 'play date' at her home with friends, was arrested.

She was initially told she could face charges relating to his death after admitting she hit him on the back of the head with a metal stool.

However, the police later said Mrs Rathbone would not face criminal charges in relation to his death since prosecutors had concluded she had acted in self-defence. A file has now been passed to the coroner ahead of the inquest proceedings.

The family of Mr Jones said they still had 'many questions' regarding his death and hoped these would be answered at the inquest.

ENDS

COMMENTS (959)

@redwall4
Lets see what comes out now never feel like we got the true story TBH

@laidback
Feel sorry for the boy's family still having to go through all this
@hatchetjob
We know the truth about what really happened. Alice Rathbone is a murdering bitch
@hatchetjob
I'm coming for you, Alice
@hatchetjob
U can't hide from me

[CLICK FOR MORE]

ALICE

Alice is sitting in the staff kitchen at the Cunliffe Institute, trying to reach DCI Barnes for the third time that day. While she waits to get through, she wipes at a mark her coffee cup has made on the pristine white sideboard. Alice started her new job a week ago, and somehow she is struggling to settle into her new environment. The kitchen is huge and nothing like Stanley's. It looks brand new. Alice has started to suspect she is the only person who uses it. The mark is not coming out. Alice wonders if she could smuggle in some turpentine solution.

'Oh, hi. Hi. DCI Barnes? It's Alice. Alice Rathbone.'

She stops scrubbing. She can tell it takes Barnes a moment to remember who she is.

'Ah, Alice. What can I do for you?'

His tone is polite, but Alice senses she will not get much of his time.

'I'm sorry to bother you,' she gabbles. 'I just need to ask you again about these online messages.'

Alice tries to explain about the latest ones that have been posted. Reads him a few of them.

'It's this one account, hatchetjob,' she explains. 'It's happening all the time now. I mean – "I'm coming for you… you can't hide from me" – doesn't that count as a threat, or something?'

'Hmm. OK.'

Barnes takes down the links to the articles where the comments have appeared.

'I will take a look at it for you, OK? I can't promise anything.'

'Thank you. Thank you so much.' The line has gone dead before Alice finishes speaking. She stares at her phone. She has another missed call. From Jade. Why on earth is Jade calling her?

Alice looks up and sees her new boss, Rollo, standing in the doorway. His hands are on his hips, chest puffed out a little, so that his broad shoulders pull at the expensive fabric of his pink posh-boy shirt. The beginning of a midlife paunch is visible over his belted chinos. Alice suspects Rollo played rugby at his private school, then thickened around the middle at university when he replaced sport with beer.

'Morning, morning,' he says in a faux-formal voice. 'Everything all right?'

Alice shoves her phone into her pocket. She will think about the call from Jade later, and in the meantime, she will try to swallow the lump in her throat, the sensation of pressure in her chest.

'Morning, Rollo,' she smiles. 'How are things?'

'Super, thanks.'

Rollo is the sort of bloke that Alice is used to encountering in the restoration world. Moneyed, entitled, but affable and basically harmless. He is about her age, maybe even younger – apparently, he is the godson of the lead curator, which probably explains his seniority. Alice has already worked out why Rollo sought her out to work for him. Despite his connections, his social gloss, Rollo knows he doesn't have the eye that she has, can't fix a painting the way that she can.

'Just making a coffee,' she says. 'Would you like one?'

He smiles tightly. 'Oh, no thanks. I always have mine before I come in.'

There is an uncomfortable pause.

'Because of the paintings,' he says slowly, as if speaking to a child. 'I presume you had a no-hot-drinks rule at Stanley's place, too?'

Alice pauses, embarrassed. She isn't an idiot. She knows you shouldn't really have hot coffee in close proximity to any canvas, hot drinks being one of the worst things that you can spill on paintings, especially anything modern that hasn't been treated with a thick varnish. But Stanley always said that coffee was a basic human right and they were all grown-ups and he trusted them to be careful. She'd never known of any spills at Stanley's in the time she was there.

Rollo lets out an amused laugh.

'Honestly!' he chuckles, shaking his head. 'Stanley, old man. What sort of place is he running over there?'

Alice tries to smile, even though the slight against her old boss has got her back up. Stanley might be old-school and eccentric, but he is a better restorer than Rollo will ever be, and it's annoying to be scolded – even mildly – by someone younger than her.

'I'll just get a glass of water,' Alice says, through gritted teeth.

'No worries. Is now a good time to have a look at the piece that's come in from The Hague?'

Rollo slaps his hands together and rubs them briskly, waggles his eyebrows to indicate his excitement.

'The Vermeer is here?'

'That's the one. It's just been brought up to my office. I was hoping you could get started today.'

'You want me to look after it?'

Rollo raises his eyebrows. 'You're our new restoration lead. Who else?'

Alice feels a frisson of excitement. She has never worked on a Vermeer before – there aren't many, only about thirty-six, she thinks, from memory.

She stands up quickly, wipes her hands on her apron, immediately forgetting about the coffee. She takes the temporary pass security gave her this morning from the countertop – her usual one has gone missing, and Rollo had to sign her in, just to add to the aura of chaos and incompetence she fears she has started to emit. The temp pass is clunky, barely fits in her pocket.

Alice follows Rollo through to his office. Two men in white gloves are unwrapping the canvas and placing it carefully onto an easel. Rollo indicates a chair in front of his mahogany desk.

'Do sit.'

'I'm fine. I'd rather stand.' Alice positions herself by the tall window, with its gorgeous view of the river, and waits for the men in gloves to unwrap the painting. Rollo is jiggling with nervous excitement, pacing this way and that to get a look at it as it emerges.

'Fabulous. Absolutely fabulous.' He looks up at Alice roguishly. 'Filthy though, isn't it?'

Alice is silent, eyes fixed on the canvas. It's not his best, and Rollo's right – it's very grubby – but still, it's a Vermeer, and it is heart-stopping. A group of three servant girls, seated at a wooden table. Two are absorbed with one another. The third, though, looks away, as if bored of the conversation, towards a sunlit window in the back left. And it is this girl's face, the luminosity of it, which gives the painting its extraordinary quality. It is, as Stanley would say, box-office.

'Where has it been?'

Rollo gives her a quick history – first identified in 1880, lost in the chaos of war, then found after the fall of the Berlin Wall in the Soviet Union, and now being sold by a private Dutch collector to the Old Masters Picture Gallery in Dresden – the Gemäldegalerie Alte Meister. The museum want it restored ahead of a major new retrospective next summer in Amsterdam.

Rollo pulls a pair of gloves on, then takes out a UV torch, so that they can examine the marks of previous restorations.

'It'll need some work over here,' he says, pointing to the worst area. 'And there.'

Alice nods. She can see for herself exactly what needs doing. It might be a Vermeer, but it is like any other canvas. She is relieved. Excited even. She is the right person for this job, she reminds herself. She can do this.

'Can I have the torch?'

Alice guides the light slowly towards the top left corner of the painting where the window is. There is something wrong with that corner. The varnish isn't quite the same, the paint a little too fresh. Surely she can't be the first to notice it. This is a famous picture. Surely someone else has thought to look.

'Has it been X-rayed?'

'Presumably,' he says. 'Why?'

'I think there's something underneath there,' she says.

Rollo frowns. 'An underpainting?'

'Maybe.'

He picks up the papers on his desk. 'Nothing in the notes,' he says. 'I think we should have another look.'

Alice is being bold, here. X-rays are expensive. But she is starting to feel excited. If Vermeer painted this another way originally, if Alice were to uncover some previously unseen element – well, then, it could give the gallery a headline for their retrospective.

'All right,' Rollo nods, after a moment. 'Can't hurt to look.'

Alice is so focused on the canvas she doesn't check her phone all day. Only when she is about to leave does she look, and finds four notifications stacked, one on top of the other, in urgent, yellow little boxes on her home screen. And only then does she remember the missed call from Jade.

Message: Jade.

Can U call me pls thanks

Missed calls: Jade.

Alice takes a breath, hesitates, then calls Jade's number.

Jade picks up instantly.

'Hey.'

'Hey, Jade. What's up?'

There is a pause. She tries to make out the background noise. There is muffled conversation. Then Jade's voice.

'The baby's coming,' she says heavily. 'And they are saying something's wrong, the baby might not make it.'

Alice takes a breath.

'Is there someone with you?'

'No.' Jade takes a gasp.

'What about Ryan?'

Jade lets out a dismissive noise.

'He's not here.' She exhales heavily. 'Can you come?'

Alice is stunned. She hasn't heard from Jade in weeks. After the missing picture, and what happened in Rye, plus these weird messages cropping up online – she'd made up her mind to steer clear of Jade for good. She had also promised Jamie that she would not contact her or Linda ever again.

'What about Ryan? Why isn't he with you?'

'He's not coming,' Jade mutters. 'I haven't seen him in... argh!'

'What about your mum? Can't she come?'

Jade gasps, then exhales heavily.

'Mum's sick,' she pants.

'Sick?'

'Cancer,' Jade manages. 'Came up on some tests, when she fell – it's bad. They won't discharge – say she needs – oh, God! Oh, help me, please!'

Alice can only sit silently, listening to the girl's howls of pain down the phone. It is agony to hear, like a wounded animal. Alice cannot imagine why she, of all people, would be the person Jade would call. But despite everything, she begins to feel a trickle of sympathy. Jade is a young girl, giving birth alone. She must be utterly terrified.

'Jade?'

Alice can only hear a muffled moan, now. Has Jade gone? She thinks about hanging up, but then she hears her again.

'I think maybe they got it wrong, when they did the tests.' Jade sounds like she is hyperventilating now.

'What tests?' Alice is confused.

'The tests they did on the baby. They *said* she'd be normal. They *said* she was fine. But what if they got it wrong?'

Jade isn't making sense. She must be talking about the scans.

'Slow down, Jade,' Alice says. 'I'm sure the baby is going to be fine. What exactly have the doctors said?'

'I don't know,' she moans. 'I don't know... He's gone now... I was... It's so painful. I feel like I'm dying.'

'It's OK, Jade.' Alice feels wetness under her arms. 'And... there's really no one with you?'

'No one.' She pauses, lets out a sob that melts into a howl of pain. 'Uh, uh,' she pants. 'Can – can you come?'

There is no part of Alice that wants to go to the hospital, to see Jade again. But then again, Jade is, despite everything, a lonely, frightened girl, and she sounds desperate. Alice can hear her breathing, can hear that she is gasping in pain. Jade does not seem prone to melodrama to Alice – maybe there really is something wrong with her baby. Alice doubts that Jade's own life is in danger, but she remembers the same thing crossing her own mind during the utter, ripping agony of labour. And Jade is completely alone. It's unthinkable.

Alice closes her eyes.

'If you really want me there,' Alice says hesitantly, 'then, um, I guess I could…'

'Yes.' Jade sounds desperate. 'Yes. I want you to come. Please.'

ALICE

After a signal delay on the tube, a lift to the wrong floor and a fruitless search for Jade on the postnatal ward, Alice finally locates her in something called the recovery bay. She has not yet made it onto the main ward, but things seem calm and quiet. Jade's curtain is already pulled back, so Alice sees them both straight away. Jade and, to Alice's surprise and relief, an apparently perfect, sleeping newborn, all wrapped up in a little cot beside her.

'Oh, you're both OK,' Alice says cautiously.

'Yeah.'

Jade is slumped in a crumpled hospital gown on the bed, little guard rails either side of her like a child. Whatever urgency prompted her call to Alice seems to have dissipated. She looks pale, tired and ordinary. Her eyes are stripped of their false lashes, and she is blinking as if newly adjusting to the light.

Alice leans over for a look at the new baby, who is lying in the same clear perspex box that Alice remembers from having Martha. She is swaddled in a white hospital cloth, a cotton hat with a daisy pattern on her head that Alice realises, with a thud of emotion, was also Martha's first hat. The baby is making little wheezy, snoring noises. A card in her box-cot, shaped like a teddy bear, states her weight, 3,450 grams, her length, 51 cm, but next to 'NAME' there is only a blank space. Her birthdate and time are recorded as 16.16 on 14 September. Two months, to the day, since Ezra's death, Alice realises with a jolt.

Alice doesn't want Jade to have to sit up to greet her, and she isn't sure about the idea of hugging her, so she settles for an awkward hand on Jade's arm. Jade barely reacts.

'You did it,' Alice says gently. 'How do you feel?'

'I'm all right.' Jade lifts her water bottle, takes a sip and glances warily over at the baby.

'So it was all... OK, in the end?'

Alice wonders what the panicked call was prompted by. Whether Jade had a section, or tore, or was cut. But she is not a relative of Jade's, or close friend – *not any kind of friend*, she reminds herself, firmly – and so all these things are too intimate to ask. Perhaps Jade was just unprepared for the pain, which is understandable. The baby looks like a normal newborn, which is to say a little alien, but not obviously abnormal. And Jade looks OK, if a little pale.

'It was scary,' Jade croaks. Words flood out of her suddenly, tripping over each other, like a dam has burst. 'Her heart rate kept dropping. At first they said it was all fine but I knew it wasn't. Then suddenly it was an emergency, and they had to get her out. I just panicked. I was so sure it meant there was going to be something wrong, even though they said there wouldn't be. Because all the time, the whole time, I've been waiting for them to say, she's not right.'

Alice wants to reassure her, but she is struggling to follow what Jade is saying. She just nods, tries to look sympathetic.

'The last doctor said she was all right,' Jade adds gruffly.

'That's wonderful,' Alice says encouragingly.

Jade shuffles up in her bed and glances suspiciously at the crib, as if trying to work out whether the doctor was lying. Alice feels a surge of sympathy for her. Jade is a difficult person, but even so. How frightening it all must have been for her on her own.

'You did really well,' Alice tells Jade. 'It's very overwhelming, isn't it?'

Jade shrugs, which Alice chooses to interpret as agreement.

Alice looks at her watch. If she leaves now, she will be able to see Martha before bedtime. She feels her shoulders drop with the relief that she can leave now.

Alice looks around the ward. All the other mothers have their babies in their arms.

'Can I pass her to you before I go, Jade?' she asks, nodding at the crib.

'No,' Jade says flatly. 'Can you get me my phone? I dunno where it is. I think the midwife put it in my bag, maybe, when they wheeled me in here.'

'OK. Let me have a look.'

Alice starts to sort through Jade's hospital bag, full of neatly folded baby clothes, cereal bars, a faded make-up purse. Her hand closes around a phone, and she pulls it out. She nearly hands it over, but pauses. This phone is ancient – a Nokia 5110. It's the sort of phone Alice had as a teenager, when all you could do was send texts and play 'snake'. Jade's phone does not look like this. She has an iPhone with a leopard-print case – Alice has seen it before. This must belong to someone else.

'Not that. Give it here.'

Jade leans forward, panicked, gesturing for Alice to hand her the bag.

'Sorry,' Alice says, taken aback by her tone. She replaces the phone in the bag, and hands it to Jade.

'That's just my mum's old phone,' she mutters, glancing at Alice.

'Right,' Alice says. It seems a curiously old-fashioned phone, though. Linda isn't that old.

The baby stirs in her cot, a spray of tiny fingers appearing just above the perspex rim. She draws her tiny knees up to her chest, her blanket unfurling, and starts to grizzle.

'I'll move her closer for you, shall I?'

Alice slowly wheels the cot towards Jade. Jade, who has now extracted her phone and dropped the bag on the floor next to her, looks up at Alice.

'Why don't you pick her up?' Jade says.

Alice blinks. 'OK. I'll hand her to you.'

'No.' Jade glances at her phone screen, then flicks it off, places it on the bedside table and looks back at Alice. 'I think you should hold her.'

Jade's voice is strangely firm. The baby starts pulling her legs up and crying harder, that awful, nerve-shredding newborn cry. Alice finds she is itching for someone to pick the baby up, comfort it, but Jade shows no reaction.

'OK,' Alice says. She slips her hands under the baby's neck and bottom. She can't remember the last time she held a newborn. She feels awkward, out of practice. Instinctively, she presses the baby upright, in the centre of her chest, against her heart, where Martha used to like to be held. Instantly, the baby stops crying, and softens. A cushiony cheek pressing against Alice's collarbone. It stills her, for a second, the feeling of it.

'Do you have a name for her?'

'Not yet. She looks different to what I thought.'

The baby starts wriggling. Alice shifts her position so she is cradling her, looking at her face. The baby's eyes open, two pink, puffy slits. She has lots of dark hair, poking out of the sides of her little daisy hat, like Martha did when she was born. Same hair, same hat. Alice knows that all newborns look basically the same. But the similarity is unsettling.

'Does it remind you,' Jade says, as if reading her mind, 'of your baby?'

Alice is not sure what to say. There is something goading, almost bitter in the way she asked the question. Alice cannot work out what Jade is asking. What she wants from her. Why she asked her here.

'Here.' Alice passes Jade the baby, wanting to rid herself of it suddenly. Jade hesitates before eventually taking her. Within seconds, she is holding up her phone with the other hand, above her head, for a selfie. She pouts, sucking in her cheeks, opens her eyes wide like a doll. She looks ridiculous, but it's tragic, also, and the sadness of it kicks Alice in the stomach. Jade has no one to take a picture of her with her new baby.

'Here,' Alice says. 'I'll take some pictures. I'll send them to you.'

Alice takes a few quick snaps, supressing the urge to tell Jade to smile naturally, instead of in that silly, pouty Instagram way. The instant the phone is lowered, Jade's smile drops from her face, like the fall of a curtain.

'All right,' Jade says. 'Take her for me a minute, will you, so I can tell you which ones to delete?' Alice hesitates, then takes the baby. But before she can hand over her phone, a midwife arrives, pushing a trolley, in a swish of purple polyester curtain.

'Hello, hello,' she calls out cheerily. 'Just here for blood pressure check, OK? Hello, Granny, congratulations.'

Alice stares at the nurse. *Dear God. She thinks I'm Jade's mother*, she realises. Alice is too stunned to say a word. And where is the real granny, Linda? Jade said something on the phone about her having cancer? It doesn't seem like the time to bring it up. Also, Alice just wants to get out of here now. Not get drawn further into Jade's dramas.

'Everyone all right?'

The midwife takes a quick look at the baby in Alice's arms, then fixes her gaze on Jade. 'How is Mum doing?'

Jade takes a moment to realise the nurse is talking to her, that she is Mum.

'I'm OK,' she croaks. She pulls herself further up into a sitting position, wincing a little.

'Grand.' The midwife pulls the Velcro band on the blood pressure machine. The ripping sound startles the baby in Alice's arms, and she does that newborn reflex that Alice had forgotten about, fingers splayed and arms outstretched. Alice would like to hand the baby back.

'When are we going to get the baby check?' Jade asks the nurse.

'Hmm?' The midwife fastens the band, holding Jade's skinny arm up awkwardly like a piece of hospital equipment.

'I was told there'd be a children's doctor, that they'd check the baby over to see if everything was normal,' Jade says. 'I want to do that part. When can the doctor see her?'

'Baby will get the full check when you're ready to be discharged,' the midwife says distractedly. 'That won't be today. We'll need you in overnight. Now, let's talk about you, Mum. How is the pain now? Let's have a look at your stitches.'

The midwife is indicating that Jade should lower the sheet so she can check her belly. This, Alice decides, is the time to leave. She lays the now sleepy baby back in the perspex box, gives Jade a quick wave, takes her phone and bag and slips away before Jade can protest.

Walking out of the maternity wing, past the couples sitting in the lobby with tiny infants in huge car seats, pink and blue balloons bobbing on strings, Alice feels light with relief. That will be the last she will see of Jade. She hopes.

Alice worked all through lunch on the Vermeer, and is now starving. She spots a coffee shop with a pleasing sage-green paint job and a neat line of paper-wrapped muffins in its window, and ducks inside.

She studies the items under the glass counter while she waits in the queue. At the end, she spots a tray of giant coconut macaroons. The coconut macaroons from the bakery in Haggerston that she loves, the ones Jamie walked for hours to find for her on the day Martha was born, that he'd brought her in the hospital.

That is what he said, isn't it? That's why he was gone, in the hours after Martha was born, for all that time. He was looking for the macaroons for her. She is sure that's what he said. Only, he must have got the macaroons here. Less than a minute's walk from the hospital doors.

Alice has reached the front of the queue. A young-looking girl with olive skin and curly hair throws her a cherubic smile.

'What can I get you?'

'Do you know how long you've had these macaroons?'

The girl raises her eyebrows, points at the macaroons. 'These? They're fresh today. We get them every morning from this bakery in Hackney. They're immense. You want one?'

'No.' Alice clears her throat. 'I meant, do you know how long you've been stocking them?'

'Oh.' The girl looks confused. 'I – sorry, I don't really know. I only started here a month ago.' She glances at the people behind Alice, waiting to be served. 'I can... try to find out?'

'Yes. Please. It's important.' Alice is not sure whether this is true really, but it feels important to her. It has become part of their mythology that Jamie walked the streets of London for two hours after Alice gave birth just to find her favourite coconut macaroons. Alice has told everyone this story. Everyone.

Now she rehearses the anecdote in her ears, though, she can hear it doesn't really make sense. Why would he have walked the streets aimlessly for two hours, looking in shops on the off chance that they might stock these specific macaroons? Surely if he knew he was looking for them, he'd have gone back to the bakery in Haggerston, where he knew he'd find them, and come back? He'd still have been gone less than two hours.

How long had Jamie *actually* been gone that day? It was all such a blur, that time in the post-natal ward. Alice had been in labour more than two days, had lost a lot of blood. She can believe she passed out, exhausted, for a couple of hours after the birth. Jamie must have been frazzled and exhausted, too. Of course it made more sense that he just popped out to this little bakery, found the macaroons, came back. But why would he have lied? What would have been the point?

Alice stands her ground, gripping the counter. The girl turns to a tall boy behind her in an apron, who is working the coffee machine, and says something into his ear.

The tall boy lumbers over. 'You wanted to know about the coconut macaroons? The ones from the Violet bakery?'

'Yes,' Alice says, ignoring the tutting she can hear behind her. 'Sorry if this is a weird question. I just wanted to know how long you'd been stocking these specific ones.' She swallows. 'Would you have had them five or six years ago?'

'I've been here eight years,' he says. 'And we've always done them. They come in fresh, every morning. They're gluten-free as well.' He pauses. 'Would you like one?'

Alice leaves the cafe, the handle of the paper bag digging into her skin, her coffee slopping burning liquid over her fingers through its ill-fitting lid. *It is just macaroons*, she tells herself. *It is just macaroons.* As she reaches the Tube station, taps her card at the barriers, Alice tries to make it funny, tries to make a joke of it with herself. First key rings, then dead birds, now baked goods. *You can't lose your shit over macaroons now, Alice. Get a grip.* So Jamie was exaggerating when he said he walked for hours. So what? Maybe he said it as a joke, and Alice, in her post-birth hormonal exhaustion, had taken him literally, banked it as some sort of epic demonstration of love at a time when she craved it most, and Jamie hadn't ever had the heart to correct her. She tries to push the sick feeling down inside, forget the words that Stella said to her.

If they lie about small things, it means there are bigger things, too.

On the Tube, Alice finds herself scrolling her phone. She clicks on her photographs, and is momentarily startled as Jade's face fills the screen. Of course – the pictures she just took, of Jade with her new baby. Alice should send a couple over to Jade, then delete them. Leave the girl and her nonsense behind, for good.

As her finger hovers over the send button though, Alice notices something which makes her stop. Instead of sending the photo, she sits up, enlarges it. Zooms right in on Jade's face.

There is no mistaking it. Jade's gold earrings, the ones she was wearing in the hospital. They are Alice's. The ones that belonged to her mother. And went missing from her house.

ALICE

On the dot of six, Alice leaves the office, slinging her bag over her shoulder. She jogs down the grubby steps to the Tube, slaps her phone on the Oyster card reader and heads for the pale blue signs of the Victoria line. She taps out a message, confirming she is on her way.

Jade replies with a thumbs up emoji, just before the signal cuts out.

When she'd suggested a visit earlier, Jade had replied immediately.

Yeh. you can come. I could do with some nappies and food, if you're passing the shops.

Alice had almost laughed at the cheek of it. She'd tapped out a message to Jamie next.

Work v busy here on the Vermeer! Mind if I stay a bit late?

The blue dots had sprung up almost instantly.

No problem. Martha's had a great day. She's drawn you a picture – it's on the kitchen island. Hope it's going well, superstar x

Alice hates lying to Jamie. But she is utterly furious about her Mum's earrings. She is determined to get them back from Jade, plus anything else that nutcase has stolen from her. And then, she is washing her hands of all this, and never going back.

When Alice arrives at the flat, she is taken aback by the sight of Jade. The girl looks haunted and exhausted, deep circles pinched under her eyes. Her hair is lank and unwashed.

The baby is slumped against Jade's shoulder, floppy as a doll, in a spotty sleepsuit too big for her, and rolled up at the sleeves. As Jade moves out of the way to let Alice pass, she flinches, as if in pain. The baby's head lolls to one side – Alice has to resist the urge to reach out and cup it. Jade doesn't seem to notice.

'All right?'

'I'm good, Jade. How are you?'

'Yeah, all right.' Jade is speaking quietly. 'Bit tired.'

Alice steps into the living room and has to supress a wince. Linda's previously neat and tidy flat now resembles a squat. Used muslins and unwashed baby clothes are slung over the backs of the sofa and chair. Plates smeared with ketchup and baked bean juice litter the floor, along with coffee-stained mugs, nappy sacks that have grown pungent and need putting in the bin. Alice is going to have a job on her hands finding the earrings.

'Is your mum here?' Alice asks.

'She's in bed.'

'Oh.' Alice lowers her voice. She glances down the hallway and sees that Linda's bedroom door is slightly ajar. Alice can hear the faint wheeze of her snoring, can just make out the dim glow of a bedside light, the heft of her body under the covers.

'How is she doing?'

Jade shrugs. 'The doctors say she's got blood cancer. She says she don't want the treatment, so they've let her come home. She's bloody stubborn.'

Alice nods. 'I'm sorry.'

'It is what it is.'

Alice sets her bag down on the sofa gingerly, pretending not to notice the mess. 'How are you and the baby getting on?'

'All right,' Jade says. 'Her name's Taylor.'

'Lovely,' Alice smiles. She happens to be a fan – of the singer and the name.

'Her dad don't like it,' Jade mutters.

Alice thought she had detected the faint whiff of Ryan – a pair of trainers by the front door, the sickly aroma of blueberry vape.

'Good that he's been round to see her, though.' Alice is barely listening. She needs an excuse to look around for the earrings. She hears the beep of the tumble drier. 'Shall I get the bits out of the dryer for you?'

Jade shrugs. 'Suit yourself.'

Alice heads to the kitchen, where she makes a cursory effort to empty the laundry into the plastic basket and fold it, balling up the tiny pairs of socks. As she does so, she looks around the kitchen, trying to work out where to start. Perhaps a sideboard drawer, so she can just say she was looking for a pen? Or wait until Jade goes to the bathroom, so she can search her bedside table? Alice glances back into the living room. Jade is sitting on the sofa, staring blankly into space. She looks like she might fall asleep.

'I'll make you a cup of tea, Jade.'

Alice flicks the kettle on, so the noise of it will drown out the sound of her searching the kitchen drawers. She goes through them, and the cupboards, one by one. But the kettle flicks off, the water boiled, and she has found nothing. She needs to try another room.

She makes two mugs of tea and carries them into the lounge.

'I folded the laundry for you,' Alice says. 'Shall I put it away in the baby's room?'

Jade looks up at Alice as if she has just woken up. She hesitates. 'No. I'll do it.'

'No worries.'

Alice decides to perch for a few moments, make conversation while she considers her next move. Jade has placed Taylor in a baby chair and is bouncing her with a socked toe while she sips the tea and stares at her phone.

'Have you had many visitors?' Alice says, as a cursory stab at conversation. She can't see much evidence of it. Despite the amount of time Jade spends on her phone – she must be communicating with *someone* in all that time, Alice assumes – she seems very isolated. When Martha was born, Alice had been inundated with friends and colleagues wanting to see the baby. Her surfaces had been covered with pink cards, her vases all taken up with flowers.

'Not really,' Jade mumbles, without looking up from the screen. 'I don't really like people's germs around her.'

Ironic, Alice thinks, glancing at the state of the flat. Alice tries to think how to steer the conversation into calmer waters.

'Isn't Ryan excited now, about being a dad?'

Jade gives her a strange look, then turns away. She cups her mug and drinks her tea in large gulps. Baby Taylor is asleep in the bouncer now, her head slumped to one side. Jade finishes the drink, sets her mug down and picks up her phone again.

Alice collects up the dirty plates and mugs from the floor as best she can, then picks a path over to the kitchen, and surveys the toppling tower of plates and cups, the streaked sideboards, the sticky floor, the knobs on the oven filmed with grease. It is much worse than it had been on previous visits. Alice wonders whether Handhold would class Jade as 'coping'. *Not your problem*, she reminds herself sternly. *Get the earrings and get out.*

Alice thinks about where to look next. She's searched almost everywhere in the kitchen now. She flicks the kettle on to disguise the noise again, then pulls a chair over to the worktop, stands on top of it to check the dirty tops of the cupboards, the space over the fridge.

'You looking for something?'

Jade is in the doorway, staring at Alice, down at the chair she is stood on, then up again.

'Just your cleaning products. Are they here somewhere?' Alice steps down from the chair, trying to keep her tone cheery.

'Why would they be up there?' Jade mutters. 'They're under the sink.'

'Of course they are.'

It is impossible to miss the hostility in Jade's voice. Alice crouches down, takes out a bottle of surface cleaner spray and a sponge, heart racing.

'If I didn't know better,' Jade says, her hands on her hips now, 'I'd think you were having a good old poke around.'

Alice turns around. 'What? Ha!' She forces a laugh, but immediately regrets it.

'Like I said,' Jade says. 'Only if I didn't know better.' She gives Alice another look, then walks back through to the front room.

Alice feels cold all over. The kettle flicks off, a cloud of steam gathering condensation on the window. *Calm down*, she tells herself. She is pushing things too far. Taking too many risks.

She makes another tea and carries it in to Jade.

'Thanks,' Jade says.

'No problem.'

'Thanks for coming, I mean,' Jade says haltingly, not meeting Alice's eye. She is bouncing Taylor with her foot again, a little too hard to Alice's eye for such a small baby.

'I'm glad you came,' Jade mutters without looking up. 'Even though I'm such a moody bitch.'

Alice laughs uncomfortably. 'You're not.'

'I am. I know I am. I just… I never know if I can trust people, you know?'

Alice feels the hairs stand up on the back of her neck.

'I sometimes get this feeling people must want something from me,' she says, looking levelly at Alice now. 'You know? Like they're not who they say they are. Do you know what I mean, Alice?'

Alice has an overwhelming urge to leave. Leave, and never come back.

'I need to use the bathroom.' Alice barely manages to force the words out. She stumbles from the living room, down the hallway into the bathroom, and locks the door behind her. She sits on the toilet, gasping for air.

She tells herself to calm down. This was a mistake, she thinks. She should forget the earrings, make her excuses, and leave.

Alice throws her head back. She tries to remember the breathing exercises from the yoga classes she barely ever makes it to. She looks up at the ceiling of Jade's tiny bathroom. There are wisps of cobweb in the corners, a grubby extractor fan, a water mark suggesting a leak from somewhere above, its edges a stomach-churning yellowish brown.

There is also something else. A panel set into the ceiling. Alice had one like this in the house she grew up in. It was a little storage space – her dad used to keep the Christmas decorations in there. And this panel is slightly ajar, like it's been recently opened.

Alice slips off her shoes, and carefully climbs onto the toilet lid, and reaches up. The ceiling is low, and she reaches the panel easily. She presses it, and nothing happens at first. She tries again, but it feels jammed. The third time, she hits it, hard, with a flattened palm. The panel gives way.

It's just a piece of plywood. Alice pushes it to one side and reaches up into the space inside. It feels dusty, cool, damp. She feels around three sides, finding nothing but dust. On the furthest edge, though, she brushes against something. A cardboard corner, smooth like a gift box.

Alice coaxes it out with her fingers, then pulls it down. A cloud of dust follows, and Alice coughs.

'Everything OK in there?'

Jade's voice is sharp, but Alice knows she has time. The door is locked.

'Fine,' she says. 'Thank you.'

Alice sits on the edge of the bath, sets the box on her lap. She opens it, her fingers shaking. She actually feels as if she might vomit.

The things that have gone missing from her house – they are here. Her silk camisole. Her lost sunglasses. The notebook where she has written things down about Martha since she was born. And other things, that she hadn't yet missed. A miniature bottle of perfume. An old tube of hand cream she thought she'd left in her old desk at Stanley's. And – this one makes Alice catch her breath – a picture of Jamie and Martha. Until a few days ago, Alice is sure this photo was stuck on the fridge in their kitchen.

Her heart pounding, Alice presses her hand underneath the photo, feeling for the gold earrings. But she can feel only a stack of papers. She pulls it out. There are pages and pages. A printout of Alice's professional profile from Stanley's studio, her face circled. Articles featuring Jamie, talking about poverty. And then copies of article after article about Ezra's death, with Alice's name underlined.

And then, at the very bottom. Something else, something that is giving off a smell of meat.

Alice lifts the papers, then pulls her hand away immediately. It is a clutch of bird feathers, their ends bloody and rotten.

Alice claps her hand over her mouth, suppresses the wave of nausea that is rising up her body and slams the lid shut.

Alice places the box back carefully, hardly knowing how she is doing it. Her hands are filthy and they are shaking now, so much she fears she won't be able to put the plywood back. There is a fine coating of dust on the floor of the bathroom. She tries to clean it with a wad of tissues, but there is too much; her fingers don't seem to work properly, and she is just spreading it around, making it worse. Instead, she sweeps it under a damp bathroom mat, then washes her trembling hands as best she can in the sink.

Alice tells herself to breathe. There is no pretending, now, that she has been in the bathroom for a normal amount of time. The most important thing that Alice can do now is get out of the flat, and never return. She might have been lying to Jade, but Jade has been lying to her too, this entire time. Jade knows exactly who Alice is. And she is planning to make Alice pay for what she did.

Alice listens at the bathroom door, but all seems quiet. Carefully, she opens the door. She looks down the hallway. Her backpack and coat are hanging by the front entrance. All she has to do is get them and get out.

She is there before Jade can get near her. She drops her coat, her hands clumsy, and snatches it up again. Her hand is on the lock when she hears Jade in the hallway.

'Hey,' she hears her call. 'Alice? Hey! Hey!'

But Alice is gone, into the night, running along the canal, in the darkness.

LINDA

It feels better being out of hospital, even if Jade isn't the most sympathetic nurse. I messaged her to say I was coming home, but she didn't even reply. I had to get the taxi man to carry my things, help me up the steps.

'What did you tell them?' Jade snapped at me, as soon as I'd staggered through the door, and the taxi man pulled off outside.

'What do you mean, what did I tell them?'

'You know what I mean.'

I sighed, steadied myself on the back of the armchair.

'Nothing,' I muttered. 'I told them I didn't remember how it happened.'

Jade nodded. 'Good,' she said.

'You didn't need to tell them I was an alcoholic.'

'Whatever,' Jade muttered.

'My house keys,' I told her. 'They're gone. I think they fell out of me bag, when I fell.'

Jade shrugged. 'I didn't see any on the floor.'

'I'll need some new ones cut.'

Jade shrugged again. I sighed.

'Oh, Jade. Just help me into bed, will you?'

The truth is, it all happened so fast that I *don't* really remember it now, not properly. I just remember her face on the steps outside, the way it changed when she saw what I was holding. The way she raised her hand. And then the feeling of falling, my head slamming into the concrete.

Once I was settled in bed, Jade came in with a cup of tea. *Guilty conscience*, I thought. But I held my tongue.

'Thanks.'

Jade sniffed, plucked up the clear bag of meds the doctors sent me home with and held it up to the light.

'What did they say would happen, the doctors?' Jade asked. 'If you kept refusing treatment?'

I didn't answer.

The baby started to whimper in the next room. The nursery, Jade calls it, like we live in a bloody palace. Only, it's not a nursery, is it? It's Ezra's room.

'Bring her in here, Jade, will you? I'll hold her while you wash your hair. You look a state.'

Jade rolled her eyes, but she did as I asked. Once Jade was gone, I held the baby close, shushed her till her watchful little eyes dropped, and she fell asleep. Her hair just like Ezra's was, when he was born. I let myself imagine that it was eighteen years ago, my little Ezra in my arms. Before I knew it, the tears were rolling down my cheeks.

Now, Jade's gone out with Taylor in the pram, so I've got a bit of peace to get on with the writing. It's harder, now. The pain is getting worse, like they warned me it would. But I haven't got too much longer, anyhow.

I shouldn't have got so angry with Jade, the day of the fall. I know it wasn't her fault, what happened to Ezra. I know that really. But the way she just moved all her things into the house, took over his room, like he'd never existed. It just got too much.

Maybe I should've been more supportive. The silly girl seemed to have been under the impression the council would hand her a flat of her own overnight just because she was up the duff. She didn't seem to realise there were waiting lists, full of a million daft idiots like her and Ryan.

'Well I'll live here then,' she'd said sniffily. 'You'll have to pay the bedroom tax otherwise, if you've got that room spare.'

I snapped, then. The room wasn't *spare*, I told her. It was Ezra's. And I told her she was to blame, for all of it.

Jade went mad.

I'm not a murderer, she screamed at me. *That's your department.*

Sometimes I wonder if it's my fault, the way Jade turned out. That's what everyone thinks, isn't it? It's always the mother to blame for everything. The truth is, John was always the one who could talk sense into her. When we lost him, I lost her too. I lost control of her.

I don't think Jade ever really got over watching her dad die. I wish she hadn't seen it. She was only fourteen, and it did something to her. She was never quite right, after that.

The school were sympathetic, for a while, after John died. When she first started getting in trouble, they turned a blind eye, at first. I tried grounding her, stopping her allowance, taking her phone off her, that sort of thing. But nothing worked. She started running away from home, coming back drunk, or worse. Boyfriends. God knows what.

Then, one day, Jade hit a teacher and broke his nose. The school weren't sympathetic any more. They had to think of the other pupils, they said. She'd had enough chances.

They made Jade go to a pupil referral unit on a reduced timetable, said she only had to do five GCSEs. Even that, she couldn't stick to. Then she ran away from home again. This time, I called the police. And of course, the social got involved.

They found her in some bedsit, drunk, or worse. There was a big meeting then, me and social services and the teachers and that, and Jade as well. And that's when Jade spoke up. She said she wasn't living with me any more, and if we made her, she'd run away for good.

People judge me for letting her go. But she was nearly sixteen by then. She'd be able to do what she wanted soon. It was pointless fighting. And I know how this sounds, but when they placed her in care, it was such a relief. With it being calmer at home, I could do my own grieving. And be there more for Ezra.

Of course, now that I had more time to focus on Ezra that's when I realised. Things weren't right with him. Things weren't right with him at all.

ALICE

Stella arrives at the Rosemary Branch pub twenty minutes late. Alice's tea has gone cold. Hers is one of the only occupied tables. There aren't many people around at this early hour. A couple of people with headphones and laptops cluster at the wall tables, making use of the plugs as if it's a coffee shop. At the bar, a single purple-faced day drinker sits on a stool, gammy hands clutching a copy of the racing post.

Stella is wearing a loose linen shirt and gold earrings, her hair pulled into a tortoiseshell clip.

'So sorry I'm late,' Stella breathes, sitting down opposite Alice.

'No worries. Drink?'

'Dry white wine. Thanks, hon.'

Buying the drinks feels like the least Alice can do. When she returns a few minutes later with an ice bucket, bottle and glasses, Stella is pulling a brown envelope from her bag.

'You managed to get off work, then. Nice one.'

'I said I'll stay late tomorrow. It's fine.'

Alice worries it's not fine. She is still on probation. And there is so much work to do on the Vermeer.

'Anything new to report?' Stella asks. 'Did you ever hear from Jade again?'

'Oh, no,' Alice lies. 'Nothing.'

Alice had so nearly gone to the police after she'd found the box at Jade's. It would have felt like a relief, to tell DCI Barnes everything. Even how she'd gone to Ezra's house that first time, and lied to Linda about who she really was. It might even have felt good, coming clean. He'd always been on her side, she'd felt. And then at least, maybe, he'd finally listen to her about the messages, the threats to her family. Maybe he'd be able to stop Jade.

But even as she went to dial the number, her fingers had stilled on the keys. What exactly would she be reporting? The theft of some earrings, of sentimental, but not much monetary, value – earrings she hadn't managed to even locate in Jade's house? She had the photo of her wearing them of course, but then Barnes would ask why she'd been with Jade in hospital, a question to which Alice had no good answer. And a few other items, none of them worth anything. What if Jade had thrown the items away, or just said they were hers – what then? Wasn't it likely that the police would have more questions for Alice than they would for Jade? They could still charge Alice for breaking her bail conditions. Alice couldn't risk going through all that again. She couldn't.

Now the box has confirmed her worst fears, she sees with awful clarity how stupid she was to ever go near Ezra's family. She wishes she had listened to Jamie.

Since finding the box, though, she has become desperate to see Stella. She needs Stella more than ever now. She needs to know everything she possibly can about Jade.

'Last night,' Stella says, fiddling with the stem of the wine glass, 'I was wondering. Other than Ezra, and his family – is there anyone else who might have had a grudge against you guys? From something in the past, maybe?'

Alice is taken aback by the question. 'I don't think so. Why?'

'Just worth thinking about all the angles,' she smiles. 'So – no unhappy exes, from previous entanglements? You or Jamie?'

Alice shakes her head. 'Nope.'

'What, really? No horrible exes?' She laughs. 'Lucky you.'

'I don't have many exes at all,' Alice shrugs. 'I spent most of my twenties dating a guy called Tag, but he's not horrible. We're not on bad terms. We're still friends on Facebook.' She laughs. 'Whatever that means.'

'OK. How about Jamie?'

Alice shakes her head. 'He's never really said much about past relationships. I got the feeling he was always, uh, married to his work, sort of thing.'

Stella nods, writes something down. 'Where was it that he worked before Handhold?' she asks, without looking up. 'It was abroad somewhere, right?'

'Tanzania.' Alice tells Stella about Jamie's previous role, with the anti-poverty charity. 'Obviously, it's a big charity. Jamie was the country manager in Tanzania, then its regional manager for East Africa.'

'Wow.'

'Yes. He loved Africa. He talked about it non-stop when we first got together – he'd only just moved back to London, when we met.'

Stella taps her pen on her pad. 'So he left his job there in which year?'

'It was in 2016. The year we met.'

'And you got married in...'

Alice clears her throat. 'That was the following year. In 2017.'

'Oh, wow.'

It was fast, everyone had said so – especially Aunt Sarah. But Alice had never had a doubt, and it felt good to have proven everyone wrong.

'Do you have any idea why he left his role in Africa and came back to London, just before you met?'

Alice glances at Stella, wondering what has prompted her to hone in on this detail.

'I think it was just the right time to leave,' Alice says carefully. But she can see straight away that Stella isn't buying it, and Alice has never been good at lying.

'There wasn't anything specific?' Stella leans in slightly.

Alice hadn't thought about all this for years – the details are sketchy in her mind. The girl. The volunteer. The one who had gone missing.

Stella takes a sip of her wine, then replaces the glass carefully on a coaster. Something tells Alice that she should steer clear of talking about all that to Stella. Not because she thinks for a moment that Jamie did anything wrong. But because she knows he found it hard to talk about. He might see Alice divulging it to Stella as a betrayal. And Alice doesn't really remember what Jamie had said about it now, not properly.

'I think he just wanted a fresh start,' she says eventually. 'He was over forty – I guess it was time to come home, start his real life, you know?'

'Sure.' Stella seems to be waiting for something more, though.

'Look, Stella,' Alice says. 'I really don't think it could be relevant to any of this stuff – to Jade and Ezra. Do you?'

'Do you think he has many photographs from that time?' Stella speaks over her, her voice slightly louder now. 'In Tanzania? Has he ever shown you any?'

Alice is a little taken aback. 'Um, maybe? I don't really know. Maybe in a drawer somewhere. I'd have to ask him.' She pauses. 'Why do you ask about this, Stella?'

'I just wondered if there was something from your past that was relevant,' Stella gives a little shrug. 'Seeing as we haven't found anything else to connect Ezra to you guys, you know?'

'I see.' Alice sighs. 'Sorry – this has been a waste of your time, Stella.'

'No, I'm sorry,' Stella says, shaking her head. 'I'm sorry I couldn't figure it out. What might have connected Ezra to you.' She pauses, takes a breath. 'Listen – I do have something to show you, though. I think you'll want to see it.'

Stella puts a hand in the brown envelope, pulls out an official-looking piece of paper and hands it to Alice. Alice stares at it.

'I spoke to my police contact,' Stella says. 'He couldn't find anything on Ezra. But I got him to check Jade out, like you asked me to.'

Alice stares at the sheet Stella has placed in front of her. There are four headings: Date, Offence, Force, Disposal. Under each, there are a few words, not much more. But enough to make out the basic picture. Enough to make Alice's stomach molten with dread.

Complaint of harassment.
Restraining order sought and granted.

Complaint of breach of restraining order.
Complaint of criminal damage to property, common assault.
Complaint of harassment, ongoing/ breach of restraining order.
Trespass.
Suspected assault.

'It's a bit of a record, isn't it?' Stella says. 'She's got away with most of this stuff so far, because of her age. But there's quite a lot.'

Alice puts down the sheet on the table, so that Stella won't see that her hands are shaking. She thinks about the key ring. The photograph. The dead gull.

'How did you get him to give you this?'

Stella shrugs. 'He owed me a favour.'

Alice swallows. Her throat feels almost too thick to speak.

'Who was the victim? Was it always the same person?'

'No idea,' Stella says. 'Sounds like one person, though, doesn't it? Sort of like a stalking and harassment campaign. I'd guess a boyfriend.' She gives a laugh. 'Ex-boyfriend, presumably.'

Alice runs her fingers across the dates, rests on the final one. The last record is incomplete.

'This is the only one that doesn't have a discharge date. What does that mean?'

'That one is ongoing, apparently. They couldn't tell me much about it.'

'It says assault.'

'Suspected assault,' Stella corrects. 'A domestic thing. They think Jade pushed someone down some stairs or something, apparently.'

Alice's mouth is dry. Linda.

Linda didn't fall down the steps. Jade pushed her. Her own mother. Alice wasn't being paranoid. Jade has done all this before. And now, she has Alice and her family in her sights.

Alice sees now, with nauseating clarity, that the trouble they are in is all of her own doing. It's like Jamie said all along – Ezra was just a troubled kid, and the break-in, and his death, was a terrible thing, but a random one. But what Alice has done now – that is different. She has ignored the advice of her husband, her lawyer, the police, and brought a dangerous stalker into their lives. A person with a history of violence, who has reason to hate Alice, to want her dead. If Jade is capable of putting her own mother in hospital, what is she capable of doing to the woman who killed her brother?

ALICE

Alice was right about the painting. Tests have revealed that the window section was altered after the artist's death. There is something underneath.

Alice has been working around the clock with her scalpel and microscope. She won't be able to say officially for some weeks, but she has seen enough to make up her own mind. There is a man's face behind the glass, Alice is almost sure of it. The girl in the picture was not looking, bored, towards a window. She is looking up because someone is there. A face that has been covered up for three hundred years.

If Alice is right, then this painting was never a scene of quiet domesticity and ordinariness. It is something much darker, much more loaded. Sinister, even. If Alice gets this right, it could prove to be one of the most important restorations for years.

Alice loses herself in tiny pixels of colour, setting about solving the problems one by one – removing dirt with a saliva-soaked cotton bud, filling areas of paint loss with tiny feather-strokes of pigment. When she is in her painting, so close to it, like this, she can stop thinking about Jade, where she might be, what she might be planning.

Since talking to Stella, Alice is thankful for Jamie's new security obsession. At least it means Martha will be safe at home. She has even started to wonder whether Jamie might be right about them moving out of London. The thought of taking Martha somewhere far away from Jade is suddenly incredibly appealing.

During the lockdown, a number of families they knew had – with no warning – moved themselves and their families out of London. Including their next-door neighbours, who had just renovated the whole place. Alice couldn't believe it when she'd seen the For Sale board. Apparently, they'd just decided they fancied a different life, in the end. Alice had never seen them again, and no one on the street seemed to know where they'd gone.

Maybe they could just do that. Jade would have no way of knowing where they'd gone. And maybe what had happened would feel smaller, further away, too. Maybe Martha would be better off overall, learning to make bird boxes and makeshift fishing rods. A charming village primary school among rolling hills. Alice could commute. Jamie could do something from home. On weekends, they could build dens in the woods, eat roast lunches in cosy pubs with chalkboard menus and crackling fires.

Alice's fantasy dissolves as she realises she has got pins and needles from sitting in the same position for a long time, her neck bent over the painting. She feels cramped and a little shivery. She stands up, plucks out her headphones, picks up her temporary pass. The restoration studio has emptied out of people. No one said goodbye to her, which is typical. There is very little conversation here. At Stanley's, they had taken turns to do lunch runs, listened to Radio 4 together, shouted at the politicians on *World at One*.

Alice makes a cup of instant coffee in the small, weirdly clean kitchen. She is still shivering, even though it's only just October and not really that cold – Rollo keeps it cool in here for the paintings.

She obviously won't risk a cup of coffee near the Vermeer, but finishing the section she has started today is going to take the rest of the evening, and Alice hasn't been sleeping well. She needs something to wake her up a bit.

Alice hears a noise from the studio downstairs, like someone is moving big canvases around.

Alice sets her coffee down a suitable distance from the painting, and decides to go down, on the pretence of needing some chemicals, and see who is there. She had thought everyone had gone home, but it would be no bad thing if it was Rollo, and he saw that she was pulling a late finish. Or maybe it's one of the other restorers working late. Alice wouldn't mind some company. The studio is too quiet.

She makes her way to the downstairs studio. It is different in here; the smell of varnish and chemicals stronger, the walls painted a bright white. She looks around for the person who was making the noise. She was sure it sounded like a large canvas being moved. But nothing looks out of place. Alice glances at the stack of canvases, lined up in the storage area by the door. Hundreds of millions of pounds' worth of paintings, just lying on their sides.

As Alice turns back to the stairs, she hears the creak of footsteps in the studio above. The noise is not loud, but it is unmistakable – the floors are poorly insulated, and it's not unusual to hear snatches of discussions between one floor and another. Alice tracks the tread of the footprints from the far side of the studio to directly over her head. Whoever it is must be roughly where Alice sits at her easel. Then there is another noise, like something being dropped, or scattered.

For the first time, she feels a little tremor of unease. Could someone from the downstairs studio have made their way up there just now without her crossing paths with them? They'd have to have been pretty determined to stay hidden.

She climbs back up the stairs, pulling the heavy door to behind her. The doors are reinforced, secured by codes regularly changed and closely guarded by the staff. Alice has been instructed to memorise the codes, and never write them down, but she has secretly stored them in her phone, just in case. It is all a far cry from Stanley's studio, where the code was his birthday, hadn't changed in a decade, and where the security door was mostly propped open by an old bit of cork in any case.

When Alice gets to the upstairs landing, she finds the lights are off in the studio. That's it, then – there will be some friendly caretaker Alice hasn't met yet, who has come to switch everything off, thinking everyone has gone. But when Alice flicks the light switch, nothing happens. She flicks it again, and again, but the studio stays in darkness. The fuse must have gone.

'Is someone here?' Alice calls out. No sound, no answer.

Far downstairs at the bottom of the building, she hears a door slam.

Alice gasps, startling at the noise. She makes her way through the studio, feeling a path from table to table in darkness. She looks out of the window and down at the street below, tries to see who has just left the building. But she cannot see anyone walking away from the office. Just a few tourists, an old man locking up the library opposite, a street sweeper outside the sandwich shop.

When she reaches her own painting station, she can barely see a thing. She fumbles on the table for her phone. When she has found it, she flicks on the torch with a trembling hand.

It takes a while for her to process what she is looking at. It takes a few beats for the full enormity of it to dawn on her, for the slow trickle of terror to enter her bloodstream and for her hands to start to shake. At first, she cannot accept that what she is seeing is real. And then, for a moment, it is as if she cannot see, or at least process, what is actually in front of her eyes, through the white heat of terror in her mind.

It is an image that might have been cut directly from her worst anxiety dream. Streaks of hot black coffee, cutting through the paint. The peasant girl's beautiful, illuminated face melting down the canvas. A nightmare made flesh.

Alice tries to quiet the panic, to breathe. To think of the remedies, the solutions. There will be – there must be – there always are, with paintings. But no. There is no solution to this.

The Vermeer, her Vermeer, has been destroyed.

ALICE

Alice directs Martha to a table at the back of Farm to Fork, the cafe round the corner from Martha's school. She mumbles her order quickly, eyes on the floor, to avoid conversation with Sam, the owner. She likes Sam. She is just simply not up to the task of interacting with him – with anyone. She just wants someone to bring her a hot cup of tea, and something Martha can eat for dinner. Even feeding her daughter feels beyond her lately.

Alice can't help feeling Jamie has missed the enormity of what has happened to her. 'At least they suspended you on full pay,' he'd said, as if the pay was the main thing. He'd also commented, more than once, that her being suspended would temporarily solve their childcare problems for free. Never mind the fact that Alice's career was effectively in tatters. That a priceless artwork lay in ruins. And everyone thought it was her fault.

'We'll pull the CCTV,' Rollo had said, rubbing the back of his head, as Alice had emerged from a bruising meeting with several people from the Cunliffe Institute's HR team plus their humourless lawyer, Julian, who had steel-rimmed glasses and the demeanour of a prison officer.

'No doubt things will be much clearer after that. Until then, though – well, I'm sure you'll understand. It's a question of our relationship, with the Dutch. We have to be seen to be taking action.'

'But surely security *must* remember someone else coming in?'

Rollo had made a face. 'Seems the desk was unattended. But according to the computer system, the only security pass used that night was yours.'

'You mean my temporary pass?'

'No, your usual security pass.'

'But I lost that security pass. I didn't have it…'

Alice had trailed off, hearing exactly how she sounded.

Jade, she thought. It must have been. How and when had she got hold of Alice's security pass?

Rollo had stood up, reached over for an awkward arm-squeeze.

'It might do you good, Alice, to have a bit more time at home,' he'd said. 'After everything over the summer, I know you didn't want to delay your start date further, but perhaps…'

Rollo had trailed off, staring down at his dreadful tan suede Chelsea boots. And Alice had seen with a sinking clarity how he must regret ever hiring this basket case of a woman, this magnet for drama. How they would now be preparing the strongest possible grounds for getting rid of her. How many restoration experts would pass their probation after overseeing the destruction of a Vermeer?

'I swear, Rollo,' she'd said again. 'I didn't *do* this. There was someone else there that night. There must have been.'

Even as she said it, though, she could hear in her own ears how ridiculous, how hysterical she sounded. What was more likely? That an intruder had somehow stolen her personal security pass and used it to get into the restoration wing of a highly secured, internationally regarded art institute at night, when she was the only one there, and – on encountering a valuable painting – decided to sabotage it then leave undetected?

Or was it more likely that a relatively new employee, who had – earlier that week – had to be reminded about the rules about hot drinks around paintings, decided that she could take the risk and have a cup of coffee with no one else in the studio. And then, had tripped and spilled it, with disastrous consequences?

Her only hope was that some CCTV – or something – would prove that Jade did this, that Jade was out to get her – and prompt the police to take action. Her feelings about Jade – once complicated by guilt over Ezra – have now been reduced to simple terror. Jade had been in Alice's house, in her studio, had followed her on her family holiday. She had photographs of Alice's husband and child. What next? Jamie's office? Martha's school? Alice grips the edge of the table until the skin around her nails turns white.

Sam comes over with a tub of coloured pencils.

'For the artist,' he says. Martha smiles shyly. Alice thanks him. It is sweet of him to remember that Martha likes to draw. Was Martha drawing something last time they were here? She can't remember. Maybe it was when Martha was with Becca.

Alice watches her daughter colouring, her impossibly smooth, perfect face in its familiar portrait of concentration, her hair dishevelled, the collar of her school polo shirt all askew. Alice reaches out to correct it, and Martha flinches.

'Mum,' she complains, pulling away from her.

'How was school, love?'

'Fine.' Martha is speaking through gritted teeth, not wanting to be disturbed, lost in her picture. Alice smiles despite herself. There is so much of her in her daughter.

Yas enters the cafe, with Iris and Archie in tow. Alice waves. To her relief, Yas looks genuinely pleased to see her.

'Hey, Alice! How are you? I'll just order, I'm starving – are you OK for food?'

Alice is about to answer when her phone rings. It is an unknown number, which means it is probably Barnes calling her back.

'Yas, can you watch Martha for a sec? I need to take this.'

Alice steps outside, even though she has no coat on. The air is cold.

'I know you must be so busy,' Alice gabbles. 'It's just – I wondered whether you're getting anywhere, with working out where these threats have been coming from.'

'Oh. That.' Barnes clears his throat. 'Yeah – so social media, it comes under malicious communications – it's looked after by another team. Is there something more since we spoke?'

'Not... not an online threat.'

Alice swallows. She can hear in Barnes's voice that he has a finite amount of time and patience for this, that she needs to make sure she doesn't waste it.

'Something's happened to me at my work.'

Alice explains briefly. Barnes listens, notes down the case number.

'OK. Your boss says they're providing CCTV?'

'That's what he said.'

'All right. Well, if it's a criminal matter, I'm sure they'll get to the bottom of it.'

Alice bites her lip. She can't risk mentioning Jade. Alice is the one who has broken the law by initiating contact.

'The thing is – even before what happened with the painting, I've been getting this sense that maybe I'm being followed,' she says carefully. 'Also, things have been going missing from my house.'

'Valuables, you mean?'

'No, just random things. A notebook, an – item of clothing.' Alice is embarrassed to say camisole to Barnes, in case she has to explain what that is. 'A pair of sunglasses.'

'I see,' Barnes doesn't say anything more. Alice can hear the scepticism in his voice.

'There was also a dead bird,' Alice blurts. 'That was left outside our holiday let, when we were in Rye.'

There is a pause.

'A bird?'

'A seagull. A dead seagull.'

'I see,' Barnes says. 'But not at your home address?'

'No...'

'Did you see someone leave it there deliberately?'

'No. I heard, it was like a slamming noise, or a bang. I was asleep – it woke me up. And then I found the gull.'

There is a pause. Alice finds herself cringing at how deranged she must sound.

'I know it probably sounds like it just flew into the house,' she says. 'But it was all – it had been dead a while. Someone left it there.'

'And did you report this to the force down there? At the time?'

Alice pauses.

'No. Jamie thought it was nothing,' Alice says quietly. 'You probably do too.'

'I'm not saying that.' Barnes's voice is not unkind, but Alice can feel she is testing his credulity. 'It's just that this could be any number of things. I mean, it's a holiday home, yes? The locals hate them, especially on the Kent coast. I know because my brother lives down there. We avoid the subject with him to be honest.'

Alice attempts a laugh.

'What I'm saying is, even if it was deliberate – it might not have been personal.'

'I suppose.'

'Look. Last time I spoke to your husband, he sounded like he was putting in a number of security measures at your home. All sounded very sensible to me. So I think you should be reassured by that, all right? But look, I will look into what's happening with these online messages. I apologise that we've not been quicker on that. It's just, you know. A lot on everyone's plates.'

'I know, I can imagine. I'm sorry.'

'Like I said, I'll chase it. You've got my number, if there's something specific.'

Alice hears the slight admonishment in his final word, and cringes for a second time.

'Got it. Of course. Thanks.'

'We'll be in touch.'

Barnes hangs up. Alice puts her phone in her back pocket, a sense of dread coiling in her stomach. Barnes can't help her, she realises, because she can't tell him the whole truth – about Jade. About what she has done, and the danger Alice has put herself in. Alice has told too many lies. Even the police can't help her now.

Yas is sitting with Iris and Archie, plus Martha, in a booth. She has distributed stickers, paper and pens, reminders about sharing. Within a minute or two, all three have tired of the colouring, and run off to the children's play area.

'That was easy,' Yas smiles. 'This place is great.'

'I hope it survives,' Alice agrees. 'It's always so quiet.'

Yas dunks a biscotti into her cappuccino. 'I give it six months, on this road. Sweet as they are. How's the new job? You bunking off early already?'

'Not exactly.'

Yas sees her face. 'Oh, no. What?'

Alice tells the story of what happened.

'Jesus,' Yas exclaims when she has finished. 'And – do they believe you, that you didn't do it?'

'I don't know,' Alice admits. 'But they felt they had to suspend me, pending the investigation.'

'What investigation, though? Can't they just look at the CCTV?'

'You'd have thought,' Alice says glumly. 'But the police are involved, so it's all going through them. At first, I was sure that it would all be on CCTV. But then I remembered the lights went off, just before it happened. So I don't know. I don't know how much they'll see.'

Yas puffs out her cheeks and exhales loudly.

'Wow. I'm so sorry. It's the last thing you needed, what with the other drama this summer.'

Actually, Alice thinks, *there is a pretty clear line from that drama to this one.*

'Did you guys at least manage to get a bit of a break?' Yas asks. 'On holiday?'

'Sort of,' Alice says. It had been a strange holiday. She thinks of Jamie's sudden obsession with moving. The dead gull.

Yas sighs, reading her face.

'You're still struggling then,' Yas says. 'With the break-in. Moving on.'

Alice looks up at her friend's face, sees the stiffness in it. She knows that it would be pointless going over it again.

'A bit,' Alice admits, with a shrug. 'But it's fine. Stella has been doing some digging for me, actually. Which has helped clarify things a bit.'

'Stella?' Yas's face tightens even further, a neat line forming between her dark brows.

'Yeah?'

'What sort of digging?'

'Into Ezra. Into who he was, what he might have wanted.'

Yas fiddles with a paper napkin, folding it in on itself, then again. Alice wonders why Yas is so uncomfortable whenever she talks about this.

'Why is Stella doing this for you?' Yas asks, after a pause.

'Well, she's a journalist,' Alice says. 'She has access to stuff.'

Yas stares. 'Like what?'

Alice realises she doesn't really know what the answer to this is. 'Electoral records, financial stuff, I don't know exactly.' Should she have asked a few more questions?

'And she offered to do this for you, did she? It was her idea?'

'Well, sort of.'

Yas sniffs. Alice looks at her. 'What?'

Yas unfolds the paper napkin, then presses it to her lips as she swallows.

'It's just,' she says slowly. 'How well do you really know Stella?'

Alice is caught off guard by the question. 'I guess – OK, not super well. But she seems nice. And she is a proper journalist. She works for the *Sunday Times*.'

Alice had found Stella's byline in the magazine pages most weeks, usually a long piece on a knotty subject. Each article was accompanied by a black and white head-and-shoulders picture of Stella beside her name at the top, her arms folded, her expression serious, like she had something big to impart.

'I just think maybe you should be careful there,' Yas says.

'Careful? Why?'

Yas is twisting the napkin into a long, thin tube now. She makes a face. 'Just something Rosa said a while back. I didn't think much of it at the time.'

'Rosa, your nanny?'

'She said she was at the park with Iris a while ago and Stella came over to her, insisted on buying her a coffee.' She pauses. 'She said that Stella seemed to have a lot of questions.'

'What kind of questions?'

Yas pauses. 'Mainly questions about you.'

Alice feels unsteady. 'Me?'

'And your family.'

'Like what?'

'Just lots of questions about you. Where you lived. Stuff about Martha, and Jamie. She seemed interested in your jobs. Where you worked. How you'd met. How we all knew Jamie.'

Alice frowns.

'I mean, look – you know Rosa,' Yas says. 'She likes everyone. But I got the feeling she'd found the interaction... awkward. She made a point of telling me. I wondered if maybe she was being oversensitive. But Rosa – well, she doesn't often mention things like that, you know?'

Alice shifts in her chair uneasily. Could Rosa have got it wrong? She thinks back to her drink with Stella in the pub recently, how she'd been taken aback by some of Stella's questions. About their ex-partners. Photographs of Jamie in Africa. But then again, that was her job, wasn't it? To ask questions. It was what Alice had asked her to do.

'I think Rosa must have been reading too much into it,' Alice says. 'Stella is chatty. It's probably a journalist thing.'

Yas has abandoned the napkin now, its edges frayed and twisted. She busies herself with a sugar sachet which Alice knows she has no need for.

'There was another thing,' Yas says hesitantly. She makes a face like the conversation is almost giving her pain. 'Rosa told me that Stella asked about other things, to do with Jamie's past. About why he left his job in Africa. Rosa said Stella had asked this in quite a pointed way.'

Alice shifts in her chair, unable to meet Yas's gaze. Yas obviously knows, then, that something happened out in Tanzania before Jamie left. Why would Yas know? From Arlo? She wonders how much Jamie talked to Arlo about it. How much Arlo told Yas.

Alice thinks back to the last time she saw Stella, about the way that Stella had pressed her on whether there was something 'specific' that had prompted Jamie's leaving his old job in Africa. Almost as if she already knew what the real answer was.

ALICE

Alice is sitting in the local library, with her thermos of tea, at the desk with the plug socket by the radiator. She has been coming here most days since she was suspended, pretending her life still has purpose and routine. Alice fears for herself without the rigging of work, feels sure that without it she will start to unravel and collapse.

She clicks open a browser window, and googles her husband's name combined with 'Africa'.

Yas's story about Stella – and the questions she'd been asking about Jamie – has made Alice uneasy. She has started to wonder for the first time whether there is something Stella isn't telling her. Something about her husband that even Alice doesn't know.

Alice tries 'Jamie Rathbone Tanzania'. She tries combining the name of the charity with Jamie's name, then with Tanzania, then with Arusha, the town where she knows he was mostly based.

There is loads of stuff about Jamie's current role at Handhold. Article after article with Jamie posed next to politicians, in children's centres, drug treatment programmes and mental health clinics all over the UK. But there is nothing on Africa.

Alice tries hard to remember what Jamie actually told her about what happened out in Tanzania. He'd told her the story on one of their earliest dates – the place on Store Street, with the natural wines and the tiny sharing plates – a chill in the air outside, Jamie lending her his palms to warm hers between. She doesn't remember the details all that well, but she does remember how sorrowful Jamie had seemed as he recounted the story over the bottle of strange-tasting wine – even though it had been absolutely obvious to Alice that none of it could have been his fault.

Essentially, as far as Alice remembers, one of the charity's volunteers had gone missing – a young woman. Jamie hadn't known her well, or for very long, but had been told by her friends that she had been troubled, in some way – Alice struggles to recall the details. Her body was never recovered, but it was widely assumed she'd committed suicide. And Jamie, who was responsible, he said, for all the volunteers, for their well-being, had felt he had to resign.

'I wanted a fresh start either way,' she remembers him saying, with a sad smile. 'It was a difficult time.' Alice remembers thinking how kind and decent a person Jamie was, to have felt so deeply over something so entirely outside of his control. And what a sad and unfortunate end it was for his time in Africa, given how much he'd loved it there, how much he'd obviously cared about the work his charity had been doing.

Alice tries to think whether she knows where Jamie might have photographs of his time in Africa, where he would keep things like that. Does he even have anything like that, photos, mementos from his life before her? Alice doesn't think he does. For the first time, she wonders whether that is odd. Jamie was into his forties when they met. So much of his life lived without her. Why did he have so little to show for it?

Jamie had talked a lot about Tanzania, about climbing Kilimanjaro, living with the Maasai in Longido, but she can't remember seeing photos for a long time. If he still has photos, Alice hasn't seen them around anywhere. He'd shown her a few pictures, she thinks, in the early days – of him at the top of Mount Kilimanjaro, him surrounded by his team of young volunteers. One of him digging a water well for a remote orphanage. Him with a whole host of smiling Tanzanian children, waving pink-palmed at the camera, school bags worn proudly across their bodies. Her mental image of Jamie in Africa is basically that of a Comic Relief advert from the 1990s, with Jamie as the white-saviour celebrity lead. Had he painted it that way, or was that just her mind filling in the gaps?

Alice has almost given up on the Internet search when finally, on the third or fourth page, something new appears – an article from a local newspaper, back in 2015, now buried deep in the algorithm.

TRIBUTES TO WINCHESTER GIRL MISSING IN AFRICA

Alice clicks on the article. It is about the volunteer, the girl. Clara Layward, her name was. The article doesn't make it clear what happened. It says she 'went missing' following 'a New Year's Eve camping trip with friends in the Arusha National Park'. But although it says 'missing', it is written as if Clara is clearly dead.

The bulk of the article is about a candlelit vigil held on the anniversary of her disappearance. It recounts a string of tributes from friends, teachers, people at the charity. She was described as 'an amazing person' who would 'do anything for anyone'. She had achieved top grades at a Winchester girls' school but deferred her university place because she wanted to travel in Africa and 'help people,' a friend added. 'She was really passionate about poverty, social justice and development.'

Alice scrolls down, looking for Jamie's name.

Jamie Rathbone, the charity's country manager, sent a message which was read at the vigil by a representative from the charity. He said Clara was an 'incredibly hardworking volunteer' whose 'passion was an inspiration to everyone at the charity'. He said the thoughts and prayers of all her colleagues were with her family.

Alice has the uncomfortable realisation that she had only ever processed the idea of this girl's disappearance – and probable death – through the lens of her own early infatuation with Jamie. As a terrible thing that had happened to *him*. A sad misfortune that had burdened Jamie – because he was so decent and honourable – with a misplaced guilt that led to him leaving a job he loved. But that – happy ending! – had also provided the twist of fate which allowed him and Alice to meet and fall in love.

How little mental space she has ever devoted to this poor girl's life, and to her death. She had never even bothered to ask Clara's name. Instead, she had glossed over this chapter of Jamie's past, because it had felt convenient to do so.

The newspaper has a photograph of Clara at the top of Mount Kilimanjaro. Alice guesses this must be something lots of the volunteers do – she remembers Jamie going on about how amazing it had been. In the photo, Clara is grinning widely, a smattering of pale freckles across her nose and cheeks, one hand pulling at the edge of her yellow beanie hat, her long hair loose underneath.

She doesn't look very depressed. Not here. But Alice squashes the thought. You can't tell these things from one photograph, of course. She knows this.

Alice scrolls down further to another photograph of Clara, standing in front of a Christmas tree with her mother. Her mother, her family – another thing she'd never thought about. Alice looks at the photo of Clara's mother. She tries to imagine waving off a teenaged Martha at Heathrow airport with a backpack on her shoulders. Having her return in a coffin.

Alice looks at the girl's face, and the mother's face, the clear similarities between them – the curve of their smiles, the rise in the apples of their cheeks. For a second, she is sure there is something familiar about their faces, but when she looks at the picture again, she dismisses it. She has never known a Clara, or a Layward. The mother's name – Carol Layward – rings no bells.

Alice scrolls still further, hoping for another picture that might trigger something. Some clue as to why Clara and her mother look so familiar. But there is only one more image. Not a particularly good one – which is probably why it's been left until last. Another photo of Clara on the Kilimanjaro climb, this time in a group, all their arms interlinked. It looks like they're at a sort of base camp in the foothills, about to start; the scenery is green and they are lightly dressed, laden with gear.

And Jamie is there, in the picture. The photo is a little unfocused, but there is no mistaking it. He is right there, next to her, their arms laced around each other. And Jamie's hand is curled around Clara's waist. She can see his fingers touching the small slice of bare skin at her waist, where her fleece and T-shirt have ridden up.

ALICE

Later that evening, Jamie is making a curry. Rice bubbles on the stove. He is chopping onions and peppers, a tea towel over one shoulder. Martha is standing next to him, on a stool.

'That's right, Squidge. We just want the leaves. You can pick them off for me, like this.'

Jamie shows Martha how to pull the leaves off the coriander and put them in a little bowl. She starts to do so, dropping bits of stalk on the floor.

'Great job Martha,' Alice says weakly. She heads to the fridge, pours herself a wine, then sits at the kitchen table, where Jamie has spread out a load more security brochures.

'What's all this?'

'Just some more stuff I've had installed. There's a camera at the back now, as well as the front.' Jamie looks around at her. 'I'm away for that conference in Scotland this week, remember? I wanted to get them in before I go away.'

Alice make a face. 'That's this week?' Jamie had vaguely mentioned a conference he needed to go on, but she hadn't paid proper attention.

'It was a lot cheaper than I thought to get a full security system,' Jamie goes on, turning back to the stove. 'Lights, cameras, the lot. They did me a really good deal.' He starts talking about monthly fees, different levels of cover, and Alice can't bring herself to feign interest.

Martha soon tires of the coriander task, wanders off to her room. Alice takes her place, leaning against the worktop. Jamie ignites the stove under a frying pan of sesame oil and adds the onions and peppers. A column of steam swirls underneath the spotlights.

'Can I ask you about something?' Alice asks.

'Sure.'

Alice takes a breath. 'You know that girl in Africa who went missing?'

Alice thinks she sees Jamie's hands still over the pans, then he continues stirring, without looking up.

'Clara,' he says.

'I don't think you ever actually told me her name.'

Jamie looks up now, sensing an accusation. 'What makes you ask about her?'

'Nothing. It's just that someone was asking me about your work, and...'

'Who asked you about that, though?'

Alice is taken aback by his tone. 'A mum at school,' she says.

'Who?'

'Does it matter?'

Jamie tips the paste into the pan with the onions and peppers. It hisses and spits. He turns the heat down.

'It just got me thinking,' Alice persists. 'I never really asked you about her. Were you friends?'

'Not really,' he says, without looking up. 'I was based in Arusha and she was up in a village called Ngaramtoni, where we were installing a well at one point. I only saw her occasionally, when she came into town.'

'But you climbed Kili together?'

He pauses for a second, then carries on stirring.

'As part of a big group,' he says.

'Were you on the camping trip, too? At New Year? Where she went missing?'

Jamie turns towards her. Then he sighs, turns all the hobs down, so he can focus on her. He folds his arms.

'What are you asking me here, Alice?'

'I was just wondering how close you were.'

'We weren't close.'

'So nothing ever… happened, between you two?'

Jamie's face contorts. 'What? No! She was much younger than me, for one thing…'

'I'm younger than you,' Alice says quietly.

'OK, fine – but no, Alice. There was nothing romantic there. We did Kilimanjaro as part of a group – it's what everyone did – it was cheaper. Clara wasn't a friend. She was just a posh, gap-year girl from the home counties doing a short stint of volunteering. Even for her age, she was young, you know? Naive. Far too young to be doing what she was doing, really. That was the problem – the gap-year kids were uniformly hopeless – they just couldn't hack it. After what happened with her, they stopped placing anyone under twenty-one in Tanzania. It was too much for them.'

Alice bites her lip.

'You sent this lovely tribute about her,' she says. 'You said she was an inspiration to everyone.'

Jamie sighs. 'That was for the family, Alice,' he mutters. 'I had to say something. They expected it. I got her friends to help me write something nice. Is that so terrible?' He rubs his eye. 'Do we have to talk about this?'

'Why don't you want to?'

His shoulders sag. 'Because it was a million years ago, and it was sad, and difficult, and because I'm tired. OK, Alice? I'm very, very tired.'

He does look tired. Pallid, almost grey in the face. She has sensed lately that Jamie has not been getting much sleep. When she wakes in the night – she often has nightmares, since the break-in – she often gets the feeling he is awake, too.

'OK,' Alice says. 'I'm sorry.' She slips her arms around Jamie. 'Only, is everything OK with you?'

'I'm OK.' Jamie encloses her in a big hug, hooking his chin over the top of her head. 'Just a bit fed up.'

'With work?'

'Mm-hmm.'

'That's no good.' Alice nuzzles into his arms. 'Anything I can do?'

'No. It's all right. I just need to sleep on a few things.' Jamie gives her a squeeze, a kiss on her hair, then pulls back. 'Let's eat, shall we?'

'Sure.' Alice looks up at his face. 'Everything will look better in the morning.'

It's something Aunt Sarah used to say to her. She is not sure why she is saying it now. She knows it is not always true.

Jamie doesn't speak much over dinner. He mumbles something about being tired and pads off to bed early.

As she loads the dishwasher, Alice hears footsteps outside. There are always footsteps on the pavement, but this is different. They sound closer. She looks up sharply towards the basement window which looks out over Stonebridge Gardens, and she is sure she sees a flicker of movement, at the edge of the window.

Alice's pulse climbs.

'Jamie?' she shouts.

He is downstairs immediately, in his socks, jogging bottoms and T-shirt. She meets him on the ground floor landing. He looks on high alert.

'I thought I heard someone outside,' she breathes.

'Stay here.'

Jamie throws the front door open. There is nothing there. Alice watches the rise and fall of Jamie's shoulders. He is panting, as if he's been running. She feels guilty for frightening him. Frightening them both.

'Sorry,' Alice mumbles.

It must have been a dog walker, or a couple, stumbling back from the pub. And yet her mind went straight to Jade, to an image of her pushing her own frail mother down the stone steps on the estate.

Jamie looks at her, concerned. 'You want me to stay here with you until you come up?' Her pulse slows a little, her adrenaline curling into unease. She used to feel so safe here in this house. But she doesn't now, she realises. Not any more.

Alice shakes her head. 'No. It's OK.' He is going away on this conference soon, Alice reminds herself uneasily. She will have to get used to being here by herself.

Jamie goes to bed and Alice goes back downstairs, makes herself a herbal tea to settle her nerves. While the kettle boils, she wanders around the kitchen, looking at the pictures on their walls. She passes them so often that she has stopped really seeing them.

They used to have photos of all the places they'd travelled, but they'd now mostly been crowded out by pictures of Martha: Martha in her first outfit on the baby blanket with the pompoms. Martha on a trike in the gardens opposite their house, aged two. Martha on the dunes at Camber Sands, fat legs poking from her little puffy shorts, a wide grin on her face, an azure sky behind. Becca had taken most of the best ones of Martha. She is a far better photographer than Alice.

The only one from before Martha is a black and white picture from their wedding day, of Jamie and Alice dancing at their reception in the Narrowboat Pub, string lights and bunting over their heads. Alice is wearing the white silk sheath wedding dress she'd chosen in the snooty shop in Islington with Yas and Aunt Sarah. She was just a few weeks pregnant, not yet showing. In the photo, the dress looks as smooth and reflective as water. Alice's head is thrown back as they dance, her cheeks creased with laughter, Jamie's face buried in the dip of her collarbone.

Alice chose this picture to frame mainly because of how unusually lovely and happy she looks – she has never considered whether it's a good picture of Jamie. It isn't. His expression is, presumably, one of happiness, but you can't really see it from the line of his face. He could be smiling, but he could equally be grimacing. Most of his face is buried in shadow. In this picture, her husband could be anyone.

ALICE

Alice closes the basement door behind her and secures Jamie's new heavy lock. Becca's last day was the week before. Alice has dropped Martha at school and has no plans for the six hours until she needs to pick her up again.

How many times in the past has she longed for a day off, for some space, some peace like this? But now the silence feels deafening, the experience of being alone in her house unsettling. She feels listless, directionless. She can't stop thinking about that girl, Clara. And how weird Jamie is being. How on edge he'd been last night, when she thought she'd heard something outside.

Alice goes through the post, checks her emails, to see if there is anything new from Rollo, or anyone from the Cunliffe Institute's HR department, with which Alice is now on embarrassingly familiar terms. There is nothing.

She decides to tidy the house. It will make her feel better to tackle the disorder that has crept into their lives since the break-in.

She starts with the piles of jackets, coats and endless tote bags that have gathered on the hooks by the basement door. Things Becca used to deal with. She goes through them one by one. She discovers PE kit that needs washing, wet swimming things. A letter about a class trip Alice has heard nothing about. A ham sandwich that has started to bloom with green mould, enclosed in a curl of tinfoil. A pungent, blackened banana.

Alice is missing Becca almost as much as Martha is. On Becca's last day, Martha had sobbed into her pillow, making them late for school. Alice had tried to be upbeat about it, taking Martha to choose a cake from Farm to Fork, so they could do a little party for Becca at home. Martha had sulkily chosen a pear and raspberry tart that she muttered was Becca's favourite – correctly, as it turned out, and Alice had been surprised and touched that Martha had remembered such a thing. Martha had made Becca a card, using some of her most prized unicorn stickers and filling a whole side of paper with plus plus plus kisses, and Alice had given her a gift card and a framed photograph of her and Martha together in Stonebridge Gardens, eating an ice cream. Becca had gone pink and tearful, throwing her arms around Martha, and then Alice, squeezing so tightly Alice had been briefly winded.

Alice works through the house room by room, feeling better as the bin bag starts to fill, her taps begin to shine, the floors and surfaces clear. In Jamie's study, she throws open the curtains, tidies the cushions on the bright patterned sofa, opens a window to let in some air. The last time she was in here, Jamie's papers were everywhere, but today it's unusually tidy. All that's left on the top of Jamie's desk are an espresso cup, a photograph of the three of them in a mosaic frame Martha made at her art club and a small, neat stack of paper.

Alice picks up the papers to wipe underneath. They appear to be copies of Becca's employment contract, and her handbook of employment. Alice hasn't seen these in years. She wonders why Jamie had printed these out now, when Becca was leaving.

Alice decides to put the papers away. But when she pulls at one of the desk drawers, she finds it is jammed. No – locked. She pulls at another, then the third. They are all locked. She is sure she doesn't remember these drawers having locks. She certainly doesn't have a key.

Alice shivers. The room is cold now, with the window open. She pulls her cardigan tighter around herself, sits down at the computer and tries to log in. But the password has been changed. It probably just expired, she tells herself. But for some reason, her mind goes to the photograph of her husband with Clara Layward. His hand on her waist.

She sends Jamie a text, asking him what he has changed the password to, but she can see her message is unread. Jamie rarely looks at his phone during the day. Alice suppresses a wave of irritation by slamming the window sash shut harder than she needs to.

She decides to tackle the guest bedroom next. Jamie and Alice have never had many visitors, so over the years it has morphed into Becca's room, where she stays over sometimes if she is working late, or babysitting, rather than trekking all the way home to Archway, where her shared flat is. Becca had started hanging a few things in the wardrobe, leaving a sponge bag with a toothbrush and modest, supermarket-brand toiletries in the en suite.

But now Alice opens the door and sees that Becca has stripped the linen from the bed, vacuumed the floor, cleaned the en suite. She has left her things in a neat holdall by the window as she said she would – she's coming to pick it up next weekend. Seeing the holdall and the empty room makes the loss of Becca real, and Alice feels a twist of sadness.

On the back of the door, Alice spots a cardigan of Becca's that she must have missed. She takes it, folds it carefully and unzips Becca's holdall to place it inside. As she does, she feels something rustling at the bottom of the holdall. She slips her hand inside, and finds the thing that is crackling. A folded piece of paper.

Alice hesitates, then unfolds it. It is a full-page colour printout of an image she has seen before. It is an advert for Jamie's charity – a campaign that Jamie had led on, and featured in. *A handhold, not a handout*, was the slogan – Jamie was the one who thought of that. Alice had thought it was clever. In the picture, Jamie is seen with some young volunteers at a youth centre funded by Handhold. Laughing together, one of them holding a basketball.

Alice can't figure out why a copy of this old advert would be inside Becca's holdall.

As she refolds it, there is something stuck to the back of the paper. It is a small piece of card. She turns it over. It's a business card.

Alice runs her finger over the embossed words. The number and email underneath.

Stella Glass. Journalist, Sunday Times.

BECCA
Three weeks after the break-in

'It's a no,' Becca is saying. 'I'm not doing it again. I don't know how many times I can say no.'

Becca works a strand of hair in her fingers. The ends are split. Becca feels more and more like the edges of her are fraying.

She thought she'd made it clear she didn't want to be involved any more. But she didn't seem to want to take no for an answer. She was so intense with it. Like it was her who'd been wronged, that a bad thing had happened to, and not Becca. And honestly, what business was it of hers, or of anyone else's? Becca had tried to listen to her, to do what she'd said was the right thing once already. And look where it had got them both.

'I understand your hesitation,' the voice was saying on the other end of the phone. 'But what you need to understand is that this isn't just about you any more. And whether you like it or not, Becca, you're already involved. You know that, really.'

Becca hears a creak above her. Alice is moving around, possibly heading for the kitchen. Becca needs to end this, get this person off her back. She walks over to the window facing the basement, the furthest point from the stairs.

'No. I said no.'

Becca winds a strand of hair around her finger again.

'I know neither of us intended it to go the way it did, but we are where we are, Becca. And now, there only way we can end this is to finish what we started.'

Becca feels herself start to sweat.

'Look, I can't even – I cannot talk now.' She starts pulling at a cuticle. She has done this ever since she was a teenager, whenever she gets stressed, or nervous. She has been doing it more and more lately. Her hair, her nails, the cuffs of her jumpers. Pulling at parts of herself, until they come undone.

'Why not?'

'Because I'm there now! I'm supposed to be working!'

'You mean Alice is there with you?'

'Yes,' Becca answers, lowering her voice a little. 'Of course she's here. She's in the house right now. She's upstairs.'

Becca hears movement on the stairs. She can't bear to glance behind her, but she can just feel that Alice is coming, like an animal sensing a familiar danger.

'I've got to go. This is over, do you understand? Don't call me again.'

Becca hangs up, pressing at her phone screen with a sticky thumb. She takes a deep breath, puts her phone in her pocket, then wipes her palms on her thighs, leaving a smudge of sweat on the material. Behind her, she hears Alice clear her throat.

'Hey, Becs,' Alice says. 'Everything OK?'

ALICE

When she gets back from school pick-up with Martha, Jamie is home already.

'Hi,' he calls from upstairs. 'I'm just packing for my trip.'

'OK,' Alice calls back. She feels a twist of anxiety. About Jamie going away, leaving her alone in the house. She thinks again about the poster in Becca's bag. The weird locks he's fitted in the desk. The picture of him with Clara. The girl who went missing, and was never found.

Once Martha is in bed, Alice waits for Jamie in the kitchen. When he pads down the stairs, Alice is struck by how unwell he is looking. His eyes are puffy, too. Has he been crying?

'Are you OK? You don't look good.'

'I'll miss Marth, when I go away,' he mutters heavily. 'That's all. I'll miss you both.'

His voice sounds so sad. Alice finds herself really looking at her husband, in a way she hasn't in a while. The shadows under his eyes, the uneven pattern of stubble that is creeping across his chin. It's unlike him to have gone into work so scruffy.

'We don't have secrets, Jamie,' Alice asks eventually. 'Do we?'

'Of course not,' Jamie says, his eyes wide. 'Why would you...'

'I know I haven't been the easiest, since the break-in,' Alice interrupts, holding her hand up to him, asking him to let her finish properly. 'But, Jamie, if something bad was happening in our life, you would tell me. Right?'

Jamie pulls a chair out carefully, with both hands, then sits down slowly at the table opposite Alice without taking his eyes off her.

'I would never keep secrets from you,' he says slowly. 'You know that.'

'Do I?'

Jamie's eyes widen.

'What is that supposed to mean?'

'You've changed the password on our home computer without asking me. Why did you do that?'

Jamie blinks.

'What?' He laughs. 'Is that what you're worried about? The password expired, that was all. I wrote it down somewhere – I'll give it to you. I'm sorry, I just thought you always used your laptop these days. Is that the only thing...'

'No,' Alice snaps. 'It's not.' Although she can feel herself flailing already, the conviction leaking from her voice. 'What about Becca's contract? Why was that out on your desk?'

'Becca's contract?' Jamie frowns. 'She asked me to print it out – I think she wanted to show it to someone she's interviewing with, so they could draw up something similar.'

Alice pauses. This does make sense.

'OK.' Alice bites her lip. 'But why are there suddenly locks everywhere, Jamie?'

'What do you mean "everywhere"?'

'On all the drawers in your desk.'

'I'm just being more careful about security,' he says, a note of exasperation in his voice now. 'I *told* you all this the other day – I could tell you weren't listening. The keys for the drawers are on my key ring. You can have them any time. It's just my work stuff.'

Alice bites her lip again. 'So it's not anything to do with... with that girl who went missing? In Africa? You're not...' Alice takes a breath. 'You're not... hiding something about that from me, are you?'

Jamie stares at her, perplexed. 'What? No! I told you – that was years ago.' He shakes his head in disbelief. 'The locks – I just thought it was sensible to fit them. After the break-in, you needed me at home. So, I had a lot more work documents hanging round here. And you know, Martha goes in the study sometimes, Becca's always wandering in to charge her phone – I just thought I should be a bit more careful about confidential documents – you know, vulnerable users, GDPR – all that stuff. So I fitted the locks to store away documents relating to my work.'

He pauses.

'That's all I do in there, by the way. Work. It's all I ever do!'

'OK, OK,' Alice mutters. She has not finished yet. She takes out the picture she found in Becca's holdall.

'I was clearing out the guest room and I found this in Becca's holdall.' She turns the paper around, pushes it across the table towards him. 'I thought it was weird. Any idea why she'd have it?'

Jamie looks at the picture, then snatches it up, starts waving it in the air, agitated.

'You see?' he cries. 'This is what I mean. I don't want her, or anyone else digging around my work papers. She has no *right* to have this in her room!'

Alice is taken aback.

'Well, to be fair, it's nothing confidential, is it? It's just that advert they made you be in a couple of years back…'

'That's not the point. This is *precisely* why I put the locks on.' Jamie stands up, paces over to the fridge, the paper still in his hand. 'You know,' he says, yanking the fridge open, 'In many ways, I'm glad she's gone.' He snatches out a beer, cracks the ring pull with unnecessary force, still holding the paper in his other hand.

'Who, Becca?'

'Yes, Becca. She is very young, very immature, actually. I haven't been impressed with her for a while now.'

Alice has never heard Jamie talk in this weird, managerial way about Becca. She has been part of their family, she feels like reminding him. Not just some employee.

'No, I think we're better off. Much better off. Just the three of us.' It is like Jamie is talking to himself now, rather than Alice.

She has noticed Jamie repeat this mantra a lot lately. Is it really true, though? Most people she knows have siblings, family who babysit and help out. Old friends who come and stay for the weekend. Is it really a good thing that she and Jamie have so few other people in their life? Apart from Aunt Sarah, with whom her relationship is strained at best, who else would Alice have to call on, if something went wrong?

Jamie is standing at the worktop now, pouring his beer. She cannot see his face.

'You know,' he says, 'I have been thinking, Alice. Now you've got this time off work. Maybe you should see someone. About how you're feeling.'

Alice feels her muscles stiffen.

'That's not what this is,' she protests.

'Oh, OK. Right.' He lets out a little snort of laughter.

'It's not!' Alice feels a flare of anger. Jamie takes a sip, then puts the mug on the worktop, and turns around to face her, wiping his mouth with the back of his hand.

'Sweetheart,' he says softly. 'It is. You never used to be like this.'

'Like what?'

'Well, I'm sorry, if this sounds... but you used to be *rational*, Alice.' Jamie struggles to keep the exasperation from his voice. 'Now it's like you're seeing conspiracies everywhere. I mean, why would you assume something terrible is happening, just because I've fit a lock on my drawer, or changed a password? Why would you dig up all this stuff, that happened years ago, at my old job? Jesus, Alice. We've been married for six years! Don't you trust me?'

'Of course I trust you. Don't be so dramatic, Jamie! And I'm sorry, but it just seems weird to me, all these locks in the study, you changing the password...'

'Alice, if anyone's acting weirdly, it's not me, it's you,' Jamie snaps. 'Going to see Ezra's family, lying about who you are – is that normal behaviour?' Jamie drops his head into his hands, rubs his eye sockets with the heels of his hands. 'I really would like it if you would go and see someone.'

'For the millionth time, I don't need to,' Alice says, gritting her teeth.

'I think you do,' Jamie sighs. 'Otherwise, it sometimes feels like this... like it's never going to be over for you.'

'What won't?'

Jamie's eyes are wide with disbelief.

'Are you serious? The break-in! You're *obsessed* with it, Alice. Obsessed with the idea that there is some big crazy backstory that will mean it wasn't your fault. That will somehow make it less, that you killed him.'

Alice hears her own sharp intake of breath. She feels winded. Her lips are parted, but she has no response for Jamie.

'But you know what, Alice?' he persists, his finger pointing, an undercurrent of fury simmering in his voice. 'At some point, you just have to face it. There is no one else out there to blame, Alice. *You* killed Ezra.'

Jamie pushes the chair he had been sitting in back under the table. The scrape of it feels loud in the silence of the kitchen. He takes the advert and crushes the paper into a ball between his hands, then hurls it into the recycling with a force that makes Alice flinch. Then he heads upstairs to bed without another word.

ALICE

'Where is Daddy?'

Martha has a mouth full of cereal, her expression more curious than concerned.

'Daddy has to be at a work conference this week,' Alice tells her. 'Remember?'

Martha looks up at Alice. 'What's a confidence?'

'Conference. It's where people meet up and talk about things to do with work, share good ideas and things.'

'Like how to help people when they are poorly or don't have enough money, like Daddy does?'

'Exactly that.' Alice leans over and dabs at the milk around Martha's mouth. Martha grimaces.

'Your daddy is such a good man.' Alice is not sure why she added this last part. Martha seems unsure too. She looks, curiously, at her mother in that way that children do when the world is not making sense.

Alice hates the feeling of having fallen out with Jamie. When she played back what Jamie had said about the locks on his desk drawers, the computer password and Becca's contract, she'd had to admit it all sounded logical. She was the one who sounded unreasonable, even paranoid. Maybe Jamie was right, and she wasn't seeing things straight. Maybe she did need to talk to someone.

After drop-off, she returns to her kitchen. She puts her keys on the hook by the door, makes herself a coffee, loads the dishwasher – avoiding, as she always does, the spot where Ezra fell, where the blood spread from his head. When there is a noise outside, she jumps, grips the worktop, before realising it is just a police siren. Hardly unusual for Hackney. Alice scolds herself for being so on edge.

She decides to send Jamie a message.

Hope you have a safe flight. Call me tonight. Love you.

She hopes it is conciliatory enough. As she sends it, she sees that she has a missed call and a voicemail from Barnes. She calls him straight back.

'Ah, Alice,' he says. 'Let me just close the door.'

Alice listens to the muffled sound of a door closing.

'It's about those comments you asked me to look into.'

Alice feels her stomach lurch.

'I'm going to send some officers round to your house today,' Barnes says. 'Within the hour, OK? I'm going to need to have a look at your computer.'

'Our computer? Why?'

Barnes hesitates.

'The IP address would suggest the threatening posts were sent from your home computer.'

'Our home computer?' Alice wonders if she has heard him right. 'You mean they were sent from our house?'

'So the data would suggest.'

'But that makes no sense.'

Barnes says nothing. There is an awkward silence.

'The guys will be over as soon as they can,' he says not unkindly. 'Don't worry. They're tech officers – basically nice IT guys. They'll be able to get to the bottom of this.'

Alice swallows. 'OK,' she says. 'Thanks.'

Alice switches on the desktop computer in Jamie's office and waits for it to load for what seems like an infuriatingly long time. She sits down to type the password, then remembers she still doesn't know it.

'Fuck.' Alice tries to call Jamie for the third, maybe the fourth time. His calls are still going to voicemail; he must be on the plane still, or in transit somewhere, with no signal. She sends a WhatsApp, asking about the password. The message delivers, but the ticks don't turn blue. He hasn't read it.

She watches the screen for a while, but the colour doesn't change.

The officers arrive half an hour or so later to take the computer. They are in plain clothes, seem more like technicians. One of them pulls on a pair of blue polythene gloves, as if her home office is some sort of crime scene.

'I'm really sorry,' she says. 'But I don't know the password.'

The younger one stares at her. 'Of your home computer?'

'It's Jamie's really. My husband.'

'Can you ask him?'

'I only just realised it had been changed,' she garbles. 'I've been trying to call him, but I think he's on a flight…'

She trails off. The technician has already turned away from her, sat down in Jamie's chair and is sticking a USB into the computer.

'No worries. I've got some software I can run.' Moments later, the home screen vanishes, and the man is in the computer. It makes Alice feel uneasy.

'If you don't mind,' she says. 'Can I just – before you take it away. Can I make a copy of the photographs of my daughter?' All the photos Alice has of Martha are stored on this computer. All the pictures of her as a baby.

The man pauses, glances at his senior.

'I don't care about anything else on there,' she adds. 'I won't delete anything. I just want to copy the picture folders onto a USB.' She looks from the man to his senior, then back again. 'You can watch me do it,' she adds. 'Or – do it for me?'

'OK,' the computer guy nods. 'I'll do it. Show me which folders, and I'll make a copy for you, if you've got a USB.'

'Thanks,' Alice says.

The man returns to the screen. Alice takes a USB from her work bag, then stands behind him.

'If you just open up all the picture files, you'll see – it's just pictures of my daughter.' The man clicks on 'Pictures' and Alice sees with a twist of affection that Jamie has categorised them carefully; first by each year of Martha's life, then into further subcategories: 'Rye 2019'. 'Christmas 2020'. 'Starting school'.

'Do you want this one, as well?'

The officer points to a folder labelled 'BC', which sits separate to the others.

'I'm not sure,' she says. 'Can you open it?'

'Sure.'

He clicks, and images fill the screen.

Alice's body somehow reacts before her brain, her breaths tripping over each other, her face turning away, even before she knows really why she is recoiling, why all the air has gone from her lungs. She blinks once, then again, as if it is her vision that needs fixing. But the pictures are still there. Pictures that do not belong inside the safe four walls of her home, the house where her daughter sleeps. Pictures that cannot be really here, on the computer Martha uses for her homework projects. Pictures of a sort Alice would never send or receive, and that she cannot believe her husband, her Jamie, would ever solicit, or look at.

'Are you OK?'

Alice is too ashamed to look at the officers' faces, to register their reactions. Are they horrified? Embarrassed? Amused? Smirking? She doesn't know, and cannot face finding out. She crouches down in a corner of the room. They ask her if she needs anything, and she just shakes her head. So in the end, they just get on with it. Packing up the computer, the keyboard, into boxes. When they are finished, they show themselves out. They leave the USB stick with the photos of Martha on the desk.

Somehow, later that day, Alice manages to go through the motions of picking Martha up, asking how school was, what she had for lunch. She makes the easiest possible dinner and lets a delighted Martha eat it in front of the TV, while she swallows three paracetamol with a large glass of Sauvignon Blanc. She manages to perform as normal all through Martha's bath, the teeth brushing, the reading of bedtime stories, even though the pictures are flickering at the edges of her consciousness. There is nothing Alice can do about the police seeing the pictures. She knows they will look through that folder, like they will look everywhere. Will the material even concern them? After all, it's not illegal, is it? To have an affair. These are not the kind of misdeeds the police concern themselves with. They are the messes which belong to the women left behind to sort them out.

Once Martha is in bed, Alice knows she should tidy up the toys, wipe down the kitchen, make something to eat. But she finds she cannot. Instead, she finds herself in Jamie's study, and before she knows it, she is throwing his stupid desk with its locked drawers on its side, smashing the lamp, kicking over a side table. And then she is on the sofa, and she is sobbing. Because she feels like an idiot, and because she doesn't feel any better. If anything, she feels worse. Nothing can stop the same sick-making details that keep rising up unbidden in her mind. The bra strap over the shoulder, the clay-coloured nipple pinched between finger and thumb. The hand reaching under the strap of underwear. The wet, open mouth, glossy lips parted.

The eyes she knows almost as well as a sister's. Because Becca really is almost like a little sister to Alice.

Or at least, she was. Now, Alice does not know what Becca is.

ALICE

Alice has never been to Becca's shared flat before – what occasion would she have to go to her nanny's home? Alice has never even really thought about what it might be like.

Now, as she paces the unfamiliar roads around Archway, her head feels thick and heavy, and she curses herself for being so stupid with the Sauvignon Blanc last night. Once Martha was in bed, Alice had sat in the kitchen with the bottle of wine and called Jamie's phone, for what must be the hundredth time. It had rung, then pinged through to voicemail once, then again.

'Fucking call me,' is all she could muster, before slamming her phone back down onto the kitchen table. Jamie hadn't called back, even though she'd waited and waited, refilling her glass until the bottle had gone.

Now Alice has a splitting headache. She needs water, and paracetamol. And she needs her head to be clear. But most of all, she needs to find Becca.

Her pace quickening, Alice climbs the steep road up past the station. She passes under the high Victorian bridge, the streets flooded with puddles from the rain overnight, a thin drizzle, like mist. Every time one of the red buses roars past, a tide of grey water washes the pavement, threatening to soak her.

Alice's phone directs her to the house; a mid-terrace broken up into flats. None of the scratched buzzers are labelled, so she starts with the bottom one and works up. On the third, she hears a crackle, then Becca's voice.

'Hello?'

The familiarity of it floors her. She is here to ask about something she still cannot really believe that Becca has done.

'It's Alice.'

'Oh.'

'Can I come in?'

'Oh. Yeah. OK. Sure.'

Alice presses against the buzzing door, wipes her shoes on the grubby mat and makes her way up the skinny, dimly lit corridor. Becca answers the door.

'Come in. We can sit in here.' Becca is avoiding her gaze. She motions through to a cosy living space. There are two small mismatched sofas with a jumble of colourful cushions, side tables with lamps and little piles of books. Behind the TV is a wilted cheese plant, an alcove of painted shelves stacked with scented candles and curling paperbacks.

'Do you want a cup of tea?' Becca seems to want to look anywhere but at Alice.

'No thanks.'

Becca finally seems to register the fury in Alice's voice. She comes to sit down opposite her.

'Is everything OK?'

As soon as she says it there will be no going back to the way things were between her and Becca, Alice knows. But that was all an illusion, she reminds herself. It must have been.

'I found the pictures,' Alice says simply. 'On our computer.'

The colour drains from Becca's face.

'Oh, no,' she mutters. She stands up, turns away from Alice, buries her head in her hands. 'No, no, no.'

Alice is briefly floored again, then feels her hackles rising. What, no apology? No explanation? Why is Becca acting like something terrible has happened to *her*?

'How long has this been going on?'

'What?' Becca croaks.

'You sleeping with my husband!'

Alice's words are jagged, her voice harder and clearer than she believed she was capable of. Becca's mouth drops open.

'Alice, I...'

'Tell me!' Alice slams a palm down on the side table; the energy passes through her like a jolt. Becca flinches, recoils.

'Alice,' she says quietly. 'I can't talk to you about any of this.' Her eyes are darting left and right, as if looking for an escape route.

'What? Why not?'

Becca looks away, her face pained. 'Because I signed something. An agreement.'

'What agreement? What do you mean?'

Becca turns away, walks towards the kitchen. Alice can see that her hand is trembling as she takes a glass from the draining board and starts filling it up at the sink.

'Are you talking about some sort of gagging agreement?'

Becca sniffs. 'I don't know if I'm even allowed to say,' she blurts miserably. 'We're not – we're not supposed to be talking to each other. Me and you.'

Alice stares at her. None of this is making sense.

'What are you talking about?'

'I had no choice,' she says quietly. 'I had to agree to it.'

Alice grits her teeth. She can hear the rain on the roof, gathering force.

'Are you saying that Jamie made you sign a gagging agreement?'

Becca is silent. Anger flares in Alice's chest. She is sick of being kept in the dark.

'Show it to me, then,' she snaps. 'This agreement, or whatever it is. Let me see it.'

Becca's shoulders drop. She turns to Alice, her eyes filled with tears.

'I can't show it to you,' she says. 'And I can't talk about it. I can't talk to you at all. Please, Alice. You... you need to leave.'

ALICE

On the way home, Alice finds just putting one foot in front of the other takes intense effort. The dirty beige tiles of the underground station are slippery, criss-crossed with muddy footprints. She is jostled by commuters, tutted at when she fails to make the ticket barriers work, winded when they slam shut on her ribs.

On the escalator, she grips the handrail tightly, tries to think what to do, what all of this means. She'd been so focused on Jade that her first thought had been that maybe she had somehow sent the threats from Alice's home computer. But those pictures of Becca – Alice could hardly blame Jade for that. And now Becca was claiming she'd been made to sign some sort of gagging agreement, preventing her from even talking to Alice about whatever had been going on.

Alice thinks back to the pictures. The documents on Jamie's desk, his locked drawers. Could her husband really have had an affair with the nanny, then forced her to sign an agreement to keep it a secret? Alice just can't imagine Jamie even thinking of something like that. Wouldn't a lawyer need to be involved? Did lawyers even do that sort of thing? And could Jamie really have organised all that without telling Alice?

As Alice watches the stations of the Northern Line pass, an alternative scenario occurs to her. What if it was Becca behind the threats? What if she'd been using their computer for that – as well as sending, or storing, private pictures? Wasn't it so often the case with Internet trolls, that they turned out to be apparently mousy, unremarkable, inarticulate people like Becca?

People who lacked much of a social life of their own, who lacked the courage to properly express their feelings of bitterness, or inadequacy? There is a part of Alice that feels guilty for thinking these things about Becca. But then she thinks again of the pictures, and reminds herself that there is another side to her nanny. There must be.

Alice just can't believe that Jamie would have an affair with Becca. Jamie has always seemed indifferent to her, at best. And Becca – well, Becca is so kind, so sweet, so utterly unassuming.

But of course, Alice wanted to believe that, didn't she? Everyone wants to believe that their husband would never be unfaithful. That their personal judgement isn't so spectacularly defective to have both married a man willing to sleep with a nanny, and hired a nanny willing to sleep with their husband. And now, Jamie has disappeared. And isn't answering his phone.

As she walks home from the Tube station, Alice checks the time. It's nearly midday. In less than three hours, she will need to leave for school pick-up. She needs more time.

Alice calls Yas at work. She picks up straight away.

'Alice? Is everything OK?'

'Yes, I'm fine,' Alice lies. 'I'm just having a bit of a day of it, and Jamie's had to go away to a conference.' She pauses. 'I wondered if Martha could go home with your two? I can let the school know.'

'Of course. I'll tell Rosa. But, Alice, you sound... are you sure you're...'

'Thanks, Yas.'

Alice stabs at her phone to end the call, and picks up the pace.

When she gets home, Alice fills a water glass, drinks it in one, then refills it. She presses two paracetamol from the packet in the cupboard and swallows them.

She desperately needs to talk to Jamie. Why hasn't he returned her calls or texts? She dials his number again, but again it rings out, goes to voicemail. She leaves another message.

This time she hears something, like a shudder, coming from somewhere in the house. A short, muffled buzz. Like a message coming through on a mobile phone. It sounds like it is coming from upstairs.

She hangs up, redials, holding the phone away from her ear. She hears it again.

In the living room, the noise is louder. It is coming from the sofa. Alice pulls the cushions away, the small ones and then the larger ones on the bottom, throwing them into a pile on the carpet. And then she sees it. Jamie's phone. She takes it in her hand, hot with frustration and rage.

He has left his phone here.

When the fury subsides, Alice sits down, thinks. If he doesn't have his phone, he can't know she has been trying to contact him. He'll have no idea that she is in such a panic. His phone must have slipped from his pocket. Without it, Jamie will be frantic – surely his digital plane tickets would have been on his phone. How had he been able to board, or pass security? *I can email him*, Alice thinks. *I will send him an email.* Maybe he has his work laptop, and is checking his work emails, hoping Alice has thought of that.

Despite everything, she is flooded with the relief of this one single breakthrough.

Alice opens her laptop. No email from Jamie – maybe he doesn't have his laptop. She writes a short email to Martha's class teacher letting her know that Martha will go home with Yas's children. Then she writes an email to her husband.

Hi Jamie. Your phone is here, as you probably know. I really need to talk to you urgently. Call me.

Even though it feels like a bizarre thing to do to her husband, she types her mobile number out, in case he doesn't have it memorised. She sends the email and immediately feels better, more in control.

A reply pings into her inbox. But it is not from Jamie. It is an automatic error message.

This email address does not exist.

Alice pulls up her sent folder. She must have mistyped his address. But she checks it once, then again, and she can't find any mistake.

This is Jamie's work email, the email address she has used for him countless times.

Alice stares into the white neutrality of the screen.

She decides to check the charity's website, to see if his email is listed there. Perhaps it has changed.

She pulls up the website for Handhold, clicks on 'Who we are', then another tab, which reads 'Senior leadership'. Then she clicks on the department Jamie heads, 'Fundraising and Campaigns'.

Another error message.

This link is broken.

Alice slams the laptop down in frustration. What next? Should she go to his office? Ask them what's going on?

Alice's phone rings in her bag. She leaps at it, in case it's Jamie. For a split second, she thinks that that's what it says.

But then she blinks, and reads it properly. It is Jade.

Alice lets it ring out, but Jade rings again. And again.

Eventually, Alice picks up.

She can hear nothing.

'Are you there?'

Nothing. The call cuts out. But moments later, she sees that a message is being typed.

Can't talk. Only text. Can you come over?

Alice lets out something between a laugh and a shriek.

You must be joking.

Jade is typing.

I am sorry.

I should have told you I knew who you was.

I swear, if you just come now, I'll tell you the truth.

> *I'll tell you all about Ezra, who he was, everything you want to know.*

Alice feels cold. Jade has worked out what Alice wants. And she is using it to lure her in – to do what?
Alice types.

> *Stay away from me, Jade.*
>
> *I know you came to my work.*
>
> *I know you've been threatening me.*
>
> *Just tell me what it will take for you to leave me alone.*

Jade is typing.

> *I'm sorry I did all that. Please come tonight. I swear I'll tell you the truth about everything and I will leave you alone after that.*
>
> *I know I should of told you before.*

Alice replies furiously.

> *Just tell me now!*

Jade is typing.

> *No, you need to come.*
>
> *I need to show you some things. Or you won't believe me.*
>
> *Please. If you don't come now, I'm afraid it will be too late.*

Alice throws the phone down on the floor in frustration. There is no way she is going anywhere near Jade. She needs to find her husband.

ALICE

Alice leaves the Tube station nearest Jamie's office. She walks across the square garden with its old wrought-iron bandstand, full of office workers with their sandwiches having a late lunch, and then up past the rows of Georgian terraces. When she reaches the building with its shiny glass windows, she finds herself avoiding her own reflection.

The last time she had come here, she'd been meeting Jamie at the charity's anniversary drinks. She'd had her hair blow-dried and worn heels and a new jumpsuit, which Isobel, Jamie's colleague, had complimented her on.

Now, Alice can only guess at how unkempt she looks: her overstretched leggings, the trainers she really should replace, her chewed nails, the bags under her eyes, hair frizzing in the rain. Her head is spinning from how much has happened in the past twenty-four hours, since Jamie left for his conference. The police getting in touch about the threats, coming for their computer. The pictures of Becca. Her claim she'd been silenced. And now Jade wanting to talk. Alice badly needs to speak to Jamie, to hear him tell her she's got it all wrong, that there's an explanation she has somehow missed.

The revolving doors stop as Alice steps inside. She can't remember pushing the glass, but she has obviously done something wrong; she is trapped, and the dreadlocked security guard has to come and let her out. Alice is flustered, apologetic. At the reception desk, the woman looks vaguely surprised to be bothered. It's the sort of time when most people will be going home.

'Hi, there. I am here because I need to get in touch with Jamie Rathbone. I'm his wife. Can you just confirm the name of the hotel he is staying at for me, please?'

The receptionist blinks at her. She is wearing a strange little scarf tied on one side of her neck, like an air hostess.

'He went away to a conference yesterday morning,' Alice explains. 'The charity will be aware – but he has left his phone at home, and now there seems to be some problem with his work email.'

'I see,' the receptionist says, in a tone that implies the opposite. Her eyes dart to one side, as if searching for someone who can tell her what to do with this odd woman.

'Is the company email working OK?' Alice persists. 'I wondered if, maybe there was an IT problem or…'

'Not that I'm aware of.'

'Right. Well, could someone get me the contact details for where he is staying, please? His hotel or the conference centre… Wherever.'

'You don't know the name of where he is staying?'

'No,' Alice says curtly. *I'm not that sort of wife*, is what she would like to say to his woman. *I don't ask him where he is staying when he goes away with work. I don't need to. I trust him.*

The receptionist hesitates, then seems to decide that sending an email would be all right. 'Just one second.'

She types something, then something else. The corners of her lipsticked mouth turn down, like a face in a child's drawing.

'You said Jamie Rathbone, right?'

'Yes. It might be down as James.'

'Can you spell the surname, please?'

Alice spells it, suppressing a spasm of impatience. Jamie is a senior executive. The head of campaigns, for God's sake.

A little comma of concentration between the receptionist's eyebrows deepens.

'I'll just call up to the main office,' she says slowly. 'Could you take a seat, please?'

Alice goes to sit on the other side of the reception room, on one of two colourful sofas. Alice crosses and uncrosses her legs, looks out of the window at the square opposite, the silver birch trees against the flat, grey sky. She picks up a copy of *Third Sector* magazine, then puts it down again almost immediately. Alice can only see the top half of the receptionist's head, but she can hear her speaking in a low voice to someone on the phone. Then there is a long pause, as if the other person is speaking.

'Hi, sorry?'

The receptionist is calling her. Alice goes over.

'I'm sorry. There isn't an active email on our system for a Jamie Rathbone,' she says. She is speaking slowly, deliberately.

'OK,' Alice says. 'That's – that's very strange, because he is the head of campaigns for the charity. It's an executive role.'

Alice tries to keep the frustration from her voice, but in the silence of the office reception, she is intensely aware that it is her that sounds unreasonable, irrational.

'I tell you what, can I speak with one of his senior colleagues, please? Richard, perhaps? Richard Jenning?' Jamie can't stand Richard Jenning, the deputy director, but presumably he will, at least, be able to tell Alice what is going on.

'Richard Jenning is in meetings all this afternoon, I'm afraid,' the receptionist replies, without missing a beat. *Oh, right*, Alice thinks. *So you know who Richard Jenning is.*

A crackle of static bursts from the radio attached to the dreadlocked security guard's lapel. It makes Alice jump.

'Someone else, then,' Alice insists. She leans over the reception desk, and the receptionist's eyes widen in alarm.

'Tim Lockwood? Or how about the secretary, Belinda – Belinda, um—' Alice grits her teeth with frustration. 'Bright! Belinda Bright. Is she…'

'Tim is working from home today,' the receptionist says. 'And it looks like Belinda is on leave.'

'Well, do you know who else is available?'

'Again, I have no information on that,' she says. The woman's eyes flick towards the guard, and Alice sees him take a tiny step towards them.

'I'm sorry that I can't help, Mrs Rathbone,' she says smoothly. 'I hope you manage to make contact with your husband.'

Alice catches a look in her eyes which is somewhere between pity and distaste. This is ridiculous, Alice thinks. This is surely just some big misunderstanding, a weird IT error. Yet there is something in the air between her, the receptionist and the security guard which feels off-key.

A clicking sound from beyond the security barriers makes all three of them look over.

A red-haired woman in a navy coat and trainers emerges, digging in her shoulder bag for a security pass. Alice is flooded with relief. It is Isobel – sad Isobel! Isobel who works with Jamie, who left it too late to start trying for a baby and had all the miscarriages. She saw Isobel at those drinks. Isobel has a different haircut now, much shorter, but it's definitely her, someone Alice knows. Isobel is a solid thing, a raft that Alice can cling to.

Alice holds up her hand in a wave, tries to catch Isobel's eye. But she taps her card and passes through the moving glass barriers without looking up. Alice sees that she is wearing earbuds. She waves more dramatically. Isobel looks up.

'Oh! Alice!' She plucks out one earbud, then another. 'Nice to see you,' she says, after a beat.

'You too!' Alice really means it.

'So, um, what are you up to?'

'Oh, it's so ridiculous,' Alice tries to keep it light. 'I'm trying to get in touch with Jamie – he's in Scotland at a conference, as you probably know – but he's left his phone at home, and now his work email doesn't seem to work either, and I stupidly didn't get him to write down the details of his hotel or anything, so…'

Isobel twists an earbud between her fingers. She glances at the receptionist. Alice tenses.

'Jamie?'

'Yeah.' Alice forces a laugh. 'You remember my husband, right?'

He's your fucking boss, Alice feels like screaming. *What the hell is going on?*

Isobel looks at Alice again, then at the security guard, then back to Alice.

'It was really nice to see you, Alice,' Isobel mutters. And then, without meeting her eye, she twists the earbud back into her ear and walks past Alice, out of the revolving doors.

Alice follows Isobel without a backward glance at the receptionist. Outside, it has started to spit again, the sky silvery, the wind picking up. The young birch trees tremble in their little cages on the pavement outside the office.

Isobel doesn't seem to hear Alice calling her name. In desperation, Alice jogs up to her, touches her sleeve. Isobel jumps, spins around, as if scalded.

'Jesus, Alice!'

'Sorry. Sorry!'

Alice holds up her palms as Isobel takes the earbuds out, places them carefully in her pocket. She eyes Alice warily, as if she is a wild animal.

'I'm sorry,' Alice says again breathlessly. 'I just – can you please just tell me where Jamie is? There was some strange thing with his email, and the website, and the receptionist was being really weird, and I just—' She feels her voice catch in her throat. 'I just want to know where he is.'

'You really need to have this conversation with Jamie, Alice.' Isobel shifts her weight from one foot to the other, her eyes pleading.

'I've told you, I can't... Hang on, what do you mean? What conversation, Isobel? What's going on?'

'Oh my God,' Isobel mutters under her breath. She stuffs her hands in the pockets of her coat, looks down at the pavement, then back up at Alice, squinting, as if she is being forced to look directly at the sun.

'You really don't know?'

Alice shakes her head, feeling close to tears. 'I really don't,' she murmurs. 'Please, I'm begging you, Isobel. Tell me.'

Isobel looks behind Alice at the doors of the building, then back at Alice's face.

'Alice,' she says. 'Jamie hasn't been at the Handhold office for... a while now.'

'Of course he has.'

'No, he hasn't,' Isobel says. 'He's been – well, he has been – on leave. For some time.' Isobel is speaking slowly, with care. 'As far as I understand it, Jamie is going to be leaving the charity. Or has left already. I'm not across the exact details.'

'That's not possible,' Alice says. But Isobel's face is so pained that she can tell that she is telling the truth.

'What – what happened?' Alice asks, her voice choked.

Isobel's eyes dart behind Alice towards the doors again. 'I can't talk about it,' she mutters. 'None of us can. For legal reasons. We've all been told not to discuss it. With anyone.'

'But, surely you…'

'No, Alice,' Isobel says firmly. 'I've already done too much, said too much. Find Jamie. Talk to *him*.'

And with that, she turns around and walks to the Tube quickly, leaving Alice gaping on the edge of the square.

Alice checks her phone, willing there to be a message, by now, from Jamie. A voicemail. An email. But there is nothing. The last messages she has received are Jade's.

Please come tonight. I swear I'll tell you the truth about everything.

If you don't come now, I'm afraid it will be too late.

ALICE

Alice moves quickly along the canal path. The darkness around her is thick and moonless. More than once, bike lights seem to appear from nowhere, cyclists nearly knocking her into the foetid water. The canal stinks of piss, beer, rotting leaves.

Martha is staying at Yas's house tonight. Martha will be thrilled to be having a sleepover with Iris, Alice tells herself. She'll be fine. Alice presses the guilt down inside her chest. She cannot think about Martha now.

Alice reaches into her bag, and then pulls her hand back quickly when she feels the blade of the kitchen knife against her fingers.

Possession of a bladed weapon. It's a crime in itself, isn't it? Alice and Jamie had replaced their knives since what happened; Alice hadn't been involved in the purchasing of this new set. The knife is awkward in her bag, probably too big to be really useful. If she was stopped and searched, on this dark canal path, Alice could be – what, fined? Maybe. Taken to court, certainly. Irrelevant, of course. Alice is a white middle-class woman, a mother, in Chelsea boots and a smart wool coat from Jigsaw. No one would suspect Alice of carrying a knife. Alice will not be stopped and searched.

Most kids caught with knives say they're doing it because they fear for their own safety. A memory of Jamie's voice on the radio being asked about knife crime among Handhold's vulnerable service users. It's always sounded a bit implausible to Alice. But now that's her excuse too, isn't it? She has only taken the knife to defend herself against a person she knows wants to harm her.

If you were so worried about your personal safety, why go to her home? she imagines Barnes asking her.

Alice has no good answer for him.

Jade's estate is different in the darkness. Alice passes the brick stairwell beside the row of flats that leads to Jade's. Is this where Linda was pushed by Jade?

Alice picks her way through the front garden. The potted plants are now long dead, the drying rack turned over in the wind. She goes to knock on the door, but it gives way before her hand. It is unlocked, not even closed properly. And then Alice sees the brownish handprint on the edge of the door.

In a brief moment of disbelief, she reaches out to touch it.

Two things happen. The door swings open, as if she had pressed it harder than she did. She guesses it was flimsier than she thought, or maybe a gust of wind has caught it, but it is unsettling how it seemed to move like that at only the slightest touch.

And then Alice notices that the brownish colour from the handprint she'd seen on the door is reddish, rather than brown, on her palm.

Alice steps inside. There is a quivering energy in the flat, a terrible, screaming silence. The lights are on, illuminating unwashed plates piled up on the carpet, clothes slung over the furniture. A lamp is smashed on the floor, and there is something else broken, too – a mug or plate, perhaps. Jagged edges of white porcelain are scattered across the hall. A dripping brown spectre on one wall that smells like coffee. And the smell of something else, too. A metallic smell that Alice cannot place.

'Jade?'

But even as she calls her name, Alice knows that Jade is not here. No one is here but her.

She checks Ezra's old room to see if baby Taylor is there. But there is no sign of her in her cot – just a crumpled sleeping bag, an upturned bunny toy. She checks Linda's bedroom, and the lounge. No Taylor. The flat is empty.

Shaking now, Alice heads towards the kitchen.

She becomes aware, after a step or two, that something is sticking to her feet, that she is trailing it all over the kitchen. She looks down, and it is the same red she saw on the door; the red that is already on her fingers. She gasps, horrified, grips the kitchen counter.

'Jade? Jade!'

No answer. Alice hears footsteps in the hallway. She quickly turns to face the open door, fear pulsing through her. She reaches into her bag, her trembling fingers clumsy as they clutch at the smooth handle of the knife.

And then she sees a figure in the hallway, blocking the light, and then she is breathing fast, and then she is holding up her hands, because that is what he – what all of them – are shouting at her to do. And then she looks at her own hands, one bloody, one gripping the knife, and she turns to the police officers, and she sees what they see. And then she swallows, and her fear becomes a horror of another kind.

ALICE

Alice is held for what feels like many hours. They take fingerprints, photographs. They take swabs from inside her cheek, pluck hairs from her scalp. They keep her in a room with a lukewarm cup of tea for a very long time.

Then the door buzzes loudly, and when Alice looks up, it is Barnes.

'Hello, Alice.'

Barnes pulls up his trouser legs, and sits down opposite. A female officer joins him, one Alice has not seen before. She has blonde hair scraped back in a bun, pale eyelashes and eyebrows. She smells of spearmint chewing gum.

The officer introduces herself as DI Clarke. She sets about sorting out the recording machine, murmurs to Barnes about whether she thinks it's on or not. Beside Alice sits a duty lawyer, who has been assigned to her case until Jessica arrives. He is a man with a crumpled suit and coffee breath, who doesn't seem to know much more than Alice about what is going on. Alice watches him rummage for a biro and notebook in his battered backpack and silently wills Jessica to get here quick.

Barnes speaks first.

'Can you state your name for the recording, please?'

'Alice Rathbone.'

Barnes gives her a little nod, as if he is pleased with her.

'Now, Alice,' Barnes says, 'you and I know each other a little, don't we?'

'Yes,' Alice hears herself croak.

'And I know you're a very intelligent woman, so I know you're going to understand what I'm telling you now. You're potentially in a lot of trouble here, Alice, OK? And what you need to do now is to tell me absolutely everything, all right? Otherwise that trouble is going to get an awful lot worse.'

Alice's insides plummet. She glances at the lawyer, who gives her a slight nod, so she does the same to Barnes.

'For the recording?'

'Sorry. Yes. I understand.'

'Good.' He pauses. 'Where is Jade Jones, Alice?'

'I don't know.'

This is not the answer that Barnes wanted. The muscle in his cheek flickers, but his voice remains even for now.

'When did you last see Jade Jones?'

'I didn't see her. When I got to her flat, she wasn't there. None of them were – Jade or Taylor. Or Linda.'

'You didn't see Jade last night?'

'No.'

'You didn't argue?'

'No, I swear. I got to her flat, and the door was open, and there was no one there. And I could see there was blood. On the door. And on the kitchen floor.'

Barnes looks at DI Clarke. She produces a plastic bag, labelled, with Alice's kitchen knife inside it. Alice closes her eyes.

'For the tape, DI Clarke is showing the witness exhibit PDM292-A, a kitchen knife.' Barnes looks up at her. 'Do you accept this is your knife, Alice?'

Alice nods miserably.

'Can you answer for the recording, please?'

'Yes.'

'Where did you get this knife, Alice?'

'From my kitchen at my home.'

Barnes pauses.

'And why did you have this knife with you last night, Alice?'

Alice swallows.

'I was going to see Jade, but I was worried she might want to harm me. The knife was just in case – in case I had to defend myself.'

Barnes sighs heavily.

'Alice, help me understand. If you thought Jade Jones was going to harm you, then why did you go to her property?'

'Because I wanted to know what was going on. I just want to know what happened...'

Alice's composure collapses, her body wracked by sobs. She feels so confused, so exhausted, so frightened. DI Clarke produces a small, folded Kleenex from a packet in her trouser pocket and passes it wordlessly to Alice.

'I think there was some reason for the break-in,' Alice manages, recovering a little. 'The burglary. I had this anonymous call, saying there was a reason Ezra was there that day...'

'When was this?'

'A few months ago.'

'And you didn't report this to police?'

'I should have.' There is a tremor in Alice's voice. 'I thought I could... I wanted to figure it out myself.'

'I see,' Barnes says slowly. 'And how exactly did you set about "figuring it out yourself"?'

Alice can't tell if he is mocking her.

'I went to Ezra's address.'

'And when was this?'

Alice is silent.

'Presumably you are aware that your bail conditions explicitly forbad you from making contact with Ezra's family?'

Alice pauses, then nods.

'For the recording, please, Alice.'

'Sorry. Yes, I did know. I am sorry. I wasn't intending to actually knock on the door, I was just going to... to look, which I know was stupid enough. But then Linda saw me and asked me in. It was... It was so hot.'

Alice knows, even as she says it, how pathetic it sounds. She can't even bear to look at the lawyer, so she has no idea what he is thinking. Barnes looks at Alice in a disappointed sort of way.

'And once inside her address, did you identify yourself to Linda Jones?'

'I... I didn't. I wish I had.' But Barnes, she can see, has no time for what she wishes she had done.

'What date was this, Alice?'

'It was... it was July. I can check...'

'And what did you talk about?'

'Nothing. It was hot...'

'You said that already,' DI Clarke says with a sudden and unexpected flash of hostility. Alice feels the heat rising to her cheeks.

'Yes. So, um, we talked about that.'

'You talked about the weather?'

'Yes, we did. I know it sounds ridiculous,' Alice sighs. 'She gave me a glass of water. And then she ended up – I can't remember how – she ended up telling me she'd recently lost her son.'

'And what did you say, when she told you that?'

Alice can feel a tear rolling down one cheek. When she opens her mouth to speak, she finds that it is difficult.

'I said,' she says with an effort, 'that I was sorry.'

The air in the room feels heavy. Barnes waits before speaking again.

'Is that when you met Jade Jones?'

'No. I didn't see her that first time. Only Linda.'

'So you went back?'

'Because I wanted to tell her the truth, to say sorry for lying... but then she wasn't there. Only Jade was. And Jade thought I was someone else, and I just sort of... didn't tell her any different. I know it was wrong...'

Alice says nothing. Barnes makes a whistling noise, gives a little shake of his head.

'Help me understand, Alice,' he says.

As Alice tells them the whole story, she tries with her eyes to blur their faces, so she doesn't have to process their reactions to what she is saying. She tells them how she'd ended up lying, first to Linda, then Jade, about who she was. But then she'd started to wonder whether Jade knew who she was all along. And then the things started going missing.

'And you say you found these items in Jade's flat?'

'Yes,' Alice says. 'In a box in a gap above her bathroom ceiling. There were newspaper cuttings and photographs of me, and things of mine – I don't know how she got them. But I think… maybe she was stalking me. I think she had been coming to my house…'

Alice lists what she found. The sunglasses, the notebook, the top. Fleetingly, she remembers her mother's earrings. She'd never found those. She wonders what Jade did with them. Then, again, it hardly matters now.

'So from that point,' Alice goes on, 'I knew she knew who I was, had probably known all along. And there were a load of bloody feathers in the box, too. So I knew it must have been her behind that dead gull.' Alice looks pleadingly at Barnes. 'I told you about the gull, remember?'

DI Clarke gives Barnes a questioning look, but he ignores her, continues to stare at Alice. The lawyer looks hopelessly confused.

'So she'd followed us to Rye. And been inside my house, taken things of mine. And then the threats – you said those had been sent from my home computer – I thought probably she was behind that too.'

Alice takes a breath. The effort of explaining it all feels exhausting. She feels as if she wants to curl up on the floor.

'And then a few weeks ago, someone broke into my workplace and destroyed a painting I was working on – your colleagues will know about that, and I mentioned it to you – there is a case number… I'm sure that was her too. I think she stole my security pass. She'd taken things from my bag before.'

Barnes and his colleague exchange a glance.

'I still don't understand, Alice,' Barnes says. 'If you'd come to believe Jade was stalking you, stealing things from you, following you on your holiday, breaking into your house, your work – that she wished you harm – if you were scared of her, as you say, then I really don't understand why you went to Jade Jones's flat last night, Alice.'

Alice takes a breath.

'Because she sent me a text saying said she would tell me the truth,' Alice says. 'About everything that had been happening.'

Barnes takes Alice's phone from his pocket and passes it to her.

'Can you show me the message, Alice, please?'

Alice's lawyer nods at Alice, eyes wide, so she pulls her phone out and scrolls through to find the message. The lawyer takes it from her and reads the messages, frowning. Barnes crosses his arms impatiently.

'I wasn't going to go at first,' Alice says, as the lawyer finally passes the phone to Barnes. 'But then I found out that something had happened with my husband's job… I was struggling to reach him, so I went to his office, and they said he doesn't work there, that he's… he's been suspended or something.' Alice shakes her head, still in disbelief. 'As soon as I heard that, I felt sure it must be something to do with Jade. It was the last straw. I just felt desperate.' Alice is sobbing now. 'I couldn't go on just waiting for her next move – I needed to find out what was going on. I thought maybe I could make her stop what she was doing. Destroying our lives, our careers…'

Barnes is frowning. 'Just pause there a second, Alice,' he says. 'Are you telling me you weren't aware that your husband had been suspended from his job, until yesterday?'

Alice shakes her head again, sobbing. Barnes and his colleague look at each other.

'And what does your husband, Jamie, say about it?'

Alice looks down. 'I can't get hold of him.'

'You can't get hold of your husband?'

Alice rubs her eyes. 'He left his phone at home, so I can't contact him. It was – it had fallen down the back of the sofa.'

'I see.' Barnes glances at DI Clarke, then leans over to say something into her ear. She leaves the room. Barnes turns back to Alice.

'When exactly did your husband leave for this – this conference?'

'Tuesday morning.'

'Where did he tell you the conference was?'

'Scotland. He was flying there.'

'Scotland?' Barnes looks at Alice, as if he is waiting for something.

'Yes,' Alice says. 'Scotland.'

Barnes sighs. 'Anything more specific?'

Alice blushes. 'Oh. Sorry. I… no. I assumed Edinburgh, or… Glasgow? I didn't really ask…'

'Is it usual for him to leave for days and not take his phone?'

Alice shifts in her chair. 'Not really,' she admits.

DI Clarke returns with some new paperwork, and says something in his ear.

'When was the last time he had to attend a conference for work before this?'

Alice pauses. 'I... can't remember.'

Alice feels as if the ground is sinking.

'How much contact has your husband had with Jade Jones, Alice?'

'Forgive me, officers,' the laywer says, finally sitting up. 'But that is a question for Mr Rathbone. My client cannot speak to—'

'None,' Alice interjects, holding a palm up to quiet her lawyer. 'None whatsoever. This was just me.'

The lawyer frowns, leans towards her, but she ignores him, keeps her eyes fixed on Barnes.

'You're sure about that?' Barnes asks.

'Yes. Absolutely positive.'

He told me never to speak to her again, when he found out, she nearly says. And then she realises that if she says that, it shows Jamie knew she had been going to see Jade. Alice doesn't want to get Jamie into any trouble. This is her mess.

Barnes and his colleague exchange a look.

'OK,' says Barnes. 'So your husband leaves his phone at home, and he tells you he's going to a conference. And then you don't hear from him. At all. And it's now Thursday.'

Barnes pauses.

'Doesn't that strike you as odd, Alice?' he prompts. 'Wouldn't you be calling friends, relatives, the police, if you really hadn't heard from him in all that time?'

'I did!' Alice protests. 'That's exactly why I went to his work. I assumed they'd be able to tell me where he was. I... I believed that he was at a conference. I had no reason not to believe it.'

'So you didn't think to alert anyone that he was missing?'

'Well, no, because at first I was calling him and calling him and I thought maybe he just wasn't looking at his phone. It was only yesterday that I found his phone, that he'd left his phone at home. So then I thought, well, that's why I can't get hold of him. And it was only when I tried his usual work email, and that didn't work, that I thought something strange was happening. And I went straight to his office, and that's when someone told me he was on leave, and I just thought, that can't be right, unless something has happened to him, unless Jade has done something – like what happened to me with the painting, and he hasn't had the heart to tell me – and that's why I went to Jade's last night in the end, because I couldn't get hold of Jamie, so... I wanted to confront her about all this weird stuff that's been going on, because I'm sure she's behind it.'

There is a pause. Alice feels exhausted with the effort of so much speaking. The lawyer is slumped in his chair, as if he has given up on her entirely. Barnes considers her for a moment.

'You sound like you were very angry with Jade, Alice.'

'Of course I was angry, but...'

'So you admit you were angry. You admit you held her responsible for the incident at your work where a painting in your care was destroyed. And you say you believe she had been stealing from you, even stalking you, to use your words. You also say you suspected her of doing something to somehow damage your husband's career. You admit that last night, after you learned your husband had been suspended from work, you went to her property to confront her about all of this. And you admit that you went home first, to retrieve a knife to take with you.'

There it is again, the sinking feeling.

'But despite that – *despite all that* – you say you weren't intending to hurt Jade Jones?'

'Absolutely not.' But she finds she is unable to meet his eye.

Barnes pauses, and for a moment, Alice thinks maybe he believes her. But then he leans over the table, resting on his elbows, as if he needs to impart some bad news, and takes no pleasure in doing so.

'Here's our first problem, Alice,' Barnes says. 'Jade Jones is missing, and there's blood all over her flat. The flat where you were found last night, holding a knife, with her blood smeared over your hands and clothing.'

Barnes lets this sink in. Alice is sweating so much that her clothes are sticking to the skin on her back, underneath her arms.

'The second problem, Alice, is that your husband is not at a conference in Scotland, because there is no conference. There has been no Jamie, or James Rathbone on any flights departing from London airports in the past week. And in addition to that, Jamie is no longer authorised to travel or attend conferences on Handhold's behalf. He has been suspended for some time. He has not been permitted to enter the charity's offices. They haven't heard from him in some weeks.'

Alice grips the table, feeling like she might vomit. She thinks about him at home, on Zoom calls – had that all been fake? All the times he's been home early lately. All the times he's been able to get out of things to take Martha to school, or pick her up, when he never has before. How had she not seen it? How had she not guessed what was going on?

'When we were in contact over the summer, Alice, you and your lawyer repeatedly assured me you were abiding by your bail conditions in full. But that was a lie, wasn't it, Alice?'

'No, it wasn't. Not... most of the times I said it...'

'Alice, you went to see the family of the man you killed while charges were still pending!'

Alice opens her mouth to speak, but nothing comes out. Barnes is looking at her steadily, in a disappointed sort of way.

'Put yourself in my shoes, Alice. It's looking very much like Jade Jones has been seriously hurt. You admit to going there, that you were angry, that you armed yourself with a knife. A neighbour calls us, reports that Jade has not returned to collect her child. And then we get to the flat, and there you are, covered in her blood. And Jade Jones's blood is all over the house.'

'But...'

'No one has seen Jade Jones since she dropped her baby off at the neighbour's house yesterday afternoon. The only person known to have been at her address in that time is you.'

'But the door was open,' Alice says weakly. 'I swear. And there was no one there.'

'But you see our problem, Alice.' Barnes leans forward. 'Are you absolutely sure, Alice, that you don't know where Jade is?'

'I swear.' It comes out as a whisper.

'Let me tell you what I think,' Barnes says. 'I think you know your husband didn't go to any conference. I think he's been at your home, with his mobile phone, this entire time.'

Alice stares at him. 'What? No! God, I wish! I...'

'I think you have become obsessed, Alice, haven't you?' Barnes continues, cutting her off. 'With Jade Jones, and her baby.'

'No, that's not...'

'Have you heard of projection, Alice?'

Alice gapes at Barnes.

'I'm not an expert on psychology, myself.' He pauses, a tight smile. 'But I do think it's interesting that you say *she* is the one stalking *you*.'

'She is!'

'Because the truth is, Alice, that you've been visiting Jade's flat, and pretending to be someone else, haven't you?'

Alice is silenced.

'You even followed her to the hospital, didn't you? Hours after she gave birth?'

'She – she asked me...'

'You passed yourself off as her mother,' Barnes snaps, 'according to the hospital staff. They say they witnessed you picking up Jade's newborn baby, even though she was only a few hours old. You're right there, on the hospital CCTV, Alice, lifting Jade's newborn out of its hospital cot.'

Alice is stunned. 'That's not...'

'I think at first you were probably just a bit curious, weren't you? Maybe it started with that. And guilt, about her brother. Was that it, Alice? Maybe at first, you really did want to help her, and her baby, to make up for what you did.' Barnes pauses. 'But I think it ended up going wrong, didn't it, Alice? You lost control of it. Things turned sour between the two of you, didn't they?'

'That's – no, that's not how it was.' Alice is shaking her head so much that it is starting to hurt. 'I'm not...'

'She didn't appreciate your saviour routine, Alice, is that it? She wasn't grateful enough? Or maybe she asked too many questions, about what you were really doing there.'

'DCI Barnes,' the lawyer says, 'could we kindly avoid these sorts of wild—'

'That's just not how it was!' Alice cries, ignoring the lawyer. 'She was trying to destroy my career, my—'

'Ah, yes, your career. DI Clarke has spoken to your employers, Alice.' Barnes shuffles the papers in front of him. 'They've told her all about why you were suspended. About how you are under investigation for damaging a valuable artwork, either deliberately or through serious negligence. A Vermeer, no less.' Barnes raises his eyebrows. 'Even I've heard of *him*.'

DI Clarke smirks at this. Alice would guess she has little idea who Vermeer was, but there is no space for Alice to feel superior. Not in this room.

Now Clarke speaks.

'Your boss told me he already had some concerns about your mental state,' she says. 'That you'd been frequently absent, distracted, unfocused, even unbalanced. They've told us that when you joined the company, you were offered counselling for your trauma over the summer, but that you'd declined that help.'

'I didn't need it,' Alice croaks stubbornly.

'They also told me how, just a few days before the incident in which the painting was damaged, you were caught preparing a hot drink to consume around the artwork in contravention of basic rules.' Alice's lawyer sighs quietly.

Alice stares down at the table. *Thanks, Rollo.*

'Being suspended from work, it can't have been good for you, Alice,' Barnes cuts in. 'For your state of mind.'

Alice says nothing.

'When things like that happen, it's hard sometimes to face up to what you've done,' Barnes goes on. 'Sometimes it's easier to blame others, to believe that someone is out to get you.'

Alice grips the table. 'None of this is right,' she says now, almost shouting. 'That just isn't how it was. Jade was stalking *me*. If you look in her flat, you'll find my stuff. It's in a box, in the loft above her bathroom.'

'This box, you mean?'

DI Clarke produces some A4-size photographs. Showing the box, where it was found, and then laid out on a grey table, with all its contents.

'You found it! Yes,' Alice nods encouragingly. 'That's the one.'

Clarke goes to put the photos away, but Barnes hovers a palm over them, as if to say: *Wait.*

'If Jade stole these items from your home,' Barnes says, 'can you explain why we found no DNA, no fingerprints matching Jade's, on them at all?'

Alice stares.

'I can't explain that,' she says honestly.

'We found plenty of your fingerprints on these items, though, Alice. And around the opening to the loft, where they had been placed.'

Alice stares at him.

'What? No!' Alice feels her pulse climbing. 'Maybe Jade... wore gloves, or...' Alice trails off. Barnes sighs, gives his head a little shake.

'You put this box in Jade's home,' he says quietly. 'Didn't you, Alice?'

'This is ridiculous!' Alice cries. 'Of course I didn't – I found it up there, like I told you.'

Barnes sighs more heavily. He starts to collect the pictures.

'I think,' he says, tidying them into a neat pile and tapping it on the table, 'the truth is, that since you killed Ezra Jones, you've been struggling, haven't you, Alice?'

'You don't...'

'Your job,' Barnes says. 'Your husband's job. Your marriage.' Barnes gives her a look. So he's seen the pictures of Becca on Jamie's computer. Alice feels the sting of humiliation.

'I think you wanted someone to blame, didn't you? And Jade – well, she was an easy target. She was the closest person to Ezra. I think you decided to blame her for everything. For what happened with Ezra, and for all the challenges you have been having since, in your life, your job, your marriage.'

'No,' Alice begs. 'That's not...'

'I think you went out last night in anger,' he continues. 'I think you wanted to punish Jade, for your life falling apart. I think that's why you took the knife.'

'No! This is ridiculous. Jade has been stalking me. Threatening me...'

'Is that why you killed her?' Barnes asks. 'Is that why you killed Jade Jones?'

'No. No! I didn't lay a finger on her. I didn't even see...'

'Where is your husband, Alice?'

'I don't know.'

'Did he take her body somewhere, Alice? Was that what happened, after things went too far?'

'No!'

'I don't think you meant for it to happen, did you, Alice? You just got too angry.'

'No!'

'Jamie, then? Was he the one who snapped? And then afterwards, you both panicked? He took her somewhere, and you agreed to stay behind to cover his tracks?'

'That's not... I would never!' Alice stammers.

'Alice,' Barnes says, leaning forward on his elbows again, 'you need to start helping yourself out now. It's all over, Alice. You *need* to tell us where Jamie took her body.'

'My client has been extremely helpful, DCI Barnes,' the lawyer says. 'She has been clear she had no part in the harm or disappearance of Ms Jones. Clearly, she cannot speak to her husband's actions. She has been in no communication with him whatsoever.'

Alice stares at the lawyer, then at Barnes.

'This is madness,' Alice cries. 'Jamie would never kill anyone. I would never kill anyone.'

'You killed Ezra Jones.'

His voice is ice-cold. Alice grits her teeth.

'Ezra was a stranger who broke into my house,' she says, with an effort.

Barnes tilts his head to one side, then the other, as if he is considering this.

'That's certainly the story you told us at the time,' he says slowly. He leans back on his chair, just a little.

'But – well, I don't know what to say, Alice. It all looks a bit more complicated than that, now. Doesn't it?

ALICE

'They want your passport,' Jessica says, swooping into her cell. 'You need to stay at your address, report to this police station once a week. If you don't do this, you'll be back in custody.'

'They're letting me go?'

Alice almost collapses with relief.

'For now,' Jessica adds sternly. She nods at the guard, who closes the cell door behind them. It buzzes shut. Jessica sits at the small table and turns to face Alice, who is slumped on the hard bench at the side.

'Look, Alice,' she says in a lowered voice. 'To be honest with you, I'm surprised. Given you admitted you flouted your bail conditions before. I would have thought they had enough to hold you. But I guess the CPS must want a body.'

'A body?'

Jessica adjusts her glasses and gives Alice a condescending look. 'The police believe that Jade Jones is dead, and they think you or your husband killed her, or that you killed her together. They are looking for her body as we speak.'

Jessica pauses, glances towards the door. There are the sounds of police officers talking outside, another inmate shouting.

'Alice, if I'm going to represent you, I need you to be honest. I need to know everything that the police are going to find out about you and your husband.'

'I am being honest. I've told you everything!'

'Good.' She places her hands one on top of the other in her lap. 'How much do you know about the circumstances of Jamie's departure from his job?'

'Nothing,' Alice says helplessly. 'I only found out yesterday that he hadn't been in the office for months. He must have been... he must have been pretending.'

Alice's head spins when she thinks about the extent of Jamie's deception. She thinks of the Zoom call in his office, where she could only hear his voice. The police say he has been suspended since the middle of June. He has been faking going to work for five months.

Alice can only imagine that he had been looking desperately for a way to tell her, and losing his nerve. And then the break-in had happened, and he'd decided it was the worst possible time, that he had to protect her from it. But Alice still doesn't understand *how* he could have lost his job. Jamie was so good at what he did. What on earth could have got him sacked?

'You've really had no contact from him?' Jessica asks sternly again. 'Nothing, since he went away? Absolutely nothing?'

'I swear.'

'And you really have no idea where he could be?'

'Like I told you, he told me he was going to a conference.'

Jessica tilts her head to one side. 'Why do you think he lied about that?'

'I don't know! Don't you think I want to know the answers to these questions? Jesus!'

'All right, calm down.' Jessica unfastens her large Mulberry Bayswater, slots her papers inside, then stands up, belting her neat camel coat. Everything about Jessica seems to belong to a world that Alice is no longer part of.

'I'll be in touch,' Jessica says. She looks at Alice over the top of her glasses. 'Do you have a way of getting home?'

'I'll get an Uber.' The police have returned Alice's phone after an argument, although Jessica says they have made some sort of copy of it and will be going through it now, every message, every photograph.

'Fine.' Jessica gives her a hard final look. 'And, Alice? Any contact from your husband, you contact the police, and myself, immediately. No exceptions. We need there to be no slip-ups from here on in. Is that clear?'

Alice nods. All she wants is to lay her hands on Martha, who must be so confused about where her mum is, and why her Aunt Sarah is here looking after her with no warning. Alice is desperate to hold her close and feel the warmth of her, the softness of her hair and skin, to tell her it'll be all right. Even though she is not sure that it will.

When Alice opens the door she can smell lasagne. Aunt Sarah is on her knees, muttering something at the oven window. The oven timer is going off. Martha is in her school uniform and her socks, one plait coming loose. When she looks up and sees Alice, her face crumples into tears.

'Mummy!'

Alice scoops her up and holds her tight, then backs into the sofa without taking off her coat or bag and holds Martha close.

'I missed you so much,' she tells her daughter. She looks up at Aunt Sarah. She mumbles a hello, tries to say 'thank you', but her face feels tight. Alice knows that at some point, she owes her aunt a real explanation. But just now, she does not feel up to offering one.

'My tooth fell out.' Martha pulls her mouth wide. 'I put it under my pillow, but the tooth fairy didn't even come.'

'Oh, my goodness! Maybe she couldn't find it. She'll be back for it tonight.'

'Really?'

'Definitely. Let me see!' Alice looks into her daughter's mouth and marvels at the gap. Martha looks back at her.

'Are you in trouble, Mummy?'

'Of course not, sweetheart,' Alice busies herself tidying Martha's plait. Martha studies her face, desperate to believe her.

'When's Daddy coming back?'

Alice's stomach plummets. She should have thought all this through. She'd been so fixated on seeing Martha that she hasn't thought properly about the questions she will have, and how on earth she is going to answer them.

'Daddy will be back as soon as he can be.' She strokes the tops of Martha's arms. 'How about we have some of that yummy lasagne now, and then we can do you a bubble bath, and then we can both get into our PJs and watch *Frozen*?'

Martha would usually like this suggestion. But today, she just presses her face into Alice's chest, unwilling to let her go.

Martha falls asleep on Alice's chest partway through the film, a blanket over her. Alice carries her into her bed and turns out the light. In the bedroom next door, Sarah has made up the guest room herself, and has found her own clean towels. Alice walks slowly down the stairs. She longs to run a bath, pour a glass of wine and just think, but she owes Aunt Sarah an explanation.

'Let me wash up,' she says weakly, but she can see that Sarah has already done it all; the pans upside down on the draining board, bubbles slipping down their sides. The kitchen is spotless, Martha's reading and homework books stacked neatly on the worktop, her coat on its peg, the washing machine humming away with her PE kit inside.

'I think your water pressure needs looking at,' Aunt Sarah says. Alice nods. She knows this is true, but she had been putting it off, because it means calling out a plumber, and now Alice is not sure how much longer she will need to last on the money that is currently in their joint account. She checked earlier – as expected, Jamie's pay for the month has not arrived. And now she is home, Alice can see that the stack of letters on the worktop has grown in her absence, at least one of which, she suspects, will be about a council tax payment which hasn't gone through, because there isn't enough in their account. Their mortgage payment is due soon too, and Alice has been getting emails about payments for Martha's after-school clubs, which are yet to be made, plus other payments she has missed – their veg box subscription, their Amazon prime. Luxuries now, that Alice can ill afford.

'Let's have a large drink, shall we?'

The suggestion is so welcome, and so unlike Sarah, that Alice almost smiles.

Aunt Sarah pours a glass of red wine for herself, and takes a large gulp before she pours another for Alice.

Alice tries to think how she can even begin to thank Aunt Sarah. To express her gratitude, and her embarrassment, too, about the chaos she has introduced to her well-ordered life.

'Who's looking after your shop?' Alice asks weakly.

'I've a good team,' she says briskly. 'They'll be fine.'

'I don't know how to thank you.'

Aunt Sarah takes another mouthful of wine.

'It has been a pleasure really,' she says, in a tone of mild surprise. 'Martha is a very sweet girl.'

Alice wonders if she was a sweet girl, when she landed on Sarah's doorstep as a teenager. Whether she was no trouble. She doubts it. It occurs to her that Aunt Sarah has twice now been called upon to clear up after the chaos of Alice's life.

'How is she, really? I mean, how has she been?'

Alice is desperate to know how Martha is coping emotionally, but this sort of conversation is not Aunt Sarah's strong suit.

'Oh, she's not too bad. Up and down,' Aunt Sarah looks away. Alice sighs.

'What sort of things has she been saying?'

Aunt Sarah's voice tightens. 'Exactly what you'd expect, Alice. She's been asking where her mother and father are. She's been asking and asking. And I haven't known what to say.'

Alice feels a sob catch in her throat. 'I'm sorry.'

Neither of them says anything for a moment.

'I can stay as long as you need,' Sarah says gruffly, brushing some imaginary dust from her tailored trousers.

'I'm really grateful.'

The truth is, Alice would rather it was just her and her daughter. But she does not know what is going to happen. If Jamie is ever going to come back.

'So,' Aunt Sarah says, sitting down heavily. 'Do you want to tell me what's been going on?'

'I promise we will talk,' Alice begins slowly. 'In the morning. I just – I really need to sleep.' Aunt Sarah is quiet, her mouth in a pinched, straight line.

'All right,' she says. 'But please… Martha has been asking and asking. Where is Jamie, Alice?'

'I don't know,' Alice admits. 'I wish I did.'

Aunt Sarah smooths her trouser fabric again, avoiding eye contact. 'He lied to you, then, I gather. About going to this conference.'

'Yes.'

'And about his job. He must have been lying for months…'

'I know, I know,' Alice says. 'But I *know* him, Sarah. He will have been trying to protect me and Martha.'

'Protect you? From what?'

Alice looks out of the sliding glass doors. She can hear the overground train rush past, see the faint blue and orange blur of it behind the black skeletons of the trees at the end of her garden.

'I don't know,' she admits.

But she is going to find out.

ALICE

It takes her a while to find the coffee place Isobel has specified is near Liverpool Street station, a good walk from the Handhold offices. 'It would be better if we could keep this discreet,' she'd said.

Alice weaves her way through the area's tall glass towers, every doorway guarded by someone with an earpiece connecting to a wire that snakes under their clothes. Alice sees her haunted reflection in every polished surface.

She is relieved to finally arrive at the cafe – a minimal Scandinavian sort of place, facing out to a square of granite, with a jagged water feature that cuts along the back of a blocky bench. Alice orders a coffee and sits at a side table, staring up at a window cleaner dangling from one of the towers. In the courtyard, a group of pigeons jab at an abandoned croissant.

Isobel appears ten minutes later.

'I got you a cappuccino,' Alice says. 'I thought you might be in a rush.'

'I'm not drinking coffee at the moment,' Isobel replies coldly. 'Can we sit in the back?'

She indicates the table furthest from the windows.

'Oh.' Alice stands clumsily. 'Sure.' She follows her, feeling admonished.

'Can I get you something else, maybe a…'

'No, I'll get my own.'

A few minutes later Isobel returns. She is wearing a black polo neck tucked into a long satin skirt, and suede boots. Her slim body is like one smooth, upholstered swathe of expensive cloth. Her new, shorter hair swings forward when she sits down.

Alice has also dressed carefully for this meeting, determined not to come off in a deranged manner as she did at their last encounter. She is glad she wore her expensive boots, washed her hair, brushed some mascara on.

Isobel places a cup of decaffeinated tea down in front of her.

'I didn't mean to be rude,' Isobel says. 'Sorry. I'm about three months' pregnant. The smell of coffee makes me want to puke.'

Alice breaks into a smile. 'Oh, Isobel. That's wonderful news. I'm so happy it's worked out for you in the end.'

Isobel stares at her.

'What?'

Alice regrets her clumsy choice of words. 'I'm sorry,' she says quietly. 'Nothing.'

'No,' Isobel snaps. 'What did you mean – "in the end"? What are you talking about?'

Alice sighs. 'Jamie mentioned how long you'd been trying to have a baby, that it hadn't been easy. I'm sorry. Perhaps he shouldn't have shared that with me.'

Isobel laughs, looks away. 'Bloody hell,' she says. 'That man. He lies about everything, do you know that, Alice?' She tuts quietly, still looking away from Alice. 'Although I wonder why he'd lie about that. No, I haven't had any difficulties getting pregnant. This was basically our first try – it was more like an accident, to be honest.'

Alice is thrown. She cannot think what to say. Three or four miscarriages – she was sure that's what Jamie had said. Why would Jamie have lied about that? Then, with a twist of pain, she remembers what they had been talking about: having another baby. Why couldn't Jamie have just said he didn't want another child? Why make up a horrible lie about someone else?

'So,' Isobel refocuses on Alice, stirs her drink. 'Jamie told you he's at a work conference, did he?'

'He did.' Alice clears her throat. 'Obviously, I now know that isn't true.'

'And I presume the police have asked you all the same questions they've asked us. About where he might be.'

Alice nods miserably. 'I honestly have no idea.'

'Oh, well.' Isobel taps the spoon on the side of her cup, then sets it on the saucer, and sits back in her seat. 'At least you've worked out by now that you're married to a pathological liar. That's a good start.'

Alice blinks.

'Honestly – I don't know what to think.' She tries hard not to sound defensive. 'Jamie has – clearly been under enormous stress. For reasons he hasn't shared with me.'

'So you really knew nothing? About why he was suspended from his job? About the investigation?'

Alice shakes her head. Isobel rolls her eyes in disbelief.

'It's remarkable,' she mutters. 'The way they've managed to keep it out of the press. I mean, he's a senior executive, for God's sake!' She shakes her head. 'Well. They've certainly succeeded in terrifying everyone at the office into silence. They warned us about it again, after your visit the other day. They know I spoke to you, outside the lobby. They are keeping an eye on me, I can tell. Hence the need to meet here. To be careful.'

Alice is struggling to follow what Isobel is saying. What has been kept out of the press? What have they been keeping quiet about?

'It can only be a matter of time before it gets reported,' Isobel goes on. 'But as it stands, he's technically still just on gardening leave, as far as I can make out.'

'But why, Isobel? What is he supposed to have done?'

Isobel sighs. 'Probably any number of things, Alice, over the years,' she says, in a hard tone. 'Except he's always managed to brush them off. Men like him often do. It's just that this time, he hasn't quite managed it.'

'Sorry,' Alice stutters. 'What do you mean – "men like him"?'

'I just mean I've seen men like him before in charities,' Isobel says thoughtfully, as if she is outlining an academic thesis, rather than mounting a character attack on Alice's husband. 'Though usually they work out in the field. They are attracted to the charity sector because they love the idea of saving the world. They enjoy the power imbalance between them and the people they help. The idea of themselves as supermen. The sense of *extremis*, of urgency. I've never known anyone quite like Jamie, though.'

'I don't really understand any of this, Isobel,' Alice says awkwardly. 'I thought you and Jamie were friends.'

'Did you?' She leans in a little over the table, gives Alice an odd sort of smile. 'I was one of Jamie's longest-standing colleagues, Alice – he and I have worked together for years. And you and I are the same age. We live not far away. Have you never wondered why we've never – I don't know – been out for dinner, or anything?'

Alice bites her lip.

'The truth is, Jamie doesn't have any friends among his colleagues.'

'He does have friends,' Alice protests, although just at that moment, she struggles to think of any examples. Everyone loves Jamie. At parties, he talks to anyone. But now Alice is struggling to think of a single real friend. Arlo, perhaps? Is Arlo a real friend of Jamie's? At their wedding, Arlo was Jamie's best man. But then she remembers Arlo and Yas's wedding, a few years earlier. Arlo had his brother as best man, his best university friends among the ushers. Jamie wasn't even there.

'He doesn't have friends, Alice. For good reason.' Isobel rotates her shoulders, sits back on her seat.

'How much older than you is he, Alice?'

'What?' Alice is genuinely confused.

'Ten years? More?'

'No, nothing like that much. I'm forty-two, so six years.'

Isobel makes a face. 'That surprises me.' She gives Alice a quick, flicking look up and down her body. 'You're young-looking, though, aren't you, Alice? Petite. Nubile. I get the impression that's what he likes.'

Alice is speechless.

'When Jamie first got the head of campaigns job, everyone was surprised. He was inexperienced – but it wasn't just that. People were very unhappy about his management style. Also, there were claims about him. From his time at the previous charity.'

'What claims?'

'It only emerged after he'd been here a while. The story was that volunteers out there had been bullied, money misspent, poor behaviour hushed up. One female volunteer had tried to blow the whistle on it all, and then that girl had gone missing, thought to have killed herself. A young girl – only eighteen, I think. There were also rumours she'd been in some sort of a relationship with Jamie.'

'That's ridiculous.' But Alice feels a lump in her throat, thinking about the picture of Clara. Jamie's hand on her bare waist. 'Where did these claims come from?'

'Something a journalist dug up. They sent a list of questions via the press office. The usual thing – giving a right to reply.'

Alice immediately thinks about Stella.

'Do you know the name of the journalist?' Alice asks quickly. 'Or where they worked?'

Isobel frowns. 'No idea.' She pauses. 'It was a woman. Might have been the *Sunday Times*. I couldn't say for sure.'

Alice finds herself gripping and regripping the edge of the table.

'Jamie swore it was all rubbish,' Isobel goes on. 'He said he'd never bullied this volunteer, never been in a relationship with her. That the girl had mental health problems, and had developed some sort of crush on him. He said that it was a tragedy, but he'd had nothing to do with it.'

Alice nods. That's what he told her, too.

'On the basis of Jamie's denials, the lawyers decided it was a fishing exercise by the journalist. Apparently, you could tell by the way she asked the questions that she didn't really have enough to run such a defamatory piece. Our lawyers thought it was unlikely that any of it would be reportable if we just stonewalled. So that's what we did, and the article never materialised, so I guess the lawyers were right about that. After that, no one spoke of it again.'

'When was this?'

'Oh, a few years ago, now. Early 2019, I think. It was before Jamie was made head of campaigns, at the end of that year.'

Alice tries to think quickly. She and Stella had been friends for what – a year? Only since Martha and Frankie had been at school together. Stella had only moved to the area shortly before that, Alice knew.

'So, despite all that fuss with the journalist, he was given the head of campaigns job.' Isobel makes a face. 'Jamie knew how to climb the ladder, cosy up to the donors, the board. I guess he was young, handsome, charismatic, an heir-to-Blair type. And he was cultivating contacts in parliament, too. You will remember that part.'

Alice does. She had questioned sometimes whether it was really necessary – all these dinners in Westminster, when she was at home with a baby, tearing her hair out. But Jamie had told her it was all for them, for his career. She had trusted him.

'Almost as soon as he got the job, he announced this big change in our campaigns direction. He said we had a massive opportunity, with the election coming. He felt we should start parroting his messages, cosying up to the Conservatives in the hope of a deal. It was win-win, he said. The government would get to detoxify their image, steal the left's clothes a bit, look like they cared about the poor. And in return, we'd get this huge bump of public money when they got in. Hundreds of millions of pounds.'

Alice is silent. She remembers Jamie rehearsing these arguments to her, too.

'Of course, Handhold had always been about grass-roots community action. It had always been proudly non-party political. Proudly unglamorous, to be honest.' She gives Alice a rueful smile. 'Jamie didn't like that, you could tell. He kept talking about global ambition, which made people nervous – the whole point of Handhold is that it's a UK charity, it deals with the UK's social problems, you know? But Jamie wasn't interested in any of that – it was obvious. He said all the right things on the radio. But in the office, it was a completely different story. It was like he thought we were a business.'

'You're making him sound like he had more power than he did,' Alice says, shaking her head. 'He wouldn't have been able to change the charity's strategic direction on his own.'

'Not on his own. But he did drive his strategy through, despite all the opposition. And on its own terms, I have to say, it worked brilliantly. Handhold started getting massive amounts of public funding, Comic Relief money, Save the Children cash, lottery funding – you name it. Even more, once Covid hit. It made him untouchable. We were awash with all this cash. We had the opportunity to do all the projects we had always wanted to, expand our successful services, recruit more grass-roots workers. Except Jamie had other plans. He started getting his revenge on anyone who'd opposed his ideas. He went for all the people who'd expressed doubts – said their attitudes about the charity's scope – about its limitations – were parochial, outdated. He wasted a fortune getting rid of people who opposed his ideas, paying them off with gagging agreements.'

Alice swallows. 'Gagging agreements?'

'Yep. Jamie loved them. They were his specialty. Good people were just disappearing from the charity, and other people appearing in their places who owed everything to Jamie, and did everything he said.'

Alice stares at the knots in the table. Thinks about Becca, what she said about not being able to speak. But why would Becca need to be gagged? What did she know that Alice didn't?

'And then, last year, Jamie brought in this ad agency,' Isobel continues. 'These Mad Men type people in shiny suits to do a massive advertising campaign. It was going to cost an absolute fortune. But Jamie and all his new hires signed it off.'

'You mean "A handhold, not a handout"? That one?' Alice thinks of the poster Becca had in her bag.

'That's the one.'

'But that was a big triumph, wasn't it?'

Isobel sighs. 'Yes, it was certainly seen that way at the time.'

It had been everywhere: buses, taxis, the billboards in Leicester Square. The timing had been perfect – it had come amid a massive row between the government and a celebrity footballer who'd grown up poor about holiday hunger and child poverty. Handhold was suddenly 'part of the conversation', as Jamie had put it. Celebrities and footballers started plugging it on social media, doing the heart thing with their hands in a mimicry of Handhold's logo, which secretly made Alice nauseous, even when Martha did it. And that was when Jamie had started getting profile pieces in the papers, popping up on the *Today* programme.

'Jamie had to be front and centre, of course,' Isobel says wryly. 'You'll remember that.'

'Oh, that wasn't his choice,' Alice tells her. 'Jamie didn't want to be the face of the ads – they told him that's what would work best.'

Isobel laughs. 'No, Alice. Why would advertisers want a boring old white guy as the face of the campaign?'

Alice feels herself blushing. That's not what Jamie is, she thinks. Isobel rolls her eyes.

'What the Mad Men wanted,' Isobel continues, 'was service users. Real ones, telling their tear-jerking backstories, *X Factor* style. The ad people told Jamie if he was going to be in the advert, he could only do it if he was sitting and chatting with the service users. Like a front-line worker. It was ridiculous, but there you go – Jamie was the paymaster, they were doing what he wanted. And what he wanted was for it all to be about him. He had a wardrobe consultant come in with a little rail of clothes. It was a circus.'

Given everything Alice has learned over the past few days, this particular revelation – that Jamie wanted to be front and centre of the ad campaign he'd always told Alice he'd been pressured into fronting – shouldn't perhaps be as shocking to her as it is. But it *is* shocking to her. The cognitive dissonance between her idea of her husband, and Isobel's portrait of him as a narcissistic corporate paymaster with a wardrobe consultant is so great that Alice feels as if her brain is breaking apart.

'Anyway,' Isobel continues, 'the ad people told us to gather kids that were young and attractive. We did explain to them we weren't a kids' charity' – Isobel throws Alice an eye roll – 'and that using under sixteens from troubled circumstances was problematic. So they asked for the next best thing: pretty teenaged girls, aged sixteen to eighteen.'

'Oh,' Alice says stupidly.

'Yes. The charity workers were basically asked to model-scout our hugely vulnerable young service users, and decide which ones were the best-looking, and persuade them to be in an ad. That's the strategy Jamie signed off on.'

'OK.' Alice can't deny that this sounds grim. 'But I mean, he was just taking advice. That's not his fault. I imagine that's what advertising is always like.'

Isobel gives Alice a withering look, but carries on.

'So, on the day of the photo shoot and the filming – you'll remember, there were both TV and billboard ads – they wheeled out these pretty teenaged girls and had them all sit down with Jamie, chatting about their problems, crying into his cashmere shoulder.'

Alice is getting irritated. 'I don't see what this has to do with anything,' she says. Isobel gives her a look, and Alice is silenced. Isobel is not going to be hurried.

'Fast forward to earlier this year,' she says. 'And in comes a new press allegation from the same journalist. About a service user. A girl who was vulnerable, lost a parent and had gone off the rails. Drugs, alcohol, crime, the usual. She'd been put in touch with Handhold by her social worker, and was apparently engaging well – a classic success story. Except now the allegation was she'd been having an inappropriate relationship with Jamie.'

'That's ridiculous,' Alice says. 'Not possible. Jamie doesn't even have contact with service users.' She knows this, because it's the line the charity have trotted out over Ezra time and time again. Even if he was a service user, he'd have had no contact with Jamie. It wasn't possible.

'He'd had contact with this one,' Isobel says. 'Because she was one of the ones put forward for the ad campaign.'

Alice's mouth feels dry. She supresses a wave of nausea, forces herself to focus.

'But...' Alice clears her throat, 'you said they were teenagers.'

'She was sixteen when they met,' Isobel says quietly. 'She spent a day filming with Jamie. There is footage, photographs of them together.'

Alice drops the spoon she has been twiddling in her hand. She hears it clatter against the table.

'The allegation was that they'd started a sexual relationship soon after she'd filmed the video for the charity. She was only just over the age of consent.'

No, Alice thinks, *this is not possible.*

'Who was making this allegation?'

'That I don't know.'

'The girl?'

'No. The girl wouldn't talk. She cut all contact with the charity. And Jamie denied it. It was something else. They'd been seen together, something like that.'

'Someone could have got the wrong end of the stick then,' Alice says, but it sounds weak, even to her own ears, and Isobel's look is one of pity.

'Look,' Isobel says slowly. 'Senior charity executives are not suspended from their jobs lightly. Not unless something pretty serious has gone on. Something that can't be ignored, or swept under the table. You must see that.'

Alice is silent.

'They wanted it done quietly. He was suspended, pending the investigation. No one heard anything for a while. And then, well, they found out that it was true, basically. So that was that. From what we heard, the deal was he'd leave nicely, he would get a bit of cash, and sign an NDA. I think the charity's lawyers were finalising it when he vanished into thin air.'

'That makes no sense,' Alice protests. 'If there was a single shred of proof, of something like that, they'd have sacked him.'

'But then it's a news story,' Isobel says, as if Alice is an idiot. 'A high-profile charity sacking its head of campaigns over a sex scandal? The reputational damage could be enormous. Especially now, if anyone ever found out who the girl in question was.'

'What do you mean?' Alice asks. 'Who was she?'

Isobel looks at Alice, almost as if she is disappointed in her.

'This is the bit which I do find extraordinary,' she muses. 'Especially now, when so many people in the office have worked it out. And given the police investigation. The charity can't still be denying it. The police must know. So I guess it's only a matter of time before it reaches the papers.'

'Before *what* reaches the papers?'

Isobel gives Alice a hard look.

'I did try to warn you once, about all this.'

Alice stares at her. 'What do you mean?'

'I didn't go about it the right way,' Isobel sighs. 'I called you, once. I didn't tell you who I was.'

The anonymous phone call at the pool. It had been Isobel.

'It was the first day Jamie had come back into the office, after it happened,' Isobel says. 'Everyone was being so nice to him, asking if he was OK. But I knew what had really happened with your break-in. What had really been behind it. I couldn't stand it. I was so angry. He was saying how cut up you were. I wanted you to know the truth.'

'So you made that call?'

'I did,' Isobel says. 'I wanted you to know that Jamie wasn't who you thought he was. I wanted you to know that you should be careful.'

Alice thinks back to that day at the pool. *He isn't who you think he is.* She hadn't been talking about Ezra. She'd meant Jamie.

'I like you, Alice,' Isobel says, looking away uncomfortably. 'I always have. I guess I was hoping you'd figure it out on your own.'

Isobel reaches into a bag under the table, pulls out an A4 photograph, in a cellophane folder, and places it in front of Alice. Alice looks down.

The same advert Becca had in her holdall. Only once she has noticed, Alice can't believe she hasn't registered it before. But then, she hadn't thought about this image in years until recently. And sometimes, if you're not looking for something, you simply don't see it.

In the picture, she is younger, of course. Her hair longer, and styled differently. She looks so childish, so fresh-faced, so different to the way she is now. She, Jamie and a few other young people are standing together in some outdoor sports centre, a youth club, probably, funded by Handhold. She isn't the main focus of the picture. She is off to one side, a basketball under her arm, her head thrown back in laughter. The charity's logo cuts across the bottom half of her in the corner; the hashtag along the bottom: #handholdnotahandout.

'Did you never notice,' Isobel asks, 'how carefully worded the denial about Ezra from Handhold was?'

'They said he'd never been a service user,' Alice croaks, still staring at the picture. 'And nor had anyone in his family.'

Isobel shakes her head slowly. 'No, Alice. They said Ezra Jones had never been a service user, and "nor had anyone in his household". That was the line they stuck to.' She pauses. 'But Ezra's household was just him and his mum.'

Alice experiences a feeling of weightlessness, of unreality.

'Jade Jones,' Isobel says carefully, 'was living in hostel accommodation when she came into contact with Handhold.'

Alice feels as if she is no longer tethered to her physical body, as if she is about to float away from it.

'He just wouldn't have,' she manages eventually, through the dryness in her mouth, her thick, clumsy tongue. 'He would never. Not Jamie. Not the Jamie I know.'

'Maybe not the Jamie you know,' Isobel says slowly. 'But where is the Jamie you know now?'

Alice stares again at the image. The image of Jamie. Standing next to a girl in side profile, and smiling at her, their eyes connecting. A girl whose face Alice has never paid any attention to. And who she only now sees is a younger, happier-looking Jade.

'That's the thing, Alice,' Isobel says, tilting her head to one side. 'I'm not so sure your Jamie was ever real.'

LINDA

Since Handhold had been in the picture, the social worker told me, Jade had really calmed down. She'd started attending appointments, she hadn't been in any fights or trouble and had even signed up for a course at college. The charity even let her feature in some glossy ad campaign they were doing, as one of their success stories.

I'm sure they picked her partly because she was pretty. And she did look pretty. She was on posters, on buses, everything. It was like she always wanted: a model at last. A star.

I thought it was great. Of course, I had no idea what was really going on.

I asked Ezra to keep the truth from his sister, just while she was doing so well. *Just give her another year*, I told him. I hoped by then, she'd be in a better place to hear it. I thought we had more time.

I see now that I asked too much of Ezra, that I shouldn't have put all that on him. He was so isolated. They were so tight knit, the two of them, it was sometimes like there was no room for anyone else. Jade less so. She had the odd friend, and boyfriends, of course – it would be Ryan, then another one, then Ryan again. But Ezra, he didn't have many mates at all. Jade was his best friend – in some ways, his only friend. And Ezra had gotten so withdrawn at school. Poor kid didn't really have anyone to talk to. Only Jade. And I'd taken her away from him.

Jade was always going to work it out, I suppose. One day, out of the blue, she said she was coming round for dinner. That she had something to tell us. I thought she was going to say she'd got the place on the college course, and I was so pleased. I made her favourite, toad in the hole.

When we sat down, the three of us, Jade looked different. She'd had her hair done all nice, new clothes, nice gold jewellery– a necklace and a matching little bracelet. Where's Ryan got all that from, I'm thinking. I hoped he hadn't nicked it. I didn't know then, all that I know now. About – what do they call it?

Grooming.

I never got to ask about the necklace, though. Because as soon as he started eating, Jade was staring at Ezra, at the hand he was holding his knife in. He was trying to cut his food, and he couldn't. It happened again, and again, and then in the end, he managed to flip his plate somehow. The whole thing went flying, sausage and batter and gravy and peas and carrots. The plate ended up on the floor, gravy splattered all up the wall.

'What's wrong with you?'

Jade looked at her brother, then me, as if whatever it was, it must be my fault.

'What the hell's going on?' she shouted.

And then Ezra started to cry.

ALICE

Isobel was right. Within days, the papers have got the story. Before Alice has had time to process what she has found out, it is everywhere. All about Jamie and Jade, that he was sacked over a suspected relationship with her, one alleged to have started when she was sixteen. The papers also report that Jade was the sister of the man killed in a 'high-profile burglary' at Alice and Jamie's home months before. And that Jade has now gone missing. That Alice has been arrested. And that Jamie has disappeared.

Reporters come to the house, one by one, the doorbell ringing again and again. One day, Aunt Sarah loses it and snips the cord roughly with a pair of garden shears. For about twenty minutes, the pair of them feel the giddy thrill of minor rebellion. But it makes things worse, because when the doorbell doesn't work, they hammer at the door, and Alice's nerves are set even more on edge.

When Alice leaves the house to take Martha to school, it sometimes looks like there are no photographers, but usually there is one lurking somewhere. There is a constant click, click, click of shutters. Sometimes, she can see them, other times, she can't, but she still hears the clicking noise, sees the flash. Alice notices they mostly come in the morning, when the light is good, and disappear when it fades. But she cannot avoid the school run, and for a while, the pictures make the paper every day, her face looking increasingly lined and grey. Next to the handsome head shots of Jamie, and pictures of Jade from her social media – with her perfect skin, curly lashes – the subtext is obvious. *Maybe she should have looked after herself a bit better*, one commenter writes.

Alice is glad to have Sarah around as she adjusts to her new reality. Not only is she a murder suspect, but a humiliated wife, a tabloid character at the centre of a huge national scandal. Stella gets in touch, asks if she can help. Alice no longer trusts Stella, but such is her desperation for this madness to go away, for things to be normal for Martha, that she allows Stella to help her contact some people called IPSO, who are something to do with press standards, and who send out a notice on Alice's behalf to say she doesn't want to talk, and noting the intrusion and the age of her daughter.

The notice stops some of the journalists. But not all. And it does nothing to deter the weirdest ones, the worst ones, the TikTok detectives who come to film at her house, outside her basement, even in her front garden, until she threatens to call the police. Stella says those people aren't regulated. They don't care. They have no boundaries. The way she says it makes Alice shudder.

Martha watches at the window for reporters before they leave for school. She starts thumb-sucking, chewing at her hands and fingernails. At night, she wakes with a wailing noise that moves from her dreams into her waking: red-faced, confused and ashamed, sheets urine-soaked. In the day, she seems permanently exhausted and tearful. She begs not to have to go to school.

Martha asks constantly when Daddy is coming home, and Alice has no good answer. She tells her daughter it will be OK. In reality, she wonders whether it ever will. It seems almost certain that Alice will lose her job. Without her own income, or Jamie's, how will Alice pay the mortgage, the bills, alone? How will she look after Martha? What will happen to them both?

Jamie has been missing for just over a week when Martha's question changes.

'Mummy,' she asks, hugging her pillow at bedtime, avoiding Alice's gaze. 'Did Daddy kill a lady?'

Alice takes a breath. 'Who told you that?'

'Olivia, at school. She heard her mum say that Daddy had another girlfriend apart from you and he killed her.'

Alice takes a deep breath. 'Of course Daddy didn't do that,' Alice says. But Martha is searching her face, and Alice's cheeks burn.

Having read everything that has been in the newspapers since Jamie went missing, Alice is no longer sure what exact combination of things she believes. She has been forced to accept that there was a relationship between Jamie and Jade. It also seems likely Ezra came to their house to confront Jamie, on the night of the break-in. Ezra was protective of his sister, Linda had told her that. So Alice knows the truth now, about that at least. The truth she wanted so badly, that she thought would bring her peace.

It hasn't. It has brought whatever is the opposite of peace.

Despite using the word 'allegedly' in almost every sentence, it's obvious what the newspapers believe. Jade is dead. Jamie killed her and is 'on the run'. And Alice knows the truth and is helping him somehow.

The coverage is so compelling that Alice actually has to remind herself that she knows this last part to be untrue, so the rest of it is no more likely to be accurate. Alice still can't bring herself to believe that Jamie would have hurt Jade. But it is impossible for her faith in him not to be shaken by the lurid coverage, the way it seems to go on and on and on.

'Mummy?' Martha is tearful. 'If he didn't do it, why can't he just come home?'

Alice touches her face.

'Daddy is scared, I think, about what people are saying. So he has run away somewhere; the police are trying to find him and when they do they will ask him all those questions.'

'And then if he tells the truth they will let him go?'

'I hope so.'

Martha sniffs.

'How do you know Daddy didn't do it?'

Alice combs her daughter's hair lightly with her fingers. 'I don't for sure,' she admits. 'I guess I just love him very much, and I believe in him, and I don't think he would do that and I think there must be another explanation. But the police will get to the bottom of it, Martha, they will find the truth, that's their job.'

She pauses.

'It's really confusing and hard, isn't it, sweetheart?'

Martha nods. Alice watches as something in her face hardens, a little kernel of mistrust taking seed in her heart.

'You can go now, Mummy.' Martha turns over in her bed away from Alice, curled up and facing the wall. Her small, quiet voice breaks Alice's heart.

Alice starts to hate her house, the house she used to love. The home she created for herself, her husband and daughter. She wishes that she and Martha could leave London, get away somewhere. But she is still on bail, and is not allowed to leave the city. She asks Jessica what can be done about this; Jessica says she is 'working on it', but that Alice 'shouldn't hold her breath'. Alice gets the distinct impression Jessica thinks she should consider herself lucky to be at home at all, rather than in custody.

At the end of the second week, the story is at last fading from the front pages in the absence, Alice assumes, of any updates. Most of the journalists and cameras seem to have moved on. Alice decides she has to take the chance to get out, if only for a takeaway coffee. As soon as it occurs to her, the idea feels wildly exciting.

Somehow, she manages to escape without the click of a camera. She had tugged on a cap, pulled her scarf over her nose and mouth and paced down the road. She feels lighter, giddy with freedom.

Alice feels a bit weird being in Farm to Fork during school hours, without a child. She sits right at the back, her cap pulled down, scarf up, mumbles hello awkwardly to the other parents who recognise her from school, or Martha's tennis camp. They are all just as keen to avoid her as she is them by the looks of things; even the ones who are usually friendly, the ones she'd have down as giving her the benefit of the doubt.

She sits at the back and flips open her notebook and laptop – she is not sure if that's really the done thing here, but she feels sure that Sam will let her off.

She combs through her email inbox. She has no contact details for Jamie's family members, but deep down she knows he wouldn't go to them. She tries to think of friends he might have called on. Other than Arlo, she draws a blank. Jamie has never spoken much about friends from before her. He always used to say their little family of three was enough for him. She searches her emails, scrolls her phone address book. But she can't think of anyone. Isobel's words echo in her mind. *Jamie doesn't have any friends.*

Sam comes over, carrying a coffee. Alice looks up in surprise.

'On the house,' he mumbles. 'I'm so sorry for what you're going through, Alice. If there's anything I can do, just say.'

Alice feels her throat thicken at his kindness.

'Thank you,' she manages.

'Martha at school today?'

'She is. Not that it's much fun for her right now.' After their last conversation, Alice had wondered whether Martha would be better off at home, away from the things kids are saying in the playground. But for now, she has decided to persevere with whatever semblance of normal life she can.

'Martha is a lovely girl,' Sam says. 'I'll never forget that picture she drew me.'

Alice looks over to where Sam is gesturing: the wall of kids' artwork behind the play kitchen. Sure enough, there is a picture that is unmistakably Martha's: Alice can tell by the way she has drawn the stripes on the tiger, the shoelaces on the little girl.

'Does she always draw that well? I was amazed. She's what, four?'

'Five,' Alice says vaguely. She is trying to remember if she has ever seen this picture, whether she was here when Martha drew it. She doesn't think she was.

'Did Martha come here with our old nanny?' Alice asks Sam.

'Yeah. Becca, right? She used to bring Martha here all the time. Usually with her friend.'

'Her friend?'

'Yeah. I forget her name. She's got a little girl too, wears that leather jacket – I think she works for a magazine?'

'Stella?' Alice asks. 'Her little girl is Frankie?'

'I'm not sure on that.' Sam's eyes drift to a customer waiting at the counter. He gives Alice an apologetic smile. 'I've just got to...'

'Hang on.'

Sam freezes, startled by Alice's tone. She quickly googles Stella's name.

'Her? Is this who you mean?'

She pulls up the byline picture of Stella, arms folded, eyebrow raised. She spins the laptop round, shows it to Sam. He frowns.

'Yeah, that's her,' he says. 'Why?'

'How many times would you say they'd been in together?'

'Oh.' Sam glances nervously at the waiting customer. 'Lots of times.'

'Lots?'

So Stella and Becca did know each other before the break-in. Alice thinks quickly, tries to work out what this means. If it means anything at all.

'Yeah. I assumed they were mates. I remember, because…' Sam scratches the back of his head, smiles awkwardly. 'I didn't know if I should say anything, really.'

'What? Please – Sam. Tell me.'

Sam throws the tea towel in his hands over one shoulder and sits down awkwardly in the chair opposite.

'Look,' he says. 'I don't want to say anything bad about her, but you said she wasn't working for you any more? The nanny?'

Alice nods encouragingly.

'It's just that I did think, once or twice, that they didn't really seem to be paying much attention to the kids, you know? They seemed very deep in conversation.'

Alice stares at him.

'The kids were on the other side of the cafe, climbing on the soft play and stuff, and I was having to sort of keep an eye on them, but obviously I'm working, and then the other little girl…'

'Frankie?'

'Yeah, she fell off the platform bit at the top and hurt her elbow; we had to ice it. And I did sort of say something to your nanny, you know, about supervising the kids?'

'Do you know what they were talking about?'

'No idea. Sorry. They were sort of apologetic, but I got the sense there was a bit of an atmosphere, like they didn't want to be interrupted?'

'OK,' Alice says, trying to absorb what she is being told, what it might all mean. 'Were they in again after that?'

Sam nods.

'Yeah. There was one other time.' He sighs. 'There was some sort of drama that time, too.'

'Oh?'

'Yeah. No idea what. But they were having this intense conversation – an argument I guess – and then suddenly Becca stood up, and stormed out of the place.'

Alice blinks. This doesn't sound like Becca.

'She didn't pay for her food and drink,' Sam says. 'Just grabbed your daughter and left. And everyone was looking, because the girl – your Martha – she was saying "why are we going, what about my cake" – she was kicking off a bit. But your nanny basically dragged her out of there. She looked furious.'

'When was this? Before the summer holidays?'

'Oh, yeah. Well before the kids broke up for the summer.'

But this makes no sense, Alice thinks. On the day of the break-in, they'd made out they barely knew each other.

'Any idea what they argued about?'

Sam shakes his head. 'No. I held the door open for Becca, but she didn't even say thanks. But as she left, she shouted something back to the magazine woman. Something like, "I'm not doing it."' He pauses, fiddles with the tea towel on his shoulder. 'Does that make any sense to you?'

BECCA
Nine weeks before the break-in

The flat is in a block that looks like a copper-clad shoebox. It feels to Becca like it might blow away in a strong wind. This stretch of the canal is all run-down office buildings and abandoned warehouses. From the windows, you can see the huge industrial curves of the old gas towers.

This is much further down the canal than Becca would ideally want to live, in a neighbourhood she doesn't even know the name of. But it was her decision to come here, to look further afield in search of two bedrooms, reasoning that it might be a better long-term investment.

Caz, as usual, is in raptures. 'I can just really imagine us here,' Caz sighs. 'Can't you?'

Becca cannot, and she is exhausted by pretending.

'Just look how nice the bathroom is!'

Caz is calling out from next door, while Becca is in the kitchen. Becca wants to laugh at how Caz is raising her voice, as if they are at opposite ends of Buckingham Palace, rather than in two poky rooms separated only by plasterboard. The shiny-suited salesman – evasive when Becca asked how many of these units they'd actually sold – keeps nodding at Caz encouragingly, unable to believe his luck.

'And check out the bedrooms!' Caz cries now. 'The windows look right over the water! Oh, wow, there's a heron – that must be a good omen!'

Becca tries, really tries, to see what Caz can see. But the whole place feels like an illusion to her – a conjuring trick, and not a very convincing one. When she runs her fingers over the worktops, she can feel they are only chipboard with a plastic coating that looks like marble. She can feel the flimsiness of the doors on the kitchen cupboards, can hear the echoey thinness of the walls when she drums her fist above the headboard in the main bedroom. And all she can think of is her parents' disappointed faces, when they see how little their money – which felt to them like a fortune – would buy for their daughter in London.

But Caz always loves everything. In the poky, damp Victorian ones, she says: *But look at the floorboards! The ceiling roses! That fireplace! Look how the light comes into the bedroom from between the branches of that tree!* Then, in the crappy, characterless, overpriced new-builds – like this one – she says: *Just look at that new kitchen! The bathroom's so shiny! I love the big windows! The area's not that bad! The ceilings aren't that low!*

And then, finally, she always ends with: *Just think how amazing we could make it.* Becca is starting to feel that talking to Caz about flats is like talking to her parents about God.

Despite this, Becca really is excited about them having a place of their own. Becca has always nursed a secret dread that sooner or later Caz will wake up to how ordinary she is really, how much better she could do for herself. Becca has never loved anyone before Caz, has never shown anyone else the side of herself that they have shared. And this deposit on a flat that her parents somehow have managed to save, and have miraculously given to her, feels like the first real thing she can offer, the first thing that even comes close to what Caz has given to her.

Becca has been trying hard not to think about the complications, trying to hush the voice that tells her that her parents would never be giving her this money if they knew the truth.

Her mother is still asking about coming up to London for the weekend. She keeps sending Becca potential dates and train times. Eventually, Becca will have to say yes to one.

She has thought about asking Caz to play along with the lie she has told her mother, namely that Caz is just a flatmate, that she sleeps in the other room. Becca could buy a cheap bed and put it in the study for the weekend, make it look like a bedroom. But

Caz would go bonkers, as much about the lie as anything else. She should have told Caz the truth from the start, about how her parents are, about how hard she would find it to ever tell them the truth. But she hadn't wanted Caz to know she was really just a backward country bumpkin, with mad religious parents. She'd been desperate to window-dress her life for Caz, to make it as easy and smooth as possible. She was terrified of giving Caz any reason to change her mind. So she'd told Caz her parents were happy with her being with a girl, like Caz's parents were. She sees how stupid this was now, but can't see a way out.

The estate agent gives them his card, and leaves them standing outside the small mini-mart on the ground floor. There is also a coffee place with a sort of bar facing the water at the front.

'You don't like this one either, then?' Caz asks, as the agent walks off. She sounds disappointed, and a bit frustrated. Becca does not want to disappoint and frustrate her.

'It's OK,' she says weakly.

'Oh, good.' Caz cheers up. 'I thought you hated it. Shall we grab a coffee here, get a feel for the area a bit?'

'Sure,' Becca says, although she is not sure there is much more of a feel to be had from this grey stretch of canal water, this post-industrial landscape. She is pretty sure the only people they saw on the canal towpath were selling drugs. But Caz has adopted a look of comical seriousness and focus, clutching the developer's brochures, shoving her knock-off sunglasses into her short, curly hair so she can look more closely at them. She is wearing her simple gold nose ring today, instead of the chunkier pieces from Camden market that she usually favours, and has kept her hair and make-up natural, a slick of nude lipstick, rosy-blushed cheeks.

'Just trying to look like the respectable future homeowners we are,' she'd giggled. Becca thought she looked beautiful.

Caz goes to hunt for a table by the window, and Becca walks up to order. And that's when she sees him.

Jamie is sitting at a table tucked away at the back of the cafe, almost in darkness. He is with a woman – no, a girl. Not Alice. A girl, who is much younger than Alice.

Becca immediately knows that this is not just nothing, that she hasn't got it wrong. She can tell by the look on his face as he talks to this girl. It is obvious even before he moves his hand, creeping under the table towards the girl's bare white leg.

Before Becca can think for even a single second about what she is going to do, Jamie looks up straight at her. His face flickers a little, a tightness in his jaw, and for a moment, it is as if Jamie is a sort of hologram of himself, glitching as his two separate realities collide.

It is Becca's turn. She fluffs her order, forgetting Caz's detailed instructions for how she wants her hot chocolate. She taps the wrong card, which is then declined – it is getting to the end of the month, and she'd had to pay the mortgage adviser £300. Becca digs in her bag, flustered, for the credit card she tries not to use. And then, when she finally looks up, Jamie and the girl have gone.

Becca sets the drinks down awkwardly. Caz's hot chocolate spills, a marshmallow sliding down over one edge like a pink slug.

'This place is so cute,' Caz trills. 'They do a brunch menu on the weekend, look!'

'Oh, yeah,' Becca mumbles, trying to sound enthusiastic, dutifully looking up at the chalk board on the wall and pretending to study the options. The word 'avocado' has, she notices, been misspelled.

'I reckon prices in this area will come up loads in the next few years,' Caz goes on, as she flicks through the agent's brochures.

Becca stirs her coffee, a sick feeling pooling in her stomach as she tries to work out what the right thing to do is, in this scenario. She thinks about the wedding photograph that hangs on the wall of Alice and Jamie's beautiful kitchen. It is a picture Becca has looked at so many times, thinking how perfect the two of them look together. They are younger in the picture, of course, but not much. They'd met later in life than most, and had got married quickly – *the maddest thing I've ever done*, Alice had told Becca once. *But I just knew. Before Jamie, all my relationships had been hard, but with Jamie, meeting him just felt like relief. Like coming home.*

Becca hadn't really understood what Alice was saying, not then. Not until she'd found Caz.

'You OK, Becs?'

Caz has exhausted the brochures and finished slurping her hot chocolate. She is like a puppy, tail wagging, waiting for their next adventure.

Becca shakes the glum expression from her face. 'All good,' she says. 'We should probably get on to the next place.'

'Oh, yeah. What time is it?'

Becca pulls out her phone to check the time. Her heart sinks as she sees a message flash up from Jamie.

We need to talk.

ALICE

When she hears the guest bedroom door close behind Aunt Sarah, Alice feels guiltily washed with relief. She heads to the kitchen, where she can now fill a wine glass unobserved, and take out a notebook and pen.

Her conversation with Sam in Farm to Fork has unsettled her. She tries to work out what Stella's part has been in all this, what she could have wanted from Becca all those times.

From a drawer in the kitchen, she retrieves Stella's business card, the one she found in Becca's holdall, and the key ring she found at Ezra's flat. She places them on the kitchen table next to her notepad and laptop, and decides to go through everything she knows so far.

There is plenty of information online about Stella's professional life. She was a news reporter before she was a features writer, started out at the newspaper, then moved to the magazine. She has been nominated for awards, and won at least one. Most of her stories are about things that touch women: surrogacy, adoption, home-schooling during Covid, the #MeToo movement, male violence.

While Stella's professional footprint is considerable, her social media is more locked-down. Her timeline on X is just retweets of her journalism, her biography has only her job title and the professional head shot she uses at the top of her articles. Her Instagram is private, so Alice is unable to view her friends, or contacts. But her profile picture is different, at least. Alice zooms in.

This photo is a classic summer holiday snap, light-filled, with a glorious vista of vineyards behind where Stella is standing – it looks like Italy, maybe, or France. Stella is tanned, wearing a strappy summer dress, holding a straw hat in one hand and laughing into the camera, as if whoever took the picture has just said something funny.

Alice studies the picture for a few minutes. She is sure there is something about this picture that is familiar, but the pieces won't connect in her brain.

What has Stella told Alice about her personal life? Not much. Stella and Frankie had lived in Leyton, before they moved here. She now lives by the canal in an apartment. Stella is close to her sister – Alice is less sure about parents, or other siblings. She has an ex-husband, Hugo, surname Glass, who was 'extremely unfaithful'.

Glass. That's Stella's married name. But what was her name before she married? Alice doesn't know. But maybe if she could find that out, the Stella from before might still be on the Internet somewhere. An old Facebook profile, perhaps. Something more revealing than what Alice has been able to find.

How did you find out that sort of thing about a person? Alice realises that what little she knows about this, she knows from Stella. You can get birth, marriage and death certificates online, for a few pounds. Isn't that what she said?

She tries to find Stella's marriage certificate but has no luck – she guesses they could have married anywhere. She looks for a birth certificate for Frankie Glass, but there are no results in the first few London boroughs she tries. She tries Frances. Nothing. Finally, Francesca. And there is a match. One, born in 2017. The dates would fit.

Hungrily, Alice taps in her card details, pays the necessary £10, plus a £3 processing fee. Clicks on the box to have it sent to her as a PDF file. Instantly, a notification pops up.

She clicks through, reads the details on the Birth Certificate.

Francesca Amelie Glass, born March 2017, at Whipps Cross Hospital, East London. Father is listed as Hugo Glass. Mother Stella Glass, born in Hampshire. Mother's maiden name: Layward.

It takes her another moment to make the connection. But when she loads up the article she found about Clara, she realises there is no real doubt.

She clicks from the photograph of Clara Layward, standing in front of a Christmas tree with her mother, to Stella's Instagram picture from a few years back. The line of their smiles, the rise of their cheeks.

Clara was Stella's sister. The sister she'd been so close to as a child; the sister she'd had a secret language with, whole imaginative worlds that belonged only to them. The sister who had made Stella long for Frankie to have a sister too.

Stella's adored sister was gone. Disappeared, presumed dead, in Africa. Volunteering, on Jamie's watch.

Before she can think properly about what it all means, Alice hears footsteps on the stairs. She looks up and sees Martha in her too-short pyjamas, her hair messy, her feet bare.

'I had a bad dream, Mummy.'

Alice sees the wet patch on her pyjamas.

'Oh, love. Come here.'

Alice removes her pyjamas, cleans her up and bundles her into a blanket on the kitchen sofa. She goes upstairs, changes the sheets and shoves the wet ones into the wash with the mattress protector. There are no clean pyjamas in Martha's wardrobe – in fact, her room is a tip. Alice feels a sting of shame. She plucks an abandoned pair from the bedroom floor.

Downstairs, she dresses Martha in the pyjamas, then holds her daughter on her lap like a baby, except her legs are so long now that it feels awkward, skinny ankles sticking out of her pyjama cuffs, her hair tickling Alice's face. Then abruptly Martha sits up, noticing something. She walks over to the table, where the key ring is. Alice realises she never actually told Martha she'd found it.

'I told you I'd find your key ring, love,' she says.

'This isn't the key ring I made for you.' Martha holds it up for her mother, as if this should be obvious.

Alice blinks. 'Yes, it is,' she says stupidly.

'Mum!' Martha is annoyed. 'My one wasn't like this! I did rainbow colours on the front *and* the back, and it was *neat*, remember?' She turns the key ring over, gives a sniff of distaste. 'Why have you got Frankie's one here?'

Alice stares at her daughter, pushes the hair from her face. 'What do you mean, Frankie's one?'

'She copied me,' Martha says. 'She always copies me at art club, I *told* you that. Because I have good ideas. It's *so* annoying. I said mine was for my mum, so she said hers was for her mum too. Then she saw I was doing mine like a rainbow, and she did hers exactly the same, except hers is all messy, look. And I told her she was copying all my ideas, and she was a copycat, and then she got embarrassed, and that's why she did plain with glitter on the other side, so hers would be different.'

Alice turns the key ring over in her hand, sees the glitter on the other side.

'This really isn't yours, Martha?'

Martha gives an emphatic shake of the head. 'No way.'

Alice looks into her open face and knows that she is telling the truth.

Martha picks up the key ring from Alice's hand, and looks at Alice. 'Why is it here, Mummy?' she asks. 'Did Frankie's mummy lose hers, too?'

ALICE

The rain starts up as Alice crosses the road from the police station. She has mistimed it; a cyclist swerves, a bus driver sounds his horn. Alice bows her head, scuttles towards the other pavement, makes her way up Church Street.

When Alice had said she was reporting for bail, the woman at the police station counter had almost laughed. She'd pushed the form under the perspex screen for Alice to sign, then blandly recited the same four questions. *Are you Alice Rathbone. Are you still residing at the agreed address. Are you refraining from contact with any of the individuals named on the form. Do you understand the conditions of your bail, the violation of which will likely lead to your arrest and imprisonment.* Yes, yes, yes, yes.

Dodging through rain-soaked office workers, prams with their waterproof covers on, Alice tries to clear her head, think about what she found out last night. Stella's adored sister was Clara – Clara Layward, the girl who died in Africa, on Jamie's watch. It must have been Stella, Alice thinks, who contacted Jamie's charity, trying to make allegations about his time there. She must despise Jamie, want to punish him for her sister's death. But she'd failed, hadn't she? The article had never been published. So maybe Stella hadn't given up. And had looked for another way to get Jamie punished.

Is that how Becca fits in? Alice wonders. In the weeks before the break-in, Sam had seen Stella harassing her at the cafe, trying to get her to do something she wasn't comfortable with. And she must have been in contact with Ezra and his family too – which is how the key ring her daughter made for her had ended up at their flat. So had Stella found out about the affair Jamie was having with Jade, somehow, months before Alice had? But how? Had Becca told Stella? Had Becca *known*?

What doesn't make sense, Alice thinks, is why Stella would seek out Alice's friendship, if she actively hated Jamie so much. But then, after a beat, Alice sees that it makes perfect sense. Stella had never really wanted to be her friend at all. Getting close to Alice – getting into her house all those times – it hadn't been about friendship. It had been about encroachment. Gathering information on them. Is all this why Stella moved to Hackney, and moved Frankie into the same school as Martha? Had it all been part of a bigger plan, to dig into Jamie's life? Alice is stunned by the audacity of it. And it had worked, hadn't it? Stella had found Jade. Had she gone to try and get Jade to sell her story? Is that how the key ring had ended up at the flat?

How ironic, Alice thinks, that she had actually asked Stella to investigate Ezra, to try and find out what had linked him to her and Jamie. Stella's key ring had been at Ezra's *before* that. Which meant Stella must have had contact with Ezra's family before Alice asked her to look into them for her.

Stella hadn't needed to investigate the connection between Ezra and Jamie. Stella had already *known* what that connection was. Long before Alice had.

What was still a mystery, though, was *when* had Stella been to Ezra's flat – and *why*. Had she met Ezra, spoken to him, before the day of the break-in? Was it Stella who had alerted Ezra to what was going on between Jamie and the sister he was so protective of, and inadvertently brought him, raging, to Alice's door? But even that wouldn't explain what Stella had been doing with Becca all those times at Farm to Fork. Or why Becca had that photograph of Jamie and Jade in her holdall. How did Becca fit into all this?

Looking back, Alice is staggered by the extent of Stella's duplicity. She'd acted her part so convincingly – pretending to share everything she knew with Alice, showing her all those documents and cuttings. But now that Alice really thinks about it,

Stella hadn't given Alice any more information about Ezra than what she'd already found for herself. A few news cuttings. The pictures of him as a kid, playing football. And Ezra's birth certificate, which had named his mother as Linda, and father as a John Jones.

Alice stops suddenly. A man behind tuts at her, and so she takes shelter under a shop awning, and thinks. There had been a document that she'd wanted to look at, hadn't there? And Stella had stopped her, tidied it into a pile so she couldn't look. That's right – it was John's death certificate. Why wouldn't Stella have wanted Alice to see that?

Alice looks at her watch, then out at the rain. If she leaves now, she can just make it before it's time to collect Martha.

The records room at Hackney Town Hall is warm and sleepy, a thick smell of paper and dust in the air. Alice is given access to an ancient blocky computer and instructions on how to search. Her heart sinks as she realises that there are dozens and dozens of death certificates with the name John Jones. Of course there are – how stupid to have thought this would be easy with such a common name.

Eventually, though, she gets the hang of the computer system, and realises she can filter it by his middle name – which she remembers was Ezra, from the birth certificate – and year of death, which Alice knows was when Ezra and Jade were fourteen. Eventually, she is left with one entry. The death of a John Ezra Jones in 2019.

She pays another £10 plus the processing fee, and the PDF appears in her inbox. She recognises it from Stella's pile of things – black-bordered, official.

She scrolls down to cause of death, and squints, reads it over again. So this is what Stella was hiding from her. The cause of death does not say heart attack, or cardiac disease, as Stella told her. It says something else entirely.

LINDA

I'm back in hospital. Started getting these fevers. All part of it, apparently. But I needed to be hooked on to a drip for antibiotics. Another one for pain relief.

For the first time in days, I feel well enough to type. But now that same bloody nurse is here again. Says one of the other patients is complaining, about my tapping away.

I know exactly which one. Graham, that cancerous old misery-guts on the other side of my curtain.

'Is she typing or playing the bladdy organ?' I heard him muttering to her earlier. I hear him complaining about the food, too. I don't think he's eating much. I don't think it's looking too good for Graham. His eyes have gone all purplish the last couple of days, his cheeks sunken. I recognise those purplish eyes from my John.

John was in his fifties when the first signs came. He kept stumbling on steps, dropping things. I just joked that it was old age, he was getting doddery. But deep down, I knew it wasn't right for a man his age. And then, he found he couldn't write, that he was forgetting things, appointments, messages. Of course, you think, maybe Parkinson's, maybe dementia.

I'd never even heard of Huntington's.

When they told us, I couldn't process what the doctor was saying. A disease that would eat his brain, cell by cell, so that in the end he would lose everything. His control of his body, his mind, his muscles. And his personality, too. That would be replaced, by something else. And there was no cure, no stopping it.

They call it the devil's disease. It would take everything there was of him. Paranoia, violence, shadows. No hope. No future.

And then the doctor asked us: 'Do you have any children?'

As I write this, I know I don't have long left. They've told me as much already. Stage four liver cancer – it ain't messing around. There is talk of *making me comfortable*. I know what that means. They keep telling me to rest, asking if I want them to put my laptop away, somewhere safe. But I won't let them. I need to get this all down before it's too late.

It's a fifty-fifty coin toss, if you're a child of Huntington's disease. Heads you escape. Tails you don't. Of every two children, one will get it.

John and I agreed we'd tell Jade and Ezra when they were older, and give them the choice, if they wanted to be tested. Things will be different then, I told myself. There'll be a cure.

After I lost John, it was like I was in a fog. I couldn't see through it a lot of the time. I should have seen sooner, what was happening to Ezra.

When he gave up his football, I thought maybe it was normal teenage boy stuff, you know – him starting to be alone in his room a lot, interested in girls, things on the Internet. There were conversations I didn't know how to have with a teenage boy. John would have known what to say, but I didn't. He was getting so tall, towering above me already. I didn't know that inside he was still just my scared little boy.

I wondered if he was a bit depressed, about his dad. I asked about counselling, but the GP said there was a long waiting list, and Ezra insisted he didn't want it. Meanwhile, Jade's antics were taking up most of my time. She was the one who kept me up at night, worried sick. Not Ezra. He was my good boy.

When the school called me in I assumed it was Jade, as it usually was – the social was involved with her by then, and it was constant: the meetings, the updates, the dreaded phone calls. But this time, it was different. They wanted to talk about Ezra.

I knew Ezra's grades had slipped a bit, but it was worse than that, they said. He was on course to fail all his GCSEs. I was shocked. It's not that he was ever big into school, but he'd always done OK.

The teacher had all his exercise books on the desk, while we were talking. I hadn't kept an eye on his homework, on what he was doing, not properly. So I looked in his English book – when I opened it up, I nearly dropped it. His handwriting had gone like a five-year-old's.

And my first thought was: John's writing went like that.

When we got home, Ezra looked at me like he was in trouble.

'Why did you give up football?' My voice was shaking as I asked it.

Ezra burst into tears. He wiped his face with his sleeve, like when he was littler. And then it all came out.

'I can't balance, Mum,' he said. 'I keep falling over.' He'd quit before he was taken off the team.

The falling over, the clumsiness, the depression. It was all the same.

'I've got what Dad had,' he said. 'Haven't I, Mum?' That wobble in his voice. I'll never forget it.

It was rare, the doctor said, for it to start so young, but no, there was no cure as such. Something like an apology in her voice. Ezra asked the doctor how long he was going to live. She paused. An average of ten years, she said, from diagnosis.

I could see Ezra adding it up in his head. His mind already working slower, the disease stopping his eyes from moving properly. He already had to move his head if he wanted to look at something.

He was sixteen years old.

The night, the dinner with the toad in the hole, when Jade found out. The horror of it, dawning on her face. I tried to be gentle with her. But there is no gentle way with something like that.

Jade stood up, stepped away from the table, away from the gravy stain on the wall. She was white, and shaking head to toe.

At first I thought she was worried for her brother. But no, Jade wasn't like that. And then I realised her hand was on her stomach.

ALICE

Alice and Martha are under a blanket on the sofa, watching *The Polar Express*. Alice has pulled the curtains closed against the blackness of the windows. On the way home from school, the pavements had been slippery, and even at half past three it had already felt like the darkness was coming.

Jamie has been gone for three weeks. In the same amount of time, Alice will have to face Christmas without him. The thought of her and Martha opening presents alone on Christmas Day is so sad and wrong that Alice cannot bear to imagine it. And how is she supposed to afford presents? In the absence of Jamie's salary, their last mortgage payment has bounced, and yesterday, when she'd gone to buy food in Sainsbury's, two of her cards had been declined.

Aunt Sarah has gone out for dinner with a friend in central London. Alice has made her and Martha pizza and hot chocolate, and prays silently that they can have a nice, calm couple of hours. Lately, Martha has been so up and down, bursting into tears about small things – the wrong water bottle, the need to wear a winter coat – shouting at Alice that she hates her. But at night she crawls into bed wordlessly, next to her. In the past, she has pushed back against this habit, but now Martha's warm presence next to her is a comfort.

As Martha snuggles up to her on the sofa, Alice tries to avoid the temptation to reach for her phone. All day, she has been googling Huntington's disease and connecting the symptoms she is learning about to her memories of Ezra during the break-in. His stumbling gait. The slur of his words. The way he gripped and regripped the knife.

Alice had previously recruited all these details to fit the picture she'd made in her mind: an out-of-control, drunken criminal. An addict, a waster. A character, rather than a person. But Ezra had been none of those things. He'd been sick and desperate. He'd seen his father get sick and die and known, she guesses, that he was headed for the same. Alice had read that people with Huntington's sometimes died alone in institutions, because their relatives were unable to cope with the changes brought by the disease, how it made people psychotic, pacing, aggressive, unpredictable. Alice can imagine a person feeling they had nothing to lose.

There is a knock on the door. Alice flinches. Martha looks up at her longingly.

'Is that Daddy?' she asks, in a quiet voice that tells Alice she knows deep down, it isn't, and that makes Alice's heart ache.

'I don't think so,' she says softly. 'I'll just see who it is. It might be Aunt Sarah.'

But Aunt Sarah has her key, and is not the sort of person who forgets it.

Alice opens the door, and a rush of cold air enters the hallway. Two young-looking uniformed officers stand on her doorstep, radios crackling. The man on the top front step, filling the doorway; the female officer side on, a few steps down, as if she's already getting ready to leave. A police car is parked just beyond Alice's bike shed, the honeysuckle plants that grow on her trellis.

Alice's first thought is the same one she keeps having in recent days, that will not leave her alone, in the small hours of the night.

'Is it Jamie?' she asks. 'Is my husband dead?' Alice has had this feeling in recent days, this sense that Jamie is gone. It is a cold, set sort of dread, creeping through her like rising damp.

'Mrs Rathbone,' the male officer says. 'I need you to come to the station, please. There's been a development.'

'What development?'

'We can discuss that at the station.'

'You seriously aren't going to tell me if my husband is dead?'

Alice's heart is pounding.

'I can't come now,' she says when he doesn't reply, 'I'm here on my own, with my daughter.'

'Is there anyone who could look after her? A neighbour, perhaps?' The male officer looks at her blankly. He must still be in his early twenties – there is a smattering of acne across his chin.

'A neighbour?'

Alice suddenly feels uncontrollably angry with this man, this youth. Who has no idea, no *clue*, of what it is to be a mother, of what it is like trying to protect your precious child from a potentially life-altering trauma, a trauma that still – fairly or unfairly – feels like it is really nothing to do with Alice, but has come for her, and more importantly, her child, nonetheless.

'My daughter is five years old,' Alice says. 'Her father is missing. She is extremely unsettled. She needs me. I am not leaving her with a neighbour.'

The police officers exchange a look.

'If a family solution can't be found,' the female officer says, 'then it would usually be a case of us looking into a temporary foster placement.' But as she says it, Alice watches her take in the details of Alice's hallway – the book bag and Boden winter coat hanging from a hook, the scooter leaning on one side, the neat rack of child and adult shoes and wellies – and hears her resolve waver.

'My aunt will be able to look after my daughter once she returns home,' Alice says icily. 'She's gone out for dinner. I'll call her and ask her to return, but you might have to wait half an hour or so. She is in central London.'

The male officer hesitates, then pulls his radio up from his jacket lapel to his mouth and starts to mutter into it. Alice stands in the hallway, resenting the intrusion more with every minute that the freezing air is permitted to stream into her house.

'OK,' he nods at her, when he is finished. 'We'll wait inside if that's all right.'

'No,' Alice says, quickly. Then, with an effort, she resets her tone. 'If you don't mind,' she manages, 'I'd prefer if you would wait in the car.'

She hears a sound behind her.

'Mummy?'

Martha is in the hallway.

'It's all right, darling. Go back and watch TV.'

'No.' Martha runs over to Alice, burying her face in her trousers. Alice glances at the female officer, pleadingly.

'Look,' she says. 'You're parked right there. I'm not some sort of flight risk. I am right here looking after my daughter. I would not leave her on her own. I will come with you as soon as my aunt is here.'

The female officer looks down at Martha, then back at Alice, and gives a small, almost imperceptible nod.

Alice closes the door, and swallows the lump in her throat as she crouches down to hug her daughter close.

'I'm going to call a lady who has been helping me,' she says. 'Can you stay here for me? The film's not too scary? You can watch something else.'

'It's OK. I've seen it before,' Martha says bravely, even though Alice knows it's getting to the part that Martha doesn't like. The strange men on the roof of the carriage; the train malfunctioning, careering off the tracks onto the thin ice of a glacier.

Once she has settled Martha on the sofa, Alice looks into the hallway mirror and uses her fingers to correct the smudges of mascara, cool the pink of her cheeks. Then she walks down into her kitchen. Her hand hovers over the light switch, but then she looks through the front basement window at the parked police car, and decides against it. She would rather not allow them to see her.

Instead, she stays in the blue darkness while she messages Aunt Sarah, who comes back straight away with 'OK. Coming now.'

She finds Jessica's mobile number. Jessica picks up within three rings, sounding only slightly throatier than usual.

'Alice, hi. I was about to call. Have you had a visit from our friends in uniform?'

'They just turned up at the house. They say they want me to come to the station. They tried to make me leave Martha with a neighbour but they've agreed to wait for my aunt...'

'Good. Glad they're being sensible.'

'What's happening, Jessica?' Alice feels the thickness in her throat again. 'They won't tell me if Jamie's dead or not.'

'Hang on, Alice. Keep calm. I'll meet you at the station – I'll be there within the hour – we can talk about it then. Don't worry. They'll want to ask you all the same stuff again, that's all. You just tell them what you told them before. Remember – polite, helpful. If you don't remember, say that. Don't speculate. Especially not about your husband.'

Alice notes the curl of distaste in her voice, whenever she refers to Jamie.

'OK,' Alice says. 'But why are they here, Jessica? What's the development?'

Alice hears the muffled voice of Jessica, talking to one of her sons. *Get yourself a snack, for God's sake*, she says. *You know where the kitchen is. This isn't room service, Theo.*

'Sorry about that,' says Jessica wryly. She shuffles some papers, clears her throat. 'I'll find out more when we get there. But no, I don't think there's anything new on Jamie. I think this is about Jade.'

'Jade?'

'Yeah. It sounds like they've found a body.'

STELLA

Stella watches from her window as they pull a checked bag out of the canal. It is wrapped in a sort of dripping sling, attached to the big hook of a cherry picker on the banks. Weeds and other things slide off the thing in the sling; it rocks a little in the wind. For a strange moment, the sling reminds Stella of the one the midwife used to come and weigh Frankie when she was a newborn.

There are police watching from the side of the canal. Plainclothes, but they have a look about them – mostly blokes in half-zip woolly things under navy puffer jackets, folded arms, expressions grim. A few no-nonsense, ponytailed women, dressed just like the men. A gaggle of teenagers, one on a bike, are watching too, from behind the police tape.

The forensics people stand in the water, in waders and white suits. More of them now something has been found. They comb the banks, although what they are looking for, Stella has no idea. Finally, there are the divers, slick black stick-men in a little boat. The divers have been here for days. They are packing up now, peeling wetsuits off to their waists and pulling on long-sleeved tops, letting the rest of them take it from here.

The presence of the divers has been making her nervous, even though the phone is not here, is nowhere near here. And even if it was, she reminds herself, they are not looking for a phone.

What will she say, she wonders, if she ever has to account for herself? She could say, she supposes, with all honesty, that she never intended it to turn out this way. No one ever wants anyone to end up dead – that's the official line, isn't it? Even though,

Stella suspects, the truth is that most of us have wanted exactly that at some time or other, whether we are willing to admit it or not. That the world would be a better, more harmonious place, if some people simply did not exist. The dictator who nods assent to guns and gas. The abusive father who drove your mother to an early grave. The smirking dealer at the gates of your child's school. Who among us can honestly say they have never longed to point a godlike finger and smite some people from the face of the earth?

Stella only ever hoped for something painless – or if not painless, at least quick. A random motorway crash, a stroke, a lightning strike. What they used to call an act of God. That would have been her preference. Something sharp and clean.

Stella sips her coffee and wonders what will happen next. She fantasises about taking Frankie somewhere far away, where nobody knows who they are. But it would look worse if she left suddenly. She knows that. Besides, no one is looking at her, are they? The police haven't asked her any questions about Ezra since it happened. Her statement was made, and accepted. Stella is nothing more than a minor footnote in a case that has closed.

But Stella wants it finished, this thing that she has started. The bag is on the banks of the canal now. A detective gestures to a colleague, and something is carried over. Moments later a white tent is erected around it. Stella shivers, and turns away.

Her mistake, perhaps, was getting anyone else involved.

Stella should have learned by now that she can't rely on other people. She must do what needs to be done herself.

LINDA

Towards the end, I'd look at John and wonder whether it could really be him. The handsome man I'd married. Watching him shuffle, his swollen tongue hanging out, his head jerking all the time. The skin all purplish-brown and speckled around his eyes.

Then, one day, I realised it really wasn't him any more. The John I'd known was gone. All the good parts of him had faded, like colours in the wash.

Ezra stayed away from him. He hated his moods, his shouting. Jade said it wasn't his fault, that he was still Dad, just ill. He was better with her. She could short-circuit him sometimes, bring him back to himself. But with me and Ezra, it was like we were the enemy.

One morning, John shouted at Ezra, accused him of making noise, when he wasn't, and of stealing his money, which didn't even make sense – he was so paranoid by then. He snapped at our boy like a dog, a line of drool hanging from his mouth. Ezra ended up in tears, packing his school bag. His dad a stranger to him.

I wiped Ezra's tears, and my own. I told him to be a brave boy. But as I watched him walk out into the cold, covering his face with his sleeve, so his mates at the bus stop wouldn't see he'd been crying, something hardened around my heart.

John had his tablets with his lunch. He'd argue about taking them, and struggled now to swallow, so I'd got good at working out how to mix them into his food. I'd worked out which things were best to disguise the flavour – meaty stews, shepherd's pies, things like that. John liked his food still. The only time he'd behave was when I was feeding him. Porridge and meat and gravy and mashed potato slipping down his chin. I had to put him in a bib like a baby, wipe him down after, my stomach rolling with disgust.

It didn't feel like a big thing, really, when I was doing it. I mixed in his pills as usual, and I just found myself just adding more, and more. Sleeping tablets, strong ones they don't let you have any more. The muscle relaxants that helped with his chorea, the jerky movements Huntington's people get. I kept going, adding and mixing. And then I fed it to him, spoonful after spoonful until the whole bowl was gone.

After, it felt important to keep my hands occupied, to stop the shaking. I cleaned and polished the kitchen until it shone. I even got down on my hands and knees, cleaned all the skirting boards, then started on the windows, rubbing and rubbing until there were no streaks. Surely, I thought, it won't be much longer.

I thought it would be a good death for him, a calm death. I thought he would just fall asleep and not wake up. But something started happening. He started fitting in his chair, his eyes rolling back into his head, his whole body jerking and shuddering, like he was malfunctioning.

I couldn't call an ambulance. They'd know it was me. The pills were right there, on the side. His spine was jerking now, his mouth foaming. I panicked.

I put my spray and cleaning cloth down, and I picked up a cushion.

It was easier once I couldn't see his face. I don't remember him really resisting. Just jerking and twitching, until the jerks got less, and finally stopped. I kept pushing longer than I needed to. I only stopped when I realised my hands had gone stiff and numb, my jaw sore from clenching my teeth. I had sweat under my armpits, and on my forehead – my fringe was all stuck to my skin. The house still smelled of glass cleaner, the skin on my hands sore with it.

Slowly, I lessened my grip on the pillow, and tucked it down where it usually went, to the side of his head. John had no need of it now. He was gone.

And only then did I look up, and see her there in the doorway, in her school uniform, her lips parted. I don't know how long exactly she'd been there, how much of it she'd seen. But I knew she'd seen enough.

I wondered at first if she was going to tell someone. Go to the police. But she never did. She just sat there, looking at me, like her father's ghost, all through the funeral, the will, and all the rainy days afterward. And she never forgave me, and she never forgot.

That moment at the dinner, her hand on her belly, I knew I'd never get her back. Jade hated lies, and in her mind, I'd lied to her, and to everyone. About her Dad, about how he died. About Ezra being sick too. About the chance that she might have the same thing, and that if she did, she could pass it on to her own child.

For weeks, Jade ignored my calls. Ezra was cagey about whether they were in touch. But he insisted he didn't know what she was planning to do about the baby, or even if she and Ryan were still together.

I'm not proud to say, but I thought she should get rid of it, and I said so, God help me, even though that's against everything I was raised to believe. Jade acted grown up, but she was only a kid. Unemployed, with no qualifications, living in a hostel – she'd have been mad to have a child. Even without the complication of Huntington's.

We didn't know then if she was a carrier – it was fifty-fifty. If she wasn't, her baby would be safe too, but if she was, her baby also had a fifty-fifty chance of getting it. And I knew that Ezra was going to get worse. I knew I couldn't look after him and her, and her baby as well, even if she wanted to move back in with me.

I tried to talk to her once about it, told her about genetic counselling. I even got her a booklet on it from the hospital. She just crumpled it up and threw it in my face. Then she went mad, screaming at me, saying I'd ruined her life, and that she would never forgive me for not telling her the truth about Ezra.

She told me the baby's father loved her, that he would take care of her.

'Hang on. What do you mean, the baby's father?' I said. 'Isn't Ryan the dad?'

ALICE

Alice is in the police station for more than twelve hours overnight. They keep asking her the same questions as before. And asking her, again and again, where Jamie is. She keeps telling them she doesn't know – don't they think she wants to know, too? When she asked about the body, they just ignored her. Alice doesn't know what is coming next. She is frightened.

Alice would badly like to go home now, but Jessica is insisting on a 'debrief' at the chain coffee place across the road. The air is thick with central heating and the sickly scent of cinnamon-spiced drinks; there are early Christmas decorations over the counter, little star-shaped lights, the sort of thing Martha would love. Alice should get some lights up in the house, make an effort for Martha. But how can she, when she doesn't know if she will even be around at Christmas? Or if Jamie will be. Where Jamie is. If he is even alive.

Alice supposes it is past nine in the morning. She won't see Martha before school, even if she goes home now.

Jessica sits down, places a coffee and a pastry in front of Alice.

'Well, don't look like that,' Jessica says. 'It wasn't so bad.'

Alice blinks at her. What could possibly be worse than being suspected of murder?

'I don't think they have any real evidence you killed her,' Jessica continues brightly.

'Because I didn't,' Alice points out.

'Yes, yes. Exactly.' Jessica taps at something on her phone, distracted. Alice tries to take deep breaths.

'Do they definitely think that Jade... that she was...?'

'What? Murdered?' Jessica says the word loud enough for the people on the next table to look over.

'Of course she was murdered, Alice. They found her body in a weighted bag at the bottom of the Regent's Canal.'

Alice opens her mouth, then closes it again. She thinks of Jade, the last time she saw her, just a couple of months ago. Baby Taylor flopped over her shoulder, so tiny and helpless.

'They've got the post-mortem now. Looks like someone slammed her head against the wall, then strangled her. She only weighed about 53 kilos. It wouldn't have taken much. Then they zipped her into some sort of laundry bag, and chucked her in the canal.'

Alice looks up. 'A laundry bag?'

'Yeah, one of those big checked ones. They're trying to trace where it came from.'

Alice stares at her in horror.

'That was from my attic,' she blurts.

'What?'

'The bag. I took her some baby clothes over in it.'

Jessica buries her head in her hands. 'Right,' she says. 'Brilliant.' She sits up, pulls out her notebook, makes a scribbled note.

'Sorry,' Alice whispers.

'Eat your pain aux raisins,' Jessica mutters back. She nudges the plate towards Alice, rips open a sachet of sugar and tips it into her cappuccino. The granules sink slowly, disturbing the star shape on the surface.

Alice stares at the pastry she didn't ask for. She was starving a minute ago. Now, she doesn't think she could eat a single bite without vomiting.

'Did you know that Ezra had Huntington's disease?'

'Yes,' Jessica says casually. 'Although I can't remember when I found out. Why?'

Alice stares at her. 'But... Why didn't the police tell everyone that? Why didn't they tell me? Why didn't you tell me?'

Jessica considers this. 'I didn't realise we hadn't discussed it, to be honest. But it wasn't material to your case. His behaviour led to your reasonable assumption was that he was violent and unpredictable, and your reasonable action in stopping him from entering the room where your child was. It wasn't relevant whether that behaviour was due to drugs and alcohol – as we first thought – or illness or any other reason.'

Alice bites her lip. How clear, how unemotional Jessica manages to be about this.

'The papers never found out about his illness, either,' Alice mutters. 'They always seem to find out everything.'

'Not stuff like this,' Jessica says. 'Someone's private medical information would never normally be released unless it was firmly in the public interest. At the inquest, something like that would come out, but not necessarily while an investigation was active. I can certainly see why they'd decide the public interest just wasn't there.'

'Why not?'

'Well, because they were dealing with a family affected by a serious and stigmatising genetic condition. They'll have been thinking of the surviving sibling – Jade – who was young and potentially affected by the same condition. By releasing Ezra's private medical information, they could have compromised hers.'

Alice can see this. She thinks again about poor Jade. How much she'd been through. And then her battered body, dumped in the freezing canal. Who could have done such a thing?

'What about Ryan?' Alice asks. 'Are the police not looking at him?'

Ryan had been on TV the day before the body was found, tracksuit-clad, sitting at a little table between two police officers, making a tearful appeal to the cameras. *If anyone has any information, please, I'm begging you*, he'd managed before sobbing into his elbow. It had seemed heartfelt, but surely the police had their suspicions.

'Ryan was ruled out early, I believe,' Jessica says archly. 'Due to the unimprovable alibi of having been in police custody on the night in question.'

'Oh.'

'Yes. Drunken disorder, I believe.'

Alice realises Jessica is looking at her with something like sympathy. She sighs, and stares at Alice as if she is waiting for something.

'What?'

Jessica sighs. 'Alice,' she says, 'you know that the person they are looking for is Jamie, don't you?'

Alice frowns, shaking her head. 'No – no. Ryan is the boyfriend. He's the baby's father. Jade told me he was.' Alice isn't 100 per cent sure this is true, now she thinks about it, but it was implied, wasn't it? 'Jamie is nothing to do with this, Jessica, I'm sure of it. There must be some... some other...'

Jessica sighs, tilts her head to one side.

'Alice,' she says. 'Jamie is not *nothing to do with this*. Jamie is the father of Jade's baby. It's been confirmed by a DNA test.'

When she thinks about it later, Alice wonders why this feels like such a shock. She thinks of Jade telling her to pick Taylor up, asking if she reminded her of Martha. And she had. It hadn't just been the clothes. Jade had been showing Alice the truth and Alice hadn't seen it, even when it was right in front of her eyes.

'You need to help yourself now, Alice,' Jessica says slowly.

'But how?'

'By helping the police find Jamie.'

Alice stares at her.

'I don't know where he is! And Jessica – I know Jamie did not do this. Whatever else he has done. He could never have done that to Jade. He isn't capable of it.'

'I'm afraid it is looking increasingly likely that he is,' Jessica says bluntly. 'Which means that if you hear anything from him, Alice, anything at all, you need to tell the police *immediately*. Do you understand?'

'I understand,' Alice says weakly.

They sit in silence for a moment.

'What is going to happen to Taylor?'

'The baby?' Jessica dabs her mouth with a paper napkin. 'Not clear. Jade's mother is a no-go – she's got stage four cancer, apparently, had just been readmitted to hospital before Jade was attacked. Close to the end, I'm told. So, foster care for the baby, probably. Then adopted.'

Alice thinks of Taylor asleep in Jade's arms, unaware of the darkness that was awaiting her life, of the fault that could be hiding in her genes. What will foster care be like for a baby? Alice wonders. It's the sort of thing she would ask Jamie normally, except now, of course, she can't.

Jessica sees the look on Alice's face, and softens.

'The baby will be OK,' she says. 'She won't remember any of this. Adopters queue up for little babies. She'll be all right.'

For a fleeting moment, Alice entertains a fantasy of taking Taylor home herself, when all this is over. After all, she is Jamie's baby. Not Alice's, but maybe that wouldn't matter. Alice imagines taking her home all wrapped in the pink pompom blanket, a sister at last for Martha. Alice wonders whether she is losing her grip on reality.

'Alice, focus on what's important, please.' Jessica is stern now. Alice jerks her head back to face her.

'If you hear from Jamie – any contact from him whatsoever – you need to call the police *immediately*. And then call me. Have you got that?'

'Yes,' Alice says more firmly this time. 'I promise.'

When Jessica leaves, Alice messages Aunt Sarah to let her know she is out. She checks the time. It's hours until she needs to collect Martha.

She thinks again about what Jessica said.

Jade's mother readmitted to hospital. Stage four cancer. Close to the end, I'm told.

Alice picks up her things. She knows where she needs to go.

BECCA
Nine weeks before the break-in

Becca opens the door quietly, closes it softly behind her. Jamie is sitting on his chair, tapping away at something.

'Becca, come in. Here, take a seat.'

Becca sits down on the sofa in the study carefully, as if by resting only lightly on it, she can somehow ensure this won't take long, that she can still leave on time. Not only is she dreading this conversation, but she is desperate to get away this evening. She and Caz have a second viewing on a flat down off Holloway Road.

For the first time, they have found something Becca really loves. It was one they'd seen online but dismissed as out of their price range. Then, a few days ago, the agent had called them, told them it was being reduced, and the vendors wanted a quick sale, and were favourable to first-time buyers. It needed work; it was probably damp. The second bedroom was tiny. But it had a garden – a garden! And a real wood floor in the lounge – well, lounge-slash-kitchen – that Becca was sure she could sand down. An easy walk to the Tube for work. But more than that, it just *felt* like it could be her and Caz's place. She could be happy there.

They were going to see it one last time tonight, but Becca had realised this morning that she had already decided. She wanted that flat. She was going to make an offer. Maybe even offer the asking price.

'Just. One. Sec.' Jamie is tapping away, making a show of finishing an email before giving her his full attention. 'There we go.'

Abruptly, Jamie spins on his wheelie chair, turns and looks straight at her. He is leaning forward a little, his shirtsleeves rolled up. He is flushed in the face. Sort of wired, like he is ready for combat.

Becca hopes he isn't planning to drag this out, get into the finer details, which would just be awkward for everyone. She knows what he has done. He must know that she can't keep the information from Alice. Surely he will see that he just needs to tell Alice himself, and then Becca can stay out of it.

'So,' he says. 'There's no easy way to say this, Becca – I wanted to discuss some performance concerns with you.'

Becca opens her mouth to speak, then shuts it as she registers slowly what he has just said.

'Performance concerns? You mean – *my* performance?'

'Yes. That's right.'

To his credit, Jamie has the grace to look embarrassed, guilty, just for a second. But then he pulls his spine straight, his cheeks flushing afresh, grabbing at papers on his desk in a pantomime of control.

'Just to be clear, this isn't a *disciplinary* conversation at this stage, but it is an official conversation, if that makes sense?'

It doesn't, in all honesty, make a lot of sense, but now Jamie is handing her several sheets of white paper – her contract, plus an appendix listing her professional duties. Becca hasn't seen this document since they hired her. Years ago, when Martha was a baby.

'I see you're looking at schedule 1 – duties and responsibilities. Let's start there,' he says. He is talking too fast, as if he's been sped up. 'Read them out loud, please, if you don't mind.'

Becca feels herself shrinking under his eye contact. She feels hot and cold at once, something coursing through her which she realises later must have been shock. Unsure what else she can do, she finds the start of the document and starts to read, her throat dry, her voice sounding dull, automatic. She reaches a section called 'nursery duties'. She pauses, looks up at Jamie. Surely this isn't relevant any more?

'Keep going,' says Jamie, without looking up from his copy.

'"Keeping the children's nursery, bedrooms and bathroom clean and tidy,"' she reads. '"Laundry and ironing of the children's clothes and bedding. Ensuring that the children's clothes are kept in good repair. Shopping for the children's needs. Preparing and cooking the children's meals. Keeping the kitchen, breakfast and any other room clean and tidy after use by the child or children (at a minimum, surfaces should be wiped down, and the dishwasher loaded at the end of each day)... "'

'You can stop there,' Jamie says. He places his copy of the contract on his lap. 'When was the last time you did the ironing, Becca? Or tidied Martha's bedroom?'

'I...'

'What about the food shopping?'

'Well, Alice always does it online, so...'

'Shopping for Martha's things?'

'But Alice likes to buy Martha's clothes, and...'

'OK, let's just talk about the basics then,' Jamie snaps, cutting her off. 'How often would you say you tidied and wiped down the kitchen and loaded the dishwasher by the end of the day?'

Becca blushes. If she is totally honest, she knows she is not good at this. She knows it bothers Alice, and it has been a source of tension between them.

'I mean, I always try to,' she says. 'But sometimes I'm just so busy with Martha, and these days she has homework, too, and I just always got the feeling you wanted me to focus on...'

'It's hardly ever done, Becca,' Jamie snaps.

Becca takes a breath.

'OK, understood. I will do better on that. I will load the dishwasher.'

Becca feels furious now. She wants to scream at him. *You're talking to me about dishwashers when you're the one having an affair!* But Jamie is in control, not her – that's what he is telling her. She *has* to load his dishwasher whether she likes him or not. And she needs to be careful.

Becca clears her throat.

'OK, Jamie,' she says. 'I get the point. Is that everything?'

Jamie's demeanour shifts just a little. As if even this small defiance from Becca was a step too far.

'No.' Jamie's voice is cold now. 'Let's return to the main contract. Let's start at clause 4.3.'

He points down, indicating she should read it out loud.

'You want me to…?'

'Please.'

Becca clears her throat. '"You will not allow the children to watch television or use screens or electronic devices to entertain the children without the express permission of the employer."'

'Would you say you comply with this part of your contract all the time?' Jamie asks. 'Most of the time?' He pauses. 'Or none of the time?'

'But this was all drawn up when Martha was a baby,' Becca protests. 'She's nearly six now. You've never said you minded her watching TV for a bit, after tea. If it's a problem…'

'Let's keep going,' Jamie snaps again. 'Clause 4.4 please, Becca?'

'Sorry?' Becca clears her throat again, fumbles through the pages. One falls to the floor, and she bends to collect it. She is flustered, grappling for the appropriate response. She reads aloud.

'"You should not use your mobile for personal use whilst the child/children is awake and in your care."'

Jamie tilts his head. 'Do you feel you're complying with that all of the time? Most of the time?'

'I…'

'Or none of the time?'

When Alice had just hired Becca, she was particular about limiting Becca's phone use around Martha. Becca had respected her wishes. But honestly, it wasn't realistic to expect someone not to use their phone in the day at all. Surely no one really had to do that?

'Jamie, like I said… this contract was for when Martha was a baby.' Becca feels heat rise to her face. 'When we agreed I'd keep phone use to her nap times. There are no nap times now, and I need to communicate with the school, with other nannies and mums for play dates, to find the details and addresses of her activities. I need the app to book her swimming, I look up videos and things that help with her homework… I need the phone all the time.'

'So you admit you are on your phone *all the time*, while she is in your care.'

'Look, Jamie…'

Jamie holds a single finger in the air. 'If we could just stay on the same subject, Becca, please.'

Becca is silenced. He has never spoken to her like this before. Like a child.

'There's something else on the topic of your phone use that I'm afraid I need to discuss with you. Unfortunately, this is much more serious.'

Jamie gives her a hard look. Then he places the contract carefully on his desk, using the tips of his fingers to tidy the edges of the stack of paper. Becca's own copy is out of order, creasing in her moist palms.

Jamie turns to his computer. Becca is sure his hand on the mouse is shaking.

'You have been using the charging lead attached to my work computer to charge your mobile phone during working hours, correct?'

'My… my charger was broken,' she stammers. 'I… I didn't think you'd mind.'

'I see. I suppose that would explain this, then.'

'Explain what?'

Jamie clicks on a folder, and the screen is flooded with pictures of Becca, her mouth open, her breasts exposed. Pictures of her in a tangle of bedsheets. A selfie, taken in her bathroom mirror, and this one makes her cringe the most, for some reason – the cheap bath products she hadn't even cropped out, her furry toothbrush, the amateurish white glare of overexposure, the phone camera's flash beamed back from her grubby glass.

'Those are private,' Becca croaks. Her throat feels thick, constricted. She tries to think whether this could have happened by accident. But it can't have done. Jamie has done this. He has been through her phone. She was so stupid to leave her phone here. How could she have been so stupid?

Because she felt safe with him. Because she didn't know what he was.

'Becca,' says Jamie. 'This sort of content – if Martha were to see it – I hardly need to say how distressing she'd have found it.'

Becca's head is heavy with humiliation. The thing she wants most now is to be away from here. Away from him.

'I've given this a lot of thought. And I think I've landed on the solution that will be best for both of us.'

Jamie leans under the computer. He takes a document from the little plastic tray and places it in Becca's hands, still warm from the printer. The document says 'severance agreement'. It includes a payment to Becca of several thousand pounds. And then it states other things. Things that Becca must do, and not do.

Severance. So Becca is going to lose her job. She will never see Martha again. She will lose the flat, too. She needs to be in a job that she has held for two years or more. Otherwise, she can't get a mortgage. No mortgage means no flat.

Becca glances at the clock. Caz will be arriving at the flat viewing, wondering where Becca is, trying to persuade the agent to wait. Becca sees how all the things she thought were within touching distance are now impossible. She'll have to tell Caz there will be no flat after all. It will break her heart. Maybe Caz will break up with her. Becca will have no job, no Caz, nowhere to live. She will be completely alone.

'Have a quick read if you like.'

Becca reads the document. She looks up at Jamie.

'I don't understand.'

'Don't understand what?'

'This part.' She points to a section entitled 'confidentiality'. 'How am I supposed to keep this a secret, from Alice? I can't just leave, and not tell her why.'

Jamie shrugs. 'Just tell her you've got another job. Or that you've decided it's the right time.' He pauses. 'I don't want her to have to see these images. I'm sure you'd prefer that too.'

Becca's face flames. The thought of Alice seeing the pictures is unbearable.

'She's always worrying you're going to quit,' Jamie adds. 'She won't be surprised.'

Becca's heart twists in her chest. Anger flares and makes her briefly bold; she has nothing to lose now. He has taken everything from her.

'This is all because of you,' she snaps. 'And that girl.'

Jamie looks at her, his face as blank as a white page.

'How old is she, Jamie? She... she looked like a kid! Alice will find out, you know. She will...'

But Becca is losing momentum, and Jamie leans forward towards her, his elbows resting on his knees, his face so close that Becca can feel the warmth of his breath on her face. If you'd asked her before this, Becca would have said Jamie's eyes were blue. But they aren't. She sees now that they are, in fact, two different colours: one is green, and the other is a greyish-blue flecked with yellow. How strange, she thinks fleetingly, the things you don't see about a person.

'I'd read it carefully, if I were you,' he says. 'It's extremely important that you understand the implications.'

'And what if I won't sign it?'

Jamie shrugs, gives a little sneer. Motions back to the screen. Becca can hardly bear for her body to be there on his flickering screen. She is made small by this. She has made herself smaller.

'I'll just close these away for now,' he says lightly. He gives a few little clicks, too quickly and deftly for Becca to see where the pictures have ended up. 'I wouldn't want them getting into the wrong hands,' he says, with a false smile. 'My wife. Your parents. Horrible men on the Internet. There are some awful websites out there, full of this sort of... *home-made* material.'

Her heart is beating so fast. It can't be good. Can't be normal. She feels like she might be sick.

'We are both adults,' he says slowly. 'Both entitled to our personal privacy, Becca. Aren't we?'

Becca can't sit here any more. She snatches up her phone and stands to go. She is late, irrevocably late. She has three missed calls from Caz, messages with a string of question marks.

Agent threatening to leave! Where are you?????

Jamie spins his chair back round to face his computer screen. 'I'll give you until the end of tomorrow,' he calls after her.

Becca steps outside the front door. She gulps in the air, leans against the short walls either side of the steps up to Jamie and Alice's front door. Then she walks down the road, and around the corner, until she is standing by the railings of the pub. She stuffs the document into the pocket of her coat. She orders an Uber. Then, while she waits, she dials Stella's number.

'OK,' she says, when Stella answers. 'I'll do it.'

'Yeah?'

'Yeah. Anonymously, like you said. But yes, I'm ready. I'll do what you wanted.'

ALICE

Linda looks like a picture taken in greyscale. Her skin is thin and translucent, bruised aubergine purple where IV lines connect the tops of her hands to the drips by her bedside. When Alice enters the cubicle, she winces in pain with the effort of turning her head. Alice knows, the second she lays eyes on Linda, that she has not got long.

'I didn't know if you'd remember me,' Alice says. 'I'm Alice.'

Linda stares at her, then closes her eyes.

'I know who you are,' she says.

Alice sits down carefully in the chair beside Linda's bed.

'Actually, Linda, I need to explain about that,' Alice says softly. 'I'm afraid I... I didn't tell you the truth, before. I...'

'I've always known who you are.' Linda's eyes are still closed.

Alice gapes.

'Can you pass me that water?'

Still lost for words, Alice stands and passes Linda a clear plastic cup with a paper straw in it from the adjustable table by the side of the hospital bed. Linda takes the straw in her mouth and sucks. Alice glances around at the machines, the chart, the monitors that surround her.

'Are you in any pain?' Alice asks, when she has recovered.

'Comes and goes.' Linda glances murderously at a passing nurse. 'I wouldn't mind a proper drink.'

Alice smiles, despite everything, remembering the strength of Linda's gin and tonics. 'I should have snuck one in.'

'That would have been nice.'

The two of them almost laugh.

'Really, though,' Alice says. 'I should have thought. To bring you something. I brought flowers – I was thinking of your plants. But they were confiscated. Infection control, apparently. Sorry.'

The flowers are now at the nurse's station at the end of the corridor. Along with a nurse who is texting on her phone, and eating chocolate biscuits from a box that also looks suspiciously like a confiscated gift.

'I'm so sorry, Linda. For lying. For Ezra. For all of it.'

For a while, Linda doesn't say anything. When she finally speaks, her voice is heavy with pain.

'Ezra was a good boy, you know,' she says. 'I'm sorry if that makes it harder for you, but he was. He was my good boy.'

Alice sees a tear is forming, pooling in the deep crease underneath Linda's eye. Alice bites her lip, nodding. The little boy in the paper, in his football kit. Her eyes, too, are filling with tears.

'I am not asking you to forgive me,' Alice says, her own voice thickening. 'It's too much to ask. I know that.'

Linda sighs. The tear falls down one grey cheek.

'I did think I'd never forgive you,' Linda croaks. 'But I don't feel that way so much now, not really. He came to your house, at the end of the day. Your kid was there. You're a mum. Mums protect their kids.' She swallows. 'If you want my forgiveness, you can have it.'

Alice is crying silently, now, grappling in her backpack for a tissue, but unable to see properly. She finds she cannot even thank Linda, for what she has given her. Linda's forgiveness feels like a gift, more valuable than anything. The fog of guilt that has enveloped Alice's life feels for the first time like it is starting to lift.

'Jade had the baby.' Linda's voice is hoarse. 'So there was that, at least. Before...'

Alice's stomach lurches.

'Taylor, she's called,' Linda adds vaguely. 'Such a pretty baby. I don't know what'll happen to her now.'

Alice stares at the floor, her vision blurred, tries to get herself under control. How can Linda manage it, the pain? Both of her children. It is monstrous, unimaginable.

'Do you think,' Linda croaks, her voice suddenly far away, 'that your husband killed my daughter?'

Alice looks up, forced to wipe her face with the cuff of her jumper. When she speaks, her voice is thick.

'I... I don't know, Linda.'

It is the first time she has admitted the possibility of this out loud. Or even in her own head. But Alice knows that Linda is owed the truth now, at the very least.

'I find it very difficult to believe that he would,' she adds weakly. 'But to be honest with you, I don't really know any more. I thought I knew who he was.'

Linda looks away. 'That can happen with people.'

Linda shifts in her bed, then turns to train her gaze on Alice. Alice finds it almost painful to look into Linda's face, at the bruises under her eyes, the concave cheeks. But she forces herself to do it, all the same. Linda looks her hard in the eye.

'Anyone can kill a person, you know,' Linda says. 'You think it'll change you, that it will make you into someone else. But sometimes, it don't feel like that. It just feels like any other thing you do. It feels like nothing.'

Alice glances at the tubes in Linda's hands, the chart above her bed, the list of drugs Alice has never heard of. She isn't sure what Linda means. Perhaps she is getting muddled.

'Linda, if it's not too painful,' Alice asks. 'Do you mind if I ask you something about what happened before the break-in? About my husband. And Jade.'

Linda is silent.

'I didn't know about it, obviously. And, I don't know how much you knew?'

Something beeps on a machine by Linda's side. Alice's eyes flick towards it.

'Do you need me to call someone?'

'I'm OK. I don't know what that noise means.'

Linda looks so exhausted, so weak. Alice should stop this. She should leave. But she needs so badly to know what Linda knows, about what happened before the break-in. She needs to know who her husband really is. What he has done.

'Look, that bloody nurse will be over in a minute,' Linda says. 'There's something I want you to have. In that bedside table.'

Alice looks over at the table. In a cubby hole under where the water jug is sitting, she can see something wrapped in a tote bag.

'This?'

Linda nods. Alice slides it out carefully. Whatever is inside is rectangular and heavy. She looks inside. It is Ezra's laptop.

'I've been writing it all down,' Linda explains. 'As much as I know, anyway. I didn't know who I was doing it for at first. There was a time when I thought… when maybe I was going to give it to that journalist.'

Alice looks up. 'You mean Stella? Stella Glass?'

'Stella Glass,' Linda nods. 'Yeah. We thought she was on our side at first. That was before Jade told me. About what she'd done.'

Linda's face clouds with anger. The machine beeps again.

'What do you mean, what she'd done?'

The beeping turns into something more high-pitched. An alarm.

The nurse rushes in, biscuit crumbs on her blue tabard. She looks at a monitor, frowns, makes some adjustments, looks at Alice.

'Hello, sorry, your mum, is it? She needs a bit of rest now, OK? It's not visiting time, anyway.'

Alice mumbles her apologies, and stands. She wonders if the nurse will notice her taking Linda's bag, but the nurse is opening a vial of something, connecting it to a needle. Linda's eyes are pressed tightly shut – she seems to be in pain.

'Is she… going to be OK?'

'If you could just wait outside.' The nurse doesn't even look up. Another nurse comes in, then a third. Alice steps back. A papery purple curtain is pulled abruptly across.

As Alice follows the signs along the bright corridor of the hospital, she finds herself squinting at the lights, a headache gathering behind her eyes. She realises she is breathing fast. The laptop feels heavy on her shoulder.

Alice finds a pub, not far from the hospital. She messages Aunt Sarah, checks she can do Martha's pick-up. She orders a glass of wine and finds a corner with a plug socket. She takes the laptop out, finds the file already open. She starts to read.

LINDA

Ezra's illness was vicious. It progressed quickly. His personality was changing, too. I never knew how much was the illness itself, and how much was what the diagnosis did to his head. But he had been a quiet lad, sensitive. Suddenly he was angry, flying off the handle at the slightest thing. And he was big by then, Ezra. He could have hurt you, if he'd wanted

He started saying strange things. People were following him, shouting – he would say he could hear them, even when it was just the two of us in the flat. He didn't let me have the telly on because he said people were trying to talk to him through it, trying to control his mind.

He was my good boy, my best boy. But I had started to dread him being at home.

I had started to feel frightened of him.

I knew I was getting sick too, a different kind of sick. I'd worked it out, before the doctors told me. They get very sniffy about this, doctors, but the truth is, it's all online these days. You type in your symptoms and you get your answer. Stage four cancer. It had spread to my liver, my blood, my bones. It was going to get me, sooner rather than later.

They'd told me I needed this and that. Radiotherapy, to shrink the tumours, give me a bit more time. I didn't want all that radiation. No thanks. But I did worry about Ezra, about who would look after him when I was gone. So I told them I'd have a think about it, and they sent me off with something for the pain. *Not to be taken with alcohol*, the packet said. *Very funny*, I thought to myself.

I was looking forward to being home in my own chair, pouring a large gin and tonic. When I got home, Jade was there, with this posh-looking woman.

They both looked at me when I walked in.

'Hello,' the woman said all sprightly, like a TV presenter. 'You must be Linda. Pleased to meet you.' She stuck her hand out for me to shake but I ignored it, so she put it back.

'I told you already, I don't want to do any fucking article,' Jade was shouting.

'What article?' I asked.

Jade didn't answer. The woman looked from Jade to me, then stood up and said she'd leave us to have a talk. On the side, by the drinks cabinet, she left a little white card, embossed with her name. Stella Glass.

She's clever, Jade, but she was naive, and stupid, too, of course, in the way all young people are. In the way that all young girls are, about men.

She'd been seeing one of the bosses at this charity. Married, of course. They'd met at the photo shoot, then later at some hotel in East London, the sleazy bastard. When she'd told him she was pregnant, this man – this *Jamie* – had gone mad. Wanted Jade to get rid of the baby. More than that, it sounded like. He wanted Jade to disappear. He'd even asked her to sign one of those non-disclosure agreements.

I told her what I thought. She had her whole life ahead of her, didn't need to be saddled with a baby so young. But Jade wouldn't listen. She was having it, she said, and that was that.

I poured myself a double, after that. Maybe more like a triple.

Jade was sure Jamie would come round, except there was this journalist on the scene, making everything difficult. The journalist, Jade said, had got it all wrong. She was going on about grooming, abuse. It was a load of rubbish.

'No it's not,' I told Jade. 'That's exactly what it is!'

The journalist – Stella Glass – wanted Jade to do a big interview, playing the victim. She even offered her money. Thousands.

Jade wasn't daft. She wasn't interested. But she did want to know what Stella Glass knew about Jamie that she didn't. This Stella was hinting about some other scandal, you see. Something Jamie had done before. Jade had strung her along a bit, wanting to find out more. She was obsessed with knowing all about Jamie's wife, too, and his child. She said they had this big house in the nice bit of Hackney with all the cafes and whatnot. This lovely life. Jade was mad as hell about it. I overheard her once asking Stella, the journalist, if she had a picture of the three of them. Imagine! And then, as it became more obvious Jamie wanted nothing to do with her, she started talking differently about it. Saying she would make them pay somehow. Him and his family.

I told her to leave it, but I knew there was no point. Jade does what Jade wants.

Eventually, this Stella realised Jade was messing her around. And she got tricky then, started talking about doing the article anyway, saying she didn't need Jade, that she'd found someone else who could 'stand the story up', as she put it.

Well, me and Jade agreed on one thing – we needed to stop the article. Because of Ezra. Me and Jade could both see what would happen if Ezra found out about all this. He'd go for Jamie, we knew he would. He was unstable by now, unpredictable. I didn't want Ezra in trouble. And Jade, well, she didn't want Ezra going off to beat up her lover boy. She didn't want him getting hurt. She was so bloody naive, Jade. I could tell she still secretly thought this bastard might leave his wife, once the baby came. Of course, there was about as much chance of us winning the bloody lottery. But there was no telling her that.

I decided I would sit this journalist woman down, and explain it all to her. How our Ezra was having these problems, how he'd become violent, unpredictable. How all this stuff coming out, about what this man had done to his sister, could trigger him to do something bad.

She seemed like a reasonable person, I thought. Bit pushy, but basically all right. I thought she would get it. I thought she would back off.

Turns out I was naive, too.

ALICE

Alice stands on the walkway outside Stella's flat. Rain drips down the edge of the glass balconies, makes the surface of the canal fizz. The towpath is quiet.

She rings the doorbell once, then again.

By the time Stella answers, Alice is so cold her hands feel numb. She must have a hole in one of her boots – one foot is wet. The laptop, Ezra's laptop, is heavy in her bag.

As Stella opens the door, Alice can feel the seductive warmth of her flat, the faint smell of cooking with fried onions, ginger and garlic. Stella's hair is piled into a messy bun, her face make-up free. She is wearing a jumper over exercise leggings, large UGG-style slippers which accentuate the skinniness of her legs.

'Hi, Alice. Come in.' Stella ushers her inside, as if she'd been expecting her all along. Alice hesitates, not keen on the idea of actually going in. But she supposes they can hardly talk in the rain, so eventually, she follows Stella inside, through the hallway and into a large open-plan kitchen diner, with windows out to the canal.

'Frankie's with her so-called father tonight, so we can talk properly,' Stella says, switching off the pan that was bubbling on the stove. 'Come and sit! I'll make tea.'

Stella motions to a bench seat beside her dining table. Behind it is a wall covered in colourful art prints and photography. On the other side of the room are sofas dressed invitingly in a colourful tapestry of cushions and throws. Her stuffed bookshelves are painted purple. It is the sort of flat Alice herself might have chosen, in another life. It had never occurred to Alice to wonder why she had never been invited here. Why Stella had always preferred to come to her house.

'I've just been catching up on the weekend papers, looking for ideas,' Stella says, scooping up a pile of newspapers from the dining table. She flicks a kettle on, then turns to Alice.

'Do sit.'

But Alice stays standing.

'I know what you did,' she says.

Stella turns around, the newspapers still in her hands, but there is a slight tremor in her fingers.

'And I know why you did it. I know all about the past. About Clara.'

Stella's face changes. She places the papers slowly down on the worktop. For a few seconds, neither of them says anything. Stella looks towards the window, the rain running down the glass, and sighs.

'I'll show you something,' she says, and disappears into the bedroom.

Alice doesn't particularly want to sit, but in the end her exhaustion wins out, and she sinks onto the bench seat. When Stella returns, she is holding a folder. She sets it in front of Alice.

'After my sister disappeared,' Stella says, her voice cracking a little, 'my family hired a private detective to try and find out what happened to her.' She nods at the folder. 'You can look for yourself.'

The first page has images of Clara, some with Stella. The two of them are so alike. There is a record of her travel to Africa, a report from the charity about her role, email correspondence about the training she received. Pictures of Clara doing volunteer work. Followed by a different set of pictures, headed: 'retrieved from CL digital camera'.

The pictures are nearly all of Jamie, of Clara and Jamie together. In one, Clara has her arms around his shoulders. In another, they are in some sort of outdoor bar with a thatched roof and wooden masks on the walls. Clara is sitting on Jamie's lap, her face buried in his neck. And another, of Clara in a sparsely furnished hotel room, dressed only in a threadbare towel. She looks young enough in the picture for Alice to feel uncomfortable even looking at it. The taker of the picture is reflected in the glass behind Clara, a starburst of the flash in the corner. It's not the clearest shot, but Alice isn't in any real doubt. The person who took the picture is Jamie.

'Jamie was the first man my sister had ever really fallen for,' she says. 'She'd only ever slept with one other person. She thought she was in love.'

The anger in Stella's voice is palpable.

'He didn't even bother ending the relationship,' Stella says. 'A new girl volunteer arrived, he just started sleeping with her instead. When Clara confronted him, Jamie told her that what they had was never a real relationship, that it was just casual. He and this other girl had a "real connection".'

Alice stares at the pictures. Clara looks so young. Could she have overinterpreted things? Most young girls do that, don't they? But then, she stops herself. Thinks uneasily of Jamie and Jade. Of course Jamie behaves like this. She just didn't see it.

'Clara felt humiliated,' Stella continues. 'Jamie was her boss. He was at all the social events, all the meetings. She had to socialise with them, pretend like nothing had ever happened. Once, when she got upset, he told her she was embarrassing herself and the charity. After that, the other male volunteers started to call her "the psycho".'

Stella taps the file.

'All this is in the emails she sent me. Other things, too.' Stella turns some pages in the file in front of Alice. 'Here – this is where she wrote to me about the way Jamie ran the charity. The culture was toxic. Male volunteers saw nothing wrong with using local prostitutes – really vulnerable women. Jamie was doing nothing about it. She said that there was weird stuff going on in the orphanage where she'd been working, too. They placed men there who she knew were using local sex workers – sex workers not much older than some of the kids. No real safeguarding. And then there was the question of money.'

'Money?'

'Clara couldn't understand why the kids in the orphanage ate rice and beans every day and didn't have proper shoes or mosquito nets, when there was loads of money pouring into the charity which was supposedly helping them. She found the accounts. It didn't add up. Meanwhile Jamie and his mates were swanning around in branded Range Rovers and going out every night. They told everyone they were drilling wells for water pumps, in the villages around Arusha. But Clara said in most cases, locals were paid to drill holes for the wells, and then sites were left abandoned because the pump equipment never showed up.'

Alice flicks through the file, scanning the emails from Clara to Stella. They are well-written; the allegations are detailed, and specific. Some of them have images attached. Jamie's name crops up a lot.

The pictures are on the next page of the file. One, captioned 'Bahati Orphanage', shows a run-down single-storey building, kids without proper clothes and shoes, the mosquito nets on their windows filled with holes, no blankets on their bare metal bunk beds. Another picture, captioned 'Ngaramtoni well', shows a deep brick-built well in red, dusty earth. In the first picture, it looks freshly built, with Clara standing by proudly, holding up a water pipe of some kind. Then another picture, taken a few months later, shows the well abandoned with makeshift cordons and signs around it in English and Swahili warning locals not to come near.

'I was doing my journalist training by then, so I started helping her look into it,' Stella says. 'When we'd got as far as we could, Clara decided to confront Jamie with what we'd found. She demanded a meeting with the charity and Jamie's bosses.'

'And she got one?'

'Yes. About a week before she disappeared. She said that Jamie had denied everything. He admitted there were delays on some pump equipment, but he said all the rest of it was a mixture of invention and Clara not understanding "how things worked in a developing country". He said Clara was letting her feelings about their former personal relationship get in the way of the truth. Clara was humiliated again.'

Stella sits back in her chair.

'The night she went missing was New Year's Eve. They were all on a camping trip, Jamie too, in Arusha National Park. Everyone there said that Clara had been drunk, and upset, and had wanted to go back to town, so Jamie offered to drive her. The other volunteers said he hadn't been drinking. That Jamie rarely drank. And that he never got out of control. Unlike her.'

Stella gives Alice a look.

'Jamie told the police he drove Clara from the campsite back into Arusha. He said they argued, and she told him to let her out of the car. So he did. He dropped her at the roadside on the outskirts of Arusha – which on that side is basically a shanty town. In the middle of the night. She was eighteen. Alone, vulnerable. She'd been drinking. And he just left her.'

Alice stays silent. Jamie had never told her this story.

'The local police accepted his account. They found witnesses who had seen her slamming a door, wandering off.' Stella looks Alice straight in the eye. 'No one knows what happened to her after that. But there is a big quarry nearby. The police speculated that she could have been killed, and her body dumped in the quarry. It would have been impossible, apparently, to find it.'

Alice takes a deep breath. Tries to process what Stella has said.

'Stella,' Alice says quietly. 'It's horrendous – awful – what happened with Clara. I can't imagine anything worse than losing your sister. But it's not as if Jamie...'

'He did kill her.'

Alice stares at Stella.

'There is no doubt,' Stella says slowly, 'in my mind, or the minds of my family, that Jamie was responsible for the death of my little sister. He had a duty of care, and instead, he had an inappropriate sexual relationship with her, humiliated her, destroyed her, made her desperately unhappy, and then left her unsafe, alone, drunk, young, vulnerable, in the middle of the night.' She pauses. 'If he had taken care of her that night, she would still be alive.

But because of his actions, Clara is dead. I don't care if he didn't physically murder her, Alice. He may as well have done.'

Alice swallows.

'Did the police never find her?'

'I don't know how much they ever really looked,' Stella says, with an effort to squash the emotion leaking into her voice. 'The embassy lost interest after it emerged she'd been drinking, that she'd "gone walkabout", as one of them put it, in a dangerous part of town at night. The police say her disappearance was "most unfortunate", but that the case is now closed.'

Alice winces.

'I thought, as a journalist, I could do something about it all,' Stella goes on. 'I tried for years to get newspapers – including my own – to publish a story about the charity, about Jamie, and his role in my sister's disappearance.' Her cool demeanour has collapsed now, her words thick with pain.

'They have all refused. They say there is no evidence to suggest any wrongdoing over her death. And that her emails, the allegations in them about Jamie, don't represent real evidence. Especially since she can't make these claims in person. What with her being dead.'

Stella pauses to gather herself.

'I was allowed to ask my questions about Jamie's conduct. I put the questions to the African charity where he used to work, and also to Handhold where he was working by then. The lawyers warned me we wouldn't be able to run a story if the charities just flat-out denied them, but I thought it was likely they'd at least pledge to investigate what Clara had written before her death. And that would have given us a way of getting something in the paper.

'But I was wrong. The charities stonewalled. They denied everything, claiming all these matters had been investigated years before and there was no evidence any of it was true. And they got lawyers on us, in a pretty heavy way. In the end, I was told it was legally impossible for us to publish.' Stella looks away, unable to keep the sting of it from her voice.

'Even then, though,' she goes on. 'I thought it would at least have some sort of impact on his career, the fact a journalist had asked these questions. I assumed they'd think twice about promoting him, at least. But soon after, I heard he was being made campaigns director! He started appearing on the radio all the time – a champion of the vulnerable! I even saw a poster of his face on a fucking bus!'

Stella makes a noise of disgust, then fixes her gaze on Alice.

'Jamie,' she says, 'got away with everything he did to my sister.'

'So you kept going,' Alice says, slowly. 'You kept trying to punish him.'

Stella juts her chin. 'I just realised a simple truth, Alice,' she says. 'That if he did this once, he'd do it again.'

Alice feels a twist of nausea.

'And I was right,' Stella says. 'Wasn't I? Another vulnerable teenager. Of course, you know all about that now.' Stella looks at Alice intently. 'Can you blame me, for wanting to see him exposed this time? Given what he did to my sister? Given *everything* I knew about what sort of man he was?'

Alice feels her sympathy harden.

'You knew, or you thought?' she snaps. 'Don't journalists have to report both sides of the story?'

'No one can ever hear Clara's side,' Stella snaps back. 'My sister is dead. Don't you understand? Clara, and now Jade as well. Both dead. And it's all because of him! Your husband!' Stella jabs a finger at Alice, her cheeks pink with fury.

'Look,' she says more gently. 'When you're in love with someone, Alice, it's impossible to see who they really are. You're a victim of him, too – you see that, now, right? We should be allies, Alice. Not enemies.'

Alice feels her anger resurface. 'I'm not here to talk about me,' she says curtly. 'I came here to talk about what you did.'

Stella frowns. 'What is it that you think that I did?'

'You went to see Jade, tried to get her to do a story on Jamie. She said no. She begged you not to do it – and her mother, Linda, did too. They begged you not to report it, or to tell Ezra what you knew. Because of how he might react. But you ignored them, didn't you?'

Stella looks at her patiently, as if she is struggling to see what the point is.

'It's because of *you* that Ezra found out about Jamie and Jade,' Alice says. 'If it wasn't for you, Ezra would never have come looking for Jamie. He'd never have come to our house that day. He'd still be alive!'

Stella frowns. 'I see,' she says slowly, a pantomime of disbelief. 'So now I'm to blame for you killing Ezra, am I?'

Alice is momentarily silenced.

'And what about Ezra? Is he absolved from blame, too? The man who broke down your door, picked up a knife and headed for the room where our daughters were watching a Disney film?'

Alice opens her mouth to speak, but can find no answer.

'What about your husband, the man who had sex with Ezra's vulnerable sister when she was a teenager? Who is now on the run for murdering her, and leaving their child motherless? And who was responsible for the death of my little sister?'

Stella's voice is breaking by now.

'Yes, of *course* I went to see Jade and her family, Alice,' Stella says, with emotion. 'I wanted to tell their story because I wanted to expose Jamie for what he was. I am a *journalist*, Alice. That's what we *do*.'

'This is nothing like normal journalism, Stella,' Alice says, shaking her head. 'You pretended to be my friend…'

'Like you did with Jade?'

Alice is thrown off-balance. 'This – this is nothing like that and you know it!' Alice is stammering. 'You came to my house. You moved your *child* to the same *school*! That wasn't you being a journalist. That was you pursuing a vendetta against my husband.'

Stella looks at her evenly. Then she leans forward, and lowers her voice.

'You know what, Alice? I think you'll look back and realise I was the best friend you ever had.'

Alice is silenced again. Stella is deluded. This, she realises, is the real her. A person shimmering with anger and resentment; her easy charm discarded like a costume. And perhaps she is right, about Jamie. But Alice is determined to focus on what *Stella* has done. She isn't going to let her off the hook.

'What happened when Linda and Jade wouldn't do the story, Stella?'

Stella's expression flickers, then resets. She shrugs. 'Nothing. I looked for another way to do it, without their cooperation.'

'But they explained to you that they didn't want the story out full stop,' Alice says. 'Because of how vulnerable Ezra was, how volatile. How likely he'd be to seek Jamie out, to get violent.'

'Alice, I can't think of a single worthwhile story I've ever worked on where there wasn't someone who'd rather I wasn't doing it,' Stella sighs. 'Stories like this are always uncomfortable for someone. The truth is uncomfortable. Often it hurts.' She pauses. 'But the truth matters, Alice.'

'Oh, really?' Alice laughs darkly. 'Perhaps you could start telling the truth then, Stella.'

Stella glares at her, but says nothing.

'I'll tell you what I know to be true. Jade and Linda were desperate for Ezra not to find out about Jamie and Jade, because of what they feared Ezra might do. And yet somehow, he *did* find out. Not only that, but he found out where we lived, too. And he turned up at our house. On a day when you were there. You were literally in our house. A bit of a coincidence, isn't it?'

That same flicker on Stella's face, a glance to the left as quick as a knife. Then she recovers, tilts her head to one side, pulls a puzzled smile.

'You're making some pretty big leaps there, Alice,' she says.

'No, I'm not.' Alice is convinced, now. 'I see it. You don't care about the truth at all. You've lied to me from the day we met. You pretended to be my friend so you could dig up dirt on my husband. And then when Jade refused to do your damned story, you decided to use Ezra instead. A sick, vulnerable kid. You used him, to have Jamie punished.'

Stella's eyes flicker.

'You lured Ezra there that day. Deliberately. I think you *wanted* him to lose it. You'd tried to punish Jamie for what you believed he'd done. And you'd failed. So now, you were angry. I think you wanted Jamie dead. You just wanted someone else to wield the knife.'

'That is utterly ridiculous,' Stella says coldly. But Alice is no longer listening.

'What about Becca? What were you talking to her about, in Farm to Fork, all those times? Were you trying to get her to help with your plan? Trying to persuade her to be in on it, somehow?'

Stella gives an amazed laugh. 'What plan? You've got this totally wrong. Yes, I took Becca for a few coffees in the hope that she'd tell me what she knew about Jamie. I felt sure the nanny would have something to say on the subject of his predatory behaviour towards women. And guess what, Alice? I was absolutely right. She had *plenty* to say.'

Alice feels a lurch of nausea. She thinks of the pictures on his computer of Becca. *Oh, Jamie*, she thinks. *How could you?*

'You do realise that it's not OK for men to act like this, don't you, Alice? To take advantage of people when they're in a position of trust? You do realise he fully deserves to lose his job? To lose everything?'

Alice clenches her fists under the table. 'You don't get to decide what people deserve, Stella.'

Stella tilts her head to one side, thoughtfully.

'I don't agree,' she says. 'I think we should decide what he deserves.'

Alice stares at her. 'What?'

'I said, I think we should decide,' Stella says slowly. 'Now. You and me.'

Alice is not sure, exactly, how she gets home. By the time she gets to her house, it is dark, and the house looks unwelcoming somehow. The lights in the downstairs are out. It must be later than she thought.

She only thinks to check her phone when she steps through the door and finds the house silent. She finds a message from Aunt Sarah saying that she and Martha are both having an early night. There is some dinner in the microwave for Alice. She hopes that Alice is all right.

Alice walks down into her kitchen, turns a light on.

When she senses the person behind her, stepping out of the shadows of the kitchen, she tries to scream. But she cannot, because a hand is clamped around her face, hot, strong fingers inside her gasping mouth.

ALICE

'I'm sorry,' Jamie whispers in her ear. 'I'm sorry, I'm sorry, I'm sorry.'

He is saying it, but he still has his hand over her mouth, the other around her waist. She twists, but his grip is tight.

'This is so fucked up, Alice, I know, I'm sorry.' As he speaks, she can feel the heat of his breath, the wetness on his cheeks, smell his unwashed hair. 'I'm so sorry. If I let go, do you – do you promise not to scream?'

Alice nods as much as she is able, jerking her head back into his. He hesitates, then releases her.

She reels from him, brings her hands to her neck, where he was holding her, not because it hurts particularly but because she cannot believe what just happened; that her own husband was holding her like that, like some kind of predator. She keeps her promise not to scream, but the thump of her heart feels deafening in her own ears.

'I am sorry,' Jamie pants. 'I promise I didn't kill Jade. I didn't.' He pauses. 'I slept with her.' His eyes dart away from Alice's face in shame. 'I know… it was a terrible mistake. But I didn't kill her, Alice. And I am so sorry, I am…'

Alice stands in front of him, her body rigid, her fists clenched. *You knew this*, Alice tells herself. *You knew this already. You knew he slept with her.* But somehow hearing him say it is still winding.

Alice clutches at one of the stools on the island, and uses her hands to guide herself onto it so she can think. Jamie is shaking his head, pacing like he is losing his mind. He looks haunted, unshaven. There is dirt under his fingernails.

'Where the hell have you been, Jamie?' Alice demands, when she eventually finds it in herself to speak. 'And what the fuck happened?'

'I can explain everything... Let me explain.' He holds his palms up, then brings them together on top of her hand. Alice snatches it away immediately, shaking her head.

'I will explain,' he pleads. 'I promise. But – listen.' His eyes dart around the room again. 'You, me, Martha. Can we go somewhere, the three of us? I've found somewhere, a place that we can go. Where we'll be safe.'

'What? What are you *talking* about?'

'Look – I was there that day,' he hisses. 'She... I went to see her. She asked me to. We argued... and then I left,' he says. 'I don't know who killed her, I swear, but it's no good. They won't believe me, won't believe either of us. But if we leave now...'

Alice stares at him. 'Jamie, you must be completely fucking insane if you think I am going anywhere with you!'

Jamie's heartbreak is etched on his face. *Oh my God*, Alice thinks. He had convinced himself that she would do this. That she loves him enough. Enough to risk going to prison, if there is a chance it can mean them being together.

'They are saying her baby is yours.'

Alice feels the lump rising in her throat, as she speaks.

'I'm sorry, Alice. I'm sorry...'

'So you keep saying.'

'It was a terrible mistake...'

'She was a *teenager*!'

'It wasn't... She was seventeen when we... when we... I didn't do *anything* illegal.'

Alice looks away, disgusted. She takes a breath, forces herself to look into the face of the man she married. *Who are you?* she thinks. *Who are you really?*

'Tell me the truth, Jamie. Did you kill her?'

Jamie's eyes are wide, his voice emphatic. He speaks slowly, deliberately.

'I swear on my life... on *Martha*'s life, I did not. I did *not* kill Jade.'

Alice had thought that if she could just hear it from him, that would be enough. That she would know then, if he was lying or not. But words are just words. She sees that now. She doesn't know what his words count for, not any more.

'Why did you go to see her?'

'To tell her to keep the fuck away from us!' Jamie explodes. 'From our house, our daughter! She was completely obsessed with you, Alice. And after the painting – it seemed like she was going further than before. I thought she would go for you next time. Or Martha.' Jamie pauses. 'She'd already attacked me once.'

'What?'

Jamie sighs.

'Months ago. Before the break-in... before everything. I tried to break things off with her for good. I told her I'd support the baby...'

Here he gave Alice an agonised glance.

'... if she was determined to have it. But I asked her to never come near us, near you.'

'And?'

'Well, she was having none of it. She went mad, attacked me, started smashing up my bike...'

Alice blinks, remembering.

'When was this?'

'A couple of months before the break-in.' Jamie looks down, ashamed. 'I told you I'd fallen off my bike.'

His black eyes, the scratches all over his face, his arms.

'She was out of control,' Jamie says. He is agitated, a shine of sweat on his forehead, dampening the ends of his ragged hair. 'She smashed up my bike, and my laptop, and then she came at me. I... I didn't know how to explain it to you.'

Alice remembers now, how she demanded Jamie report the incident to the police, so that they could investigate the Uber driver who had been at fault. But Jamie had said he hadn't got the reg; he was rubbish at cars, couldn't even guess what sort it could have been. He had said it was just one of those things, that they should forget it.

'I was hoping that... maybe it would all be over after that,' Jamie goes on. 'But then somehow my work found out about me and her, and I was suspended. I didn't know how to tell you. I thought maybe I could ride it out...'

She'd thought it was her fault, Alice thinks dully, that he wasn't cycling any more. She thought it was because of her anxiety. But no. He was no longer cycling because he no longer had a job to go to.

'I was... I was just trying to figure out how to deal with all that.' Jamie can barely even look at Alice. 'How to tell you about my job. And then... the break-in happened. And then, Ezra was dead, and you were so... so devastated about what had happened... And you needed me. You and Martha both did. But the whole time, I was worried about Jade. I knew she was going to blame us for Ezra, that she wasn't going to let this go.'

Alice nods miserably. And then she had gone to see Jade, and had made everything worse.

'She'd always been obsessed with you, always asking me questions about what you were like, about our life together. So when I found out you'd gone to see her, and she'd pretended she didn't know who you were – I just felt sick.' Jamie hangs his head. 'I knew she would use you to get closer to our family. And I was right. Luring you over there, dressing her baby in Martha's clothes... it was twisted! And she was coming to the house – I know she was, because the security sensors kept picking someone up, someone coming down to the basement door, at night. Then, when you started noticing little things going missing, I knew deep down, that she must be behind it. I started to suspect she'd got hold of a key somehow. I changed the locks. I tried to make it safe. But it kept happening.'

'This is why you wanted to move,' Alice says flatly, a jigsaw in her mind starting finally to fit. Jamie cradles his head in his hands.

'I know you thought I was going mad,' Jamie says miserably. 'I just thought, if we could go somewhere, and never tell her where – then maybe it would all just end.'

They'd both come to the same conclusion for different reasons, she realises. But Alice had been so focused on the secrets *she* was keeping about Jade, that she'd failed to see what her husband was hiding. Something so much worse. So much bigger.

'Then those messages started turning up online. A dead bird outside our fucking holiday cottage. I was losing it, Alice. I *knew* she was playing some sort of game. I just wanted her out of our lives. When that thing happened at your work, I was terrified. It felt like she was going further and further. I was worried she might go for you next, or Martha. I had to see her. I had to try and talk some sense into her.'

'So you made up a conference.'

He looks at the floor.

'And pretended you'd forgotten your phone.'

Jamie's face contorts with shame. 'I thought you might use the iPhone tracker thing on me. And see that I wasn't in Scotland.'

Alice makes an involuntary noise of disbelief. What an accomplished liar she has been married to.

'I honestly never planned to be away for more than a day or two,' he goes on pleadingly. 'But then… I went to see her and she just… it was a complete waste of time. She denied everything, even when I caught her in her lies – that photograph of us in Rye – the one you said she took from you? She had that… I found it in her fucking handbag! I snatched it off her, and she went nuts.'

Jamie's voice is thick with anger.

'She still denied everything – all the stalking, the thing with the painting – even though it was obvious it had all been her. In the end, I couldn't stand to be in the same room as her, to listen to her lies any more. But I never hurt her, I swear. I left, and I didn't go back. And the next thing I knew, it was on the news – you'd been arrested, and she was missing, and the police were looking for me. And I panicked. I just… I just ran.'

'But where? Where have you *been*, Jamie?'

Jamie pauses. 'Somewhere safe.'

'What about Becca?' she snaps. 'I found the pictures. On our computer.'

Jamie's face flickers for a second. This, he was not prepared for, Alice can see.

'What do you mean?' Jamie says carefully.

From the darkness outside, there is a scream of sirens. They both startle, necks jerking towards the windows. The noise passes; another place, another crime. But it has shocked Jamie into a new urgency. He grabs at her hand again.

'Come with me, Alice. Please. From where I am, we can get away – I've got tickets for the three of us. Once we get over to France, we can...'

'Are you insane? I'm on *bail* – the police have got my passport, Jamie – I'm not going to fucking France with you, and neither is Martha!'

'I've got a passport you can use. It's only France. They barely look.'

'What? You're not serious.' But she can see he is.

'Alice, I'm begging you. Don't you see? The police want one of us for Jade's murder – or both of us. We were the last people to see her alive. Our DNA is in the flat. They caught you there with a knife. This ends with us losing Martha. Unless we take her. Now.'

Alice has started to shake.

'They've only let you out on bail because they're hoping you'll lead them to me,' Jamie says. 'As soon as you do that, they'll get us both, if they can.'

Alice feels as if she has been punched in the gut. Is that true? What had Jessica said? *I'm surprised. I would have thought they had enough to hold you.*

'Martha will be left with no one,' Jamie says. He is shaking too. 'Like you were. Do you want that for her?'

Alice stares at him.

'But there is another way...'

'No.' Alice shakes her head. 'That's not... we *can't*. We have to go to the police, Jamie. You have to hand yourself in. Tell the truth.'

'They're not interested, Alice!' Jamie is sobbing now, tears streaming down his cheeks, grabbing her by the shoulders. 'They don't believe me. They'll never believe me!'

'What about Clara Layward?'

Jamie blinks. 'What?'

'Why didn't you tell me you were in a relationship with her?'

Alice waits for the denial, but Jamie's mouth clamps shut, his eyes darting from one side to another. Alice realises with quiet horror that her husband is working out whether he can lie to her again, or not. This is the real Jamie. This is who he is.

'Did you kill Clara, Jamie?'

Jamie's eyes are wide. 'What? Of course not! No one knows what happened to Clara Layward. I told the police everything I knew… Jesus, Alice. Why are you asking about Clara? The family just want someone to blame… That whole thing is bullshit!'

Alice looks at her husband and thinks about the photos of him and Clara together, his hand on her waist, her on his lap. She thinks about the picture of him in the ad campaign with Jade, and how he reacted when she showed the picture to him, after she found it in Becca's holdall. She thinks about Isobel, how he'd made up that horrible lie about her having miscarriages. About the fake Zoom calls he'd pretended to be on in his study, in the days after the break-in. The cycling accident that never was. The conference that didn't exist. The fucking coconut macaroons. And she realises that she has no idea whether Jamie is guilty or innocent.

The only thing she can be certain of is that Jamie is a liar.

Alice takes out her phone without another word, tears filling her eyes. She dials 999, and holds the phone to her ear.

'No, Alice. Please!'

'You need to talk to the police, Jamie,' she says, her voice choking. The ring sounds.

'Alice, don't do this!' Jamie backs away from her towards the basement door. He is sobbing, his face slick with sweat.

'I can't live without you and Martha, Alice. Please. You know I can't, I can't lose Martha…'

Alice is crying now, too. But she does not end the call. And Jamie buries his head in his hands, crouches down so that his head is between his knees and lets out a noise of pure animal pain, somewhere between a roar and a howl. Then he grabs the battered backpack he'd left on the kitchen table, and as the call is answered, he bolts from the house, slamming the basement door behind him.

ALICE

By the time the police got to the house, Jamie was long gone. Alice had been made to go over the conversation three or four times.

Can you explain why you delayed calling the police? What exactly did he say about Jade Jones? Did he give any indication at all of where he was going? What was his state of mind? Do you think he is likely to be at risk of harming himself, or others?

Martha had woken up, of course, and Aunt Sarah, with all the noise and the door slamming, then the arrival of the police, sirens strobing blue through the downstairs blinds. Aunt Sarah had stood in the kitchen in her long towelling dressing gown, making tea and shaking her head over and over. Martha had clung to Alice and buried her face in Alice's chest, and Alice had stroked her hair and tried to somehow murmur reassurances. Even though it was almost impossible to manage the disconnect between what she was telling Martha – 'The police are just trying to find Daddy, to help him come and explain everything' – and the words coming through the crackles of the police radios, calling Jamie a 'suspect' who had 'fled the scene on foot, heading west'. After a while Alice had stopped saying anything at all, and had just held her daughter close.

Alice walks Martha to school, holding tightly to her hand. The sky is a piercing blue, the air so cold it catches in Alice's throat, Martha's little breaths showing as puffs of steam. Yas offered to take Martha to school, but Alice declined. She wants to hold Martha's hand until the last possible minute this morning. Martha has an energy bar shoved in her pocket along with a pair of mismatched gloves, which is the best Alice could do. Martha refused to eat breakfast, or brush her hair, or teeth, and Alice hadn't had the energy to force her, so the two of them look equally wild and unkempt.

Alice is glad that the cold has given her an excuse to wear a huge scarf, a hat pulled low over her face, an overlarge coat. Part insulation, part armour, part disguise. It doesn't work entirely. Even Martha's nice class teacher gives Alice a slightly pained look these days, and the head teacher, who has a cheery smile for almost everyone at the front gate in the morning, averts her eyes from Alice. A few days ago, Alice had tried to pull up the school WhatsApp group, to ask a question about Martha's homework, and been unable to find it. Have she and Jamie been deleted?

'Bye, sweetheart. Have a great day. I love you.' Alice tries to give Martha a hug as she says goodbye, but Martha shrugs her off, wincing, and stamps into the classroom, failing to return the teacher's welcome. Alice gives an apologetic eye roll to the teacher, but gets barely a nod in return before the classroom door is closed.

Alice doesn't know if it is really the right thing, making her go to school. She feels a bit jittery at the thought of leaving her. But then what is the alternative? Alice has to keep their lives on track somehow.

Alice spends the day at home. She should do something useful – cook some food for Martha, wash the sheets, clean the house, maybe even start looking for a new job – but finds she is distracted, can't settle to anything. Aunt Sarah has gone out – Alice can't remember where – and won't be back in time to pick up Martha from her art club, so Alice does, at least, have that to do.

By pick-up time, the temperature has dropped further, the sky threatening snow, so Alice decides to drive. She gets there early, wanting to get Martha home as quickly as possible, and ends up having to stand awkwardly with the other art club mothers. Stella is there, wrapped up in a leopard-print coat, heeled boots and a crochet hairband. She catches Alice's eye and attempts a smile. Alice supposes she should be grateful. None of the other parents have even made eye contact. But Alice does not return the smile. As she turns away she is sure she hears Stella give a faint sigh.

A thin confetti of flakes starts over the playground. The parents turn to look. It is barely snow, nothing that will settle. Alice tucks her face further inside her thick bundle of scarf, checks the time again on her phone. Inside the classroom, paper stars hang from the ceiling, rainbows of home-made paper chains stapled across wall displays on the Tudors, minibeasts, Diwali. Alice feels a surge of gratitude to the school for providing her daughter with its precious haven of normality. Inside the classroom, she can see Kirsty and Lucy, the lovely art club girls, collecting up the paint pots and clipping artwork to clothes lines to dry.

After what seems like an eternity, Kirsty throws the door open. Alice pushes to the front, ahead of Stella, not caring if she is being rude.

Kirsty gives her a confused look. 'Hi, Alice,' she says. 'Is – is Martha not home with you?'

Alice feels a lurch of nausea.

'What do you mean?'

'She was picked up early today – we got a parent message, on the clubs app?'

Alice stares. She hasn't sent any message.

'Who? Who took her?'

'I wasn't here – I assumed it had been you. Hang on.' The teacher calls over to the art club assistant, Lucy.

'Lucy, who was it that took Martha home earlier?'

Lucy sets down the pile of books she is carrying.

'It was her dad,' she says. 'He's on your approved list, right? Why?'

There is no time for questions about how it has happened, and who is to blame. How the multiple emails from both the police and Alice to the head teacher, copying in the school admin office, the senior staff, the class teachers and all the teaching assistants, had somehow missed off the team who run the after-school art club. Leaving them somehow unaware that Martha's father was wanted for murder, that the police and Alice should be alerted if he was so much as seen near the school premises.

Alice is ushered inside, to an office behind the reception she has never been to before. The school and playground, teeming with parents and children just minutes ago, are silent now. The place feels strange and wrong without the noise of children. On the desk there is a framed photograph in a round oval mount of a little girl with bunches.

'It's important you stay calm, Alice,' the head teacher is saying. 'Do have a seat.'

Alice stares at her, this woman – Jill, her name is, who has never shown any interest in Martha until all this, who didn't seem to have any real sense of who Martha even was when Alice had first got in touch to discuss what had been going on.

'I've alerted the police, they are on their way,' Jill continues, in a voice that's clearly meant to be soothing. 'They said to wait by the phone, and...'

'Wait by the phone?' Alice is shaking. 'My daughter has been abducted!'

'I know this is all very upsetting.'

Jill is talking to Alice as if she is a primary-age child herself. The woman clearly only has one mode.

'Why don't we sit...'

'I'm not sitting anywhere! Do you not understand what is hap—' Jill's mobile phone rings loudly. She glances at Alice, then answers it.

'Yes? Yes, she is right here. Hang on.'

Jill passes Alice the phone. Alice snatches it.

'Alice? This is DCI Barnes.'

'Jamie's taken Martha,' Alice blurts, a sob escaping with the words.

'Where would he have taken her, Alice?'

'I don't know, I don't know... Last night he was talking about France, but I didn't think...'

'All right, Alice – stay where you are. Some officers will be along, and we will need to take statements...'

'But we need to find her!'

'It's better that you stay where you are, Alice. Our officers will be doing all they can. I'm going to end the call now but I'll see you very soon. OK? Alice?'

Alice hangs up in a rage, thrusts the phone back at Jill. Her hands are shaking. Jill raises her eyebrows.

'I'm sure they'll be here soon.' She pauses. 'Can I get you a cup of tea, while we wait?'

'I'm going to my car.' This woman must be insane if she thinks Alice is going to sit here and drink tea while her daughter is missing. Alice turns and heads out of her office before the head teacher can answer.

Alice marches out of the school gates, snow swirling in front of her eyes, sticking to her wet lashes, melting on her hot cheeks. She gets into her car and slams the door shut. She grips the steering wheel, and lets out a howl of pure anguish and frustration.

Jamie would never hurt Martha. She knows this to be true – doesn't she? And yet, he has taken her. He has *taken* her.

On the seat next to her, Alice's phone vibrates. A message from an unknown number. Alice snatches it up.

M is safe. Everything will be OK if you come here, with no police.

Alice grabs the phone and types back frantically.

Where are you?

The reply comes immediately.

You have to promise. No police.

Alice's hands are shaking.

OK. Please just tell me where Martha is.

Before the reply comes through, though, she thinks back to exactly what Jamie said the night before. *From where I am, we can get to France. Please, Alice.*

And now she realises exactly where Jamie is.

She calls Barnes. His line is engaged. She redials immediately. Same thing. She dials 999, asks for the police. She tells them what is happening, that her child is missing, that she knows where her child is, repeats the address. But the operator doesn't seem to understand, keeps asking for the postcode of the school, keeps getting confused by whether Martha is missing or with her father, seems to think Alice is referring to some sort of custody issue.

'I can see that the police are already on their way to you,' the operator says eventually, sounding relieved, 'so what I suggest is that you stay where you are and wait for…'

Alice stabs the button on her phone to hang up. She tugs her coat off – she is too hot in here, with the blowers on. She scans the road outside the school for any sign of the police. Why aren't they here yet?

There is a knock on the driver's side window. Alice startles, then looks up and sees Stella. She hesitates, then opens the window.

'I heard about Martha,' Stella says breathlessly. 'I'm so sorry. Are the police coming? Is there anything I can do?'

'I know where Jamie has taken her,' Alice gabbles. 'There is a place we used to go in Camber Sands – the house is called Gull Cry. It's right on the beach. I am *sure* he is there. I'm trying to phone the police, to tell them – but the line is busy…'

'OK,' Stella says. 'Slow down.'

'Can you wait here for them?' Alice asks. 'Tell the police the address where I think he is? They will be here soon, but I can't just wait here, Stella. I have to go. I have to go to her.' Alice feels like she might hyperventilate, her words tripping over each other.

Stella's eyes are wide, a tiny snowflake caught on one eyelash. Behind her, Alice can see the head teacher is still standing at the gates, talking to Kirsty, the art club leader, looking around for the police. Where the hell are the police?

'Please, Stella. Write it down.' She tells her the address of Gull Cry, and obediently, Stella taps it out on her phone. 'Will you tell the police they have to go there? Please?'

'Sure, of course, but…'

'Thank you. Thank you.'

Alice starts the engine, revs it more loudly than she means to, her hands shaking.

'Alice? Hang on, wait a second,' Stella protests. 'Don't you want to…'

Alice doesn't stay to hear Stella finish. She throws the phone onto the passenger seat, and accelerates, forcing Stella to jump back from the window in shock. Alice pulls the car around into a three-point turn, then floors the accelerator, speeding away until Stella and the school and all the other mothers and the children and the teachers are just dots in a snowstorm in her rear-view mirror.

ALICE

Alice drives fast, erratically, overtaking car after car, ignoring the many honks of protest. Finally she reaches the motorway, and then the turning for the coast road. The light is fading now, and the cars on the roads have thinned out. The snow is heavier. Alice has never seen snow over the sea before. It looks wrong, like one of those creepy computer-generated images of places that aren't real.

By the time she gets to Gull Cry, it is almost dark. The house looks different in the winter. The windows that face out to sea look gloomy and menacing in a way they never did before. In front of the house is a hoarding: the name of a builder's firm and a phone number. But there is no sign of workers here now. Nor are there any lights on in the house. No sign of a car in the drive. Or of the police.

Alice feels a sick lurch of doubt. Have the police already checked the house and left? Has she made the wrong call? She snatches up her phone, tries to call Barnes. But there is no signal.

She pulls on the brake, slams the car door shut behind her and punches her way through the makeshift door cut into the hoarding. She races to the front door and hammers at the knocker. No response.

'Jamie? It's just me. I'm on my own.'

No one answers. Breathlessly, Alice runs around the house to the back doors. They are locked. Then she remembers the small basement door off on one side. As she approaches, it swings open, revealing a room in darkness, and before Alice knows what is happening, she is bundled inside.

Jamie slams the door behind her. He is sweaty, his breath fast. It is freezing in the house, and smells of damp. There is plaster missing from the walls, wires dangling from light fittings that have been pulled out, piles of flooring, building tools, dust sheets. She can barely make out Jamie's face in the dark.

'Jamie, what the…'

Jamie puts his finger to his lips.

'Where is Martha?'

'Upstairs,' he mumbles. 'Alice, wait! She's asleep…'

Alice bolts from him, taking the stairs two at a time. She throws open one bedroom door, then another.

In the master bedroom, she finally sees her daughter.

The window is covered with a taped-up sheet, sagging to one side. A sliver of moonlight cuts across the mattress on the floor, illuminating a mound of thick blankets. Under them, is Martha. She looks exactly like she always does when she sleeps, curled on one side, hands near her face. She is still wearing her school uniform, the collar of her polo shirt curled at her neck. Alice drops down to her daughter's side and touches her forehead, the space under her nose. She is fine. Warm, and breathing. Relief floods through her.

'I gave her some of that antihistamine stuff,' Jamie murmurs. 'The stuff we gave her on the flight to America.'

Alice stares at him. 'How much?'

'She's fine. I was careful,' he says vaguely, as if it doesn't really matter, and Alice feels a cold shot of fear. He is talking like a person she does not recognise. She touches her daughter again, needing to be sure. Martha stirs a little at the coolness of Alice's touch.

'I won't let you take her, Alice, if that's what you're thinking. I'd rather die than let you take her from me.'

Alice turns around. Jamie is standing in shadow, and she can't see his face properly.

'I'm not going to take her,' she says quietly.

Jamie shuffles towards her into the light.

'Why are you here, then?'

'I thought you said you had ferry tickets.'

Jamie reaches for her hand to gently pull her towards him. The look on his face breaks her heart.

'You believe me, don't you?'

For a moment, they just stand there, facing each other. Alice can hear the swirl of the dark water outside, the wind rushing over the sand dunes.

'I believe you, Jamie,' Alice says, feeling tears on her cheeks. 'I believe you didn't kill anyone.'

Jamie takes a step forward, studies her face in the thin moonlight as if he can't quite allow himself to believe it. Eventually he exhales, his shoulders sagging, makes a noise between a sigh of relief and a sob, and pulls her into his arms.

Jamie leads Alice down the stairs into the main room. Wires hang from the ceilings where lights are to be fitted and the radiators lie on their sides, yet to be plumbed. A fire crackling in the log burner is their only source of heat, or light.

'Martha is OK under those blankets,' Jamie says, reading her thoughts. Alice shivers, draws close to the fire. It is so cold she can't think straight.

'Can we really not even boil a kettle or something?' Alice mutters. 'I'm so cold, Jamie.'

Jamie comes to sit beside her on the floor, his shadow long on the wall. 'Sorry,' he says. 'But here. Have this.'

He passes her a whisky bottle.

Alice takes a small sip. She hates the taste of whisky and this one is particularly awful, but the sensation of warmth spreading through her chest is worth it. She takes another sip. Then a gulp. And another.

There is a shifting sound in the darkness outside, like footsteps on the gravel. But as soon as it comes, it is gone again. Jamie stiffens, then slumps back.

'Probably just a fox, or something,' Alice says, before reminding herself that she is not in East London now. Are there foxes out here? Or something else? The police? Surely they must be on their way. *Come on*, she thinks. *Come* on.

Alice takes another gulp of whisky, looks up at her husband's face in the orange glow of the fire. When you are married to someone, you don't look at them, really look at them, very often. You have a picture of them in your mind's eye, that was formed long ago. When you first met, when you first fell in love. A picture from the time they became imprinted on you, became a part of who you are. Alice realises that she hasn't paid attention to Jamie's face for a long time, not in the way she is now. And that even though it is the same, it is also different in small ways. The flecks of grey at his temples – when had they appeared? The thickening of his eyebrows, the deepening parentheses in his forehead, the softening of his jawline. These changes had happened right in front of her eyes, and she had not seen them, not really.

'How have you been here all this time?'

Jamie shakes his head. 'I slept on a beach one night. Under a bridge. But it was so cold. And then I remembered about this place, the building work. I watched for a day or two, but I didn't see anyone here. I think the work must have stopped for a bit. But then yesterday afternoon, someone came round to check on the place, a builder, I think. I slipped out before they could find me, snuck onto a train back to London. I wanted to talk to you. I hoped you would come...'

'But how did you and Martha get here?'

Jamie sighs. 'When I was in the kitchen last night. Sarah's car keys were out on the worktop.' He shrugs, hopelessly. 'I was desperate.'

'Jamie,' she says, laying her hands on his arms. 'Did you really buy ferry tickets?'

'At the harbour,' he mumbles vaguely. 'We can leave at first light.'

'Which harbour?'

Jamie says nothing. He must mean Dover. If he paid by card, maybe he was caught on CCTV. Buying the ferry tickets. Or at the train station. Either way, the police will know to come here. They will be found. Martha will be OK. Stella will have told them by now, to come. Won't she?

'You know,' she continues, 'the police have got my passport, Jamie. We won't be able to…'

Jamie seems to physically wince at her words. He shrugs her hands off, waves her words away.

'It doesn't matter. We won't need it.'

Alice stares at him.

'What do you mean? Jamie?'

She can't understand what Jamie is saying. She wants to press him further, but she can no longer tell if Jamie is still listening to her. It is as if he is in some sort of trance.

Alice feels strangely outside of herself. She feels the whisky swimming warm inside her, softening the edges of her consciousness. She longs to go to Martha upstairs, to be with her, but she can't risk letting Jamie out of her sight. She tries to think what his plan could possibly be. Does he really think they can stay here until dawn, until it is time to leave for the ferry? And if they do, will they be stopped? Will the scream of sirens come, the shouts of police, the sensation of being bundled into a van? Or will they be waved through onto a ferry, and feel it pull away from the coast onto the sea? And if so, then what will happen after that?

'Do you remember,' Jamie says, 'the first time we ever came here, to Rye? When Martha was a baby?'

Alice, thickness forming in her throat, unable to speak: morning, when Martha had woken early, she'd left Jamie to sleep and taken her out in the sling to walk on the beach. The morning sea air had smelled rich, salty and sweet at once. By the time she'd reached the water's edge, Martha had been snoring softly, her tiny feet in the palms of Alice's hands, warm and soft as baby mice. She'd looked back to the house, at Gull Cry, and seen her husband on the balcony with his coffee, just smiling at the two of them, glowing with love for his wife and daughter.

'I want to go back there,' Jamie whispers, through a sob. 'I just want more than anything to go back.'

We are there, Alice thinks stupidly, for a second. And then she sees what he really means. He wants to erase it all. Go back to the way they were. Before the break-in. Before everything. She feels the tears in her own eyes now, too. She puts her arms around him.

'That's all I wanted,' he tells her. 'I wanted to go back.'

Alice holds him in her arms. She thinks she understands now.

'There are no passports, Jamie,' she asks him gently. 'Are there? There are no ferry tickets.'

Jamie shakes his head, still sobbing silently. Alice feels her lungs release all the air inside them, the muscles in her shoulders relax with sheer relief. All his delusions are at an end, at last – leaving London. Fleeing to France. Running away. He is facing reality, at last. He is going to hand himself in.

She pulls him more tightly into a hug.

'This is the right thing,' she says, after a while.

Jamie roughly brushes a tear from his cheek. She has never seen him so broken.

'I know,' he says heavily. 'I knew you'd understand. I only ever wanted to protect you from it all. You and Martha. To keep our family together. And this is the only way, now.'

Jamie pulls something out of his pocket. A small brown bottle. Alice doesn't recognise it at first. Then she sees the label, and realises. It is the bottle of prescription sleeping pills, the ones she was prescribed after the break-in.

At first, Alice doesn't understand. What do they need these for? Alice had thought she'd thrown those pills away. They had always made her feel horrible – groggy and anxious – so she had scarcely ever taken them. She'd used only one or two.

Now the bottle looks nearly empty.

Alice pulls away from Jamie. She thinks about the awful-tasting whisky she has been swigging.

'Jamie,' she says shakily. 'What did you do with the pills?'

Jamie looks up at her, blinking.

'You understand, don't you, Alice?' he says dully. 'Why it has to be this way?'

ALICE

Alice feels sick.

'Jamie, what do you mean?' she stammers. 'I – I thought... I thought you meant you were going to hand yourself in.'

Jamie stands heavily. Walks over to the window, pinches the slats of the blind open to check outside.

When he looks back at her from the window, his face is blank, as if it has been wiped clean. He looks at her as if she is mad.

'I can't go back out there.' He turns away, gesturing behind him at the glass. 'Not now. It's too late. They'll never understand.'

'They will.'

'No, they won't.'

Alice's stomach flips. Is that the answer – can she be sick? Would that stop this? How long has she been here, drinking this whisky with him? One hour? Two? How many of the pills has he put inside this bottle?

And then she thinks of Martha, of what he'd said, about the antihistamine.

'Jamie,' she says, her voice harder now. 'What did you give Martha?'

Jamie sighs. 'I told you,' he mutters. Alice feels a jolt of adrenaline, dragging her back into consciousness, even though her limbs already feel heavy. Her hands tighten into fists.

'Jamie?'

'I gave her that antihistamine stuff.'

'But how much?'

Jamie just shakes his head. 'I just wanted us all to be here together,' he says. 'Just for this one last time. I thought you understood. I thought that's why you came here.'

Her husband looks broken, but Alice no longer cares. She doesn't care about anything but Martha. How she can wake her up, stop this. Stick her fingers down her daughter's throat. Whatever it takes. She shoves past Jamie, but as she does, his whole demeanour changes. He grabs her, with a strength and solidity that she never knew he had. Because he has never shown it to her.

'I can't let you go.' There is hardness in his voice. 'You must see that, Alice. You can't leave me. I couldn't bear it.'

'Jamie, let me go! You're hurting me!'

But Jamie is ignoring her, gripping her arms more tightly, so tightly she gasps in pain. He is breathing heavily, too, and Alice cannot tell whether it is anger, or the effort of restraining her.

'Let me see Martha, Jamie!'

'It's too late,' he hisses in her ear.

Alice opens her mouth to scream. But then there is a noise from outside. And both of them freeze.

A sound from the other room, like a chair falling. For a split second, she and Jamie just stare at each other. Then Jamie twists his neck to look towards the noise, keeping Alice in his grip.

A door is thrown open. A figure in the darkness, the silver flash of metal in her hand.

'Let her go, Jamie.'

Stella's voice is calm, but thick with a quiet fury. Jamie stares at her in horror. She is holding a knife, but her hand is shaking so much that Alice wonders whether she would be capable of using it.

'It's over, Jamie,' she says. 'The police know you killed Jade. Tell Alice the truth. Tell her!'

Jamie stares at Stella.

'Put the knife down,' he says quietly.

Alice looks at him, then back to Stella. Something has happened to her vision. The room tilts and swims, as if she is stepping off a roundabout. She wonders whether she might be sick.

'Stop lying, Jamie!' Stella snaps furiously. 'It's over. The police have all the evidence they need. They are coming for you.' She takes a step towards them. 'So it's time to tell me the truth. About my sister. What did you do to her?'

Stella's presence has shaken Jamie from his torpor. His voice is clear and defiant.

'There is nothing to tell.'

'*Liar*!'

Stella jerks the knife up higher, in front of his face. Both Jamie and Alice gasp.

'You left her to die.' Stella's voice is thick with fury. 'She is dead because of *you*.'

Jamie makes a little noise of disgust. 'No one killed your sister,' he says, his tone contemptuous. 'Drop the knife, and we can talk.'

Stella ignores him. She tightens her grip on the knife, keeping it at eye level. Her whole body is still trembling. When are the police coming, Alice wants to ask Stella. But then she realises: Stella hasn't told the police where they are. Because Stella wants to finish this herself.

Alice tries to focus on how she can get to Martha. But Jamie is still gripping her tight. Every time she moves, he hardens his grip. And Alice is shaking too, and her legs feel weak, although whether it is the cold, or the pills, or the knife in Stella's hand, she can't be entirely sure. The shaking must be obvious because now Stella is looking down at her. She looks alarmed, lowers the knife a little.

'Alice? What's wrong?' Stella's eyes scan the floor, where the bottle of pills has fallen. 'What are those?' She looks up at Jamie, eyes narrowed, and jerks the knife up again. 'What are you doing, Jamie?'

Jamie takes a step towards Stella.

'You want the truth about Clara?'

His voice is soft, almost a whisper. Stella is thrown briefly off-balance. Jamie comes close to her face, so close it is almost as if he is about to kiss her. Then he throws Alice on the floor, and grabs Stella's jaw in one hand, and closes the other around her hand, the one with the knife in it. Alice feels her tailbone slam against the floor, and sees Stella gasp in pain.

'You want to know the truth about your sister?' Jamie hisses at Stella, tightening his grip. 'She was a spoilt little brat who made everything about herself. The charity were trying to help people, and she spent all her time moaning about how I'd supposedly treated her. We had a casual thing, and she turned completely psycho about it and couldn't accept I'd moved on. She tried to destroy my career, and failed. She was pathetic.'

'So you left her,' Stella spits, her words muffled, Jamie's hand still clamped around her jaw. 'You left her to die. Because she was telling people the truth about you…'

Jamie grips her harder still, and Stella winces, her face contorted with pain. Alice gasps. He ignores them both.

'There was no need,' he hisses, 'because not a single person believed the word of that silly little slut over mine. Not then, and not now.'

A noise from outside. Tyres on gravel, doors opened and slammed, footsteps. The three of them freeze, and look at each other.

'Police!'

Jamie's head jerks towards the shout from the front door. The lock breaks, the door juddering open. There is a flash of light from a torch outside, the clatter of footsteps, getting closer.

'My daughter is upstairs,' Alice screams. She scrabbles at the wall, trying desperately to pull herself up. 'He's given her something – she needs to go to hospital! Please.'

Jamie turns his head to Alice. His eyes lock with hers, his face full of betrayal.

'You sick bastard!' Stella spits at him. His hands are looser now on Stella's face and wrist, as if the strength is draining from his body. There are footsteps in the hallway.

'Police!'

Something else happens, then. Alice sees Stella's mouth move close to Jamie's ear, but she doesn't hear the words. She sees only Jamie letting out something between a gasp and a gulp. His eyes bulge, as if they are about to pop out of his head.

Alice hears footsteps, and then there are people in the room, three or four at once.

'Police! Get back! I need your hands where I can see them. Now!'

Alice pulls her upper body off the floor with an effort, and raises her hands. Stella does the same. A knife drops, clatters to the floor. The same voice shouts again.

'Hands! Now!'

Jamie has not raised his hands. He has not turned around, to look at the officers. His hands are clutching at his chest, searching for something, clawing at his clothes. And then he holds them out in front of him, and the palms are red with blood.

And only then does Alice see the dark red, spreading from underneath his ribs, soaking his top. She looks again at the knife on the floor, a handle just like the one that Ezra held that night. For a moment, she thinks it must be the same knife, but that cannot be right; she cannot be thinking straight. Things are getting muddled in her mind. Because here again is a body falling to the ground, the cool tiles of a floor clouding with blood. And Alice is falling too, listening to a scream that she only later realises is coming from her own mouth.

BECCA
One month later

Becca is standing in the kitchen of her flat, making soup, warming bread in the oven. Rain patters on the skylight window over the kitchen table, where Martha is kneeling on the padded bench seat, colouring pencil in hand. Becca and Caz's new puppy, Pip, is curled up next to her on a cushion, her silky head tucked right up against Martha's leg.

Alice is sitting opposite on a chair. She is holding her patterned coffee mug a little stiffly in her hands, and Becca wonders why Alice wanted to come, and whether she is thinking about what happened the only other time she came to this flat. Of all the things that she and Becca still have never talked about. But then Becca sees that Alice is, in fact, focused entirely on her daughter, and the pictures she is drawing.

'That's a lovely drawing, Martha,' Alice says, carefully. Martha doesn't speak. She is not speaking much since it happened. The therapist has told Alice that she shouldn't push. So Becca and Alice press their lips together, and stop themselves from pushing.

At lunch, Martha manages a surprising amount of soup, plus bread and cheese, and even – miraculously – some of the salad that Becca has made. Becca is glad to see it, and to see the relief on Alice's face, the exquisite pleasure of seeing a child you love eat well.

'Can I see your pictures?' Alice asks. Martha pauses, then passes them over. As Becca stands to collect the bowls, she casts her eyes warily over Martha's pictures, and sees Alice do the same. But today, there are only rain and puddles, trees and flowers, and in the middle, a large girl, a smaller girl and a dog that is obviously meant to be Pip. Becca says a silent prayer that this signals the end of the other drawings, the ones Alice has told Becca about. The ones of the crying people, the knives, the big black clouds.

'These are very good, Martha. You're so talented.' Becca sits beside Martha and leafs through the pictures slowly, paying attention to the details. Martha says nothing, but snuggles into Becca, who strokes her hair softly. Becca and Alice talk to Martha carefully, in a way that doesn't demand responses. Becca talks about anime and kawaii, the sort of drawings that Martha has become interested in lately, as well as gymnastics, school lunches and whether the rain might stop in time for them to give Pip a walk. This last topic elicits a flicker of a smile.

Caz emerges from her room, where she has been on a Teams call. She ruffles Martha's hair and asks if she wants to come with her to take Pip to the park. Martha, who has taken an instant liking to Caz, nods vigorously.

When the door closes behind them, Becca sits with Alice in the kitchen, and opens a bottle of wine. Today is the day, she has decided.

'Alice, I want you to know the truth about the break-in,' Becca says.

She sees Alice's spine stiffen as she holds her breath.

'Everything,' Becca says. 'You deserve to hear it.'

Alice sighs. 'OK,' she says.

And so Becca finally tells Alice the story of how she'd seen Jamie and Jade by the canal that time. How she had tried to demand he come clean. And then, how Jamie had blackmailed her, how he had forced her to hand in her notice. And, through her toe-curling embarrassment, she begins to explain to Alice about the pictures on the computer, and who they had really been for. Her flatmate, who in fact, is so much more than just that.

When she gets to the part about Caz, Alice bursts into tears. She throws her arms around Becca, and then, when Caz arrives home with Martha and the dog, Alice jumps to her feet and embraces a surprised Caz in a tearful hug too.

Afterwards, Alice pulls away, wipes her eyes with both hands and says: 'Enough. I don't need to hear any more, Becca.'

'But, wait,' Becca protests, glancing at Caz and Martha, 'I need…'

'I don't care what else happened,' Alice says quietly, a palm raised, silencing her. 'I don't want to think about the break-in any more. We all need a fresh start.'

Becca exhales. 'OK,' she says. She shifts in her chair. 'What do you want me to do?'

Alice looks at her steadily. 'What I want you to do,' she says, 'is rip up whatever stupid agreement you signed, and stay. With us. If that's what you want, I mean.'

Becca stares at her.

'Are you sure?'

'More than sure.' Alice takes her hand, across the table. 'Like I said. A fresh start. For all of us.'

Becca looks away, at the whorls in the wood of their kitchen table. At the walls covered in photographs of her and Caz, and of her parents, and some of Martha, too. And the big painting, stuck on the fridge, that Becca and Martha made together years ago, of a rainbow.

And she thinks about all the things that she has done. The things she has told Alice about.

And the things that she has not.

BECCA
Five days after the break-in

Once they'd decided what had to be done, the rest of it had felt almost like sleepwalking.

Once Jamie was dead, everything could go back to normal, Becca kept telling herself. She would get her job back, and she and Caz would get their happy-ever-after. And most importantly, no one would ever see those pictures – not her parents, not Alice, not anyone.

She knew Martha and Alice would be devastated – Becca hated that part – but Stella had said both of them would be better off in the long run, without Jamie for a husband and father. A cheater. A blackmailer. A liar. And, according to Stella, a killer.

Some men are just toxic, Becca, Stella had said. *And the world would be a far better place for our daughters, if they did not exist.*

Stella hadn't needed Becca to do that much. On the day in question, she would call in sick, thereby forcing Alice to pick the kids up and take them to the playground at Stonebridge Gardens, where Becca has told Martha they would go that day. Stella would be there, waiting, and would invite herself back for a coffee. Becca just needed to be there, having made a late recovery from her fake illness, with tea ready for all the kids, so that Alice couldn't say no. Becca would then would leave a kitchen knife out on the side, when she unloaded the dishwasher. Use the prospect of their favourite movie to get all the kids safely into the snug. Then get in with them, and lock the door.

Once Stella knew that Jamie was about to be home, Stella would text Becca on the burner phone, and Becca would use her burner to send the agreed message to the agreed number.

Stella hadn't said who would be on the end of that phone. And Becca hadn't wanted to know. But Stella had assured her it would look exactly like an ordinary break-in.

Once Jamie was dead, the only other thing Becca had to do was get rid of the phone afterwards. That was easy enough. Surely that much, she could do.

After that, Becca would be free of Jamie. They all would.

But of course, it hadn't gone to plan. Not at all. And Becca couldn't escape the feeling that Stella had lied to her. Every time she saw a picture of Ezra in the news, Becca felt sick. She'd thought Stella meant some sort of hit man would be involved. But this was just an angry kid. And it was Becca – Becca's message – that had lured him to his death.

Stella told Becca to keep calm. A hit man would have been a terrible idea, Stella had explained. If it had been a hit man, the police would have known someone had put him up to it, and come looking for who. Ezra had a motive of his own, so there was no reason the police would think anyone else was involved. Plus, Stella said, he had some sort of brain disease, which made him act irrationally, violently sometimes – so he'd have been fine – any judge would have let him off.

But he isn't fine now, is he? Becca had hissed at Stella. *He's dead! And Alice could go to prison!*

It wouldn't come to that, Stella said. They'd realise Alice wasn't to blame.

And what then? Becca had asked. *What if they come looking for someone else? What if they find out about the phone?*

Look, Stella had said, *I know it didn't go to plan. But Ezra is the only person other than me and you who knew what really happened, and he's dead, OK? Just get rid of the phone, and we're safe as houses.*

Becca hoped she was right. Already, the phone felt hot to her, like a thing with a noxious energy of its own, that was making her sicker and sicker the longer she carried it around.

She'd waited to get rid of it for a few days after the break-in, once the police had let Alice back home. Alice was still stumbling around the house, ghostlike, wandering off with conversations half-finished to stare out of the window. Jamie was barely speaking to Becca, yet it fell to the two of them to keep up the rituals of dinner, spelling, homework, reading books. Bath, nit combing, bedtime stories. Kisses and lights out.

On the night she did it, she'd got back to their flat to find Caz in the galley kitchen, with the slippers she always wore – the tiled floor was always freezing. Caz had started on one of the meals from the vegetarian recipe-box subscription she'd recently signed them up to. Becca didn't love the boxes, but Caz – who always got home first – had said they gave her one less thing to worry about, so she was trying to be upbeat about all the tofu.

They'd eaten the dinner on their laps, sitting on their sagging red sofa. Caz had been full of ideas for the new flat – paint colours, kitchen layouts, some rug she'd seen on sale that she thought would be perfect, but Becca couldn't focus. Caz wanted to know why Becca hadn't replied to all the estate agent's messages about the flat. They were supposed to be exchanging solicitors' details, getting the ball rolling. Becca's answers had been mumbled, non-committal, pleading tiredness, a headache.

In the end, Caz had given up, and switched on the BBC detective series they were watching. Becca had suggested it after reading good reviews, but while it had initially seemed interesting, it had slightly lost its way, or perhaps Becca had just lost the thread of it. When a crack of gunshots came, Becca had startled on the sofa, sending pieces of jackfruit that was supposed to substitute for chicken flying onto their rug.

Caz had sighed, started hauling herself up.

'Don't be silly – I'll do it,' Becca said, gently pushing Caz back down with a hand on her knee, and standing to find a cloth for the mess.

'Are you sure you're OK, babe?' Caz had tipped her head up to look at Becca. Her face was pinched with worry. 'I thought you were really excited about this flat. You haven't changed your mind, have you?'

'God, no,' Becca exclaimed. 'I'm sorry – I'm fine.' She forced a smile. 'Just this headache. Might get an early night.'

'Good idea. This is rubbish, anyway.' Caz held out the remote control and switched off the TV.

'I'd guessed the husband was the killer ages ago,' Caz said as she collected up their plates. 'Did you?'

'Yeah,' Becca nodded, although actually she'd been surprised by the way it had turned out.

When Caz was deeply asleep, her breath slowed to little wheezes, Becca carefully lifted her side of the duvet and tiptoed towards the landing. Without switching the light on, she'd retrieved the black clothes and face mask and dressed quickly. Then she'd taken the burner phone, closed the door softly behind her and headed towards the canal.

ALICE
April

Alice dabs her brush in the jam jar of water on her desk. She watches the tendrils of red paint detach into the water like coils of smoke until gradually they disappear, the water pinkening. She takes a cotton bud and wets it carefully. On her shoulders she can feel the warmth of the sun through the studio windows, and in the background is the reassuring murmur of Radio 4, and the smell of Stanley's coffee. Not hers, though. Alice drinks her coffee on the way in, these days.

Stanley pauses at her easel on his way to the kitchen. 'I thought you said you were leaving early today,' he says, squinting at his watch.

'I'm just going to do this bit,' she smiles up at him.

She had missed having Stanley around, teasing her about her lunches, his tuneful whistle to the *Archers* theme. He had taken her back with a squeeze of the shoulder and barely even a conversation, for which Alice will always be grateful.

Alice pulls on her coat before she leaves, but it is unseasonably warm, the trees along the canal foaming with cherry blossom, and by the time she reaches the cafe, she has taken it off and stuffed it in her tote bag.

Becca is waiting at the cafe, as she said she would be. She has brought Pip, who is sitting obediently beside her, tail wagging, happy to be out in the sunshine.

'Thanks for doing this with me,' Alice says. 'I know it probably seems a bit weird.'

Becca shrugs and smiles, combing Pip behind the ears with her fingernails. 'I don't mind. I get why you wanted to come.'

Jamie's birthday always felt like the exact moment of the year when eating outside felt right again. He loved this cafe on the towpath, so that's where they'd always come, and they'd eaten pancakes together the three of them. And Alice had realised that despite everything, she had wanted to come here today, and remember when their life had been like that.

Even after Jessica had told her everything – the DNA they'd found under her fingernails, the messages between him and Jade, the phone mast evidence that placed him at her flat – it had taken Alice such a long time to really believe it of Jamie. That the same man who'd held her hand and wept as Martha was born had done that to Jade. Had packed her broken body into a bag, had thrown her into this water like rubbish. But then she remembers the look in his eyes. How he had been ready to end it for all of them. Even her daughter.

Looking back, it's obvious Jamie was having some sort of breakdown, and that Alice had just been too focused on her own to notice. His security obsession, the sudden urge to move out of London, his abrupt loss of interest in his job – none of it had made much sense to her at the time. But she sees now that he was terrified of the consequences of what he had done with Jade, of what he thought she might do to his family. And after Alice told him she'd been to see Jade – followed by the stolen photograph, the gull, the painting – Jamie had simply snapped.

It is odd, she thinks, that he'd denied killing Jade, even at the end, even when it can't really have mattered. But Alice reminds herself that Jamie's words don't count for much. It was like Stella had warned her. If they lie about small things, it means there are bigger things, too. Jamie's lies had got too big, in the end. He was ready to die rather than face what he'd done. Alice wonders if she could have persuaded him, to turn himself in. If Stella hadn't come. Whether she could have saved Martha the pain of losing her father. But then she remembers that Jamie was ready for her to die, and Martha, too. She is sure that Stella would say this way is better. Cleaner. *Some men are just toxic. And the world would be a far better place, for our daughters, if they did not exist.*

Alice inclines her head towards the modern flats where Stella had lived, cupping a hand over her eyes to shield them from the sun. 'I wonder,' Alice says aloud, 'if Stella still lives up there.'

'No idea,' Becca says quickly. She smooths her skirt, takes a careful sip of coffee. 'Is it, um, all over now?' Her eyes dart sideways at Alice. 'The investigation into Stella, I mean. Will they let her go?'

Alice nods. 'Jessica thinks so. She says the charges will be dropped any day.'

After Stella was arrested at Gull Cry, Alice had been taken to hospital with Martha, while Jamie had gone in the ambulance behind. She found out later that they'd tried three times to shock his heart back to life on the way to the hospital. But by the time his ambulance pulled up behind Martha and Alice's, the paramedics emerging from the back doors had been quiet, their heads down, talking in hushed voices. And then Alice had collapsed.

Alice had woken in a hospital bed, her stomach pumped of the drugs that Jamie had given her, to find two officers from Kent police by her bedside. They told her Martha was safe, that she was with Aunt Sarah, who had reported her car stolen and given the detectives the lead they needed to save Alice and Martha. Alice could see Martha later. And they had asked Alice what had happened.

The questions had gone on and on. Her assigned lawyer – oh, how she'd wished for Jessica – had reminded the officers that Alice had been a bystander. That Stella Glass had been the one holding the knife, and was best placed to answer these questions. But they had kept going, asking the same questions in different ways.

Alice had tried to stick to the truth. She told them how Jamie had grabbed Stella, holding on to her jaw and her wrist. How Jamie had tried to kill her and Martha.

'Did Stella Glass know that, though?' The officer's eyes had narrowed. Alice had said nothing.

'It's just that from what you've said,' she'd prompted, 'it's not actually clear that Ms Glass would actually have had reason to believe Jamie was threatening your life, or your daughter's.'

Alice had cleared her throat. She thought of what she herself had done to keep her child safe. The blood on her kitchen floor. And then she thought of Frankie. How Frankie needed Stella, and that was bigger than one little lie.

'I told her,' she'd said in the end. 'I told Stella he was threatening to kill us.'

The officer had glanced at her colleague.

'You're sure about that?'

There had been a beat of hesitation, the blood loud in Alice's ears.

'Yes,' Alice had said. 'Yes, that's right. I told her.'

There are things, of course, that Alice has not told the police.

She has never told them about her visit to Stella's flat the day before Jamie took Martha. How Stella had asked Alice to lead her to Jamie. And had told Alice that she would do the rest.

Alice hadn't agreed to it.

Not then.

But after Jamie took Martha, everything had felt different. And Alice had found that she didn't care about anything in that moment except getting her daughter back. Had she known when she told Stella where Jamie was, that Stella would come to finish things, once and for all?

Alice thinks that deep down she probably did. A look had passed between them, as Alice had started her car. Nothing more than that. And Alice had done nothing to stop her. Just driven off, hands as clean as the freshly fallen snow.

'Did you ever find out what she was doing in Rye that night?'

Becca is swirling a little wooden stick in her coffee. Alice shifts uncomfortably in her seat.

'Stella? I guess she must have been worried about me going there alone, so she followed me,' Alice says vaguely.

She feels sure that Becca will accept this explanation. Most people have.

'Oh, I didn't mean the night Jamie died,' Becca says. 'I was thinking of what happened before.'

'What do you mean?'

'That night in Rye in the summer. When I went out and you and Jamie stayed in the holiday place. When I went out to get some food, and then, just as I was coming back, I saw someone outside your house, dressed in black.'

Alice realises what she is talking about, suddenly. Jade, and the gull.

'I... I didn't know you knew about that.'

'Yeah, it was so bizarre,' Becca says. 'I couldn't make out who it was at first, but I could see they had a bag, like a shopping bag. I saw them take something out of it – I didn't know until later that it was a dead bird.'

Alice shivers at the memory of finding the dead bird Jade had placed on the front step of the holiday house. A crushed, bloody skeleton, broken wings, a smashed skull. And then, how she'd found a clump of the bird's same bloody feathers in that box at Jade's house, and known in that moment that her worst fears were right. She was after them.

'I tried later that night to talk to Jamie about it,' Becca says. 'I told him what I'd seen. But he wouldn't let me speak. He cut me off, told me it will have just been kids messing around, that I shouldn't talk about it in front of you. He seemed really agitated about it – so – I didn't mention it again.'

'I had no idea,' Alice murmurs. 'So you – you saw her do it?'

'Yeah,' Becca says. 'Well, I saw her put something down on the doorstep – I couldn't see what it was at first. It looked like she was going to walk away, back down your garden path, but then she turned suddenly and slammed herself – literally her whole body – right against your door. It was – I don't know. Like someone possessed, you know?'

'I was asleep,' Alice remembers. 'On the sofa. The noise woke me up.'

'Right. I ran over to see what was going on. But she just bolted away down the street into the darkness, before I could see her face properly.'

'Wow,' Alice says. 'I didn't know you'd seen that.' She pauses. 'But you weren't there when we opened the door. When we found the bird.'

'That's because I followed her up the road,' Becca says.

Alice sits up straighter. 'You followed her?'

'Yeah. I wanted to see who it was,' Becca continues. 'So I followed her right up the road until she turned a corner, stopped running and took off the mask, and the hat.'

Alice bites her lip. 'I guess you recognised her, then? Jade?'

Becca looks up.

'The same girl you'd seen Jamie with that time.'

Becca shakes her head.

'No, no. It wasn't Jade.'

Alice stares at her.

'What do you mean? It wasn't Jade?'

'It wasn't.'

'Yes, it was,' Alice stutters. 'We – we know she was behind it. She was stalking me, stealing things, writing messages online, all sorts of stuff. That was why Jamie lost the plot. That's why he…'

She trails off.

'It wasn't Jade, though,' Becca says, shaking her head. 'That's what I'm trying to tell you. It wasn't Jade who put that bird outside your house.'

Alice gapes at Becca.

'Who, then?'

Becca looks straight at Alice. 'It was Stella.'

STELLA

Stella is happy to find it is so beautiful here. An azure sky, a track of red earth up the hillside. A lush, tangled forest of unfamiliar trees. And finally, the place that she came for.

Her taxi driver, Jonathan, had to ask the Ngaramtoni village children to point it out. They had been excited to see her – 'because of your blonde hair,' Jonathan had laughed. They had followed her through a grove of banana trees, shouting, 'Good morning, good morning!' But now Jonathan had somehow got them to leave her here in peace.

And he too, has left her in peace. He is standing with his back to her, leaning against his car, smoking a rolled cigarette. He hasn't asked what she is doing. She paid him the 50,000 shillings up front, and since then, he has let her get on with it.

Stella kneels in the earth. She traces the faint circle of bricks in the dry red ground with her fingers, brushing the sticks and stones away. You would never know it was here if you didn't try to look for it. There is no one still here who remembers Clara now. Or why the *wazungu* – the white people – dug a well here years ago, only to forget all about it, so that gradually the locals gave up on them coming back, and filled it with earth, to keep the children safe. No one remembers her sister, and how she built this. Thinking she could do some good, make a difference. But Stella knows she was here. And that is enough.

The village has a water pump now in the middle square. Has done for years. Plus a new primary school, a medical clinic. The only people who come here now are the children who play in the woods.

Stella closes her eyes. She does not know if any piece of Clara is here, or not. But wherever she is, Stella feels for the first time that she is now at peace. She traces Clara's name in the earth, and talks to her, for a little while. Lays down the pink hibiscus flowers she cut this morning from the gardens of her hotel, and put in her bag. Then she stands up, dusts down her trousers and tells Jonathan that she is ready to go home.

The police had never spotted the connection, never asked Stella a single question about her dead sister, or worked out that she'd been linked to Jamie. There had never been an official murder case for Clara, not even an inquest, barely any official word on her death outside of Tanzania. Stella and Clara haven't shared a surname for many years. On paper, Clara Layward barely exists.

And so, for the police, there had been no reason to believe Stella had a motive for killing Jamie, other than protecting Alice and Martha. The officers had seen the pills on the floor, the marks on the two women that bloomed into purple bruises where Jamie had gripped them. And Alice had backed her up. Just like she'd spoken up for Alice, over Ezra. Had it bothered the detectives, she wondered, the strange symmetry of that? Perhaps it had. But it wasn't evidence of anything, was it? Or certainly not enough.

Stella can never risk talking about her sister now. Or trying to get justice for her in the normal way. But she has got justice for Clara now, and that is a comfort. A justice of the oldest and simplest kind. A life for a life.

Back at the Arusha hotel, Stella orders a negroni and sits by the pool. The heat has softened, and the hotel is quiet. The few sunloungers that were used today have been long abandoned, empty water glasses and crumpled towels strewn around their feet.

Stella raises her glass in a silent toast, and sips it as she watches the sky darken and change colour, enjoying the space between the heat of the day and the coming of the night. She loves this time of day, the smell, the noise of it. A time that disappears with young children, buried under a relentless checklist – fish fingers and chips, teeth brushing and bath time, stories and lights turned out. For once, she can just sit, and take it in. The cicadas in the trees, the pink leaking into the sky, the holiday smell of the pool, the tick-tick-tick of the hotel's irrigation system, keeping flowers and banana trees lush in the borders.

Her phone pings on the little side table next to her lounger, but she resists the temptation to scroll, to check for updates from Hugo about Frankie, or from the council about her new school place, or from the estate agent about the exchange date on their new flat.

It was not a good idea, Stella had decided, Frankie being in the same class as Martha. Alice is studiously avoiding her, but she has seen Becca a few times, at drop-off. Stella always tries to smile at Becca, give her a little wave, reassure her their secret is safe. Stella is good at keeping secrets. But Becca always averts her eyes. She guesses Becca has given Alice a pretty selective account of events. Stella feels pretty sure Alice wouldn't have given Becca her job back if she knew how Becca helped Stella try to kill her husband.

Stella wonders what Alice *does* think happened now, on the day of the break-in. Maybe Alice thinks Stella acted alone. Or maybe she has finally accepted that there are some things about that night that she will never quite understand.

Such a stupid, small thing. But Stella had never imagined that Jamie would get home, only to go straight out again – for milk. She'd tried to call it off then. But Ezra had already switched his burner off, and left it behind.

While Ezra was bleeding out on the floor, Alice reeling, the stool still in her hand, Stella had searched his pockets, his trousers, everywhere. The burner *had* to be on him somewhere, she'd thought. But there had been nothing. No sign of it.

She'd been sure the police would find the burner. But amazingly, they never did. *He must have got rid of it somehow*, Stella had told Becca. Maybe the kid had more brain cells than she'd given him credit for.

'So, all you need to do is get rid of your phone, and we're safe as houses,' she'd told Becca. 'Ezra is the only person other than me and you who knew what really happened.'

The problem was that this wasn't quite the case. There was Jade. And the problem with Jade was that she was a tiny bit too smart.

Obviously, Stella had never *told* Jade what she'd done. That she'd been to see Ezra to tell him not only who had been fucking his sister, but also exactly how he could get revenge, if he felt like it. Stella certainly hadn't told Jade about the burner phone she'd bought Ezra, for Becca to let him know just the right moment, once Jamie was home.

Just keep away from the locked door leading to another room, she'd reminded him. *Away from the room with the children.*

But Jade was smart, and she knew her brother. She knew Ezra wouldn't have done that off his own back. Figured out where Jamie lived, and come up with a plan for revenge. He was too sick, for one thing. She knew he had to have been manipulated. And of course, she was right.

The burner was a loose end, Stella decided. It needed tying up. So once the dust had settled, Stella had been to see Jade, pretending she was still hoping Jade might agree to do the story. In reality, she needed to search the flat and locate the burner.

It hadn't gone well.

Stella had only managed to search the bathroom. It was clear – the attic space above the weird ceiling hatch included, which was a shame, because when she found that little nook, she had thought immediately that that was where she would have hidden a burner phone, if she'd been so inclined. When she got out of the bathroom, Jade had worked out what she was doing. As soon as she'd stepped into the hallway, Jade had been there.

'Looking for something?' she'd asked. 'The phone you gave my brother, maybe?'

Jade had found the burner when she'd cleared out Ezra's room to make way for her baby stuff. Which meant she had proof of what Stella had done. Stella had a serious problem.

Stella needed to stop Jade – or her mother, who was equally hostile – from taking the phone to the police. But she didn't know how, and she was starting to panic, to get sloppy. She went back to Jade's flat a few days later, thinking maybe she could offer her money for the phone. But when she'd got there, she'd seen Linda heading out with Ezra's laptop under her arm and a great big bag on her shoulder. Stella had panicked. What if she was taking that, and the phone, to the police?

Pushing Linda down the steps – well, that had been moronic. It was only Stella's good luck that no one saw her do it, and that the CCTV cameras had all been vandalised. Moments later, when one of Linda's neighbours had seen her and run over to help, Stella had had to run off without getting hold of the laptop, or the phone. At least she'd managed to swipe Linda's house keys, though, which she'd dropped on the ground as she fell.

If Linda remembered who'd pushed her, she seemed to be keeping quiet. And she was stuck in hospital for a while, which was useful. Jade, though, was going to be harder to stop. In the end, it was Alice who'd handed Stella the perfect solution.

Stella takes a taxi across the border to Nairobi airport, and boards the flight home. Travelling alone is a rare and exquisite pleasure. Her carry-on bag is free of all the items she usually carts around for Frankie. It is thrilling to have so little on her: other than her travel documents, phone and purse, she has packed only a Kindle, a silk eye mask and a tube of moisturiser. When Stella rummages in the pocket for her passport, though, her fingers close around something else. Something cool and metallic.

She picks them out, one, then the other, smiles as she remembers. The gold earrings, the ones that had belonged to Alice. She'd forgotten all about them.

Stella has always liked Alice. It was just unfortunate for Alice that she had unwittingly presented Stella with such a perfect scenario when she confided that, consumed with guilt over Ezra, she had been to see Jade and Linda, and had ended up panicking and lying about who she was. And that she'd then somehow become embroiled in Jade's life – delivering her baby clothes, for goodness' sake – only to then become convinced that Jade in fact knew who she was. Apparently, Alice had caught Jade taking a photograph from her purse – a photo of her, Martha and Jamie. She'd become convinced, then, that Jade had worked out she was the person who killed her brother. That she could even be preparing some sort of vengeance.

All of which meant it hadn't been very hard at all to nudge Alice towards believing that Jade was stalking her. Stella hadn't had to do much, really. A few silly messages online – those had taken seconds to post. She'd used Alice's own family computer, which was always switched on in the study, just so nothing would lead back to her. And Stella had also made sure, each time she was at Alice's, to relieve her of a few of the sorts of items your textbook stalker might take, just to increase Alice's paranoia.

It had been easy. A silky camisole plucked from a bathroom radiator. A small notebook slipped into her coat pocket from a kitchen drawer. Some sunglasses popped into her handbag, while Becca was making a pot of coffee. Alice's work security pass. And these – a pair of gold earrings Stella had spotted in a little trinket dish in Alice's hallway, which Stella had tucked into her jumper sleeve.

The earrings were particularly nice. These she'd carefully placed – thanks to the use of Linda's house keys – on Jade's dressing table. She suspected, rightly, that someone as vain as Jade would be unable to resist trying them on. And then, just in case seeing the girl in her dead mother's earrings wasn't enough for Alice to get the message, Stella had faked a suitably alarming 'criminal record' for Jade, typed it up and printed it out at work.

Possibly the dead gull stunt had been a bit over the top, but Stella had been in a black mood that day, Hugo having taken Frankie away for a week to a villa in Tuscany with his vile new girlfriend. Stella had decided that cheating bastards like him and Jamie deserved to have their holidays ruined.

Rye wasn't far to drive. And when she had seen the bird in the dunes – the black, unseeing beads of its eyeballs, the torn, bloody flesh at its neck – it had seemed like as good an idea as any. There'd even been a child's pink plastic spade on the beach nearby, abandoned in a curl of seaweed.

As for the painting – well, Stella had only intended to freak Alice out a bit. She hadn't actually planned the coffee part, or realised the painting was a Vermeer. It hardly mattered, though. Stella had never had much time for his dull Dutch domesticity.

When Jade was in the hospital to have her baby, Stella had let herself into her flat with Linda's keys, and stashed the things she'd taken from Alice in Jade's bathroom hideaway, leaving the panel just slightly ajar, of course, so that Alice couldn't help but spot it. She'd even stuck a few bloody bird feathers in there, just for dramatic effect. With a box of horrors like that, Alice would surely be convinced she had a deranged stalker on her hands.

Her next job was to find the burner. She'd searched forensically. It was nowhere to be found. Jade could only have taken the damn thing with her in her hospital bag. It was unbelievable.

Stella would have much preferred if Jade had handed the phone over nicely. But in the end, Stella's patience had run out.

Still, even on that last day when Stella had gone to Jade's flat, she'd hoped she could be made to see sense, to finally hand over the phone. Without the burner, any allegation Jade made to the police about Stella plotting the break-in would be easily dismissed. Stella needed it gone.

Jade had been annoyed when she answered the door. She'd been asleep, she'd yawned – a neighbour with kids of her own had taken the baby for a few hours so she could catch up on rest. Stella had pushed in before Jade could protest.

It was a shame Jade couldn't be won around, Stella thought. Clever, but not quite clever enough. Jade didn't see that she'd left Stella with no choice. In the moments just before, as she pulled on her vinyl gloves, Stella had thought of Alice on the day of the break-in. Of how she'd watched as an animal instinct had taken over Alice's body, a lioness protecting her cub. How she'd lifted that metal stool above her head, then brought it crashing down on Ezra's skull, like an automaton. Stella had learned from that day, that it wasn't a question of strength. It was simply a question of your willingness to step into your most primal animal self. That, and the element of surprise.

She'd thought it would be enough to grab a fistful of her hair and slam Jade's head against the wall. She was so small, so slight – even smaller than Stella, who never ate more than one meal a day and did weights and cardio each morning before Frankie woke up. But even that hadn't done it. It had just made a mess. So Stella had to improvise. Going for the neck was much easier, except that it had meant that they were face to face, which was unfortunate, because it meant she had to watch as Jade's eyeballs rolled back behind her thick lashes like the eyes of a child's doll, the red blood vessels bursting one by one, the blood from her head wound getting all over the floor.

Afterwards, Stella's hands and wrists had felt stiff and unfamiliar. She'd run them under the warm tap, waited for the shaking to subside. Then she had packed Jade's body into a big checked laundry bag she'd found under the cot in the baby's room. It had been surprisingly easy, that part. Her limbs still soft and warm, her neck, broken like a flower stem, now easily shoved into her chest.

She'd found the burner after that, plus Jade's own phone, which came in handy to message Alice, asking her to come over, promising to tell her everything. She was pretty sure Alice would come after reading that, and place herself handily at the scene. She'd left Jade's phone in the kitchen after a good wipe, just to make it nice and easy for the dear old Metropolitan Police.

Framing Alice and Jamie for Jade's murder – it was only ever a back-up plan, of course. Just in case Jade wouldn't play ball, and hand over the burner once and for all. Stella was confident the police would think one or both of them had done it. Jamie had more than enough motive to want rid of his secret teenaged lover. As for Alice, she was suspended from work and slowly losing her mind, convinced – thanks to Stella – that Jade was out to harm her, destroy her family. Stella didn't know if Alice had said anything to the police about her suspicions Jade was stalking her. But if she had, so much the better. It would just give her more of a motive.

Stella left with the bag from the steps, where she knew from last time that there were no working CCTV cameras. She stuffed the bag into the boot of her car. Later – once Alice had been arrested, and Frankie waved off to Hugo's for the weekend – Stella waited until three in the morning, and then, from a dark stretch of the canal path, popped the bag into the water along with a couple of sacks of ballast sand she'd noticed one of the narrow boats had abandoned on the towpath.

With the sandbags, Jade had sunk nicely. Stella knew the body would float in the end, bloated by decomposition, but that didn't matter so much. By then, any traces of Stella would be washed clear. On a separate stretch, she'd weighed her gloves and shoe covers down in a plastic bag with some rocks from the towpath. Then, plop, into the water they'd gone, along with the remains of Ezra's smashed-up burner.

As the plane taxis on the runway, Stella stretches out over two seats, a blanket over her legs. She gazes out of the window as they rise into the air, watches the airport, the houses, the roads and cars get smaller and smaller until they are all too small, too far away to see. The next time she looks, all she can see is the endless blue of ocean.

Stella slips her earbuds in, sets her pillow under her head and takes a melatonin pill. When she gets home, she will declutter the house, wash all the sheets, bake bread. Make everything new and fresh and clean, for when Frankie comes home. Stella is no different from any other mother, she thinks. She would do anything for her daughter. She could never have taken the risk of letting Jade live, because it meant taking the risk of being parted from her daughter, of losing her to Hugo. No girl should grow up without her mother.

With this thought, the image of Jade's baby daughter rises uncomfortably to the surface of Stella's consciousness. She quickly blinks it away.

Stella pulls on her silk eye mask and waits for sleep. She has nothing to worry about, any more. Ezra and Jade are gone, their secrets buried with them. Linda is dead now, too. It was a disease, really, that claimed her family, the devil's disease. But it died with Ezra. Jade and her daughter were free of it – Linda had told Stella that, the first time that they met. And baby Taylor is probably better off, thanks to Stella, with a proper family. Thanks to Stella, she will never really know what darkness she came from.

Alice is better off too, without Jamie, whether she knows it yet or not. Men like him are like a cancer; he would have destroyed her in the end. Alice will thank her one day, Stella knows.

Forehead against the glass of the plane window, she drifts off easily, her mind calm as a blank page. Stella doesn't care that she was responsible for Jamie's death, any more than he cared about being responsible for her sister's. Stella is sorry, she supposes, that Jade had to die. But Jade already feels unreal to her; a character in a life she is leaving behind. And Stella really believes that she, just like Alice on the day of the break-in, had no real choice, in the end. It is just something she has to live with.

STELLA

Stella is woken by the in-flight announcer. The plane will shortly be preparing for landing at Heathrow. She rubs her eyes blearily. She has slept almost the whole flight. The window blinds on the plane are up, and light is streaming in. Air hostesses are clearing away the little trays of breakfast; people are queuing at the toilet door with washbags and toothbrushes.

The plane lands with a bump, to gasps from the other passengers, but Stella is unfazed. As it taxis on the runway, she logs onto the airport Wi-Fi and scrolls her messages. There is an update on the flat – the sellers have got the survey back, and are ready to proceed. Her solicitor is proposing a date for exchange. And the council are in touch; there is a school place for Frankie, if they move quickly. Everything is falling into place.

Stella also sees that she has a missed call from Hugo, and three from Oscar at work. These can wait.

Stella takes her time in the airport terminal bathrooms, applies her make-up, brushes her teeth. While she is standing in the passport queue, she taps out replies to the solicitor, to lovely Maxine from the new school, who has been nothing but helpful on the phone. She sends a message to Hugo, asking how Frankie is, reminding him of where and when they are meeting. Lastly, since the queue is moving slowly, she decides to call Oscar back.

'Hey,' she says. 'Everything OK?'

All she hears, for a moment, is the heavy sound of Oscar's breathing.

'I – I'm sorry, Stella,' he says. 'I think I've messed up.'

'What do you mean?'

Stella is distracted by some sort of confusion, at the front of the queue. The passport control people have stopped beckoning people forward. Two armed police officers are leaning into their booth, demanding something.

'I was just trying to do what you wanted – I thought you'd be pleased. I just hadn't thought...'

'What?' Stella snaps. 'What are you talking about?'

Stella tries to will herself to calmness. The police can't know she was working on a story about Jamie. It is confidential. There are journalistic exemptions. Oscar won't have had to show them anything.

But then Oscar tells her. About how it had occurred to him that since Jamie was dead now – and you couldn't libel the dead – and Stella was exonerated, that maybe they could revive the article about Jamie's treatment of her sister all those years ago. And the lawyers hadn't seen why not, now he was dead.

'So I... I put the calls in to the police,' he says.

'What do you mean?'

'I... I asked for a comment,' he says. 'From Kent police. And then – and then I had a call from the senior investigating officer. He said he'd seen my email to the press office. He said they knew nothing about your sister, or her connection to Jamie. And... and then they came here.'

'Who came here?'

'The police.'

The passengers ahead of Stella in the queue shift restlessly. They tut as they glance at the passport control officers, who are still searching, flustered, for something the police officers are asking them for. A girl in front of Stella, wearing tracksuit bottoms and fluffy UGG slippers, decides to use her suitcase as a seat. The adults with her mutter about switching to another queue.

'What... did you tell them?'

'The truth, Stella,' Oscar hisses. 'They were murder detectives. I couldn't not answer their questions. They wanted to know about your investigation into Jamie. How long you'd been looking into him. Whether I thought you were…' Oscar pauses. 'They used the word "fixated"…'

Stella feels her phone slip from her hand, hears it clatter to the floor. A man collects it for her; she ignores him. The lights in the ceiling of the airport, the signs for the exits, are suddenly indistinct, blurring and softening at the edges.

At the front of the queue, the passport control people finally produce the paper the officers have been demanding. One of them holds the sheet, and the other one points. First at the list, running a thick finger down the line. And then he says something to his colleague, and then he turns to look straight at Stella.

Stella grabs a metal bar at the side of the walkway. She feels as if she might faint, or float away. The people in the queue are all turning to look at her, curious and slightly thrilled rather than annoyed. Murmuring as the two armed police officers stride past them, their hats pulled down, asking the passengers to move aside. Stella looks beyond them briefly, to the gates that lead out. The taxi drivers holding signs with peoples' names. The passengers streaming underneath the green sign that says 'Nothing to declare'. *I came so close*, she thinks.

And then the two officers are at her side, and they say something she doesn't quite catch, but she knows, of course, what they want from her, so she nods, as if she heard them after all. And then they take Stella gently by the arms, and lead her away.

ACKNOWLEDGEMENTS

The spark of an idea for *The Break-In* came from Patricia Highsmith's haunting short story 'Something You Have To Live With' (from her 1982 collection *Slowly, Slowly in the Wind*), in which a woman is confronted by a burglar at her deserted home, and ends up killing him with a stool. Like Highsmith, I found myself fascinated by how the knowledge that one was capable of such an explosive act of violence might eat away at a person, and thus the character of Alice was born. Like so many writers of my genre, I owe a great debt of inspiration to Highsmith and I highly recommend *Slowly, Slowly in the Wind*, as well as all her other works.

I am very grateful to everyone who assisted me in researching this novel. I am deeply thankful to the families who have shared their experiences of Huntington's disease to assist me in researching the impact of this terrible illness. Thank you to the extraordinary Hannah Yates for allowing me to observe the life of an art restorer; it was utterly fascinating, and any mistakes (or leaps of creative licence) in this regard are entirely my own. Thanks to Max, aka Digital Forensics, for your many helpful insights on investigative procedure.

I was greatly inspired, while writing this novel, by the book *Adrift: A Secret Life of London's Waterways* by Helen Babbs, a fascinating portrait of life on and around London's regent canal, which I highly recommend.

Thanks, as ever, to my brilliant agent Madeleine Milburn, the whole MM team, and to my incredible editors Alison Hennessey and Alison Callahan. Thanks, too, to all those on the Raven and Gallery teams who have worked so hard on the (extensive!) editing, copyediting, proofreading and championing of *The Break-In*, especially to Fabrice Wilmann for having the patience of a saint.

Thank you to all the extraordinary authors who have supported me and this novel, in particular Abigail Dean and Lizzy Barber for helping me to stay sane juggling a book and a newborn (again!).

Thank you to all those who support and have supported me to write: Mum, Jo, Kirsty, Sue, Rhia, Karolina. And most of all Pete, who lets me have the nice desk, who reads everything and always claims he likes it, who never complains about any of my nonsense, and who even said 'yes' to a third (baby, as well as book). And to Emma, Maddie and Arthur, who are everything.

A NOTE ON THE AUTHOR

Katherine Faulkner is an award-winning journalist turned full-time writer. She wrote her debut novel, *Greenwich Park*, while on maternity leave with her first daughter and her follow-up, *The Other Mothers*, while juggling family life and work. She lives in London with her husband and three children.